C000139745

ARC OF A SHOOTING STAR

BOOK 1 OF THE SHOOTING STAR SERIES

SIMON NORTHOUSE

FLABBERGASTED

PUBLISHING

For information about special discounts available for bulk purchases, sales promotions, fund-raising and educational needs contact admin@snorthouse.com or visit the Author's website at www.snorthouse.com or Facebook page https://www.facebook.com/simonnorthouse

Disclaimer: This is a work of fiction. Names, characters, businesses, places, events, locales, and incidents are either the products of the author's imagination or used in a fictitious manner. Any resemblance to actual persons, living or dead, or actual events is purely coincidental.

Published by Flabbergasted Publishing
Second Edition
Paperback ISBN-13: 978-0-6482884-3-5
Kindle e-book ISBN-13: 978-0-6482884-1-1

Dedication

To Mrs Fletcher

Maybe you were right—time will tell

CONTENTS

1: BLOWING IN THE WIND

April 2005

I was a bloody idiot! The snowstorm that greeted us as we emerged onto the summit soon morphed into a full-blown blizzard. I could not see more than four or five metres ahead. I glanced down at my poor old Doberman. His ears were pinned back, blobs of snow dangled from his nose and his once dark eyelashes were now a thick white. No longer the effervescent bundle of unbridled energy, he took on the persona of a ghost dog, the canine equivalent of the Flying Dutchman.

'How did we end up here, old pal?' I gasped as I bent my body double to shield my face from the blistering cold. He looked at me and let out a low whimper, as if to say, "What's all this 'we' business ... It was your stupid idea!"

We were on top of Yorkshire's second highest peak in the middle of an unusually bitter spring. I blamed my dominatrix—Madame Nicotine. I had been off the smokes for two weeks, three days and ten hours—not that I was counting—and decided a brisk walk may alleviate my withdrawal symptoms. Damn those tobacco giants!

The day started off pleasant enough with a weak sun occasionally peeking through icy clouds and a cool but invigorating breeze sweeping across the Dales. My intent had been simple enough—to complete a circular amble around the foothills of Inglegor Pike and then return to my warm farmhouse in time for the afternoon football game on TV. The

1

weather forecast predicted cold and blustery conditions with a high chance of snowfall at elevated levels. I remembered looking up at the sawn off peak of Inglegor Pike and in a rash and impulsive act of stupidity decided to tackle its arduous incline. It was a walk I'd done so many times before during the last decade, I'd lost count. However, that was in summer or autumn, never in winter and rarely ever in springtime. I was ill prepared for the conditions I now faced.

Despite the relentless attack of sleet and snow, I could just make out the grey outline of a rock formation ahead. I knew this must be the windbreak as the plateau was barren of any other structure. With great effort and much relief, we made it to the shelter. I sat down behind one of the walls and was instantly removed from the snarling teeth of the storm. Caesar shook himself violently sending a spray of wet ice and mud over me. Luckily, I had brought a backpack with a few meagre provisions. I unzipped the bag and pulled out a peanut butter sandwich, a block of chocolate and a bottle of ice-cold water. I cursed myself again and as I sat there slowly munching on my rations, I voiced out the litany of transgressions I had committed. My shivering dog listened morosely.

'Inadequate clothing, no hat, no scarf, no waterproofs, no hot drinks, not enough food or water; no matches, no compass, no map, no torch. I have not informed anyone of my destination or my expected return time. The weather forecast told me to expect strong winds and squalls and what do I do?' Caesar cocked his head to one side listening intently. 'I decide to walk to the top of Yorkshire's second highest peak. I saw the gloomy sky and ignored it. Any normal person would have turned back when they realised it was blowing a blizzard, but did I? No, not I, Will Harding, Patron Saint of Village Idiots everywhere.' I finished three-quarters of my sandwich and threw the remnant to an appreciative Caesar, who swallowed it greedily.

I assessed my situation. The visibility had now dropped to less than a couple of metres and I realised I was in a spot of bother. I needed to get off this damn peak as quickly as possible. If I had packed ample provisions and some insulation, I may have been able to hunker down until the storm abated but I realised this was no longer an option. There were only three routes off the plateau, two by established paths and a third by a hundred metre vertical drop to unforgiving rocks. I unwrapped the bar of chocolate, pulled off a chunk, and popped it in my mouth.

'Sorry Caesar old pal, but this might be my lunch and dinner.' The old dog gazed sadly at me as the chocolate disappeared into my pocket. I stuck my head above the windbreak and a sub-zero blast of air greeted me with such ferocity it stole my breath away. It was impossible! The conditions were treacherous and I felt an unwelcome wave of fear roll over me. I dropped back down behind the wall and sucked on my chocolate. *What am I to do?* I was getting colder by the second even in the shelter. If I could get off the peak, I assumed the storm would blow harmlessly over the top of us and the immediate danger would pass. I decided to head back the way we had come. There was no chance of retracing my footsteps as they were now covered with snow, but I was sure I would recognise the path if and when I saw it. At least I would have my back to the storm, therefore making visibility easier. I rubbed my numb hands together, stamped my feet and hoisted on my backpack.

'Come on Caesar, it's do or die, mate.' We set off into the milky maelstrom and I kept glancing behind every couple of steps or so, not wishing to lose sight of the windbreak. I'm not sure if I did this in a valiant attempt at keeping to my original bearing or just for reassurance, knowing the hexagon of rocks was the only sanctuary on top of the spiteful peak. After no more than ten or so strides, the windbreak disappeared from view and I felt the sharp claws of panic grip my stomach. This was it—there was no turning back.

'If yesterday was tomorrow,' I began to sing, 'then today I'd be alright …' The song was from our first album and it was an unconscious choice, but I smiled upon realising the irony of the words. I stumbled on blindly, praying I was walking in the right direction. Caesar now had icicles forming on the end of his nose and hanging miraculously from his jowls. I felt sorry for him but at the same time, his pathetic figure did make me laugh a little.

I halted abruptly. I inched forward staring hard into the whiteness and made out an edge where the ground rudely stopped. I could see no further, horizontally or vertically, and only guessed at what may have happened had I walked another metre or so. Any fall in these conditions would be fatal; a broken leg or even a sprained ankle was all it would take.

Two choices; either set off in a clockwise direction or an anti-clockwise direction and skirt the perimeter of the rock. At some point, I would surely stumble upon the trail which, would lead me to safety. The problem was, I didn't know the exact distances involved in such a circumnavigation. On my previous visits to the summit, I ate my lunch at the windbreak, took in the views and then set off back the way I had ascended. I had never orbited the entire plateau. I now wish I had. It wasn't a huge area, but would it take ten minutes or half an hour? I knew I wouldn't last thirty minutes in these conditions; ten minutes, fifteen at a push, was my estimated limit. For a moment, I thought about heading back towards the windbreak but quickly decided against it. What was the point? Even if I managed to find my way back, which was unlikely, all I would do was waste valuable energy. No, the only way was to navigate the boundary.

I set off nervously. I feared the edge may crumble at any moment or a powerful gust of wind would pick me up and toss me to a terrifying death; but, if I moved in from the rim, I was unable to make out the rock's outline and so risked walking right past the path I desperately sought.

I shuffled on and on, occasionally spotting what I thought was an exit route only to find it was a dead end, a ledge jutting out from the peak. This happened on three occasions; each time my heart began to beat faster with expectancy and excitement only to feel the crushing blow of disappointment when I realised it was merely a ruse. I struggled to keep control of my fear and began to berate myself for the life I lived.

I had no wife, no soul-mate, no children; I had only one friend from my musical past and my only immediate family was my Mother, whom I reluctantly visited once a year. What was the point of life if there was no one to share it with? I was a recluse! It was over ten years since the Shooting Tsars disbanded. I had needed time away then as I was spent, disillusioned and worst of all, I became cynical. That's when I found the converted barn in the little Yorkshire village of Whitstone. It was a great house in the middle of nowhere—the perfect place to hide away and lick my wounds. Although the cynicism and self-pity soon faded, a new attitude was born. I became insular and selfish without even noticing it. My whole life revolved around me. I was heliocentric. There was no warmth or love in my life. How had this happened? I didn't deliberately set out to create this solitary existence, it just crept up on me like a slow debilitating cancer. I thought of a cheesy poster I had once seen, stuck on the window of a gym—"nothing changes if nothing changes". I scoffed at the time and deemed it just another example of the feel-good, positive affirmation, self-help industry that plagued the world. A meaningless slogan dreamt up by consensus around a boardroom table during a brainstorming session. But now those words resonated around my head with increasing clarity, "nothing changes if nothing changes". The more I thought about it the simpler and more obvious it became. Those five words summed up the last ten years of my life. I had meandered, drifted, bobbing about like a discarded champagne cork in the ocean. If I didn't instigate change, well, then nothing would change. Days had slipped into weeks, weeks into months and months into years—if I carried on like this, it wouldn't be long before my coffin would be slipping into the cold dead earth. I always intended to get back on the musical merry-go-round, but as the years passed, my confidence gradually waned, slowly melting away like a candle in a cold dark room. Now the thought of reforming my old band, or even going solo, seemed so outlandishly impossible I always immediately buried the idea on the rare occasions it raised its mocking head. I was plagued with self-doubt, and anyway, life was too easy and comfortable. There was nothing, or no-one, to kick me up the arse, to shake me out of this apathy—until now. Mother-nature wasn't just bitch-slapping me awake, she was throwing a bucket of ice-cold water over me as I emerged from a steaming hot bath. It was a bit late to be ruminating on life at the present. I felt tears begin to sting my eyes and kidded myself it was due to the biting gale. Was it too late to change? I promised myself if I ever got off this bloody mountain, I would put things right or at least die trying. I pushed my self-pity aside and became angry.

'I will not be beaten! I will not be beaten!' I chanted as I meandered along. Caesar began to whimper. I stopped and knelt down beside him, pulling him in close to my body and giving him a big hug.

'Easy boy, you'll soon be tucked up in front of a roaring log fire chewing on a bone,' I encouraged softly. He didn't understand the words but he knew the intent and his spirits seemed to noticeably lift, and so too, my own.

I continued with renewed vigour. I navigated another dead end and at one point stumbled perilously close to an edge. Although I couldn't see the drop I narrowly escaped, I felt the vast emptiness that awaited me had I been a few inches further to my left.

I'd been walking for fifteen minutes and was beginning to get tired. The freezing cold I experienced earlier had subsided and I reminded myself this may be due to the onset of hypothermia. My body was closing down its normal mechanisms to save energy. I realised lethargy and then sleep would not be far behind, and after that, death.

I doubled back on myself as I finished exploring yet another ledge. As it rejoined the main plateau, my feet slipped on a patch of hard ice and I was sent reeling to the ground. As I landed, my head hit the surface hard and I heard a loud zinging in my ears. I rested. Caesar lay down at my side and I smelt a faint comforting aroma of damp dog. I thought about getting back to my feet but decided that maybe a five or ten-minute rest would do me good. I closed my eyes and sensed movement—Caesar had left—probably gone to chase some rabbits.

I felt something heavy yet warm on my midriff accompanied by a less than pleasant smell. I opened my eyes and stared at the snowflakes as they floated gently to the ground. They were beautiful. It brought back memories of Christmas Day when I was about ten years old. I recalled pushing my action man jeep through thick powdery snow that lay heavy on our street. I remembered Christmas dinner, Mam, Dad, and all the relatives sat around the big table. The house was bursting at the seams— paper hats, Christmas carols, the smell of cigars and stale beer, the aroma of turkey and plum pudding with a heavy rum sauce. There was a sense of magic—a magic only the very young can ever feel. My eyes became sleepy once more. The heavy weight on my stomach was suddenly lifted from me. I blinked. *What is that? Black, brown, red? No, not red, pink. Snowflakes rising? That's not right.* My eyes slowly focused on an object a few inches directly above me. *It's a God. No, not a God, I mean a dog. What's a dog doing here?* I sluggishly regained my senses. Snowflakes weren't rising, it was the dog's steamy breath floating in the cold air. His long pink tongue lolled around his jaws as he panted heavily.

'Caesar,' I called his name as I slowly became aware of the numbness in my legs and the deep throbbing from my head. I staggered wearily to my feet and shuffled forward. Caesar wagged his tail as he licked my hand. The tempest abated, the snow now a gentle dancing ballet. I could see further. I noticed a path in front of me but wasn't sure what to do. *Should I go down it? Why not.* I trudged slowly onward following the winding trail as it rapidly descended away from the peak. Within a few metres, the temperature noticeably increased and I saw a refreshing vista of greenery stretching way into the distance. The snow petered out the further I descended. Down the hill I went, slipping and sliding, panting hard. I began to feel the cold in my hands and feet once again, a good sign. My thinking became clearer, although my head still ached. I felt my hairline, something sticky. I inspected my fingers and saw a crimson stain. A flesh wound, nothing serious.

On and on I went as though trying to escape some monstrous fiend. Finally, at the point of exhaustion, I stopped. I turned and glared at the huge monolith behind me. It was grinning, mocking me, its presence overbearing, as though it still held me in its jaws. I was desperately thirsty and pulled my water bottle from my backpack—my heart sank. The bottle was all but empty and my backpack extremely wet. The jogging down the hill must have loosened the top, releasing the precious contents. I glanced at my watch—4:15 pm—I could not believe it! I must have been unconscious for a couple of hours. I tried to find my bearings by surveying the horizon for familiar landmarks but everything appeared foreign. With resigned weariness, I realised I had descended the wrong path and was now on the opposite side of the mountain. It was getting dark, and at best, there was barely an hour's daylight left. I pulled out my bar of chocolate and broke it in half.

'Make the most of it pal; it may be the last thing you eat.' I threw Caesar half the chocolate and deposited the remainder in my mouth. The glucose seemed to work instantly and galvanised me into action.

'Okay Caesar, here's the plan. We'll continue downwards and sideways in an easterly direction which will eventually bring us back onto the path we took this morning, not far from Inglegor Beck. If we can get to the path before dark, then I know the way back from there, blindfold.' I often talked to my dog—he was a good listener and rarely disagreed.

We set off at a slow jog across the damp grassland. The sun completely relinquished its right to exist and dark, heavy clouds began to sink lower and lower. It began to rain, not heavy, but steady. I stuck my tongue out feeling tender droplets fall upon it, vainly hoping it would ease my aching thirst. Caesar sauntered merrily along at my side, ignorant of our parlous predicament. My feet felt raw and blistered as they slipped around inside my boots, but that was the least of my worries. I needed to get home; my energy reserves were depleted and I was soaked to the skin, a night out in the cold would finish me off.

Occasionally, I'd throw a glance over my shoulder at the grimacing peak behind me. I had escaped its icy grip this time, but would I be able to escape my own self-built prison? I chanted the mantra I'd used on the mountain.

'I will not be beaten, I will not be beaten.'

Darkness began to smother the landscape and visibility was becoming an issue. I came across a dry-stone wall and ran along its side until it took a direction I did not want, at which point, I had to stop and heave Caesar over it before tentatively climbing over the wall myself. On the other side, I carried on in my disjointed and irregular way. A couple of stars twinkled on the horizon. I checked the time again—6:30 pm—the footy game I was hoping to watch was long gone and I idly wondered who won. I slumped down on the wet grass. Caesar stared at me sadly. I tried to feel sorry for myself but could not—I was too fatigued. I stood up and walked on, there was nothing else for it. Then... I heard something ... was it just the sound of rain on the stone walls? No ... it was a familiar sound ... distant but distinct. It was the sound of a bristling stream! I quickened my pace and tried to lift my legs into a jog but they would not oblige. I thought of water—icy cold, pure, refreshing and rejuvenating. The sound grew louder and louder. I walked up a slight grassy slope which fell away sharply on the other side. For the first time that day, I was given a break as a thin sliver of moon appeared in the inky-black sky to the east. It spread a faint glimmer of light and hope over the countryside. I saw the reflection of the lunar talisman in a stream, no more than fifty metres ahead. I covered the distance in no time, fell at its bank, and scooped up the precious liquid with my hands, gulping it down in a frenzied fashion. When my thirst was slaked, I rolled over onto my back and gazed up at the night sky. I was safe. This was

Inglegor Beck. All I needed to do was follow the stream south and it would lead me home.

I searched my backpack for remnants of food which may have been left over from previous outings. An odd piece of chocolate or a few mints, anything would do. I felt something hard and box-shaped. I quickly unzipped the pouch and pulled out ... a packet of cigarettes. Damn! I fumbled around again in the bag and located something familiar—and welcoming—a lighter. I thought of the arduous fortnight I'd gone through trying to quit smoking but the temptation was too great for such a weak man. I put a cigarette in my mouth and lit it, inhaling deeply at the same time.

'Ah fuck! That's good.' I melted back into the grass. The moon grew in size and luminescence as I lay puffing away on my cigarette. I was cold, wet, hungry and sore, but at that moment in time, for those few seconds as I lay under the moon, I was happy.

As I stared into the night sky, there was a sudden dizzying flash high to the north. A brilliant fireball slew through the atmosphere. I watched in awe as the arc of a shooting star illuminated Inglegor Pike and the surrounding countryside in a shining radiance which was both beautiful and frightening. It was gone in seconds, leaving no trace it had ever existed.

'... like a shooting star in the darkest night... you shone so brightly...' I sang quietly. I thought of my old bandmates, our music and our time together. I especially thought of Geordie and cast my mind back to that first rehearsal with him.

2: START ME UP

I met Geordie while he was working as a barman in "The Duchess" public house in Leeds city centre. I got talking to him and when I found out he played bass guitar, I begged him to come and audition for my band.

'I don't do auditions. Bands audition for me and not one has ever passed the test,' he announced in a thick Scottish brogue. He was an arrogant prick and angry with it too, but I was desperate.

Geordie, or Allan Kincaid as I knew him then, was on time for that first rehearsal. I was surprised. I'd been in and out of bands for five years and people turning up late for rehearsals and gigs or not turning up at all, was not unusual. I formed my own band, "The Shooting Stars" after becoming disenchanted with all the bullshit I'd put up with along the way. I was finished with tacky covers and lame rip-offs; I was tired of losers who thought they were the reincarnation of Jim Morrison or Brian Jones. I was sick to death of tortured, misunderstood artists who were destined to be ignored in their own lifetime but revered as deities once taken from this cruel and thankless world—wankers—every last man jack of them! They all lacked one crucial component that is essential if you want to succeed—talent!

I encountered a few good musicians along the way but no songwriter of any worth. That's when I decided that if I were to drag myself out of the gutter, I'd have to do it my way.

I recruited Robbo (Gordon Robinson) on lead guitar and Flaky (John Steele) on drums. They were good musicians, if not exceptional. They just wanted a laugh, the occasional gig, beer money and the chance to impress the girls. You couldn't call them "ambitious". Over a two-year period, I had composed about twenty songs, which I at least, regarded as pretty good. The problem was, we could never get a regular bass player. Many came and went. Some could play, some couldn't. The few that were good were typically transient and uncommitted. They realised they were in demand and were always being poached or lured away to play for the big money cover bands. My frustrations were palpable but I persevered.

#

I watched Allan Kincaid as he hauled his huge frame from the taxi outside the rehearsal studios. He handed the taxi driver a fiver then went to the boot and lifted out his amp and bass case as though they were made of polystyrene. I showed him to the rehearsal room, where I was already set up. He stopped and surveyed the empty room before staring at me suspiciously.

'I thought yer said yer had a band?' he demanded.

'I do,' I replied.

'Then where the fuck are they?' He growled.

'They're obviously not here yet,' I stated with a false air of cockiness, trying to combat his intimidating manner. I had expressly told Flaky and Robbo to be on time for the rehearsal as we were auditioning a bass player—a bass player we desperately needed. I knew this meant nought to them. If something more interesting appeared on the horizon, there was a very good chance that neither of them would show up. I was relying on it being a boring evening in Leeds to focus their responsibilities.

'Okay,' said Kincaid 'I'll give 'em half an hour and then I'm out of here. I'll set up and we can run through some of the songs—that's if you know them without your mates.'

'I wrote them, I sing them, I play them, so I think I'll be okay,' I retorted belligerently.

'Fuck me! We have Barry Manilow in the building.' He switched on his amp and it thumped into life. I was already having second thoughts about the great big, Scottish git. His negativity was overbearing.

I picked up my guitar and moved toward the microphone. I began to pick out the notes of the first song "Mad John". I began to sing. I wasn't nervous or self-conscious. I believed in my ability and the quality of my songs. If people liked them, good, if they didn't, well, I didn't give a toss. Kincaid sat on his amp, head down, looking at his bass strings. He appeared to be listening but I wasn't sure what his reaction would be. I was past caring. The thought of giving up on music altogether was becoming ever more attractive.

I'd paid a high price for being in a band. Relationships never lasted long. I was too involved with my music to pay the sort of attention that a budding romance required. I also worked "cash-in-hand" jobs whilst signing on for the dole. I'd sacrificed my full-time job to concentrate on my music. Had it all been worth it? Of course not.

I carried on playing, hitting the chorus of "Mad John". I heard Kincaid's bass begin to follow along. I shot him a glance. It sounded good—very good. His head was still down, his long greasy hair cascaded over his face as his head rocked slowly from side to side. When the song finished he took a notebook from his guitar case, turned to a blank page and scribbled away, murmuring to himself, in rapid, staccato, half sentences.

'Key of G, possibly change to D. Four-four time may work in middle eight, hmm ... lead guitar to repeat riff on chorus. Need fade out ... possible fade in, drums—backbeat, hi-hat, rim shot on chorus, maybe on outro. Studio—ah yes, studio! Bring horns in on chorus, maybe keys on mid-eight or even verse'. He carried on mumbling and scribbling. I started the next song.

'Okay, this is called, "The Flip Side of Mr Brown", join in when you want.' I got no response from Kincaid, who was still making notes and mumbling as if in some sort of trance.

As the song ended, he again wrote furiously in his notebook. This went on for the next four songs. I couldn't get a word out of him. Sometimes as he talked to himself, he would laugh aloud.

'Ha-ha! Of course ... Beatles White album, one of John's I think, yes, yes, or possibly George? It may work again. Very Dorian, arpeggio, not too clichéd. Ha! Yes, yes, "Ruby Tuesday", no not that, "Evening Of The Day", yes, that's it. Need to rework the intro though. Not enough time ... needs more space.' He was quite obviously a lunatic but at least he seemed to be enjoying himself.

Twenty minutes passed before the door violently burst open and in trotted Flaky with a tom-tom under each arm. He immediately spotted our auditioning bass player.

'Who's the Sasquatch?' he inquired. I made eyes at him and shook my head as if to say "don't mess with this bloke, he's a bit unstable". Flaky nodded, acknowledging my semaphores.

'Flaky, I'd like you to meet Allan Kincaid; he's auditioning bass for us. Allan, this is Flaky, our drummer,' I gesticulated, trying to be courteous and formal. Kincaid ignored me. A few minutes later, the door was rudely thrust open again and in trudged Robbo with guitar and amp—he was not in the best of moods.

'Bastard bus drivers! What's their problem, eh? One twat wouldn't let me on his bus because all I had was a five-pound note. Said I'd take all his change. You'd think if you were in the business of charging fares that it might be a good idea to have a bagful of fucking change!'

'Robbo, mate, chill out, bus drivers, bouncers and security guards were put on this earth to annoy the rest of us. It's a fact of life. It's like getting mad at an elephant for having a trunk. The elephant can't help it,' consoled Flaky, whose postulations on life were renowned for being of no use to anyone.

'Thanks, mate. I'll remind the bus driver of that little gem next time I see him.' Robbo began to set up before he finally noticed the strange creature sitting at the far end of the room. He stopped what he was doing and stared in disbelief.

'Who's the Yeti?' Diplomacy was not this band's strong point.

'Ahem, Robbo, I'd like you to meet Allan Kincaid. Allan, this is Robbo our lead guitarist and of course Flaky who I mentioned before.' Nothing; he was still wrapped up in his notes. For some reason best known to himself, Robbo fancied himself as a bit of a hard man and having witnessed him in a few dust-ups, I'd come to the conclusion that he couldn't punch his way out of a wet paper bag. He was more of a danger to himself than anyone else; alas, it did not alter his belief.

'Oi mate! Are you deaf, stupid or both?' Robbo growled, swaggering towards Kincaid with hands in pockets. Kincaid held up one hand as if to say, "Stop there, do not proceed any further, I have nearly finished what I am doing". Robbo stopped and turned to me.

'You gotta be joking man! Where did you dig this one up from?' Before I could answer, Kincaid put down his notes and stood up. His six-foot-six-inch frame towered over everyone in the room, especially Robbo, who was a good nine inches shorter.

'I do beg your pardon for being so rude. You see, I needed to get it all down whilst it was still fresh in my mind. My name is Allan Kincaid. You can call me Allan or Kincaid, but not Sasquatch, Yeti, or deaf or stupid. If it wasn't for the fact that I think you have a very talented songwriter in your midst I would now be in the process of inserting your head up his arse,' he pointed first at Robbo and then at Flaky. They both gawped at him, visibly intimidated even though the tone of Kincaid's riposte was of a genial nature.

'This man,' he rested his large thick hand on my shoulder, 'is a flawed genius. I have only heard your first five songs but that is enough to convince me of the potential. It's not a unique formula by any means, but I suspect an unwitting mixture of numerous genres and styles. When combined correctly, they create their own individualism, an alchemy if you like—and I am your alchemist! However, success is not inevitable, but now I'm here to guide you, it is a distinct possibility. The question is—are you two cuckoos up for it? You can come along for the ride, on our coat tails as it were, or you can spend the rest of your lives shovelling shit for a living. I don't really care either way, the choice is yours, but I will need to know tonight. Now, if you care to set up, let's get on with this rehearsal. Show me what you can do.' He turned his back and began practising scales on his bass. We all looked at him as though he were stark staring bonkers. Finally, Flaky broke the silence.

'Are you Scottish by any chance?'

'No mate, I'm a fucking Geordie!' We all laughed and the ice was broken. Kincaid became Geordie, a metamorphosis, the first of many over the next five years. Flaky sat on his drum stool and clicked his sticks together:

'One, two, three, four.' We ripped into our set!

3: ONLY THE LONELY

Caesar brought me back to reality by sticking his wet snout in my ear. I finished my cigarette, filled my water bottle from the icy waters, pulled on my backpack and strolled off, following the bank of the stream. Within a few hundred metres, I spotted the twinkling lights of Whitstone village. Another forty minutes weary trudge and I passed the Beaconsfield Arms. It was very alluring as soft light filtered through its windows, along with the distant sound of chatter and the uplifting smell of beer. It was tempting, very tempting, but I walked on by. I knew better than to go inside. Being admonished by a collective of self-righteous Dales Farmers was not the tonic I needed right now.

I fell exhausted onto the couch clutching a large glass of scotch. I relived my nightmare step by step, cursing myself between sips of single malt. Caesar, who appeared overly agitated as he sniffed around from room to room, constantly interrupted my recollections. Not until I fed him and got a log fire going did he finally settle down and drift off into a well-earned slumber.

I stood at the window and gazed at the shadowy outline of Inglegor Pike in the distance. It cast a cold hard gaze over me as if to say, "next time, show some respect." I thought about my life and the promises I made to myself on top of that rock. I knew I had to change but wasn't sure how. An icy blast hit the window followed by a sprinkling of rain. The droplets carved a streaky path down the glass. I pulled the curtains shut, threw another log on the fire, re-filled my glass and slunk into the folds of the couch.

#

I awoke to the comforting song of a blackbird warbling in the distance. A shaft of light shone through a crack in the curtains and I idly watched the incomprehensible dance of microscopic dots of dust float in and out of the daylight's illuminating path. I turned to see if Caesar was awake. He peeked back at me from his rug, staring patiently into his master's face—breakfast time.

For most of the morning, I ruminated unhappily on my life. Prior to my brush with death, I thought I had it pretty good. My life was easy going and laid back. I lived in a great house in a beautiful village in the heart of my much-loved Yorkshire Dales. I spent many of my days walking the fells and peaks with my dog. I was a keen gardener spending many hours in my vegetable garden, planting, sowing, picking and watering. I produced more than enough vegetables for a family of six never mind one man and his dog. I donated the surplus to the local church who handed it out to some of the older parishioners.

When my tomatoes were ready at the end of summer I made gallons of tomato sauce that I'd sell at the Women's Institute stand on festival days. The old dears loved me, the perfect surrogate son. I did a lot of reading, or when in the mood, writing songs. I still played my guitar regularly and had a small suitcase full of half-finished tunes that would never see the light of day. On warm summer nights, I would sit out on my back veranda with a bottle of red wine and a plate of olives and watch the sun set on Inglegor. In winter, I would relax on my leather couch in front of a cosy log fire reading voraciously as Caesar snored away on the rug. Friday and Sunday nights, I'd go down to the Beaconsfield Arms for a game of darts and dominoes with the locals. I'd sit and drink pints of bitter and join in the village chitchat. In autumn, I'd help with the Harvest Festival and in spring, I'd help with preparations

18

for the May Day Celebrations. Only a few people in the village knew of my illustrious musical past and as for the rest, hidden away in this land that time forgot, they had no idea who Will Harding or the Shooting Tsars were, most of them only vaguely remembered The Beatles. This was my life. On the surface, it was the perfect bachelor's lifestyle and I had never questioned it before. I didn't care for the past and I didn't think of the future. I knew it would be easy to slip back into this quiet and genteel existence but I kept thinking about the promise I made to myself on top of that peak. I needed to open myself up and share my life. I was a wealthy man, too much money for one single person to spend or enjoy. I needed to give more. I needed to rekindle my old friendships and try to instigate some new ones. I needed a woman, a soul mate, maybe even kids!

My first step on the road to redemption was to call my Mother and let her know I'd be setting off the next day to spend a fortnight with her. She sounded delighted and after hanging up I felt considerably more positive. With a new bounce in my step, I decided that I needed some action. Trying to find action in Whitstone on a Sunday morning was akin to digging up the dead and requesting a blood donation. After much contemplation I realised my only option was to pay a visit to my neighbour, Arthur, and see if I could coax him down to the pub for a few refreshing ales; hardly extreme sports I know, but it was the best I had.

As I sauntered the couple of hundred yards over to Arthur and Ethel's place, I happily puffed away on a cigarette. My lapse of willpower on the hike proved to be the breach in the dam wall and I conceded defeat in the battle against nicotine. I walked up Arthur's driveway and knocked on the door as Caesar urinated on a denuded plum tree. I heard gruff Yorkshire voices from within before Arthur eventually stood on the threshold.

'Eh up! Bloody 'ell lad, I thought you'd never arrive. Am I glad to see you. My Ethel is driving me round the bloody bend. Wants me to start repainting the bathroom. Says it's old fashioned. I told her, "we're

19

old fashioned", it suits us just as it is.' I smiled up at Arthur's old craggy face.

'Well, I guess it's your shout first then, Arthur.'

'Who is it, Arthur?' Ethel's blunt voice echoed from the kitchen.

'It's Will love, wants to know if I fancy a quick pint?' replied Arthur sheepishly while winking at me. Ethel's diminutive frame appeared behind Arthur.

'Get out of the way you big oaf.' Ethel flicked a tea towel at Arthur's backside and he quickly stood aside.

'Ah Will, how ya doing love, are you well? And how's your Mother keeping?'

'Hi, Ethel. Yeah, I'm fine and so is Mam. I'm heading down to see her tomorrow for a couple of weeks, so I wondered if Arthur was allowed out for a few pints before I go?' Ethel folded her arms and pursed her lips while perusing her husband with a hint of disdain. Arthur, resolutely averted her gaze.

'Well, I suppose so. But I don't want him coming back half-cut.'

'No, I promise Ethel, just two or three quick ones that's all. Cub's honour.' Arthur wasted no time and ducked inside returning with a thick heavy overcoat.

'Right then Will, let's be off.' The old man's eagerness annoyed his wife.

'And don't think that I've forgotten about the bathroom. You can start on it this afternoon. And don't be late for your dinner.' Arthur was already making his way to the gate with an excited Caesar dancing around his feet.

'It's the Sabbath woman; man should not work on the Sabbath.'

'Ha! The Sabbath he says. Last time he saw the inside of a church they were sprinkling water on his head.'

'Oh aye, and what about when I wed thee?'

'Oh yes. I forgot about that, it's not something I like to remember.'

20

'Bloody charming, I don't think.' I smiled at Ethel, turned, and followed Arthur down the path.

'Give my regards to your Mother,' shouted Ethel as we made our way out of the gate. I waved.

'Will do!'

We strolled down to the Beaconsfield Arms and caught up with a few of the locals who, in typical male chauvinistic tradition, had abandoned their wives who were all busily cooking the Sunday dinner. Over three pints of bitter, we discussed the weather, my foolhardy hike up Inglegor (toned down dramatically), the finer attributes of Ethel and whom we fancied for the football premiership. We had a game of dominoes and two games of darts before Arthur checked his watch and hurriedly finished off the dregs from the bottom of his glass.

'C'mon lad, best make lively, Ethel will have my guts for garters if I'm late for my dinner.' We left the warm comforting environment of the pub and headed outside into the fresh country air. Caesar trotted happily along at my side and Arthur ambled along on the other. He was a man of few words. He stopped and filled his pipe with tobacco before ceremoniously lighting it, sending a large blue plume of pungent smoke into the air. A few prodigious intakes later, we set off again.

'So lad, yer off to see yer Ma tomorrow then?'

He'd called me lad since I'd first moved into the village ten years ago. I didn't mind. In this part of Yorkshire, virtually everyone was a lad, no matter what their age, and if they weren't a lad, they were a lass.

'Yeah, I haven't seen her for a while and she isn't getting any younger.' Arthur chortled to himself.

'Aye, no-one gets any younger lad, they just get older.' I looked at Arthur and saw an old man, although he really wasn't that old, barely past retirement age. However, his demeanour and attitude added another twenty years. He still had his faculties and he seemed to be healthy enough, but he wore the countenance of a man who had given up, someone who had lost the lust for life, all but waiting for God. I wondered if this was to be my fate also. We sauntered slowly along the sweeping bend in the road and started on the uphill stretch back to our respective abodes. The old stone cottages of the village stood proud and defiant in the palm of the imposing fells and hills. A breeze occasionally wafted the sweet scent of apple blossom over us. Caesar's nose twitched as he investigated trees and bushes along the route. Arthur stopped to re-ignite his pipe. I gazed up at Inglegor, ever-present, unchanging; a shiver ran down my spine.

'Depends on yer mood,' stated Arthur matter-of-factly.

'Pardon?' He removed his pipe from his mouth and used it to point at the peak.

'The pike lad, the pike. Depends on yer mood.' I was puzzled. 'If yer feeling a bit down in the dumps that thing can feel like a bloody prison guard. Everywhere you go, it's there. Even when you nod off to sleep, yer know it's still there watching over you, there's no escaping it. On t'other hand, if yer feeling chipper then it's like yer best bloody pal, always by your side, giving you strength and encouragement when you need it.' He was right. I was surrounded by thousands of hectares of wide-open spaces yet I felt trapped, claustrophobic.

'You ever climbed it, Arthur?'

'Aye, long time back. Probably over twenty years ago.'

'Why so long?' I asked. He stopped and stared at me.

'Once you've done it, you've done it. Don't see the point in doing it again.' Caesar came bounding back, thrusting his snout first into my hand and then into Arthur's, reaffirming the bond of the pack. This particular trait always tickled Arthur.

'He's bloody crackers that dog of yours, bloody crackers!' he laughed loudly.

'Ever thought about getting a dog yourself Arthur? I reckon you'd love it, they keep you on your toes you know.'

'Oh no, I'm a bit too old for all that business. Maybe a few years ago but not now,' he said resignedly. I felt like grabbing him by the throat and yelling, "You're not bloody dead yet you know!" But I didn't—a bit like Arthur's reason for not climbing the pike again, what was the point.

We walked on in easy silence for a while each wrestling with our own thoughts.

'Oh by the way, did you catch up with yer old mate?'

'What old mate?' I asked. Arthur stopped, removed his pipe and turned to me.

'Didn't get his name. It was yesterday, 'bout mid-morning. Big lad, short hair.' I shook my head. 'And when I say big lad, I mean big lad. Built like a brick shithouse, ex-forces if you ask me. London accent. Great big scar under his left eye.' Arthur made a motion with his pipe tracing an arc across his cheek. There were only a handful of people who knew where I lived and none of them fitted Arthur's description. For the life of me, I couldn't think who it was. My obvious bewilderment prompted Arthur to continue his description.

'I was doing a spot of gardening in the front and this car goes up and down a couple of times. He was obviously searching for someone or something. He pulled over and asked if I knew where Will Harding lived, I said "Aye lad, next one up, who's asking?" Says he was an old mate, went back a long way. He says thanks and off he drove back down t'wards village. I thought it a bit queer like at the time but later on, I saw his car parked in your driveway so I just assumed you'd seen him otherwise I'd have mentioned it earlier.' I remembered leaving my door unlocked the previous day and also recalled Caesar's agitated sniffing when we returned from our ill-fated hike. Arthur noticed my concerned look.

'Tha's not in trouble is thee lad?' I laughed loudly, a little too loudly.

'Ha-ha! No, it's probably just some old fan who found out where I lived and wanted an autograph or a photo or something.' Arthur didn't seem convinced and neither was I. The tale unnerved me but I dropped the matter and we walked on in silence.

23

Back home I completed a thorough search of the house. If anything was missing, it certainly wasn't obvious. I eventually convinced myself that I was being paranoid and put the matter to rest.

As the daylight began to wane, I grabbed a bottle of merlot, a plate of olives, my guitar and went outside and sat on my veranda. As I strummed the strings, I thought of Arthur and his soporific existence and wondered whether I was simply a younger version of him. I shuddered at the thought. I lit a cigarette and inhaled while staring at the magnificent view in front of me. I watched the sun slide gently into the earth as I refilled my glass. Caesar was off scouting in the distance and I relaxed into the stillness surveying my modest empire. My house was high up on the outskirts of Whitstone offering a picture postcard view of the sleepy village below. The back of the house captured the striking panorama of Inglegor Pike and its neighbours. The garden was a long narrow strip that fell away in a gentle slope towards the adjoining fields that stretched for miles before merging with the rising hills. The jewel in the crown was the river, which cut a swathe through the middle of the landscape. On warm summer days, when the flow was languid, I would lay in the gentle current and let the cool water flow over me. In spring, after the snows melted, I would stand in awe on the riverbank and watch the water rise and the flow increase until it became a boiling viaduct, carrying away all in its path.

My passion was the garden. When I first arrived, it was an empty paddock, which was good as it gave me the chance to stamp my individuality on it. It was still a work in progress but now I had extensive raised vegetable beds and a sunny courtyard full of potted herbs. I planted a concoction of fruit trees, which gave me an overabundance of apples, pears, plums, and cherries come autumn. To the east of the garden was a large disused barn that was still in relatively good condition. I intended renovating it, but at present, it was a receptacle for various bits of garden machinery and paraphernalia. The house and land were extravagant for a single person and for the first time in ten years I found myself asking the question "why?" A sudden wave of melancholy washed over me. I was not one for excessive navel-gazing but I was unable to shake the emotion. I was actually feeling sorry for myself. Here I was, surrounded by the magnificence of nature, clean fresh air; sweet smells of spring, a view to die for. I had no money worries; in fact, no worries at all. If ever a man could relax safe in the knowledge that the road ahead was straight and clear, then I was that man. Still the feeling lingered. I took a gulp of wine, lit another cigarette and paused while a realisation slowly dawned on me. The truth was plain to see—my malaise was loneliness.

4: PUMP IT UP

When that first rehearsal with Geordie finished, we were all shell-shocked. We'd never played as well and sounded as good. Before Geordie came along we were three individual components, competent, steady, dull. Once Geordie arrived, he stuck us all together—he was the glue. Now, the whole was greater than the sum of the parts. His gift was the ability to see the value in a song and turn it into something special. He was our conductor, our musical mentor. He thought I was the genius because I wrote the songs, but he was the real genius. He took the songs to new heights and on different journeys that no one else in the band would ever have dreamt of and he did it quickly. There were no long tedious sessions of going over and over the same song ad infinitum. He knew after the first hearing what he wanted to do and where we should go with it. I gave him a skeleton and he put flesh and skin on it.

Robbo appeared a bit sceptical at first, but after trying out some of Geordie's ideas on the first two songs, he turned to me and gave the thumbs up. We were all invigorated by this breath of fresh air. When Geordie talked music, he was alive, communicative, articulate, sociable and likeable. The rest of the time he was a bullying, cynical pain in the arse. I suppose you've got to take the crunchy with the smooth: and that's what we did. He lectured us all that first night, not in a condescending, demeaning manner, but in a supportive, encouraging way.

'Okay, you're all competent on your instruments but that's not good enough for what we're going to do. You've got to really knuckle down and learn your trade and that means doing homework. You've got to listen to all sorts of musical styles and tastes; you've got to practice, practice, practice. Practice until you get blisters, until your fingers bleed. Know your instrument, what it's capable of, find its limitations and then push them back even further. Experiment with different chords, different progressions and alternative tunings; you may never use any of them but that's not the point, they're in your arsenal should you ever need them.

Flaky, the drums are the heartbeat and like the heart there are many different types. Fast heart, slow heart, angry heart, happy heart, sad heart, dead heart—broken heart. You need to learn the heart of each song. You are the band's heartbeat. You pump the blood to the rest of us—we rely on you.' Flaky nodded intently, hanging onto every word that fell from Geordie's lips.

'Robbo, you're a good guitar player but you need to get yourself a sound, something distinctive, it doesn't matter whether it's been done before or not, just as long as you do it better. When people hear that guitar, they need to be able to say, "that's a Shooting Stars song". It's not just the tone either, it's the way you play or don't play. A guitar doesn't have to be flat out from start to finish. It's not quantity, it's quality. Remember, silence can be your ally, and if used correctly, it will embellish your playing better than a dozen different effects pedals ever can.' Robbo smiled and nodded. Geordie turned to me. It was my turn and I thought I'd get my comment in first.

'What do you think about us getting a proper singer,' I said, 'I'm okay but it's hardly brilliant is it?' I was genuine and thought I was being pragmatic. Geordie didn't think so.

'Don't you fucking dare!' he yelled, 'If you get a singer then I'm out of this band.'

'Well, it was only an idea,' I replied sheepishly.

'I can't believe you'd even contemplate such a thought. You wrote these songs, you bloody sing them! You know what every word means, what inflexions to give and what not to give. Who else would sing them, eh? Singing isn't all about hitting the right notes, about being in tune all the time, about correct breathing patterns and clarity; sure, all those things help, but do you know what *the* most important thing is about a voice?' We all shook our heads.

'It's about this!' he jumped to his feet and slammed his fist into his own chest. 'It's about passion! And what's passion? It's emotion—envy, jealousy, love, hate, greed, indifference, spite and vindictiveness. It's about loss and grief and desperation. It's about hope and hopelessness and chasing dreams and about never having a chance of achieving them. It's about life and death, blood and guts and fucking and living. It's about new life and old life, about slow painful death and unashamed, unconditional love for another person ...' he paused. His eyes were wild and a bead of sweat rolled down his cheeks. He sat down and continued quietly as if exhausted by his own ferocity.

'It's about beauty,' he whispered. 'That's what singing is—it's passion.' He tailed away as though recalling some sad event in his life and there was an uneasy silence for a second or two. The moment passed and he jumped to his feet again with new purpose.

'We've got a lot of work to do, but if we're all committed and honest and really give it a go, then it won't be long before we're signing our names on that record deal that's waiting out there for us. I can't promise what sort of deal it will be, but at least we'll have jammed our foot in the their fucking door! We'll be on that road to nowhere—fast. So you lot need to go home and really think hard about this. Is it what you really want? If there's any doubt at all, then you owe it to the rest of us to fuck off, and we'll get someone in who really does want it.' He slowly stared at Robbo and Flaky in turn as though searching for a chink in their armour. 'Right, that's enough for tonight. Rehearsal tomorrow at six ... don't be late! Anyone fancy a pint?'

'Great idea!' said Robbo and Flaky in unison and with audible relief.

'Oh, and one more thing,' Geordie continued. We all stopped what we were doing.

'What?' I asked.

'The name, "Shooting Stars", I know where you're coming from and I quite like it, but, what about giving it just a little twist?' I was apprehensive, as I was quite fond of the name.

'Go on ...' I replied.

'Change Stars to Tsars ... Tsars with a TS, not a CZ.'

'What?' Robbo asked.

'Shooting Tsars,' emphasised Geordie with his arms extended.

'Why?' inquired Flaky with a pained expression on his face as though contemplating an unsolvable mathematic conundrum.

'It's edgier. Conjures up connotations of something radical, something dangerous.' I smiled, it was great: the changing around of two letters gave the name another dimension, more depth. Robbo turned away and began unplugging his equipment.

'Whatever,' he said blithely.

'I don't get it?' Flaky needed a bit of help.

'The Russian revolution; you know, bang, bang! The end of the monarchy, the ruling class being overthrown, a new vanguard, a new cause, a new world order ...'

'Oh yeah, I get it now,' said Flaky, although he obviously didn't.

'The Shooting Tsars it is then,' I said.

We packed away, chattering excitedly to each other, and headed off to the pub.

5: YOU CAN'T ALWAYS GET WHAT YOU WANT

I slept late the next day, waking at 11 am feeling unusually groggy. I showered, dressed, fed Caesar and enjoyed a leisurely breakfast of bacon and eggs washed down with a few cups of strong black coffee. I rarely listened to the radio, but for some reason, I turned it on while doing the washing up. A song began to play. It sounded familiar, and after a split second, I recognised what it was and turned the radio up and listened intently. It sounded vibrant and fresh, and although the song was from well over a decade ago I marvelled at its power and beauty. It ended slightly prematurely as the DJ resumed his inane prattle.

'That was "From The Cradle to the Rave" by the Shooting Tsars. Wow! That sounded good. Whatever happened to the Shooting Tsars I wonder? They were absolutely massive for a while in the nineties. They were here one minute and gone the next. I'll have to see if I can dig out any of their other hits and give them a spin, I enjoyed that. Okay, onto our hot topic of the day; is bottled water better for you than tap water ...' I flicked the radio off and lit a cigarette.

'Prick! Here one minute gone the next. We were around for years you wanker!' I shouted at the radio. I was annoyed at the DJ but felt quite proud that my song had stood the test of time. I thought about my life in the band until I began to feel the bitterness rising. *Forget it mate, it's not worth it.* I stubbed my cigarette out in the ashtray and got a sudden vision of my Mother lecturing me.

"William, don't use my saucers as ashtrays please." I emptied the ashtray, washed and dried it and placed it on the kitchen bench near the front door so I wouldn't forget to take it with me on my journey.

#

It was late afternoon and I decided it was time I set off down to Cornwall to visit my Mother. I checked all the windows and doors, removed any perishables from the fridge and emptied all the bins. I packed my bag into the boot and called Caesar, who obediently jumped into the back seat. He followed his tail around in a circle a couple of times before slumping down on his blanket. A few drops of rain began to fall as the last of the weak daylight faded. I locked the back door of the house and climbed into the car, started the engine and turned the headlights on.

'Oh shit! I knew I'd forget something.' I jumped out of the car and fumbled for my house key, unlocked the door and walked into a dusky kitchen. The ashtray was sat patiently on the side where I'd left it earlier. I was just about to pick it up when the phone began to ring. I went into the hallway and picked up the receiver. 'Hello?'

'Will, is that you?' I recognised the cockney twang immediately. My heart began to race as a cold shiver ran down my spine.

'Will, Will, are you there?' the voice reiterated again. There was only one Chas Dupont—and that was one too many! I hadn't expected to talk to the Tsars ex-manager ever again. The last time we spoke was over ten years ago outside a courtroom in London, shortly after the Judge awarded in favour of the plaintiff, GMC Records. It wasn't a pleasant exchange and I occasionally regretted the words I used that day.

'Yes Chas, I'm here. How are you? But more importantly, how in hell's name did you get my number? It's ex-directory!'

'You know me, Will, I have my ways sunshine, I have my ways.'

'Yes Chas, I know you do, only too well.'

'Now, now Will, don't be like that; can't we kiss and make up? A lot of water has passed under the bridge and I'm offering you an olive branch.' I recalled the pain he caused me and became angry.

'What is this? Dial a fucking cliché! You've got some nerve, I'll give you that. You and your buddies, GMC, ripped us off and ended our career and you want to kiss and make up!' I yelled down the phone. Chas tried to interject.

'Now, now, Will, that's not quite true is it, there's a lot …' I cut him off.

'You slapped a writ on us, we couldn't write, we couldn't play, we couldn't record. Twelve months in the courts and at the end what did we get? A great big cup of fuck all! You broke us mentally and financially. By the time we'd paid the court costs and lawyers and every other blood-sucking leech in London we didn't have a pot to piss in.' I was surprised at the ferocity of my anger. Chas tried to interrupt again.

'Will, Will, I understand how you feel. We all got burnt; I didn't come out of it too good either. I was as shocked as you were by the actions of GMC. If you hadn't sacked me, we would have been able to work it out amicably.'

'You sacked yourself, you toe-rag, when you sided with GMC.'

'Actually Will, I was trying to smooth things over and get GMC to drop the court action, that's until I received the letter from your lawyers terminating my contract.'

'And so you decided to jump on the bandwagon and sue us as well! Get your pound of flesh, as if you hadn't milked us enough!'

'I told you not to mess with GMC Will, I warned you! But did you listen? NO! I said you'd never win. But you still had to take on the biggest record company in the world. Great career move, Will. How do you think they got the nickname "Mafia"? I told you a million times, don't fight them, there can only be one winner; they are ruthless. They would rather spend ten million in court and make sure you never record again than lose face. If you'd followed my advice you'd have done the last

32

album, taken the money, shut your gob and then searched for a new deal.'

'Yeah, you mean sell our souls to the devil so you get your fucking twenty percent; that's what you were pissed off with then and that's what still riles you now. We may have lost the battle but we walked away with our integrity intact. I can sleep easy at night, can you?' I didn't really blame Chas for what had happened anymore. I wasn't sure whether he knew about the caveats and small print in our record contract or not. He advised us to use a respected (and very expensive) music lawyer to go over the contract but we opted to use Robbo's brother-in-law, who was more used to local divorce proceedings than multi-million-pound record deals. It was a bad career move, but shit happens and you move on. I pulled a cigarette out of my top pocket and lit it. Chas must have heard me puffing away.

'Still on the smokes Will? You know they will kill you.'

'Well, something has to kill you in the end. I take it you've given up?'

'Yeah, coming up for three years next week; best thing I ever did. I feel as fit as a fiddle. Even taken up running.' The nicotine focused my thoughts and I found it hard to envisage the diminutive, bandy-legged, ex-barrow boy pounding the bitumen.

'So Chas, you didn't ring up for a dose of verbal abuse, why did you call?'

'Well, I was just wondering how you and the boys were going. Do you see much of them?'

'I see Robbo occasionally, but I haven't seen Flaky or Geordie since we split up.'

'Wow! You've got to be joking? You lot were as thick as thieves, especially you and Geordie. What happened?'

'Life … that's what happened. Now let's cut the bullshit Chas, what's your real reason for calling?'

'Okay, I'll be up front; you know I always like to talk straight'. *No you don't.* I sucked on my cigarette and eased back into a chair, ready for a good dose of bullshit.

'Well, here it is, a bit of a deal, a very good deal actually, for all of you'.

'Okay, I'm all ears.'

'I'm putting together a package tour of a few of the best acts from the nineties and you were top of my list. You know the thing, play the big arenas, roll out all the hits for an hour or so, plenty of merchandise, reissue the old product. It's a license to print money. What do you say Will?'

'I need more details. How many gigs? How much money? Which other bands are going to be on the tour? How long is it going to be? There are a million and one questions to be answered before I would even consider it.'

'Will, Will!' Chas tried to interrupt but I continued.

'And it's not just up to me, is it? There are four in the band, and without all four of us, I'd definitely not do it. Robbo is probably tied up with recording work. Flaky is now a full-time psychologist and wouldn't be interested in getting caught up in that madness again and as for Geordie—well who knows where he is. He may be dead for all we know.'

'Will, my friend, you always sweat the small stuff. That's my job, all you have to do is turn up and play music, I'll do the rest. Listen; here are the bones of the deal. Thirty gigs over ten weeks, with a two-week break mid-tour. All the gigs are in the UK. Mid-range hotels, no presidential suites in the Hilton this time. We'll be doing it on a budget so that you guys get more of the money. You all get a set fee of two hundred grand. You also get a twenty-five percent share of merchandise after costs. I'm still negotiating TV and video rights. All you have to do is get the band together, come down to London for two weeks rehearsal and put together a sixty minute set of some of your finest songs—it's easy. Come on Will, it's money for old rope. You're going to be onstage for an hour a night, that's a pretty good rate of pay—I've spent longer having a shit!'

'You need more fibre in your diet, Chas,' I laughed down the phone. 'Who else is on the tour?'

'I've approached the Stoned Crows, The Green Circles and Divina so far and they all seem interested, especially when I told them the Tsars will be on the bill.'

'Bit presumptive aren't you?'

'Faint heart never won fair lady.'

'Jeez, ever thought about making a living from writing greeting cards.' My bullshit detector was going into overdrive. The trouble with Chas was figuring out exactly what he was up to before it was too late. I was intrigued by the offer but decided to nip it in the bud.

'Listen, Chas, it sounds great but I think it's a non-starter. First of all, I really don't need the money, I'm doing okay. Plus, I really don't like those nostalgia tours, it just devalues what we used to believe in and stand for.' Chas was not renowned for giving up lightly.

'You may not need the money Will, but what about the other guys? Okay, Robbo may be doing well for himself but what about Flaky and more importantly what about Geordie? Can you imagine what two hundred thousand might do for him?' I was a little puzzled on two counts; one, he assumed Geordie was skint, which he couldn't possibly know for sure and secondly, when he mentioned two hundred thousand, I'd assumed he was talking per band. However, if I understood his last sentence correctly it appeared that it was two hundred thousand each. Although wealthy, my working-class upbringing couldn't ignore that sort of money. My Father would have needed to work for twenty years to earn that sort of dough, and here I was being offered it for eight weeks work!

'And as for your image Will, people don't see you as some washed up old has-beens trying to make a quick buck; they see you as a seminal act cut off in your prime by the machinations of the music industry. You're heroes man! And there's a whole army of kids out there who have your records but have never had the chance to see you live. It's a chance to go out there, strap on your Gibson, and show the people what you've got. Once you've done the tour you can return to your life of quiet solitude. Think about it Will, think about it.' Against my better judgement, I was thinking about it.

'So, let me get this straight. Is it two hundred grand for each member? That's eight hundred thousand for the group?'

'Yes, spot on. Did you think I meant two hundred grand per band?'

'No, just clarifying,' I lied. The money, the little speech Chas just made, the thought of playing live again—I was beginning to consider it. *Yes, it might be good to strap on the old guitar again and go out there without all the bullshit and just play.* What was I thinking! Had I forgotten all the heartache being in the band caused me and how I'd vowed never to trust anyone again, especially Chas Dupont.

'Chas, we were crucified, and I'm sorry, but I don't believe in resurrection.' There was a pause and then I heard him laugh.

'Thanks, Will, I've been struggling to think of a name for the tour and you've just nailed it. The Resurrection Tour—what do you think? The kids will love it! So come on Will, how about it? For old times sake?'

'No Chas, it's a non-starter. I'm really not interested. It's not on. It's just not feasible.'

'Okay Will. I get the message. Just hear me out and then I'll go. The first gig is the Isle of Wight festival on 11th June and the last gig is the 20th August at Wembley Arena. But the crucial thing is, I need to know whether you're in or out within the next two weeks. If you're in, then you and the boys need to get down to London ASAP. I have pencilled in two weeks rehearsal time for all the bands. I'll give you my mobile number and if you change your mind give me a call. Maybe you owe it to the other guys to let them have their say before you go making any final decision.'

He gave me his number and I wrote it down more out of politeness than anything else. We exchanged farewells and then hung up. I needed a smoke and some fresh air, a contradiction in terms I know, but nevertheless. I retraced my steps, grabbed the ashtray and locked up the house for the second time. The car engine was still murmuring away and the looming rain had turned into a fine crisp drizzle. I placed the ashtray on the roof of the car as I lit up and paced up and down the driveway talking to myself.

'Cheeky bastard. Ten years. Two bloody weeks. How did he get my number? I should never have answered the phone! Two hundred thousand! Thirty gigs. If I hadn't gone back in for that ashtray, I'd never have known. Geordie, what's happened to Geordie?' I paced until my cigarette burnt down to my skin. I threw it onto the ground and stamped it out. I jumped into the car and looked at the ever-patient Caesar.

'Okay Caesar, what tunes do you want?' I flicked open the glove box and pulled out a clutch of CDs. 'Paul Weller, Beautiful South, Morrissey, The Beatles, Oasis, Motown compilation, Big Bill Broonzy? What's that you say? "Morrissey", are you sure? Some people find his lyrics a bit oppressive, a little bit depressing. Oh, is that right, you find a certain kind of comical irony in his lyrics. Okay, well Morrissey it is then, but don't come crying to me if you slip into a depressive, melancholic fog of self-absorbed reflection.' I put the CD in and reversed quickly down the driveway swinging the car around as I hit the main road. There was a grating noise on the car roof, followed by the sound of breaking glass.

'Shit! The bloody ashtray.'

6: HOMEWARD BOUND

I was racing down the motorway, engine purring sweetly, Big Bill Broonzy blasting out of the speakers. The rain had cleared and it was a cool clear night. I should have been happy; two weeks by the sea, catching up with the old girl, but I wasn't happy. I was annoyed, pissed off, confused and just a little bit excited. I was annoyed that I'd ever gone back for the ashtray, if I hadn't, I would have been blissfully unaware of the offer from Chas. I was pissed off with myself that I had even given Chas the time of day. I should have given him a big serve and thrown the phone down—but I hadn't—I had listened. I was confused because I was contemplating the deal. I, Will Harding, considering a deal offered by that double crossing, cheating bastard of an ex-manager, Chas Dupont! But most worrying of all was the shard of excitement I felt in the pit of my stomach. I kept trying to push it aside, but it kept tickling away like a light feather, deep inside. Could the Tsars really get back together and play to sellout crowds again? Would people turn up?

'Fucking wake up, you clown!' I chastised myself for having such thoughts. 'There's not a snowball's chance in hell of it happening.'

\#

Chas had become the Tsars Manager in 1990 less than six months after our first rehearsal. We'd been kicking up a storm around the country when he'd made a special trip to Newcastle to watch us play and offered his services that night. In less than six weeks we had signed a million pound recording and publishing contract with the giants of the business, Global Media Conglomerate or GMC. Three months later we had our first No 1 single, followed by a number one album that stayed in the UK charts for eighteen consecutive months. We all thought the deal with GMC was for three albums because they had three "options" on us. As it turned out the three options didn't kick in until we'd delivered our first album. We didn't even really know what an "option" was when we'd signed up. Only during the court case did we learn that it was a record company's win-win guarantee. If they wanted us to do another album after our first, we had to do it, likewise with the second and third. We couldn't shop around for another deal. Also, whatever royalty rates we'd signed up for originally, were applicable to all the options. So it didn't matter if we became a lucrative international act, we still only got ten percent royalties. We also didn't realise that we were signed to them for ten years! Even if we completed our albums in five years, we were stuck to the bastards for ten. On the other hand, if our first album had been a flop, GMC had the right to rip up the contract and wave us goodbye. Apart from their initial investment, everything was stacked their way. We were as green as cabbages. We weren't the first band to get sucked into a bad deal and we certainly weren't the last. GMC had all sorts of things in the contract's small print about restraint of trade, breach of contract, copyright and one hundred percent clawbacks. We didn't learn what any of this meant until the court case, by which time it was too late. The million pound sign on fee was recoupable. In other words, GMC gave us the money up front but then recouped it from our record sales. Not until after it was all paid back did we receive another penny from them. In fact, it turned out that every cost we incurred was ultimately paid for by the band. Rehearsal rooms, recording studios, engineers, producers, videos, the whole shooting match was paid upfront by GMC and then deducted from our sales. Anyone who thinks the life of a rock star is a gold mine needs to think again. We also learnt at our court case that for every CD sold we received ten percent of the wholesale price not the retail price, minus twenty five percent for packaging. When we did eventually receive royalties, this was to be split five ways—twenty percent to each band member and twenty percent to Chas. Then of course we had to pay the usual tax on it. It wasn't until our third album that we eventually began to see some of the money we'd earned. The real winners were the record companies. On our last tour of America, promoting our third album "Buddha's Playground", we'd secretly been approached by a large independent label, Jeffa Records. We assumed that once we had completed our contractual obligations relating to "Buddha's Playground" we were free to negotiate with whoever we liked. We had been trying to secure a new deal with GMC, with far better royalty rates, but all they offered was an extra two percent and two more options; it was an insult for such a large act. The boys from the States were offering seven million pounds for a three album deal and sixteen percent royalties. Our latest album had entered the US top twenty and we were on the cusp of becoming a truly international act. Anyone in the music business knows that if you crack America, you're made for life—if you have the right record deal.

We played the "Red Rift' festival on a private island in the UK, to 60'000 adoring fans. We were the biggest band in Europe and had finally made inroads into the States. We weren't even at our peak; we were still climbing, but we were far and away the biggest group in the country and in Europe. The world truly was our oyster. We broke the news to Chas about leaving GMC after that gig, which turned out to be our last performance together. Chas flipped his lid and immediately informed GMC. A week later we received a letter from the GMC lawyers explaining about the "options" and how we still had one more album to deliver. Chas begged us not to start a legal battle with GMC, a battle he said we would never win. Geordie accused Chas of knowing about the dodgy contract from day one and of being in GMC's corner instead of ours. In an act of rash stupidity and grand arrogance we sacked Chas and started legal proceedings to take GMC to court. Their lawyers were bigger than ours and in retaliation they issued an injunction citing the "restraint of trade" clause in our contract. This prevented us from performing or recording until the court case was settled. We initially weren't that bothered about GMC's legal machinations, in fact, in a way we were quite pleased. It would give us a break from the hectic touring schedule and free us up to concentrate on secretly recording our fourth album (provisionally and portentously titled "Dark Side of the Tune"). We figured it might take three months, maybe six at a push before the court would find in our favour, so in the meantime we surreptitiously left the country and began illegally recording in the Seychelles. We decided against hiring another manager and thought we could manage our own affairs—another bad move. Collectively we couldn't have run a corner shop never mind an international act like the Tsars. After eight weeks we returned home with not so much as a "B" side recorded. The Seychelles offered too much of a distraction. We had spent the whole time shagging, partying, scuba diving, jet skiing and snorting huge amounts of coke. When we got home we found out that we had a new lawsuit to contest, the sacking of Chas. Things were getting out of hand. We had no idea how to track our expenditure; no-one had a clue what was coming in or due out. In reality, the life of a successful rock star is a closeted, insular, selfish existence. Every whim is catered for. You want a car? Here's a car, don't worry, it's taxed and fully insured. You want a house? Pick one out, I'll do the rest, just sign this. You want to go to Greece? No problem first class or private jet? Do you want a pool with the mansion? Okay, silly question. Out of drugs? Let me make a call. You've assaulted a cameraman, no sweat, I'll sort it. You've been caught speeding and drink driving, no problem leave it to me. You want your arse wiped? Fine, hand me the tissues. All these things and more a good manager organises.

Another couple of months passed before we went back into the studio again, this time in the exotic climes of Manchester. We argued, we bickered, we got drunk, we got high and we got low. We were slowly beginning to hate each other. It took six months to record the album and it was the best thing we'd ever done and we were all ecstatic with the results. Somewhere during that time, the title had changed from "Dark Side Of The Tune" to "Bloom". Two months later and we were in the final stages of mixing. We arrived one afternoon to learn that there had been a small fire in the mixing room overnight and that our precious tape was now a pile of ash. And worse—we had never created a back-up.

While we had been secretly recording our new album our lawyers had been scrapping it out with GMC in the courts. Six weeks after the fire, the Judge was ready for his verdict. Only me and Robbo attended that day. Flaky had retreated to his London pad, refusing to talk with anyone and Geordie had disappeared after the fire and hadn't been seen since. I was still confident that we'd win the case, so when the Judge ruled in favour of GMC my whole world came crashing down. We were ordered to pay GMC's costs (over one million pounds) on top of our own costs of over five hundred thousand pounds, and we were still legally bound to GMC to deliver one more album. To be fair to the old Judge, he was sympathetic to our case but pointed out that GMC had taken a risk on us, a venture capital risk. He said we should see ourselves as a consumer product; GMC had put up all the money (which they got back through our sales) and organised all the promotion and now that they were finally beginning to see some return on their investment we were hoping to walk away and sign up with one of their competitors. He advised us to mend our bridges with the record company and in future employ a specialist music industry lawyer before signing anything. There was more legal waffling but I'd stopped listening by that point. When me and Robbo trudged disconsolately from the courts Chas was waiting for us outside. He tried his old charm but we weren't in the mood. He said that GMC were willing to talk—we weren't! He even told us that he'd drop his lawsuit against us if we'd just get around the negotiating table. It was an olive branch and Chas was GMC's little dove. I was full of bile and hate and the last thing I wanted to do was sit around a table with a conga-line of suits, discussing what was best for *my* band, *our* band! I was tired emotionally and physically, so were the other boys. My only way to get back at GMC and Chas was to take away what they wanted most, the band—and that's exactly what I did. I let Chas have it with both barrels. I accused him of being a liar, a cheat, a swindler. I said he was a Judas who had no scruples or morals, who would sell his own mother into slavery if there were enough money in it for himself. I expected stiff resistance from the little cockney barrow boy—but got none. The trouble with words is, that once said, they can never be unsaid. That was the last time I'd seen or spoken to Chas.

#

I filled the car up with petrol on the outskirts of Leeds before eventually getting onto the M1 and was now in the process of bypassing Sheffield. I lit a cigarette and inhaled. I could feel the nicotine hit the veins and pump up into my brain where it brought relief from my troubles. I replayed the phone call in my head trying to pick out the catch. I thought about Chas and Geordie and their love-hate relationship. Chas loved himself and hated Geordie whereas Geordie hated Chas and also hated himself.

'Where was Geordie? Why had no-one seen or heard from him? Was he dead?' My mind drifted back.

#

Geordie had been our Rottweiler, our bouncer, our protector and our tormentor. He fought like a Spartan and drank like a camel. Once the drugs came on the scene he embraced them with open arms. In hindsight, he was out of control from day one, but as the madness of fame and fortune escalated, his erratic and worrying behaviour was lost in the shadows. He was the only one in the band that had a fractious relationship with Chas, whom he had threatened to kill on numerous occasions. This usually happened when he was orbiting some galaxy on a

43

rocket fuel mix of dope, coke and or LSD, washed down with copious amounts of whisky. He was loud, vitriolic, argumentative, aggressive and menacing. But I could see through his tough shell. Underneath was a desperately sad and lonely man, well meaning and overly generous. On the few occasions I broke through to the other side, we had long meaningful talks about many subjects. I was the only one willing to share a room with him, and likewise, I was the only one who he'd share a room with. The others were scared of him. He often delivered blows to them when they were out of order or riding the pop star Prima Donna attitude a bit hard. Once, during a rehearsal, we had a disagreement on the arrangement of a song, it soon turned into a full blown argument. Geordie went to hit me in the face and I ducked, he fell over his amp and cut his head open. He rose in a towering rage. I knew if he got hold of me he'd as good as kill me. I grabbed a half empty bottle of Budweiser that sat on top of my amp. I smashed it on the side of a table and it shattered into a lethal weapon.

'Take one fucking step closer,' I screamed in his face 'and you'll be doing a duet with Buddy fucking Holly'.

'Okay Billy boy, we'll do it your way.' He backed off, smiling. After that he never abused me again, neither verbally or physically. I had won his respect. His verbal tirades were often more harmful than his fists. On many occasions he had Flaky in tears. Once he started, he'd never let up until he'd scored his pound of flesh or until he passed out. But the one who took the brunt of his rage was Chas. They were like chalk and cheese. To Geordie, Chas was everything he hated in a person. He saw him as a fake in a flash suit, a cockney motor mouth that would rip off his own grandmother if given half a chance. Likewise, Chas saw Geordie as a bigoted, Scottish oaf who had serious psychological problems and a chip on his shoulder bigger than the Forth Bridge. Whenever the two were around each other there was constant sniping. They were like a couple of world war one infantrymen, glaring at each other from behind the trenches, every now and then popping up to take a pot shot. It was rare when either landed a fatal blow. Both were so thick skinned that only the most spiteful attack could penetrate their armour. Unfortunately, like most wars of attrition, the biggest casualties were the innocent. It was the roadies, road managers, producers, engineers or the rest of the band that would end up in the crossfire. Geordie had suffered a troubled childhood. His Father had deserted the family when he was very young. His Mother was an alcoholic and from what I could ascertain, very violent. And his younger Brother was killed by a car one night when he and Geordie were on their way back from the cinema. Being the older brother, I assumed Geordie blamed himself for the death of his younger sibling—and this was where his rage came from. He had only ever told me the tale once and it was not something to bring up lightly. After his brother died, his Mother disappeared leaving Geordie to fend for himself. She was found a few weeks later, floating face down in the River Clyde. He ended up being taken in by his Grandparents who lived in a remote fishing village in the Scottish Highlands. This is where he gained some sort of normality. For the first time in his life he had a stabilising influence. By the time he was fourteen, he had found music, devoting most of his time to learning the bass and ripping off riffs from his favourite bands. He left school at sixteen and immediately set off for London in search of fame and fortune. He only got as far as Leeds and played in various local bands, supplementing his income with bar work in the city.

#

I pulled into a motorway service station and went inside to get a coffee. I asked for a cappuccino from a sullen girl and was given something that resembled muddy water with a layer of scum on the top. I knew better than to complain. As I made my way outside, a tall, slender, well dressed man bumped into me. The liquid passing itself off as coffee splashed over my hand; luckily it was tepid.

'Oh, I do beg your pardon, I'm so terribly sorry; here let me …' The man reached into his long cream overcoat and pulled out a tissue.

'It's fine, don't worry, really,' I replied. The man looked at me with an apologetic grin.

'Are you sure? Hope it's not too hot.'

'I'm fine, honest.' His eyes narrowed and I thought he was about to ask me a question. We were blocking the entrance.

'Let me get you a fresh one,' he offered, as I began to move away.

'No, no … really, it's okay.' I made my way to an undercover area where all the other lepers were and lit up a cigarette. The night was cold and damp and I felt a chill in my bones. I watched the motorway traffic, incessant, snaking its way to destinations unknown. Lorries continually pulled onto the slip road and made their way to the large vehicle car parks. Their loads creaked and groaned like ailing pre-historic monsters. The engines roared and brakes hissed as forward momentum was brought to an ungainly halt. People milled about, coming and going, apparent randomness to the untrained eye. The building, a large concrete and glass edifice, sat like an alien spaceship in the English countryside. A feeble looking walkway straddled six lanes of bitumen below, connecting to its sister ship on the opposite side. All lights and flashing signs, cheap tasting food at expensive prices, row upon row of porno mags, game machines and telephones. It could have been a crucible of humanity, all creeds and classes of life meeting as equals under the same roof; alas, this was not a place for discussion and communication with one's fellow man. It was soulless and guileful; its only motivation—to remove money from your pocket as quickly as possible. People passed each other by like silent spectres. Eyes rarely met and if by accident they did, immediate suspicion was aroused. Mankind's disdain for his fellow man was nowhere more evident than on this carousel of indifference. I finished my smoke and immediately lit up another one. Someone moved out of the shadows towards me. I instantly tensed up.

'Orright wac! I couldn't scag a smoke off yer could I?' A sallow man in his mid-thirties darted forward. His eyes were dead, sunken into grey skin that clung to his bones like soggy newspaper. I eyed him suspiciously. Dirty, worn trainers jutted out beneath badly faded and frayed tracky bottoms; his lightweight Ben Sherman jacket engulfed his scrawny frame, offering little protection from the bitter night air.

'Yeah, sure,' I replied positively, belying my wariness. He smiled, a big wide gaping chasm of a smile; for a second I saw someone who was once young and vibrant, full of life; a Liverpudlian laugh-a-minute. I pulled a cigarette out of the packet and passed it to him; he took it carefully as though he'd been handed the holy grail. I leant forward as I lit it for him. He smelt of stale beer, old sweat and worst of all, defeat. He sucked deeply and lustily on the nicotine.

'Aw, cheers, mate. I've been hanging out for one. I've given up but every now and then I just need a fix, know what I mean?' I smiled back and relaxed a little.

'Yeah, I know exactly what you mean.'

'Most people you ask, tell you to fuck off and buy a packet. There's no fucking courtesy these days; what's wrong with good manners eh? All they have to say is "no", I'm not going to be offended or get violent. Peace and love man, peace and love, that's my motto, no need to be fucking rude. Problem is, there's no trust; the country's fucked; the whole world's fucked; know what I mean man?'

'Yeah, I know what you mean.'

'So, where you heading?'

'Cornwall, visit my Mam. You?'

'Fucking London—glorified shithole—see my kid. He's living with my ex. Fucking bitch! You got kids?'

'No, no I don't.'

'Best way mate; don't get me wrong, I love my la, would die for the little bastard but it's the women. I can fucking do without that grief; know what I mean?' I nodded but didn't reply. He stared at me for a few seconds before smiling again. His trance was interrupted by the blast of a car horn and someone shouting.

'C'mon Bazzer you wanker! Get in the fucking car!' He puffed vigorously on the butt of his cigarette and threw it to the ground.

'That's my brother. Complete tosser, but a heart of gold. Not many of us left. Anyway, thanks for the smoke I best be off.' He half turned before ambling back to me and sticking his hand out.

'Bazzer by the way. If you're ever in the 'pool, check me out. I'll take care of you. Just ask for Mad Bazzer, everyone knows who I am; Liverpool's my city.' He shook my hand vigorously before running off to the car that was waiting. I glanced down at my palm and saw a small white piece of paper carefully folded into an envelope shape. I had a good idea what it was and had no intention of taking it. I watched as Bazzer and his brother disappeared onto the slip road.

'I wasn't sure if you took sugar or not?' The voice made me start. 'Oh sorry, didn't mean to make you jump.' It was the man who had bumped into me a few minutes ago. I looked at him as he held out a fresh coffee. I really didn't want it, but it seemed churlish not to accept. I smiled.

'Oh, thanks, you really shouldn't have bothered.'

'Not at all; I can be a bit of a klutz at times. It drives my wife mad. Always breaking things or knocking things over.' I studied him as he talked. He would have been in his late thirties; well groomed, sparkling blue eyes, a well manicured shock of blond curly hair, glasses. 'She won't let me dry up anymore. Bit of a blessing really…' I threw my cigarette butt into my old coffee cup and deposited it in a nearby bin. I lit up another cigarette and offered the packet to my new acquaintance.

'Smoke?'

'Not for me, thanks anyway. I haven't smoked a cigarette since I was at university.'

48

'Don't tell me—Salford or Manchester?' It was a facetious comment and I regretted saying it immediately. The man appeared a little sheepish.

'Oxford, actually.' There was an embarrassed silence. 'Do you mind if I ask you a question?'

'No, fire away,' I replied casually.

'Well, it's a little rude, but are you Will Harding by any chance?' I laughed. The man's eyes lit up. 'I knew it, I knew it! Yes!' he punched the air with his fist. 'Straight away I saw you, I knew; I recognised your face and when you opened your mouth to speak, I was positive.' The man was genuinely excited. He held out his hand, which I shook warmly. 'Pleased to meet you. John Peterson is my name.'

'Pleased to meet you John,' I replied sincerely.

'Wait until I tell my wife. She won't believe it. I'm you're biggest fan, well, at least I think I am. I have all your CDs. I must have seen you live, oh, at least twenty times. You probably don't remember, but I once came backstage after a gig you did at Oxford Town Hall. You signed a tour T-shirt for me.'

'Well, I obviously can't ...' he cut me off.

'No, no, of course not. How silly of me. Of course you don't remember.' I glanced at my watch and decided to make a move.

'Well, I must get a move on. Got a long way to go.' John seemed a little crestfallen.

'Yes, yes, of course. I'm sorry, I've delayed you.'

'No, that's fine, it's been pleasant talking to you. It's not often I get to talk to an old fan these days.' He smiled at this.

'Before you go I really must ask you a question; is there any chance of you getting the Tsars back together?' I should have said no; I meant to say no—but instead I heard a disembodied voice saying,

'Well actually, there is a slight possibility. I've just been talking with our ex-manager and he's offered us a reunion tour.' John slapped his leg.

'Oh my God, that would be truly amazing. You are going to do it aren't you?'

'I'm not sure. We'll see.' John reached into his pocket and pulled out a business card and handed it to me. He suddenly became serious and business like.

'Here, take my card. I'm an entertainment lawyer. I don't like to blow my own trumpet but I'm the best in the business. If you ever need advice don't hesitate to call. Anytime, day or night. Don't sign anything or agree to anything without first talking to me. I understand what happened to you in the past. Dreadful shame, really appalling. Please, promise me you'll contact me if you get back together?' I stuck the card in my pocket.

'Okay, I will. We could have done with you years ago. Anyway, like I said, it's been a pleasure to meet you, but I must get going.' John followed at the side of me as I made my way back to the car. He talked incessantly and excitedly about the gigs he'd been to, about the CDs, the singles, the videos. He knew more about the Tsars than I did. Things I'd forgotten, songs I could barely remember, obscure 'B' sides and radio sessions. As I opened my car door he grabbed my hand again and shook it vigorously.

'It's been an absolute honour to have met you. Now you won't forget, will you? Anytime, day or night!'

'No of course not. Thanks.' I opened the car door.

'Sorry, just one last thing. I'm sure it's an urban myth; it's always a friend of a friend of a friend who has a copy and when I try to track it down the trail always goes cold.' I hadn't a clue what he was talking about. 'The Bloom sessions? Is it true? Did you secretly record an album while in dispute with GMC?'

'Yeah, it's true.' He punched the air again.

'Oh my word! You must release it; it's like the Holy Grail; I've heard so much about it, but have never been able to get a bootleg of it.'

'Sorry to disappoint you, but there's not much chance of that. The master tape was destroyed in a fire. Not sure how anyone got a bootleg.' John's face dropped like I'd just told him his Mother had died. I said goodbye once more and jumped into the car, fastened my seatbelt and fired the engine. He waved enthusiastically at me as I drove slowly out of the car park. I eased down the slip road and accelerated away. I had a quick glance back at the alien spaceship in the rearview mirror. Only its lights could be discerned now, twinkling in the darkness. I rounded a bend and they were gone.

7: PEOPLE ARE STRANGE (WHEN YOU'RE A STRANGER)

Being a man of weak will, I had succumbed to the temptation of the white powder that Bazzer, the Scouser, had deposited in my hand. The only drugs I had taken in ten years was nicotine and the occasional aspirin; now, I was speeding my tits off on whizz. I was enjoying myself so much that I came off the M5 near Taunton and took the long winding coastal road adding a good hour to my journey, chain smoking my way through the south-west corner of England, mind racing. I was still on a high when I neared the drowsy little fishing village of Pugstow and realised it would be pretty hard to get much sleep tonight. I had a sudden flash of inspiration. When I got to my Mother's house, I would ring Robbo and run Chas's proposition by him, just to sound him out. I drove along and gazed out at the ocean below. I could see the white peaks and crests of waves as they continually caressed the shore. A lighthouse, somewhere unseen, spun its light over the watery sheets, distant globes flickered and twinkled in reply, the only concession to human life in the inky blackness.

I arrived at Pugstow, slowing down as I crept through the quiet town. The rows of fishing cottages stood tall and proud along the high street, a gleaming mixture of whites, yellows, pinks and pale blues; pavements spotlessly clean; it looked like Legoland. I passed the local pub, which was lit up like a Christmas tree despite the unseemly hour. The outside was locked up but I spotted a few heads still in the taproom, obviously a few trusted locals enjoying a lock-in courtesy of the landlord. I drove down by the harbour, glancing at the small fleet of fishing boats bobbing about in the swell. Some of them seemed too tiny to possibly take on the wrath of the sea but no doubt they did and had been doing so for many a year. Caesar was awake and was stood up resting his head on my shoulder, eagerly panting in my ear. He knew this place and he was probably already scheming about racing through the sand and jumping in and out of the waves. I passed the last jetty and began the steep climb out of town. As we neared the peak of the hill, I turned right onto a tight gravel track that slowly meandered its way toward the sea before stopping abruptly in a large circular hollow. This is where my Mother's house was situated; in this idyllic natural feature. Protected from the elements but still within earshot of the sea below. I parked up at the side of the house, let Caesar out and grabbed my bag from the boot. I walked around the back of the house and opened the gate to the immaculately kept garden. A long straight path led to the back door, flanked on both sides by neatly manicured lawn and a whole plethora of various flowers and shrubs, each carefully pruned and trimmed. I breathed in the sweet perfumes that sprang from the early starters and suddenly noticed how much warmer it seemed here in this southern land. Caesar had to spoil the moment by relieving himself on one of Mother's hydrangeas. Dogs, what can you do! The kitchen light was on but the moonlight was bright enough to make it unnecessary. I pulled out my keys and let myself in. Caesar noisily barged past me, plodding from room to room searching for the owner. He had a good memory for people who overfed him. I sat down in the kitchen. The smell of good home cooking lingered in the air. I opened the fridge door and as usual there sat my favourite dish, meat and potato pie with a small jug of gravy next to it.

'Ah, God bless you Mother,' I sighed with satisfaction. Despite the appetite suppressing actions of the speed, I was looking forward to this feast. I decided on a plan of action. I'd open a bottle of red, reheat my pie, have a smoke and then ring Robbo. It was half past two in the morning and most people would be in bed but not Robbo, he was a night owl. Now would be a good time to catch him; but first, food and drink.

#

I scraped the gravy off the plate and into my mouth using the blade of my knife. Caesar sat a few feet away, head resting forlornly on his paws. I could feel him watching me intently but whenever I turned to look at him, he quickly averted his eyes and put on a sad woeful expression.

'Okay mate, you win. I can't stand the self-pity anymore.' I gathered his bowl from the floor and gave him a large spoonful of the pie despite him already finishing off a large tin of dog food. He wolfed it down in a few seconds and began licking the bowl pushing it noisily around the room. *What a waste of good pie.* I was still buzzing from the speed and hadn't any second thoughts about ringing Robbo. Another one of speed's little attributes—confidence. I pulled out my mobile and searched for Robbo's number. I walked outside into the back garden and sat down on a bench underneath the protection of a gazebo. The moonlight flickered through the blooming wisteria, its agreeable scent wafting under my nose. I lit a cigarette and sipped on my merlot, relaxing for a moment while taking in the serenity. Would I regret making this call at a later date? I convinced myself I had nothing to lose, after all, I was only making enquiries. I found Robbo's contact and pressed the call button. There was a brief pause and then the familiar ringtone. After a few rings a croaky voice answered.

'Hello? Who's this?' It was Robbo's unmistakable gruff Yorkshire voice on the other end. He didn't sound in good humour and I instantly regretted calling at this hour.

'Robbo, you old bastard, how are you going?'

'Who's this?' He repeated.

'Who the hell do you think it is? You haven't forgotten me already have you?'

'Well fuck me dry, if it's not me old mate Will. What the hell are you up to calling at this time, you're usually tucked up in bed with your cocoa and slippers by eight thirty,' his voice had changed on recognition of his caller and he now sounded genuinely pleased.

'Yeah, that's true. I didn't wake you did I? You sound a bit out of it,'

'No, I'm wide awake mate, I was just having a serious love affair with my bong when you called.'

'Still a dope fiend eh, old habits die hard,' I replied dryly.

'Old habits *do* die hard. I'm just laying down some tracks for my own amusement and I always find a little bit of menswear helps the creative process. What about you though? You must be on something to be ringing at this time?' Before I could reply, Robbo burst back in with a more serious tone as though the thought had just occurred to him,

'Oh, shit, what is it, somebody's injured, or dead aren't they? I knew something was going to happen when I woke up this afternoon, I had a bad, bad, feeling. Who is it mate?'

'No, no. Calm down Robbo, you've got it all wrong. No one's dead. Well, not to my knowledge. I'm ringing up with a proposition for you. Are you in a fit state to comprehend what I'm saying or shall I ring you back later?'

'Oh thank God for that, no listen, I'm totally compos mentis, I think. What is it?'

'I had a call from Chas,' I continued.

'What did that smarmy bastard want? Has he run out of blood?'

'No, not quite. He's putting together one of those reunion tours. A few bands from the nineties and he wants us to be on it. The money is good, two hundred big ones each, and there doesn't seem to be any obvious catches. We'd have to get a music lawyer to check out the contracts though, make sure it's watertight. The trouble is we've got to let

55

him know within the next two weeks—that's his deadline.' I was talking at a hundred miles an hour trying to get my thoughts out before Robbo finally rejected the idea.

'I mean, I'm only making enquiries, I obviously wouldn't trust the little cockney wide boy as far as I could throw him. I was totally against the idea when he first mentioned it. I mean, one, I don't want to get involved with him again and two, those tours are a bit sad really aren't they. A bunch of old has-beens in badly fitting pants and bald spots still trying to be out there on the edge. Plus, I said that you were probably booked up with studio work, and then there's Flaky; I mean, he's been out of the loop for a long time, well so have I too I suppose. And then the big question is—where the hell is Geordie? It's like he's fallen off the face of the earth. I mean I might be interested if everyone was up for it, you know, just for old time's sake. I don't need the dough and I'm pretty sure that you don't, but as for Flaky and Geordie, well who knows. It's money for jam. Ten weeks work, well actually, eight weeks work, there's a two week break mid-tour. Thirty gigs and two hundred grand apiece! It's not to be sniffed at …' I was rambling at speed and on speed.

'Whoa Will! Slow down man, you're twisting my melon. What the fuck are you on? Sounds like coke or speed,' replied Robbo in mock surprise.

'Well, just a little snifter, you know. I haven't touched any whizz for years and then I bump into this mad Scouser, gave him a cigarette, and as he's leaving, he shakes my hand and drops a little wrap of speed into it. I was going to throw it away, but I suppose my old habits got the better of me and I decided to have a little snort, but that's got nothing to do with why I rung you. I was going to ring you anyway …'

'Okay, okay, I believe you. I'm not the drug squad you know, you don't have to justify it to me,' he broke into a loud laugh which then turned into a coughing fit. 'So when are the gigs?'

'June 12th to 20th August.'

'Hang on a minute.' I heard him put the phone down and scuttle off into the background. He must have opened a door as I could suddenly hear music in the background.

'Right, let me check my diary. You're in luck. I've nothing booked until mid November. I had a band booked in for the next six months but I've been stitched up; anyway, it means I've nothing much happening from now until then.'

'What do you mean, stitched up?' I quizzed.

'Oh, nothing, I'll explain later. But yeah, I'm up for it.'

'What, you mean you'd even consider it?' I was taken aback. I had expected some resistance at least.

'Yeah man, it will be a laugh. I get tired of being a fucking troglodyte, stuck in this underground world, never seeing daylight. Let's do it for the fun this time, just the music, we'll put on a really good show …'

'Yeah, that's my sentiments entirely,' I reciprocated. 'When was the last time you saw Flaky?' I inquired.

'I saw him at Christmas. He was visiting some relatives in Cumbria and he called in for an hour or two on the way through. Had the wife and the two rug-rats with him.'

'Shit, I forgot he had two kids. How was he?'

'Oh …' he paused, 'yeah, yeah good. You know Flaky, he was always pretty straight, well he's even straighter now, but he seemed happy enough.' I detected Robbo wasn't telling me the whole story but I didn't pursue it.

'Do you reckon he'll be up for it?' I heard a raucous laugh down the line, which didn't fill me full of confidence.

'No! No, I doubt it, but you've got to give it a try, eh? Do you want me to call him?' asked Robbo.

'Yes, that might be better, at least you two have kept in touch. It might sound a bit mercenary if I were to ask him.'

'Okay, I'll give him a call later on today. Of course Flaky's the least of our worries. The big problem is going to be Geordie.' He was right. I was getting ahead of myself.

'Yeah you're right. Listen, maybe he's still involved in the music business in some way. Can you put out some feelers and see if you can come up with anything?'

'Yeah, I'll do that, but don't hold your breath.'

#

After I hung up, I relaxed in the garden while I finished off the bottle of red and smoked more cigarettes. I reflected on the chain of events and marvelled at life's little games of chance. I suddenly got the urge to pick up a guitar. My first ever acoustic was still in my bedroom wardrobe. I'd given my Mother express instructions to never get rid of it. I tiptoed quietly through the house and into my room, Caesar padding nonchalantly behind me. I retrieved my guitar, sat down on my bed and gently strummed a "C" chord. It was badly out of tune. I re-tuned it and began again, quietly playing the opening chords to "Cataclysmic Overdrive" our first single and first number one. It was a happy, carefree, little ditty that I had written in response to the rise of racism and fascist symbolism at the time. I sang the words softly as I strummed along.

'We followed your burning torch, down the path to salvation, we really should have known it was the road to damnation.' I lost track of time; I was no longer aware of my own presence, no self, just a voice and guitar, as one. As natural as breathing.

8: WHISKEY IN THE JAR-O

A day passed before I got a call from Robbo. Not good news. He was unable to shed any light on the whereabouts of the Haggis worrier and even more deflating was the fact that Flaky had categorically given the idea a big NO! I was surprised at how severely disappointed I felt. A couple of days ago I was blissfully unaware of any of this, and yet now, I couldn't think of anything else. Robbo said he'd leave it a couple of days and then work on Flaky again. It sounded futile to me, but Robbo seemed cool about it. Geordie however, was my problem. I relayed my regret to my Mother who offered her usual comforting slant on things.

'Well, it's probably for the best William. You don't really want to be getting into all that rock and roll mumbo jumbo again, do you?'

'Thanks Mam; I don't know where I'd be without your guidance.' I replied sardonically.

'That's okay love. I'm always here should you need me. Boys always come home when they're in trouble.' She hadn't detected the irony and I felt a bit of a heel.

When, at the age of nineteen, I had given up my job as a draughtsman with the council to concentrate on music, she'd nearly had a heart attack. As far as she was concerned, I had a job for life and a guaranteed pension when I retired. She thought I was insane. She didn't seem to have any concept of how famous the Shooting Tsars had become and how much money had passed through our hands. She'd watched us on telly a few times but the novelty soon wore off. I remember ringing her one day to tell her to watch Channel Four on a Sunday evening. There was a two hour documentary on the band. It was an in depth interview exploring the way we wrote, how we interacted, how we recorded, the effect we'd had on our contemporaries. Next time I spoke to her I asked what she thought of the documentary.

'Oh, sorry love but it was on at the same time as Songs of Praise so I didn't get to see it.' I was gob-smacked—for about two seconds. When I pointed out that the documentary was on for two hours and that Songs of Praise only ran for thirty minutes she informed me that there was also a re-run of the "Two Ronnies Christmas Special". I never really stood a chance. Mam wasn't part of the modern generation. She had grown up during the war and no doubt the best days of her life were the fifties when she had married Dad and lived off two pounds ten shillings a week. After John Lennon was shot I remember her confessing to quite liking the Beatles when they had first started out, "they had some nice catchy, happy songs." Once they grew their hair long, that was it, they may as well have been on the CIA's most wanted list, which they could well have been. She blamed most of the ills of the western world on long hair; drugs, lewdness, violence, terrorists, litter, the fall of the British Empire—cause—long hair.

#

I took Caesar for a walk on the beach and tried to come to terms with my disappointment. I felt flat. I knew it was always going to be a long shot but I hadn't thought for one second that Flaky would have been the one to scupper the whole thing. *God, what an arrogant bastard I am!* I hadn't even sent him as much as a Christmas card during the last ten years; I had never inquired into his fortunes, his family, his health or what he was up to. The only news I got was relayed through Robbo who at least made the effort of catching up with him occasionally. What had I ever done for Flaky? Now I expected him to drop everything on a fanciful whim. According to Robbo, Flaky had matured, emotionally and intellectually. He was no longer the spotty, dopey looking student that I recalled from all those years ago. I wondered whether I had matured or had I stood still, trapped in time. Maybe Mam was right, she had a more succinct way of expressing it, but what she had really been saying was, let it be, it's gone, you have a new life, it's good, it's easy, don't throw it all away on a childish dream. Move on and leave the past where it is. Then again, knowing Mother, she probably wasn't saying that at all. She was most likely implying that should I return to the life of a rock and roll star there was always a chance that I may grow my hair long.

I walked for hours along the beach much to Caesar's delight and eventually returned through the little fishing village as night began to fall. I trudged along the wet, glistening cobblestones, head bowed and shoulders hunched against the drizzle, feeling a little sorry for myself. I passed the Three Bells and smelt the appealing whiff of beer and cigarette smoke, anathema to most people but pure fragrance to me. I couldn't resist and went inside after tying Caesar up outside. The pub was roughly rendered on the inside with low ceilings supported by thick long beams. At the far end was a glowing coal fire that had attracted a small group of old men, busily playing dominoes. Although they did not lift their heads to witness my entrance, I knew that they had monitored my arrival. As they say in Yorkshire, see all, hear all, say nowt. I walked towards the bar but before I got very far the Barmaid berated me,

'Don't leave that poor hound out there in this weather. Bring him in and let him get a warm'.

'Are you sure? Is that alright?' I asked

'Of course it is,' she replied. I retraced my steps and untied a thankful Caesar.

'It must be your lucky day mate. Shake.' He shook himself of the excess rainwater and we both trotted happily into the welcoming pub. I walked up to the bar and thanked the Barmaid and ordered a pint of bitter and a double whisky.

'Been a bad day has it?' she inquired as she got my whiskey.

61

'Oh, I've had better. I'm cold and wet and feeling just a little bit sorry for myself.' I replied.

'Anything you want to talk about?'

'No, I'll be right in the morning. We all have bad days.' She handed me my double whisky and began to pull my bitter. I downed the whisky in one and placed the glass on the bar.

'Yes, I've had my fair share of bad days I must admit. My husband was killed in a boating accident two and a half years ago, so I've struggled with three young ones since. All boys. I do a bit of part time work here because I just can't survive on the welfare. It's not cheap bringing up three kids.' I wasn't really paying attention but agreed with her.

'Yes, I can imagine,' I replied, but the truth was I didn't have a bloody clue.

'Youngest is two, middle one turns four tomorrow and my eldest is five. I'll be glad when I can get them all off to school; at least it will make things a little easier. I mean they pay me a pittance here but it's not just about the money; I need to get out and speak to adults, I need some grown up company, a bit of intellectual stimulation. Although some of the dickheads that come in here, I'd be better off speaking to the kids.' She finished pulling my pint and handed it to me. I passed her a twenty pound note.

'I'll have another double and take one for yourself.'

'Oh thanks, I'll have a white wine.' I watched Caesar as he inspected the pub, instinctively drawn to the warmth of the fire. It looked like one of the old domino players had befriended him and there was no way Caesar would give up that fire for neither man nor beast. The Barmaid picked up my glass and turned to refill it. I noticed her body for the first time. She was extremely attractive and shapely for a Mother of three. I don't know what I expected. That's the trouble with stereotypes, life keeps shattering them for you. She turned and handed me my drink and my change. She had a strong face with full lips and glossy black hair that was pulled back into a ponytail, but there was definitely sadness in her eyes, unsurprisingly, yet the flame wasn't quite extinguished. I suddenly felt myself thinking about a woman sexually for the first time in many years.

'And now they're doing tests on the middle one, Callum,' she continued. 'Eighteen months I had to wait to see a specialist. They thought it was just asthma at first but now they're not so sure. The specialist says it may be a congenital defect, whatever that means. When you do finally get a chance to talk to them they treat you like you're a bloody idiot.'

'It means, existing from birth, you know, he was born with the condition and it's not a result of his surroundings or upbringing.' I explained helpfully.

'Is that right!' She exclaimed with slight incredulity, 'you see, I've learnt more from you in two minutes than I did from that wanker specialist in half an hour,' she replied, as though I was an old mate. 'Poor little mite. He's too young to understand. My Mum helps out as much as she can but she's got a bad hip so it's a real handful for her. Dad's dead and my Brother and his family live in Wales.' It suddenly began to sink in what she was saying. They were just words a few moments ago, now it was reality. And here I was, feeling sorry for myself. I felt ashamed and facile and stared down at the ground to avoid her eyes.

'Oh I'm sorry love, I'm rambling. I'm sure you don't want to hear about my woes. We all have our cross to carry, don't we.'

'No, I don't mind, honestly.' My voice was weak and brittle and I wondered whether she detected my embarrassment.

'Oh, you're such a lovely man. I knew you would be. I used to have a crush on you when you were in the Shooting Tsars. That would have been about twelve years ago, wouldn't it? Yes, that's right because I remember bunking off school with my best mate Sally to go and see you lot in Exeter. I'd have been about sixteen at the time. Shit, I got such a bollocking when my Dad found out. He didn't let me out for weeks.' I was a little taken aback. I hadn't been recognised for years and now twice in the space of a couple of days. I couldn't remember playing Exeter all those years ago but so what; apparently we played Japan and South Korea and I certainly had no recollection of them either.

'I should introduce myself, I'm Fiona.' She held out her hand.

'Hi, I'm …'

'You're Will Harding, yes I know,' she interrupted, taking my hand and giving it a very firm shake. 'We've had a few celebrities in here. Last year Billy Brag was in, before that The Wurzels and that guy out of the Troggs. And apparently, Val Doonican once popped in for a pint and a pickled egg. Mind you, that's going back some years, well before my time.'

'Well it's good to know that I'm in such illustrious company. To think the Wurzels have drunk at this very same bar. Where the hell did they park their combine harvester though?' Fiona laughed.

'Next to the Runaway Train,' she responded. I laughed. Our eyes locked momentarily before she quickly pulled away.

'Excuse me, but I must collect some glasses.' I glanced around the pub. Four men next to the fire all with half filled pints. At the other end of the pub I saw two figures patrolling a pool table. Hardly knee deep in empty glasses. I finished off my whisky refill and lit a cigarette before beginning on my pint of bitter. I could already feel the whisky working its magic. I began to feel a warmth inside and a slight rush of euphoria as I relaxed against the bar. I watched Fiona as she walked around the pub picking up a couple of empties before returning to her post. She carried herself well; her poise and elegance appeared out of place collecting glasses. She continued the conversation.

'You're Mother is such a sweet woman. She's so proud of you.' I was intrigued.

'How do you know my Mother?' I asked.

'Oh, she's an old friend of my Mums. They used to go to school together as girls. Then when your Mother moved back here they struck up their friendship again. They go to the Women's Institute together and various other outings. She always tells anyone new she meets, that she's the Mother of Will Harding, famous rock star from the Shooting Tsars. She's as proud as punch.' I was amazed. I never realised she was actually proud of me. Well there you go, the stubborn old stick.

'So come on, you walked in here with a face like a slapped arse, what's on your mind? I'm a Barmaid, it's my job to be nosey.'

'I'm okay. Just a bit disappointed that's all.' I related the events of the previous days. I explained about Chas and his proposal and how I wasn't interested at first and then slowly came around to the idea. How I expected Robbo to flatly refuse, but instead he'd enthusiastically agreed. Where was Geordie and how could I possibly find him. How I expected Flaky to agree but of course he hadn't. And now, it was all over. A little dream gone up in a wisp of smoke.

'Jesus, I thought you were made of sterner stuff than that. As William Shakespeare once said, "if at first you don't succeed, try and try again". You can't give up just because of a few setbacks?' I was pretty sure William Shakespeare hadn't said that, but I let it go, no point splitting hairs.

'Unless there's the four of us it's not going to happen. I believe in loyalty. You know, all for one and one for all—the four musketeers.'

'Oh that's very noble of you. When was the last time you saw the other three?' she prodded sarcastically.

'Well, Robbo I saw last year and well, as for the other two ...' I fumbled for the words.

'Yeah, go on,' she insisted as she vigorously dried a glass.

'Well, the day of the fire, which would have been July, maybe August '95.' I felt embarrassed and ashamed about my admission.

'The four bloody musketeers my arse; more like the four bleeding strangers. What's all this crap about loyalty? You owe them nothing and they owe you nothing. If they want to do the gigs let them do it. If they don't, it's simple.'

65

'It is?' I asked

'Do it yourself and get another band.' I felt suitably chastised. Her admonishment had not diminished her attractiveness, in fact quite the opposite. Her cheeks flared and reddened and a spark jumped back into her eye. I must admit, I was smitten.

'How much were you offered to do these thirty gigs, if you don't mind me asking?'

'Oh a fair bit, enough to make it worth our while,' I was embarrassed to tell her the actual amount.

'You missed your vocation Will Harding, you should have been a politician. How much?' she persisted.

'Okay, two hundred has been mentioned,'

'Two hundred thousand pounds! And all your expenses no doubt?'

'Yep,'

'So that's fifty thousand pounds each?' She exclaimed, staggered at the figures. 'Fifty thousand for ten weeks work.'

'Well actually, it's two hundred each, and it's only eight weeks work.' Why had I just said that—what a berk!

'Two hundred thousand pounds for thirty hours work!' she said a little too loudly. 'Well it beats my four pound fifty an hour I'm getting here.' I could see she was a little more than pissed off.

'Hey, it's not my fault. I don't decide who gets what. You try and get the best deal for yourself whatever you do, don't you? Anyway it's not thirty hours work, it's fifty odd days on the road up and down the country and it's twenty four hours a day that you give up. It's not like you can nip home to hang the washing out or go down to the local for a few jars. Then there's at least two weeks solid rehearsal prior to the tour. Then there's the publicity in-between gigs, the radio interviews, the press interviews, the photo shoots. It's not all beer and skittles you know. I admit, it's good money, bloody good money. What do you want me to do, refuse it, tell them it's too much. Don't blame me for the inequity in

66

the world. I only came in here for a quiet drink.' I was quite worked up by now and any thought of passion had gone straight out of the window. I expected a mouthful back.

'Well you have, haven't you?' she retorted calmly, eyes staring into mine.

'Pardon?' I didn't understand the question.

'You said, "what do you want me to do, refuse it", well you have refused it, haven't you.' I thought about what she was saying. She was right, I had; I'd given up before I had started. 'I don't begrudge what anyone gets paid or what they do as long it's not harming anyone else. Good luck to them is what I say. But you walk in here feeling sorry for yourself, as though the world has dealt you a bad hand. You've just been offered two hundred grand for eight weeks work. It doesn't matter how hard it may be, in two months it will be over and you'll have all that money in the bank. So what if someone you haven't even spoken to for ten years doesn't want to do it. So what if you can't find your bass player. You wrote the songs, you sang the songs, you played guitar. Get another band and stop playing the loser. Leave losing to other folk.' I stared in to her blue eyes as they flooded over. She turned her back and busied herself with stacking glasses. Well, I suppose that had told me hadn't it. She was right. Fuck 'em—fuck 'em all. I needed to have a long hard think about what I really wanted, but first I needed to do some grovelling.

'I'm sorry. You're right. I have no right to feel sorry for myself. I'm doing pretty well compared to many. Sometimes you just take things for granted I suppose. Listen, how about I buy you another drink if you accept my apology?' She turned slowly. Her anger had subsided. A faint smile passed across her moist lips.

'Okay, it's a deal. I'll have a double Brandy mister moneybags'. We both laughed.

'Aye, okay, and make mine a double whisky'.

#

I staggered out of the pub two hours later, thoroughly pissed but imbued with a feeling of elation and freedom. I didn't care if it was the whisky and even if the feeling had left me by the morning, at this moment in time I was soaring. I felt in control of my own destiny. Yes, from now on I would dictate what happened to me. I had hidden away for ten years. I had cut off my nose to spite my face. I had retreated from my vocation, scared I might get another bad deal, lamenting the unfairness of it all. Because I was scared of failure I had done what many others do, I had given up. After all, if you never try, you can never fail.

I missed my music although I didn't miss the madness that went with it. But could you have one without the other? I had removed temptation by exiling myself, not just physically, but socially and emotionally. I had cut off the rivers flow. I had no contact with the band or any of my old music business friends. But why did this have to be so? Why should I let those bastards win, whoever *they* were, imagined or real. Why did I have to play their game by their rules? Why couldn't I live my life as I chose? I realised now in my inebriated, euphoric state, that I could have, and I should have and in future I would. I wanted to etch this feeling into my brain because I knew it would not say goodbye but merely nip out the back door when I wasn't watching.

I meandered unsteadily through the town walking dangerously close to the harbour's edge, Caesar by my side. There was something else that I was feeling. A sensation I had experienced seldom and only fleetingly. I was in love.

9: EVER FALLEN IN LOVE

I woke hot and sweaty. My head was pounding and my tongue was stuck to the roof of my mouth. A brightness shone through the curtains, radiating unwelcome heat. I could hear the distant labour of the sea and smelt the homey scent of my old room. It was like being back in the womb, apart from the self-inflicted throbbing head. I unsteadily raised myself to look at the clock—it read 11:30 am. I reached for a glass of water and gulped down the tepid liquid thirstily. I lay back down.

'Oh shit, never again.' I'd vowed never to say "never again" after breaking my never again vows a thousand times before. But the habit was embedded into some primordial part of my brain that I had no control over. I lay, momentarily hoping for the brass band in my skull to end their pomp and circumstance. They eased up on the big bass drum for a while and memories of the previous week began to flow through my brain in unconnected fragments, like sticks in a wide river. *Chas, cockney wide boy; speed, that was some good shit; Fiona, beautiful eyes, firm full tits, good listener, stunning arse; Caesar, I hope Mam's walked and fed him? Of course she has; Ah, Fiona, I've got butterflies in my stomach. What do I need to do now? Don't know, I've forgotten; something very important. I was talking to Fiona about it last night. She was telling me I had to have a plan of action. Beautiful breasts and those lips … hmm. What's that smell? Ah yes bacon, hmm, smells bloody good, better get up, need a smoke. Something important, Jesus, that bloody brass band has started up again, I must be seriously dehydrated. Not used to it anymore, getting too old. Need to give it away. It was Mam who gave me the idea, I know, strange but true; now what was it ... ah yes, that's it, of course, Bingo! I know what I've got to do.*

I made my way delicately to the bathroom and tried to enjoy a warm shower but it only made me feel worse. There was only one thing for it. I turned the tap to cold and waited for the inevitable shock.

'Holy fuckeroo! I'm singing in the rain!' I hopped around like a demented frog on hot coals. I quickly washed and rinsed. I could now feel the blood vessels in my head pulsating against my skin. The brass band had begun a quick-time version of Scotland the Brave and had also enlisted a brigade of hairy arsed, jock bagpipers. I ended the pain and quickly dried myself off. I studied myself in the mirror. Flecks of grey adorned my hair, bags under the eyes, a tired pasty appearance. I was beginning to form man-boobs, droopy little titties. I wasn't fat but my stomach certainly didn't ripple with a six pack either, then again, it never had. I gazed down at my scrawny chicken legs and my white blue veined feet. It wasn't a pretty sight, but I had seen worse. I encouraged myself by pulling my gut in and pumping my chest out. I stood straight and talked to myself.

'Come on mate, so what, everyone ages. I bet when Bowie or Rod Stewart stare in the mirror after a hard night on the piss they don't look too impressive either. Imagine what Keith Richards sees every morning, he must think the grim reapers arrived. Best foot forward pal, make a fist of it. It isn't over yet. Carp diem, tempus fugit. Right, up and at 'em.' I dressed and entered the kitchen where Mam was busily grilling toast, frying bacon and making hot coffee. Just what the doctor ordered.

'Morning love, you had a big night didn't you?' I tried to remember whether I had spoken to her when I had arrived home last night.

'Yeah, I suppose it was, for me at least.' I conceded.

'I'd been in bed about thirty minutes and was just nodding off when I heard all this banging and clattering. You must have stood on poor old Caesar's foot because I heard him yelp. Where had you been to get into such a state?' I felt a little guilty about my behaviour.

'Just down the Bells. I wasn't there all that time though, I had been for a long walk; trying to get my head straight.' Mam stopped accosting the bacon and gave me a quick glance over the shoulder.

'Meet anyone you knew? I understood Mam's loaded question and deduced immediately that she had already gleaned some useful gossip from Fiona's Mother. I thought I'd play her for a while and let her think she was in control.

'Considering I don't know anyone from this village, no, I didn't see anyone I knew. Can you stick two eggs in for me please, I could eat a scabby dog,' I replied as I glanced down at Caesar who was in the process of cleaning his balls. She reached for the eggs and carefully cracked them, letting the yolks and white slide gracefully into the sizzling bacon fat.

'Oh come on, you do know some of the villagers. There's Pete from the post office, Robert from the fish warehouse. How long were you at the pub?' The names sounded familiar but my idea of knowing someone and Mam's idea were completely different. I'd probably passed them once in the car while Mam was in the passenger seat.

'Oh, two hours, maybe three.'

'Long time to spend drinking on your own.'

'It's not illegal in Yorkshire; has the law changed down here?'

'Don't get smart. Who was working the bar?' Poor old lass—she couldn't help herself.

'Oh, I can't really remember. Some old, nondescript woman. Like I said, I don't know anyone, so I can't give you any names.' I smiled to myself knowing Mam wouldn't be able to contain herself.

'Old, nondescript woman! What utter tosh!' she erupted into self-righteous indignation. 'She's a good ten years younger than you and she's regarded as the best catch around here, but she hasn't looked at another man since her husband passed away.' I flicked through the morning paper without much interest and slurped on a cup of black coffee for a

71

few minutes while Mother planned her next route of attack. She lifted my bacon and eggs onto a plate and placed it down with a thump in front of me. I tucked cheerfully into my breakfast and continued reading the paper with an aura of indifference. Mother was still silent, although I could feel her annoyance and decided to bait her a little more.

'Best catch around here you say, well there must be some bloody ugly fish in the ocean.' I ducked as I saw Mam swing her tea towel around, but I wasn't quick enough and got a whack on the back of the head with the damp cloth. 'Whoa, take it easy Mam, I'm only joking!' I appealed.

'I should think so too. That's Fiona Watts, she's the daughter of Margaret, you know Margaret, my best friend.'

'Yes, I know. I spoke with Fiona most of the night. I think we hit it off. She's a nice lass.'

'Well?'

'Well what?' I was concentrating on my breakfast now.

'You know what.'

'Yes I do know watt, although I didn't realise that was Fiona's last name'

'Don't get smart, you're not too old for a good hiding.'

'Yes I am. Anyway, I'd report you to the authorities and they'd put me into care.'

'Did you ask her to walk out with you?' That was Mam's generational talk. In English it meant, "did I ask her for a date".

'No.'

'Why ever not? She's such a lovely girl, there's not many like her left around I can tell you. Not many that would look at you anyway.' I ignored her barb and chomped nosily on my crispy bacon and swigged on my coffee before fixing my inquisitor with a steely eye.

'I'll give you three very good reasons. She has three kids.' I dipped my toast into the egg yolk and continued eating. The old girl gave me a smile.

'Her kids are wonderful little darlings; you'll just fall in love with them. I'll put in a good word for you.' I could see Mother had worked everything out. In her mind she was already baking the wedding cake.

'Well there's no point in you interfering Mother, as I'm going to be away for quite a while. Now I need to speak to you seriously. Sit down for one minute and stop fussing around.' Her face suddenly took on an anxious expression that had always saddened me as a child. I always wanted to fix it by putting a smile on it, but there was only Dad who could do that and he was long gone.

'What is it Will? What's going on?'

'I'm going to try and find Geordie. I'm going to get this band back together if it's the last thing I do. I've some unfinished business to attend to that I should have taken care of a long time ago. If I can't get them back together, I'll go it alone. Now I only have one clue where Geordie might be and that's at the arse end of Scotland. Now, will you take care of Caesar for me while I try and sort this band out?'

'Yes, of course, I'd love to. I'm glad you have yourself sorted. I don't agree with your decision but I'll support you all I can.' She paused and still seemed a little sad.

'What is it Mam?' I took her hand and gently squeezed it.

'Well, what about Fiona?' I smiled.

'It's thanks to Fiona that I'm doing all this. She has a wise and may I say very attractive head on her shoulders. Don't you worry about Fiona. I've set my heart on her and I usually get what my heart wants.' She beamed. 'But not a word to Margaret. I want to do this in my own time and my own way. Don't interfere. You've done enough matchmaking for one year.'

'Trust me Son. I won't breathe a word.'

#

I cruised slowly down steep cobbled streets. I glanced at the address that was scribbled on the back of an envelope—6 Stable Street. I

73

pulled up outside a little white fishing cottage nestled neatly in a row of about a dozen others. Before I could get out of the car, Fiona appeared in the doorway. Dressed in tight jeans and a loose sweater she beamed broadly and waved me to come in. I got out and walked up to her, but stopped short of entering the doorway.

'I can't stop, I'm in a hurry.'

'So you're going are you?' she asked staring intently into my eyes.

'Yeah, I thought I'd best call in to say thanks—for last night.'

'No need for that, I didn't do anything.'

'You certainly did. You clarified everything for me. You gave me a wake up call. Today's the first day in a long while that I've got a purpose in my life, and that's all down to you.'

'Well now you're sorted, I guess you'll be off playing rock stars again.' I detected a slight hint of resentment.

'Well yes, but on my terms this time.' She peered down at the pavement and kicked a discarded cigarette butt into the gutter before fixing me with a steely stare.

'Will I see you again?' I moved a step closer and gently gripped her hand.

'You try and stop me. I haven't felt this way about anyone for a long time, in fact ever.' She held her gaze for a few seconds before abruptly turning away.

'Oh poppycock. You only just met me last night, you can't know anything yet!'

'I didn't say I knew, I said I felt. There's a big difference, and I know what I feel.'

She raised one eyebrow as though questioning the validity of my last statement, I didn't blame her, it was a bit Mills and Boon. I pulled her towards me and we kissed a long soft kiss. I felt the rising in my jeans and with all the will I could muster I pulled away. Her eyes were closed and her head followed mine as I broke the spell. I pulled out a wad of notes and peeled off a hundred pounds and handed it to her. She seemed surprised and a little affronted at my offer.

'I remember you saying that it was Callum's birthday today and I thought he deserves something special seeing as he's been through a hard time lately. Get him whatever you like, if there's a bit left over, take them all out for a Macdonald's or something.'

'That's very sweet of you to remember. Especially considering the state you were in when you left last night. The nearest Macdonald's is sixty miles away, but I know what you mean. Fish and chips on the end of the pier will be nice. Thanks again.' She accepted the money and stuffed it into her pocket. I climbed back into my car and wound the window down.

'I must get going. It's over seven hundred miles to Dinkiad Bay.'

'Where the hell's that?' she asked, puzzled.

'Arse end of haggis land. It's where his Grandparents lived, where he was brought up.' I turned the ignition and began to move slowly away, blowing her a kiss at the same time.

'Where who was brought up? Who are you talking about?' she yelled after me.

'As my Mother said, boys always return home when they're in trouble.'

'WHO?' She yelled after me. I stuck my head out of the window.
'GEORDIE!'

10: ROAD TO NOWHERE

As I began the long, tedious drive, I thought about Fiona and her children. If the relationship was ever going to stand a chance, her kids would have to like me and I would have to like them. Problem was, I hated kids. Well, not quite true, I was indifferent towards them, unless they annoyed the shit out of me and then I hated them. I'd never, ever, entertained the idea of having children. Now here I was, falling in love with a widow who already had three kids of her own, and young kids at that. Did I really want to get involved? Was I demented? Had I taken leave of my senses? I wasn't responsible enough to take on the burden of a family. The all consuming, dead, crushing, spirit breaking role of parenting. I sometimes struggled to put my socks in the correct drawer, that's not father figure material. I couldn't be reined in like that; I was a minstrel, a wandering nomad, an artisan. I was like a wild stallion, it would be against the laws of nature to try and neuter me; to tie me to the kitchen sink, to get me changing shitty nappies, to be dabbing bloodied knees with Dettol, fixing doors, unblocking toilets that had three rolls of toilet paper jammed in them or extracting unidentified green waste matter from the shag pile. I was a zephyr on the open dusty savannah, I wasn't a grey, dreary, responsible dullard who barked orders and suffered from tuna breath. No, I was definitely not cut out for parenthood.

#

I arrived back in Whitstone in the early evening feeling quite exhausted. I had a light meal and hit the sack early as I had another marathon drive in the morning. I awoke the next day at 5am, had a quick blast of coffee and hit the road again. I drove through stunning and spectacular countryside as I headed north. I cut westwards and got onto the M6 that intersected the Dales and the Lake District before eventually crossing the Scottish border and heading towards Glasgow. I stopped at a service station and grabbed a bite to eat, a strong coffee and a couple of smokes before I jumped back in the car for the last leg.

I listened to the radio, switching between the mundane triviality of local stations and the highfalutin, condescending tone of some of Radio Four's presenters. The country slowly changed as I headed east. The highlands were to my left as I drove and in the distance I could see the imposing mountain range far larger than anything my Dales had to offer. I wondered why I'd never holidayed in Scotland before. I'd toured with the band, I think. I'm sure we played Glasgow a few times and maybe even Aberdeen. Yes, I remember Glasgow, because Geordie took us on a pub crawl around the city; some of his old haunts. It was a good night out as far as I could remember. I don't think he even managed to get into a fight that night, which would have been unusual. I wondered if I would find him and if so, what I was going to say. I hadn't really planned anything, but then again, there wasn't much point when it came to Geordie. The best laid plans could be thrown into total disarray when he was around. He was a loose cannon, an unknown quantity, a UXB that no one knew if, or when, it would go off, or even if it still had a fuse. I'd play it by ear, policy on the run as the politicians liked to call it. I'd assess his state of mind and live by my wits.

I passed a sign that thankfully told me 60 miles to Dinkiad Bay. I'd been driving for nearly six hours and was beginning to feel weary. The road was painfully slow. Winding and climbing high westwards before falling back towards the coast. Eventually after another hours drive I came to the outskirts of the little village. It was a lot like Pugstow in size

77

and atmosphere. Rows of granite houses ran adjacent to the one road into town. A few streets peeled off to the left heading down to the foreshore. I drove slowly along what I assumed was the main high street. I passed a grocer, a butcher, a doctors surgery, an undertaker, a newsagent-post office, a fishing tackle cum-clothes shop and the obligatory public house. I noticed a sign in a bed and breakfast that read "Vacancies". It appeared clean and tidy and I made a mental note that this could be my bed for the night, if required. The road carried on about another five hundred metres and wound down to a ramp at the edge of the harbour. This really was the road to nowhere. It almost appeared as if the road carried on underneath the waves, a sub-marine track to aquatic unknowns. A large jetty penetrated out into the calm seas. A sign read, 'Keep Away From Edge While Ferry Docks'. I studied the sign and wondered why it was always necessary to state the bleeding obvious. I reflected on human nature and conceded that indeed, it was necessary. I lit a cigarette, reversed the car and headed back up the main drag. I turned down one of the side streets and did a little tour of the town, which took no more than five minutes. It was nearly 11:30am. I decided that my first stop off point would have to be the pub. Landlords always knew everyone's business, sometimes too much. Geordie might not have been seen in this town for ten years or more but someone would definitely remember him or his folks. I parked up at the harbour front car park as I felt it was a bit conspicuous to park up outside the pub. I locked the car and had a good stretch, while gazing at the pale blue pastel horizon, that melted into the metallic grey of the sea. A few distant bumps interrupted the vista. pinpointing the location of distant isles. I buttoned my jacket against the cold and walked towards the town.

11: DIDN'T YOU USED TO BE YOU?

I called into the newsagent and bought a paper. I was served by a friendly, elderly woman who wanted to talk more than I did. I gave nothing away just yet and said I was here for a spot of fishing. She didn't seem convinced; jeans, trainers, loose cotton shirt and sports jacket were hardly the attire of a keen angler. I entered the Fisherman's Way public house through a low level doorway. I blinked to try to adjust my eyes to the sudden drop in natural light.

The refreshing, invigorating smell of ale always conjured up memories of my first forays into the world of pubs when I was a teenager. Trying to get served while underage was always fraught with danger. But the fear and humiliation of being refused service never outweighed the elation I felt while cockily supping my illicit gains in a dark alcove.

There was an 'L' shaped bar to the east of the room. To the north lay a small dining area of about seven tables; a fruit machine and pool table to the south. To the west was a long bay window that stretched the length of the pub. Below the sill was velvet seating with adjacent tables and chairs, opposite was an open fireplace containing a few blackened embers.

There were no customers in the pub and the bar was unattended. A little bell on the side read "Ring For Service". I duly obliged and immediately heard voices—a man's and a woman's, emanate from an open doorway behind the bar. Shortly, a stout, plodding man emerged through the entrance. His face was fat and ruddy. He wore half rimmed spectacles and peered over the top of them towards me.

'Morning Sir, how are you today?' His voice was deep and throaty but friendly enough.

'I'm good thanks, how are you?' I replied. He smiled and ran his hand through his thinning grey hair, pushing some rogue strands back and across the top of his head, overlaying his bald spot at the rear of his crown.

'Never better Sir, never better. Now, what can I get you?'

'I'll try a pint of your local bitter please.'

'Good choice Sir, good choice.' I had a repeater on my hands, but that wasn't too bad. Repeaters were usually eager to dispense information—even if it was in duplicate. 'So what brings you to our little piece of paradise Sir? Are you here for the walking or the fishing? Lovely place for both Sir, lovely place for both.' The glass filled quickly and he eased off on the tap as the creamy dark gold liquid rushed to the lip of the glass forming a perfect head.

'Neither really, although I do enjoy both pursuits.' He placed the pint down on the mat in front of me,

'That'll be two pounds ten, please Sir.' I pulled out a fiver and handed it to him. He gave me change and I pocketed it as I lifted the glass to my mouth. 'Just visiting Sir? Just visiting?' I swallowed a couple of large mouthfuls of the dark amber nectar. It had a warm nutty flavour with a hint of liquorice. I placed the pint down and wiped my top lip and reached for my cigarettes.

'Hmm, nice drop that. No, I'm actually trying to chase up an old friend of mine.' I lit up a cigarette, inhaled and then exhaled the smoke away from the bar. I assumed the man was the landlord; he had that demeanour about him. He bowed his head and peered over his glasses and asked inquisitively,

'Who might that be Sir? If he or she lives around here I'll know them for sure, I'll know them for sure.'

'Allan Kincaid is his name. He used to live here years ago—with his Grandparents. I'm not sure what their surname was, all I know is, it wasn't Kincaid.' The landlord had a puzzled expression on his face as though mentally chewing over the name.

'Hmm … no, I'm not familiar with that name Sir, not familiar at all. You say you're a friend?' he inquired suspiciously.

'Yes. We go back a long way. We used to be pretty good mates.' He eyed me intensely as though trying to read my mind. 'Big bloke, six-foot-five or six, wild eyes, likes a drink, nickname of Geordie,' I offered more information but feared the trail had gone cold.

'Kincaid, Kincaid, Geordie, Geordie,' he pondered, while rubbing his chin thoughtfully.

'We used to be in a band together: about ten years ago: the Shooting Tsars.'

'And what's your name Sir, if you don't mind me asking?'

'No, not at all, Harding, Will Harding.' The landlord suddenly stopped rubbing his chin and beamed broadly while sticking his hand out over the bar.

'Pleased to meet you Sir, pleased to meet you.' I was slightly taken aback but shook his hand anyway.

'Stanley McAlpine, Stanley McAlpine's the name. I'm the landlord of this fine establishment.'

'So you do know Geordie?'

'Yes I do. Sorry Sir, I had to make sure who you were. You could have been from the DSS or the Inland Revenue or undercover from the Glasgow CID. I believe in people's privacy you see; yes, people's privacy.' He seemed proud of himself. 'Yes Geordie's one of our regulars. He's mentioned your name in the past, although of course I don't actually remember your band, Geordie tells me you were quite popular at one time—is that correct Sir?'

'Yes, yes, we were, that's right we were … er … yes quite popular.' I was unwittingly picking up his annoying habit of repetition and made a mental note to nip it in the bud. 'So Geordie still lives in the village? Do his grandparents still live here?'

'Well yes and no. His Grandfather died about seven years ago now. I think that's when Geordie returned to take care of his Nan, although between you and me Sir, it's more the other way around. But he's a good lad to her. He totally adores her. Yes, yes that would be right. He moved in with his Nan, after old Hamish, that's his Grandfather, passed away. Yes that'd be right, that'd be right,' he concluded thoughtfully.

'So where does his Nan live? Will Geordie be there now?'

'His Nan lives two rows back towards the harbour. No 16 Kettle Way, second to last house on that particular row. But there's no point going there now. It's Thursday and that's dole day for Geordie. Every second Thursday he gets his dole cheque and catches the 9 am bus to Aberdeen, yes to Aberdeen. Does the shopping at the supermarket there and then gets the bus back. He always calls in here on his return, always calls in. Sometimes has a couple of pints and sometimes he has a few more, yes quite a few more. Well of course you'd know all about Geordie and how he likes a drink I suppose?'

'Yes, I know Geordie alright.' I was shocked by the landlord's details. On the dole, that couldn't be right, surely?

'You said he's on the *dole*?'

'Yes Sir, that's correct. No work around here unless you're part of the fishing fleet. And I know many of the captains won't have someone as big as Geordie on board. Only little boats Sir, not a lot of room you see.'

'Yeah, yeah, I can see that. I just thought …' I stopped myself. Despite the bad deal we got from GMC and the cost of the court case, I had made enough money to live very comfortably. So why was Geordie on the dole? Then I remembered that most of my money had come from the Performing Rights Society; as the songwriter I got money from public airplay; it was a continuous, although dwindling, source of revenue. To think of poor old Geordie having to go through the ignominy of signing on for a few measly pounds every fortnight made me feel sick and more than a little ashamed of myself. I should have been here to help him out.

'Another Sir?'

'Aye, fill it up. Same again. So what time does the bus get back from Aberdeen?' I asked Stan.

'Supposed to be 1 pm, but it can be up to twenty minutes late. Yes, twenty minutes late.'

'And Geordie's first stop will be here?'

'Aye Sir, it will, regular as clockwork. He'll be pleased as punch to see you no doubt, pleased as punch'. He passed me my next pint and I handed him the money.

'So one and a half-hours possibly two,' I said peering at the clock behind the bar.

'Yes Sir that's right, that's right'. I was getting hungry and studied the lunch menu. I ordered a meat and potato pie cooked in local stout and sat down in the corner with my pint, fags and a newspaper. There were still no other customers in the pub and Stan decided to while away the time by coming over to where I sat and engaging in conversation. Well it wasn't really conversation—more of a monologue. Although I kept my head down and read the paper, it did not deter him from droning   on and on—twice. Even when his vivacious wife appeared with my lunch, it didn't stop him. She was surprisingly attractive considering Stan was her husband. She was a lot younger than him and well built in that attractive barmaid way. She wore a lot of makeup, but I could tell she would still be an attractive woman without any.

'Here's your meat and two veg Sir,' she said provocatively as she bent down to place my food in front of me. Her ample bosom was squashed into a push up bra. She caught my eye roving to her cleavage and smiled a wicked smile and winked. *Hmm, was that a come on.*

'Thanks for that,' I replied, 'it looks good enough to eat.'

Stan was still rattling away, leaning on a pillar, arms folded, totally oblivious to his wife's flirtations.

'Yes a nice lad, but a short fuse. Yes a very short fuse. I've had to bar him a few times. Not really his fault, he very rarely starts trouble, oh well, maybe occasionally. But he blows up sometimes, takes four or five of us to subdue him.' I was only half listening. The pie was wholesome and tasty, the beer rich and satisfying and I was quite enjoying myself; if only Stan would fuck off! To be fair, he was well meaning and honest, very commendable attributes, but he was a boring old prick and I wasn't in the mood for his inane ramblings.

'Once had a group of student climbers in here for a weekends walking, of course we do bed and breakfast you know, you may have seen the sign outside, although some people don't notice it, Margaret, that's my wife, Margaret keeps telling me to get it enlarged, she says I need to get a bigger one.' *I bet she does pal, I bet she does.* 'Anyway, where was I?' *Who fucking knows.* 'Ah yes, the students, they weren't a bad bunch, bit rowdy but nothing we couldn't handle. Anyway, Geordie was in having a quiet drink, minding his own business he was, yes minding his own business. He came to the bar for a refill and one of the students, the big mouthed one actually, bit of a gobshite that one if I recall, yes, the gobshite shouted over to Geordie at the bar "Oi mate?" he shouts "Didn't you used to be you", aye, that's what he shouted.' Stan insisted on doing the actions. It was like watching a bad foreign film except there were no subtitles. 'Anyway, Geordie, he ignores this gobshite. But the gobshite won't leave it alone. He shouts it again, "Oi mate?" he shouts "Didn't you used to be you". Geordie's having none of it; just pays for his pint and turns to walk back to his seat. Anyway, this gobshite follows him singing one of the songs, you know one of your songs, well I assume it was one of your songs because I'd never heard of it,' *thanks pal,* 'I think Margaret had heard of it, anyway this gobshite follows Geordie and says "Oi Pal, I'm talking to you" by now his mates have followed him over to

84

where Geordie is and are egging him on singing this song. I wish I could remember how it went, but it wasn't very catchy, not like a Roy Orbison or a Jim Reeves song, no disrespect of course,'

'None taken,' I replied.

'This gobby bastard taps Geordie on the shoulder. Geordie stops, puts down his pint and turns to look at the student. "You fucking talking to me pal?" asks Geordie. This took the gobshite aback, but he glances over his shoulder to make sure he still had his mates with him. Probably about six of them all together. Students they were, did I mention that?'

'Yup,'

'Then he says—the student that is, not Geordie, he says "I asked you a question, didn't you used to be you?" Geordie replies. "No. I've never been you I've always been me. If I had been you I would have blown my fucking head off a long time ago." Well, the whole pub erupts in laughter, apart from the students. It was a busy night, Saturday night I think or maybe it was a Friday.' I already knew the ending. Most Geordie stories ended the same way … violence. 'Well the gobshite didn't like that you see. Everyone laughing at him, so he points his finger at Geordie and says "Don't get smart you effing has-been". Well that was it, Geordie smiled at this guy and whispered something. No-one heard it, but this gobshite leans forward and at the same time Geordie lets fly with a headbutt. Ha! Ha! Ha! I can laugh at it now, but it wasn't particularly funny at the time. I've not got much of a stomach for violence. Anyway, the gobshite's head goes flying back, his nose all over the place, blood flying everywhere. He catches one of his mates behind him and that's two on the deck with one headbutt. The other mates rush at Geordie, he just sticks out his long arms and pounds the shit out of these poor guys. Six of them he took down. They were none too quick to get up either. When he'd finished, he walks over to the gobshite who is on his back holding his nose, squealing like a stuck pig, and he bends down and whispers "Didn't you hear me, it's rude to point" and with that, he turns, picks up his pint and goes back to his seat. Of course I had to bar him,

85

just to make it seem like justice was being done. Well, it wasn't actually me who barred him, it was Margaret. I thought it best to come from her as she seems to have a way with him, sort of placates him, if you know what I mean.'

'Yes, I think I know what you mean.'

'She walks over to him and says "Geordie, when you've finished your pint I think it best you leave and make sure you don't come back for two weeks. We can't be having shit like that in this pub. We're trying to run a business. If you want to fight join the fucking army." I thought she was a bit harsh myself, but Geordie just stares at her, smiles and says "Aye, fair enough Margaret, fair enough." The students were threatening to take legal action but I didn't charge them for their rooms so the matter was dropped.'

I'd witnessed many such events in the past and heard as many tales. Geordie didn't muck about when it came to fighting and one sure-fire way to send him into a blind rage was to point a finger at him.

'Anyway, I can't stand around here all day chewing the cud with you. I've got work to do,' chuntered Stan as though I had been the one keeping him.

'Yes, well don't let me stop you.' I called after him as he waddled off toward the bar.

#

I relaxed for the next hour, wiling away the time with a couple more pints while doing the crossword. Each time I went back to the bar Stan would start on one of his long meandering chronicles; seals and how they were ruining the fishing stocks; David Beckham's hairdo; the migrating instinct of the Ibis; council taxes; small business taxes; the perils of walking in the highlands; the price of beef; brewery take-overs and the construction material in modern golf balls. It seemed there was no subject that was beyond the reach of the great philosopher. I suppose it was a good trait for a publican, I just cursed that I was the only customer to benefit from his extensive and exhaustive knowledge. Even when I walked back to my seat, he would follow me, twittering away. If I tried to join in the conversation with any of my own points or observations, Stan would just talk over the top of me. I gave up trying to engage in a two-way discussion. In Stan's world there was only one worthwhile authority on all subjects under the sun—and that was himself. I glanced at the clock—12:55 pm. I just hoped Geordie was on the bus when it arrived. I walked back to the bar.

'Stan, here take this fifty and stick it behind the bar. I reckon me and Geordie have some catching up to do. Listen, can you have a pint ready for him when he walks through the door and don't let on you know who I am.' I handed Stan the fifty and he laughed heartily.

'No worries Sir, no worries at all. I won't say a word, not a word. Ha! Ha!' *Oh please God, if only that were true.* I sat back down at my table tucked away in the corner and lit another cigarette. I stared out of the window and down the high street trying to detect any sign of life; there was none. I sucked nervously on my smoke. Why was I nervous? I wasn't sure, just excited I suppose. I checked the clock again—1:05 pm. Nothing. I finished off my fourth pint and placed the glass down accidentally hard on the table. The noise made Stan stop his glass polishing and throw me a quick glance.

'Ready for another Sir?' he hollered across the pub.

'Aye, why not,' I replied. I was just about to get up when I heard a faint rumble. I gazed out of the window again but saw nothing. The rumble grew ever louder. Yes, it was definitely the sound of a diesel engine changing gears. Then it appeared. As small as a postage stamp at first but growing steadily.

'That'll be the bus now Sir, that'll be the bus now,' informed Stan helpfully as he poured the pint. An old green Bedford bus made its ponderous way up the high-street, passing the pub before pulling into a terminus fifty metres further up. I quickly went to the bar and collected my pint.

'Not a word now,' I indicated to Stan.

'Don't you worry about me Sir, I shan't give the game away, shan't give the game away at all.' I sat back down and watched as the bus did a large u-turn and came to a halt. A couple of old ladies disembarked with tartan shopping trolleys; a small boy with a dog; two teenage schoolgirls laughing and giggling; a serious looking man wearing a Homburg and sporting a handlebar moustache alighted, looking like he'd walked straight out of a 1950's film.

'Come on Geordie, come on, where are you?' I muttered under my breath. Time passed as the other passengers slowly disappeared from view. *Shit! He's not fucking on it!* Then I saw him. A tall, lithe figure dropped to the pavement carrying at least four carrier bags in each giant paw. He turned and walked towards the pub. He disappeared out of sight momentarily due to the angle of the street before reappearing outside the pub window. I shrunk back into my seat. If he turned his head left now I would be spotted, but he didn't. He hadn't changed much at all apart from the usual ravages of time. He was dressed in a large olive green trench coat, his hair was shoulder length, wild and straggly. He sported a ridiculous bushy beard that belonged in the 19th century and he had large black bags under his eyes. I pulled my newspaper up to my face and peered furtively over the top. I saw him struggle sideways through the doorway cursing all the while. Then the strong familiar Scottish brogue, all exasperation and cynical weariness.

'Fucking 'ell Stan, when are you going to get that doorway widened? No wonder you don't have any fucking customers, they cannae fucking get in the joint.'

'Geordie, how are you son, how are you?' replied Stan.

'Oh fair to middling, apart from those miserable bastards at the post office in Aberdeen.' He dumped the carrier bags of produce on the carpet and lifted two of the bags onto the counter.

'Here, can you stick this in your fridge Stan.'

'Aye of course I can. Now don't bugger off and forget them like you did the other week otherwise I'll have your Nan in here complaining again.'

'Cheers. Yeah, those pernicious little bastards at the post office. I've been going in there for over seven years, every fortnight and every fortnight they ask me for ID. Yet they never seem to ask anyone else. So I said to them today "I'm the same person I was last time you asked me, and the time before that, and the time before that". He's not so bad the old lad there, I think he only asks 'cos he's scared of his wife. She's a right miserable old shrew that one, dried up old prune, probably hasn't had a fuck since her wedding night; fucking button counters, they rule the world. Pint of the usual please.' He fumbled in his trench coat pocket and came out empty handed and then searched the back pockets of his jeans.

'Now where the fuck have I put it?' he cursed to himself. Stan disappeared out the back with the two carrier bags all the while talking indiscriminately.

'Aye you're not wrong there Geordie, you're not wrong. That's Mavis Dougal. I used to go to school with her when I was a wee lad. She hasn't changed one iota.' His voice trailed off before returning to the bar continuing the conversation. 'Yes she was a real fastidious nitpicker at school and she hasn't changed one jot, not one jot. Her Father was an elder in the Presbyterians for donkey's years. A very staunch Protestant but a big advocate against abortion, aye, dead set against it he was.'

'Aye, well, I wish someone would abort her, miserable lemon sucking old sow.' Stan began pulling a pint as Geordie started emptying his pockets searching for his money while cursing under his breath.

'No need Geordie, no need,' stated Stan emphatically.

'What do you mean no need? I've been coming to this pub longer than I care to remember and I've never had so much as a free peanut out of you. What's the catch? Have you discovered religion or something?'

'It's already paid for Geordie, it's already paid for.' Geordie stopped searching and glanced around the pub. When he looked in my direction I dropped my eyes back behind the paper. All he saw was a stranger having a quiet pint and reading the news.

'Oh aye, and who's fucking paid for it? I stopped believing in fairies a couple of years back.'

'The gentleman in the corner. Says he's a friend of yours, a friend he says.' Stan lifted the pint and passed it to Geordie who took a giant sup while glancing over his shoulder in my direction. He stopped drinking.

'And who may that be?' he asked suspiciously.

'Didn't catch his name, actually,' lied Stan.

'Fucking bullshit!' I heard his footsteps make their way over to my table.

'Thanks for the pint mate, I don't usually accept charity but I'll make an exception on this occasion.' I slowly lowered the paper while trying to keep a poker face. I could see the cogs slowly grind round in Geordie's head. For a split second no recognition, then slowly, a flicker in the eyes.

'How ya doing Geordie?' I asked softly. His eyes narrowed to a slit and then his mouth cracked with a giant smile.

'Well fuck me backwards and suck my saggy titties, you sneaky old bastard! Billy boy, me old mate!' He put his pint down and rushed towards me as I stood up. He grabbed me in a bear hug and lifted me a good three foot off the ground while shaking me intensely.

'Aargh! For fuck's sake Geordie put me down, I've just eaten.' Eventually he released his grip and I fell like a sack of shit back onto my seat, gasping for breath but with a withered smile on my face.

'It's good to see you too, Geordie!'

12: WITH A LITTLE HELP FROM MY FRIENDS

Stan brought two fresh pints over to our table and hung around telling Geordie the tale of my arrival, the tale of Geordie's own arrival and what an essential part he'd played in the whole affair. Luckily, a few locals came in and Stan had a new audience to bore, leaving Geordie and I to our reunion.

'Fuck me Geordie, how do you put up with him? I've only been here a few hours and he's driving me fucking mad!'

'Who? Oh, Stereo Stan. Ah, he's alright, you learn to switch off. He's harmless enough, I say, he's harmless enough,' we both laughed. 'So Billy boy, what, how and why?' Geordie was the only one who ever called me Billy boy. 'Don't tell me you were just passing.'

'Just passing—to where? The next stop is Norway. No, I'm here for a reason, but now I am here I realise that whatever the outcome, we need to keep in touch. It's been a long time Geordie and I guess it's no-ones fault, but when you get to our age you don't make too many new friends so it pays to look after the friendships you already have. What do you say?'

'Aye, Billy, you're right. There's no excuse for it. Ten years and not a call, postcard or kiss my arse from either of us or from Robbo or Flaky. Time just gets away from you. I never meant to leave it this long, but after the band split I just wanted some time out. Before I knew it three years had passed. All my money was gone and I'd nearly drunk myself into oblivion. I can't remember a bloody thing from that period.

Apparently, I was doing the rounds in Glasgow, just dossing at people's houses, doing shit loads of drugs and generally being a thorough nuisance to anyone who still had time for me. Then Gramps died about seven years ago. My Nan spent two days walking the streets of Glasgow trying to find me. She found me alright, unconscious in an alleyway, covered in shit and piss with an empty whisky bottle clutched to my chest. After that I did a lot of thinking. Decided I had to cut out the drugs and cut down on the booze. I figured that there could be no better place than Dinkiad Bay to do that. It's hardly a nest of temptation. And this is where I've been ever since. Anyway, I decided I owed Nan some payback. She took me in and gave me a chance as a kid and now it was my turn to repay the favour. I only wish I'd spent some time with Gramps before he died. Cancer took him, long, slow and painful. I still regret that very much. If I had been here I would have put a pillow over his head and put the poor bugger out of his misery.' He paused momentarily to take a large gulp of his pint. 'I kept meaning to get in touch but where do you start? I had no idea where any of you were living, no phone numbers or anything. After a while it all seemed too hard.' He took another long glug and finished his pint and stared at the floor. He appeared tired and old, and the anger that once raged in his eyes seemed to have been replaced with a sadness.

'Hey, what about another pint?' I said brightly. He snapped out of his memories and beamed, showing a row of teeth that had seen better days. A couple were missing, some chipped and one black.

'Aye, fucking good idea. Stan!' he shouted to the bar and nodded at Stan who duly nodded back. We drank. Then we drank some more. Then when I thought I couldn't drink anymore, we had one-for-the-road. We talked about the old days. We recalled adventures and sorrows, misgivings and successes. It was past 6 pm when I told him enough was enough. He agreed that we should be making a move and invited me to come and stay the night with him and his Nan. I didn't put up any resistance. Geordie collected his carrier bags, bid farewell to Stan and he walked, I stumbled, out of the pub.

Outside it was dark and bitterly cold after the warmth of the pub's open fire. There was a light salty drizzle that blew in from the harsh North Sea, its fine spray wetting my face and giving me a sharp wake up call. We both turned our collars up and walked along, huddled up against the elements. The street lamps shone amber halos and glowing lights emitted from the little fishing cottages giving them a warm and inviting appeal. Occasionally we'd pass a house where the smells of the kitchen escaped and teased our appetites. I thought of steak and onions, creamy mashed potato, gravy, buttered bread and strong cups of tea. I realised that I was quite famished. Geordie talked, I listened. I was concentrating on taking large deep breaths of fresh air, trying to sober up. I wanted to be at least comprehensible when I met Geordie's Nan.

By the time we reached the gate that enclosed the tiny garden I was feeling slightly refreshed. I told Geordie that my car was parked on the front and I'd need my overnight bag. He went inside and I walked briskly down to the harbour front and opened the car. The smell of stale cigarette smoke hung like a bad coat of paint on the interior of the car.

'Shit, I must give up smoking one day. It bloody stinks.' I collected my bag and headed back to the tiny terraced house. I knocked on the back door and let myself in.

'Hello, only me,' Geordie appeared and ushered me into the heat and light of the kitchen.

'Come on in Billy, come on in out of the cold.' I took my coat off and hung it on the back of a chair. I studied my surroundings. A small coffin shaped kitchen. An old fashioned stove and oven at one end with an array of different sized pans merrily boiling away. The door of the oven was slightly ajar and I could see the blue flame of gas at the back. The glass door cupboards, the chessboard linoleum, the Formica backed table and chairs, the taps with the rubber bung on the end, the old gas kettle, everything was from a bygone era. It was like walking back in time to the sixties. The only concession to the modern era was a microwave oven, stuck away, lonely, on its own shelf next to the larder cupboard.

The smell of a wholesome tasty meal permeated the whole house. It felt good—I felt good.

'Nan, come in here and meet Billy boy,' Geordie shouted through the kitchen door into the living room.

'What's your Nan's name?'

'Morag. Fancy a brew?' he asked

'Yeah, a cup of tea would go down a treat.'

'Cup of tea it is then Billy me lad,' replied Geordie with a smile. I gazed at the big man. He had removed his trench coat revealing a well worn, green denim shirt. His large wiry frame and wild mean appearance seemed out of place in this scene of busy domesticity, but I could tell he was happy. The door opened and in walked a diminutive, white haired old lady. She took short, tentative steps as though the ground was unstable. Her voice was tremulous and brittle. I stood up as a matter of courtesy.

'Ooh, so you're Billy are you? I've had to wait a long time to meet you. Allan often talks about you and the other boys. Why haven't you been to see us before now? Come on Son, sit yourself down. I've got supper on the go. I hope you like lamb chops with cabbage and mash and some homemade apple pie with custard for afters.' She took hold of my hand and clasped it in both of hers. 'I'm so glad to meet you. Now, how long are you staying?' She seemed genuinely overjoyed at my presence. I felt like royalty. Geordie stood behind her, like a huge protective tower, with his hands on her shoulders, smiling intently at me. I didn't know which question to answer first.

'Well Morag, I really must get going tomorrow I'm afraid,' I replied apologetically.

'Morag! That's not my name lad!' she said in surprise. That bastard Geordie. 'It's Iris. I don't know where you got Morag from?'

'No, I'm not sure where I got it from either,' I apologised while throwing Geordie a dirty look.

'No, that won't do at all. You'll stay at least two days. You and Allan have a lot of catching up to do. It will do the big oaf good to have some company of his own age. It can't be much fun for him living here with an old lady.'

'Don't be ridiculous Nan, I love living here. I wouldn't live anywhere else,' protested Geordie.

'Now how's that cup of tea coming Allan? Use the good pot and best china and none of those teabags, only the best tea leaves mind.' We sat and chatted away for a good half an hour until the food was ready.

She was definitely old school and believed in boiling the vegetables to within an inch of their lives. I could tell that she must have been a fearsome battler in the old days, tough and stoic, a bustling ball of energy, but now she was frail and weak, the spirit dimmed by the onset of time, the flesh tired and yielding. Geordie ran around like a good little schoolboy, draining veggies, mashing spuds, making gravy, replenishing our cups with fresh tea. I was quite amazed. When I last knew him he had trouble boiling an egg, now he was the proper little domesticated manservant.

After dinner or supper as Iris called it, we retired to the living room and sat in front of a glowing coal fire. The small TV set in the corner was on but the sound was turned down in a sign of respect to their visitor.

Iris brought out an old photo album and showed me pictures of when she was a young girl, the place she was born, her parents, her husband Hamish and her wedding day. She laughed and recalled seemingly random and insignificant events that had lodged in her mind like dog hairs on a woollen blanket. Her eyes jumped and sparkled and her brittle voice gathered strength and timbre. Geordie sat in the corner of the room in a rocking chair, smiling and laughing to himself as his Nan explored the past. The levity became subdued when she came across pictures of her only daughter, Claire—Geordie's Mother. She smiled and sighed.

'She went off the rails. She met a no-good drunk and followed him to Glasgow. I told her that he'd lead her to rack and ruin. But you can't tell a young girl anything. They know it all. She was very headstrong and stubborn, a bit like me I suppose. They got married without telling anyone. When he left her, that's Geordie's Father I mean, she really struggled. Of course, I'd lost touch with her by then, I didn't realise what a state she was in. When I did finally catch up with her she was eight months pregnant with Allan. Of course in those days it was a lot harder for a single Mother. I begged her to come back to Dinkiad Bay but she refused.' I threw Geordie a quick glance. The smile was gone, replaced by a severe frown, as he rocked back and forth in the chair.

'I sent money but I realised that all she was doing was spending it on the grog. In the end I just used to send things like parcels of food or furniture coupons. She had another child, Iain, Allan's Stepbrother. By this time Allan would have been about four. I thought she was getting back on her feet, although she always had a different fellow in the house whenever I visited. On one visit I noticed Allan, and to a lesser extent Iain, had bruising all over their backs. I mean, it's normal for wee bairns to have bumps and bruises all over the place but this was different. It was very severe. I quizzed her about it but she told me it was none of my business. Well, we had a big argument and I told her I'd report her to the welfare if I saw anything else like that again.'

The old girl stopped as if to catch her breath. She pulled a small white hanky out from her cardigan sleeve and wiped away a tear that had formed on her cheek. I glanced at Geordie again. He was now rocking quite vigorously and his face was like thunder.

'That was the last time I saw her alive. She moved flats and must have changed her name because I couldn't find her anywhere. I reported it to the authorities but there was nothing they could do if she couldn't be found. A year went by and one day I got a call out of the blue. It was the child welfare officer from Glasgow. They'd found Allan living in a flat all alone. They pulled Claire's body out of the Clyde. They couldn't tell how long it had been there, maybe days, maybe weeks. Suicide they said. And all that time little Allan foraging for himself in the gutters and backstreets of the city.

I found out about Iain from Allan. Apparently, Allan used to take his younger brother to the pictures with him every Saturday afternoon, that's right across the busy city mind. Eight years old and going all that way. Anyway, one day they came out of the cinema and it was dark. They were crossing a road and some drunk driver lost control. Allan grabbed his brother's hand and tried to pull him out of the way but the wee bairn was frozen to the spot. Allan lost his grip and little Iain was killed outright. Then a few weeks later Claire was dead.

I don't know what she was thinking; who knows what goes through a person's mind when they're muddled with sorrow and grief. I don't suppose the drink will have helped either. If only she had called, just one call, that's all it would have taken, I could have been there in three hours. Too late now.' She wiped away another tear. I felt like crying myself. I was always useless in situations like this. I was an emotional cripple. I took the easy way out and said nothing. She continued her sojourn through the past in a more upbeat resolute voice.

'I went to Glasgow and brought Allan back to Dinkiad Bay. He was in a bad way. He was malnourished, he had head lice, virtually no schooling and of course he was very withdrawn. Hardly surprising really, after what he'd been through. Well, slowly but surely he started to come out of his shell. His Gramps and I loved him to bits and spoilt him rotten, I think it was compensation for the guilt we felt over Claire. He had nightmares for a while but with lots of love and understanding he came good.' She paused to take a deep breath.

'Of course history nearly repeated itself a few years back.' She threw Geordie a disapproving glance. 'We hadn't seen Allan for quite a while, what with him off touring the world and being a big pop star and all. Then we read in the papers that the group had disbanded. Well, me and his Gramps expected to hear from him but we never did. And then

Hamish passed away. It was a painful death, poor soul, but at least he died in this house, his home that he loved so much.

Two days before the funeral Mrs Willis from down the street comes knocking on my door. She'd been to Glasgow to visit her niece. They'd been shopping in the city, it was near Christmas time and it was very busy. Anyway, guess who she spots drunk as a lord, cursing and swearing at the police in the middle of the high street? Allan! That's right, my Allan! I was so ashamed. As if I didn't have enough on my plate.'

Well, I got my hat and coat and the most recent photograph I had of him and took the next bus to Aberdeen and then the train to Glasgow. I scoured the streets searching for him. I must have been in every pub and bar in Glasgow, but no one had seen him. I visited the police station and showed them the photo. They confirmed that they'd arrested a similar looking man the day before for being drunk and disorderly. They said he carried no ID and no-one could get any sense out of him so once he had sobered up they gave him breakfast and then kicked him out onto the street again with only a caution.

I suppose they come across a lot of these derelicts and it saves them a lot of paperwork if they can just stick them back out onto the street. I stopped the night in a little hotel and began searching early the next morning. I retraced my steps but it was no good. It was like searching for a needle in a haystack, or should I say it was more like searching for an oaf in a city full of oafs.' She laughed at her own simile. I offered her an impoverished smile.

'Well, I was just about to give up. It was late afternoon and starting to get dark. I had to get back home soon as it was Hamish's funeral in the morrow. For some reason I stopped to listen to the Salvation Army band that were playing Christmas carols on the corner of the street. I'm not sure why I stopped, I mean it was hardly the appropriate time to stop and listen to carols. But I did. They were playing "Once In Royal David's City" which used to be Hamish's favourite. I stood and watched the band until the song finished. Then the band

98

began to march away down the street. I just stood there, tears streaming down my face, saying, "Oh Hamish, I wish you were here now, you'd know what to do." Well I believe he was there. There was a little alleyway that had been hidden by the band until they marched off. At first my eyes didn't focus. I wasn't looking at anything in particular. Then as I snapped myself out of my sorrow something caught my attention at the very far end of the alley. There were a couple of large dustbins to the side of a doorway, you know, the ones that they use for food scraps and such like. But sticking out from behind the bins were a pair of cowboy boots. Brown cowboy boots. Now I knew that was the only footwear that Allan had worn for at least fifteen years. I walked slowly down the alley until I got to the bins. I poked my head around the corner and there he was. In a drunken stupor, reeking of booze and filth. He was in such a state. I couldn't wake him. I went and flagged down a taxi and explained the situation but no-one wanted to drive all that way with a stinking drunk in the back. Three, four taxis I flagged down and none of them were interested. I even offered to pay double if they'd help but no one would. By the time I flagged the last one down I was in such a fury no-one would have dared to argue with me. I shouted at the taxi driver that this was the time for goodwill to all men, that I was burying my husband in the morning, that my Grandson lay in a drunken heap down a back alley as the rest of the world went about its business. Anyway, I'm not sure whether the taxi driver helped out of kindness or fear of my tongue, but whichever, it did the trick. He helped get Allan into the back of the cab and we drove all the way back to Dinkiad Bay, with the windows down mind. He reeked something terrible.

When we got home, the taxi driver, helped me get Allan upstairs, undressed and into the bath. He was starting to come around by this time, but he still didn't know what was going on. I washed him and put him to bed. I made the taxi driver a sandwich and a cup of tea. I asked how much I owed him, I knew it would be a lot of money, but he said I owed him nothing. He said that I was right, if you couldn't help someone out at least once a year you didn't deserve to be on this planet. I nearly cried. When I think back on it now, I think it was Hamish who led me to that alley. After all, they were playing his song. I think he wanted to help one last time before he left us both for good; although, some days I know he's here watching me and smiling.' She shut the photo album, sighed heavily and said, 'I'll put the kettle on.' She shuffled out of the room shutting the door behind her. I gazed at the embers.

'She's a bit of a party animal is Nan,' said Geordie sarcastically. 'If she really wants a giggle she puts an Auschwitz video on; occasionally she'll even throw the cat on the fire; aye, laugh a minute she is.' I didn't laugh.

'I've learnt more about your life in the last ten minutes from your Nan than I ever did from you after all those years on the road together,' I said incredulously.

'Yeah well, shit happens,' reflected Geordie.

13: A CHANGING MAN

I first heard the birds, then the sound of an engine and the clinking of glass. Milk being delivered—I hadn't heard that sound for many years. Then a new noise I couldn't decipher in my semi-comatose state; a rasping and low whistle, a grunt. I drifted out of reality and back into the land of dreams and screams.

The next time I awoke, it was to the vision of a large, Rasputin type figure, with long shaggy hair and a disturbingly unkempt beard.

'Billy, I've brought you a cup of tea, I'll put it here on the side,' said Geordie, playing the consummate host. I lifted my head and felt a sharp pain. Another hangover; mouth as dry as sandpaper. I sat up in bed as Geordie's huge frame disappeared out of the small bedroom doorway. I sat sipping the tea as I glanced around the room. I was in a single bed. There was an inflatable mattress on the floor at the far side of the room with a tangle of loose blankets and sheets. The big fellow had sacrificed his bed for me.

The room was done out in floral wallpaper, with a cream ceiling and a few small picture frames that contained pastel prints of Victorian children playing in the street. A more unlikely meeting of man and décor one would be hard to find. Under the window was a bass amp, bass guitar and a pair of headphones, all plugged in. A portable CD player stood on the windowsill next to a neat stack of CDs.

I finished my tea and got up and showered. I felt a little claustrophobic. The house was so small in all its facets. Little doorways,

101

small passages, tiny shower, dinky toilet. It was like the land of the little people. Geordie must have felt like Gulliver in the land of Lilliput. I went back to the bedroom and put on a fresh set of clothes. Geordie shouted up the stairs, 'One egg or two?'

'Two please!' I yelled back. The comforting aroma of bacon wafted up the stairs and into the room. I stared at the mirror—the picture of health stared back. On the far wall was a set of built-in robes with the doors slightly ajar. Curiosity got the better of me and I had a quick peek. One column of shelves was completely taken up by books. I had a quick flick through. There was a lot of non-fiction stuff; different religions of the world, philosophy, astrology, quantum physics, biographies of old film stars. The only concession to any fiction was the complete works of Ernest Hemingway. On the opposing column of shelves were countless CDs neatly stacked and indexed. Jazz, reggae, African, Latino, sixties soul, Dylan, a couple of old punk albums. Nothing that one could call contemporary. So this was how Geordie spent his time.

On the back of the cupboard door was an old picture of the Shooting Tsars. I don't remember the actual photo shoot, but it was definitely one of the teenage glossies—so it must have been not long after we entered the mainstream consciousness, maybe after our first number one. We were never comfortable in these contrived photo shoots. We were stood outside a castle, as though we were Lords of the Manor. I studied myself intently and marvelled at how good I looked. Short mod haircut, a dark blue Ben Sherman polo shirt, tight white Levis and suede desert boots adorning my feet. I seemed ridiculously young. How old was I? Maybe 23 or 24—a lifetime ago. Robbo was like a young Ronnie Wood and Flaky was a carbon copy of Keith Moon. As for Geordie, well he looked like a cross between Mick Fleetwood and Billy Connolly. Although his presence in the photo should have seemed incongruous, it didn't. In fact he added another dimension to the band's profile, albeit a dangerous one. The lords of cool! The photo shoot would have been organised by Chas and in the early days we just went along with whatever he asked us to do. We didn't know any better. I mean what else did rock stars do! They wrote, rehearsed and recorded songs. They played live, they made videos, they spouted their half-baked opinions in interviews and they attended photo shoots outside castles. What else was there? Maybe we should have tried to save the world or the lesser spotted Himalayan ant-eating butterfly, like other rock stars did—maybe, maybe not.

#

I tucked into breakfast and chatted away with Geordie as though there had never been a break between us. It was mid-morning and I was still feeling a little seedy from the heavy session the previous day, but the greasy fry up and copious amounts of tea soon began to revive my spirits.

'So where's your Nan this morning?' I inquired.

'Mothers Union trip. They come once a week and pick up a few of the old dears from around town and take them for a drive, peruse the scenery, stop at places of special interest and so on. Then they take them to the pub for their lunch. It gives the old chucks a chance to gossip and catch up and something to look forward to apart from the grave.'

'How old is she?'

'Eighty-six in September. She has a dicky heart and gets tired very easily. I'll tell you what though, you turning up has certainly put a spring in her step this morning. She does pretty well for her age but I don't know how much longer she's got. Maybe months, maybe years, who knows. Just live each day as it comes is what I say.' I finished up my breakfast and walked outside with my cup of tea and lit up. Geordie followed closely behind.

'You know that'll kill you one day,' he said pointing at my cigarette.

103

'You're the second person who has said that recently,' I replied, recalling Chas's comments from our recent telephone conversation.

'Oh yeah, who else has been handing out good advice?' I very nearly slipped up.

'Oh Cha ...' I coughed and spluttered. 'Charlie, a bloke I play darts with in my local.' Geordie seemed to buy it. He leant up against the small garden wall and stared at me suspiciously.

'So, what's the scam Billy boy? You're not here for my Nan's five star cooking are you?' I carried on smoking while staring out at the little white boats that bobbed about in the distant sea, like children's toys, so small and vulnerable.

'No, no I'm not. I do have an ulterior motive. I'll give it to you straight, if you agree to hear me out.' Geordie nodded.

'Okay, go ahead.'

'We've been offered a reunion tour. Three, maybe four bands, thirty UK dates over eight weeks.'

'Not interested,' Geordie interjected.

'We headline, sixty minute set, a best of collection.'

'I said, I'm not interested.'

'Hang on, you said you'd hear me out. Two hundred grand ...' I paused, 'each.' Geordie had been staring straight ahead, arms folded in a defensive manner. I saw his eyebrows momentarily rise when I mentioned the amount of money. 'Robbo and Flaky have agreed.' Okay, it was a white lie, but I was assuming that Robbo would have been more persuasive on Flaky the second time around. I got the same response,

'Not interested.' I carried on regardless.

'The tour starts in June. We have to have made a decision by the end of this week otherwise they'll offer it to someone else.'

'Let them. I'm not fucking doing it.'

'It's good money Geordie, and don't tell me you don't need it. You haven't got a pot to piss in. It's a one-off. We do the gigs, take the money and return to our lives, and everyone lives happily ever after.' He

104

turned to face me. He wasn't angry but I could sense that he was rankled by my persistence.

'N. O. Spells NO! Do you understand?' I had to try another tack. Guilt was always worth a shot.

'Okay, I get the picture. That's a shame because I was really looking forward to it. Plus, Flaky, well … he's doing it a bit tough at the moment. But never mind, maybe next time eh?'

'Don't feed me that shit. You can still do it without me, you could do it alone if you wanted. You are the band. You're the singer-songwriter for fuck's sake! We were just your backing group. Get yourself a session bass player. No-one will even notice.'

'Don't speak shit! It's all of us, the original band or not at all.' I stubbed my cigarette out onto the gravel path and immediately lit another one.

'Well then it's not at all. Don't try to offload your guilt on to me.' Alright, plan A and B had failed miserably, what did I have left. Maybe a good old ego massage would do the trick.

'Geordie, if it hadn't been for you, the Tsars would never have got off the ground. You were the catalyst, the glue that stuck us all together. You were, are, integral to everything. You gave us meaning and direction. Your bass playing was an art in itself. I still hear some of these scabby little bands today ripping off your runs and ideas. You're as much a part of the Tsars as I am. For me, to do it without you, would be the same as you doing it without me. It's like night and day, you can't have one without the other.' Geordie was quiet for a while, deep in thought, and then the light bulb came on.

'Oh very good, nice try Billy boy, but you've got to get up a lot earlier in the morning than that to catch me out!' he hollered angrily. Back to the drawing board.

'Give me one good reason?' I badgered. I was using the same technique Chas had used on me.

'I don't have to give you or anyone else, a reason.' He was becoming increasingly belligerent and I knew I would have to back off shortly.

'You can't give me a reason because you don't have one, do you?'

'Okay, I'll give you a good reason. I'm happy as I am. I don't want to do it. Anyway, those things are always cheap and nasty. I'm surprised you even contemplated doing it. You'll sully our reputation. You should be ashamed.' Now it was my turn to be angry.

'Well I'm not ashamed! I'm proud of our music and I know it has stood the test of time and that it's as relevant today as it was ten years ago or in ten years time. I thought we'd do it for one reason and for one reason only—the music. We were scuppered in our prime and I see it as putting a full stop to an unfinished chapter. We crawled away from those dreary Law Courts with our tail between our legs, or at least me and Robbo did, like a pair of sad, sorry, losers. Let's go out on a high, a swansong, roll back the years—go out with a bang.' I took a deep drag on my smoke and calmed down a little. Geordie said nothing, he just stared blankly towards the sea.

'I thought it might be fun; that's all,' I said passively. I put my cigarette out and headed back inside. I went to the bedroom and began packing my things. I was deflated but not particularly surprised. I thought about what Fiona had said, about going solo, and I knew that was what I must now do. I would start again, from scratch. There'd be no reunion tour, there'd be no Shooting Tsars comeback. It was pointless hanging around any longer. I would set off just as soon as Geordie's Nan returned from her outing—it would be rude to leave without saying goodbye. I would invite Geordie down to my place for a few weeks in summer. I wasn't going to let this matter spoil our re-kindled friendship. I heard footsteps on the stairs and then the bedroom door creak open.

'So, you're going then?' His voice was soft and quiet. He wasn't here to fight.

'Yeah, I've a lot of things to do and I've left my dog with Mam in Cornwall. He's a bit of a handful.'

'Yeah, sure, of course—I understand.' I nodded towards the bass amp and guitar.

'So you still play a bit eh?' I asked.

'Oh aye, it keeps me out of mischief. Once you've got the bug it's hard to get rid of it, but of course you know that.' I smiled in agreement. He walked over to the amp, flicked it on and picked up his bass. He began to play. His fingers were like giant spiders legs, nimbly climbing up and down the neck of his bass. He played a quick mosaic of famous riff lines and styles all blended skilfully into one tune. His eyes closed and he swayed back and forth. He was gone, lost in a place where time and pain didn't exist. I envied his total abandonment, no lyrics to encumber the process, just pure musicality.

#

We both sat in the kitchen, talking, but saying nothing of substance. We both kept glancing at the clock.

'She shouldn't be long now,' Geordie advised.

'Aye, not to worry, I'm in no rush.'

'Another cuppa, before you go?'

'Go on then,' I replied. Geordie got up and put the kettle on and I contemplated how different our banter was today compared with yesterday.

'Oh fuck, we're out of sugar, I forgot to get some yesterday while I was shopping.' He reached for his coat. 'I'll just nip to the grocers, you stay here, I'll be back in a jiffy.' He got up and left. I was alone with the sound of silence. I went outside and lit up another cigarette. A small minibus made its way slowly up the street and pulled up outside the gate. The bus door hissed open and I saw Geordie's Nan carefully descend the steps. She turned and called goodbye to a couple of her white haired friends who peered gleefully out of the window. She thanked the driver and walked down the path.

'Having a quiet smoke eh lad?' she asked.

'Yes, it's a disgusting habit, I know. I should really give up.'

'Don't give up on all the pleasures in life lad. We all need a little something to keep us going.' I wondered what it was that kept her going. I followed her back into the kitchen.

'Geordie's just gone to get some sugar from the shop.'

'Aye, we just passed him. He'd forget his head if it wasn't screwed on.' She sat down at the kitchen table, slightly out of breath. She noticed my bag on the floor. 'So, you're going already, eh lad?'

'Yeah, I've got a lot of things to do. I'll be visiting again don't you worry and I want Geordie to come and visit me this summer as well.'

'Good, good. I do worry about him you know. Can you promise me one thing?'

'Yes of course, what is it, Iris?' I asked.

'I've not got long left …' I foolishly jumped in with the fatuous and obligatory denial.

'Oh no, don't be silly Iris, you have a lot of life left in you yet.' I knew she hadn't—and so did she.

'That's very nice of you lad, but we both know it's not true. Just listen; when I'm gone will you promise to keep an eye on Allan for me. I don't mean take care of him or anything like that, but just watch out for him like a true friend would. Check up on him a few times a year, that's all. Can you promise to do that for me?' I wasn't sure whether the dig was intended or not, but I did feel guilty.

'Yes, I will. I promise.' I meant it.

'I think I'm already overdue. My Hamish is getting impatient. He's waiting for me but I keep telling him I can't come yet not until I know Allan's going to be alright. I wish he'd do something with his life or find himself a girl and settle down. He's not much chance of that around

108

here.' The sound of Geordie's large feet resounded down the gravel path and he re-entered the kitchen.

'Ah Nan, how did you go?' he went over and gave her a big hug and kiss on the cheek.

'Oh wonderful son, just wonderful. Now sit yourself down and I'll make us all a cuppa.' Geordie sat and perused me as his Nan busied herself at the countertop.

'So, what are your plans Billy?'

'I'm not sure. I have a suitcase of new songs, I may put a demo together and tout around for an ethically motivated record company and see how it goes.'

'Ha! Good luck with that!'

'Well, you've got to try. What else is there?'

'Here you go boys, here's your tea. Now Billy, I'm a bit tired so I'm going to go and have my afternoon nap in the living room.' I stood up and gave her a big hug.

'Now you look after yourself and remember what I said.'

'Yes Iris, I will. All the best, I've really enjoyed meeting you and hope to see you again soon.' I felt a wave of sadness envelop me.

'Oh Nan, the mail is on the table in the room, alright,' said Geordie.

'Aye, okay Allan—thanks,' she replied as she toddled off into the living room.

'She likes to open all the mail,' Geordie explained. 'She pays all the bills and makes sure everything's tickety-boo. It makes her feel like she's still got something to give.'

'Aye, she's a wise old bird as well.' Geordie smiled and nodded in agreement as we both took large swigs of our tea.

'Aargh! What the fuck!' Geordie spat his tea out all over the kitchen table. I jumped back and away from the spray and instinctively laughed, sending a river of tea shooting down my nose. 'Aye, if she's so fucking wise, how come she just filled the sugar bowl with salt?'

whispered Geordie. It broke the barrier between us that had been there since our earlier discussion about the tour.

'You'll come down to Whitstone this summer then?' I asked.

'Yeah, of course I will.' He leaned over and patted me on the shoulder. 'No hard feelings eh?'

'No. None,' I answered, grabbing his big paw and giving him a hug. A feeble scream came from the living room. We both rushed through to see what was amiss. Iris was slumped in the corner of the settee, her eyes were closed and she was breathing heavily. Clutched in her white fingers was a sheaf of paper—on the floor, an open envelope.

'Oh fucking hell, she's had a heart attack or stroke or something. Fucking hell Billy! Quick, go fetch the doctor!'

'Where, whereabouts?' I yelled as I headed out of the door.

'A few doors down from the pub. Run! And tell him to come straight away.' I rushed down the gravel path and took a right turn into the street. The first hundred metres or so was easy as the adrenaline surged me along, but I soon began to flag, puffing and panting like an old man. My legs felt weak, my heart pounded and I cursed the cigarettes. Luckily, it was only a couple of streets away. I turned right and then left into the main high street, eventually, I saw the sign that read "Dinkiad Medical Centre". I burst through the door and into a tiny waiting room. There were three old dears sat down, patiently awaiting their appointments. I must have scared them half to death, as they all gawped at me in shock. I turned and walked quickly to the reception and hit the bell. A young woman of about twenty came to the window.

'Yes Sir, may I help you.' I was bent over coughing,

'Where's ... where's the doctor?'

"Well, he's just down that corridor Sir, but you can't see him without an app ...' I was already down the corridor and outside the door. I tapped once and walked straight in; it was no time for protocol. The doctor, a dark haired man in his mid-forties, yelled out,

'What in heavens …' I stopped in my tracks and assessed the situation quickly—it wasn't good. I slammed the door shut behind me. In the middle of the room, squat on her haunches, skirt hitched up, bra around her torso, large ample tits swinging freely, was Margaret, the landlady from the pub. In her mouth was the doctor's cock. One hand gripped his balls, the other hand was on his shaft. She glared at me in astonishment and slowly retracted his dick from her mouth, a long strand of saliva created a temporary bridge between the doctor's rapidly flagging member and her lips.

'Oh, hello Margaret, how ya doing? Hope I'm not intruding?' I nodded my acknowledgement as she offered back a resigned smile. 'I'm sorry doctor, but it's urgent, you must come quickly!' In hindsight, maybe not the most appropriate choice of words. Margaret stood up and began to tuck her large bosom back into her bra. The doctor was quickly pulling up his pants and stuffing his tackle away.

'What the, who the, this is most outrageous!'

'It's Iris, Iris …' I realised I didn't even know Nan's last name. 'Iris—Allan Kincaid's Grandmother, she's had a heart attack or stroke or something.' The receptionist was now banging on the door.

'Is everything okay doctor? This man just ran straight in!' her muffled voice called out.

'Yes Sheila, it's okay, go back to your desk,' he replied. 'Iris Harris. Right, I'll get my bag.' The doctor gave Margaret an apologetic shrug of the shoulders, coughed, cleared his throat and then followed me out of the surgery as Margaret was still adjusting her garments.

'See you Margaret!' I called out. I didn't get a response. We walked briskly to the reception.

'Sheila, I've got an emergency; can you please explain to the patients. Anything non-urgent, please reschedule for tomorrow.'

'Yes doctor,' she replied, as she threw me a dirty sideways glance.

'Oh, and Sheila,' the doctor leaned forward and whispered 'make a fresh appointment for Mrs McAlpine, her session was interrupted.'

111

'Okay doctor,' she replied. I looked at him and noticed that his shirt-tail was protruding from his fly. That would give the old chucks in the waiting room something to gossip about.

We got outside and began to jog, the doctor trying to pull his coat on at the same time.

'So what happened?' he panted,

'I'm not sure Doc, one minute she was fine, the next we heard a yell and there she was slumped on the couch. She's been out for the day and came back about an hour ago. She seemed right as rain, well you know, for her age I mean.'

'Yes. She's not getting any younger. She's had two mild heart attacks in the last year but she's on medication to try and prevent them. I think she worries too much about that bloody loafer Allan. She shouldn't be worrying about him at her age.' I didn't reply. 'So are you a relative or a friend of the family? I don't recognise your face from being around here?'

'I'm Geordie's mate,' I replied.

'Geordie?' the doctor inquired.

'Sorry, I mean Allan. Geordie—that's his nickname.'

'Funny nickname for a Scotsman.'

'It's a long story.' We soon reached the house but before we entered the door the doctor grabbed me by the sleeve.

'Ahem ... what you saw back there, well, I can expect you to be discreet? It's a very small town and ...' I cut him off.

'Doctor, I didn't see a thing and I'm leaving here shortly, so there's absolutely nothing to worry about.'.

'Ah good, good.' Relief spread across his face. 'But I must say, that it is most inappropriate bursting in like that on a private consultation, very irregular indeed, despite the circumstances. Maybe next time you could get my receptionist to call through on the phone.' Quite fucking amazing! There he was, getting a gobble off the local publican's wife, while a bunch of old grannies waited outside and now he was trying to reclaim the moral high ground over my well intentioned actions.

'I'm not sure there will be a "next time" doctor. I can't envisage those exact same circumstances ever happening again, unless there's a parallel universe somewhere.'

We walked through into the living room. Geordie jumped up from the settee where he'd been sitting.

'Oh doctor! Thank God you're here. Is she going to be alright?' I glanced at Geordie's tormented face and realised that this old woman was the most important thing in his life. My heart went out to him and I made a mental prayer to a cynical God. The doctor put his bag down at the side of the settee and pulled out a stethoscope.

'If you don't mind waiting outside,' he gestured towards the door.

'Oh! Of course, sorry doctor,' said Geordie. We both made our way out and back into the kitchen. Geordie slumped into a chair. I put the kettle on like any good British bloke would. He stared blankly at the table.

'Hey come on mate, keep your pecker up. Just keep hoping, that's all you can do.' I patted him on the shoulder.

'Fuck it. Fuck it all. What will I do Billy, if she dies, what will I do?' he pleaded with me for an answer.

'Don't talk like that Geordie, it's not over yet mate.' I noticed that he was holding in his hand the same sheaf of paper that Iris had been holding in the living room. 'What's in the letter?' I asked quietly. Geordie's wild eyes refocused and he handed me the letter. It was from a solicitors in Aberdeen. The paper was expensively embossed with their ostentatious business name, "Cooper, Unsworth, Noble and Tilburg - Partners in Law". I laughed, could they really have missed the bleeding obvious? Apparently so. I read the letter. It transpired the house that Iris had lived in happily for the last sixty years was up for sale. Iris and Hamish had never owned it, they had merely rented it all these years. Now, without any prior warning, the house had been put on the open market. The letter was a notice to vacate the premises within eight weeks. Reading between the lines, I assumed that an offer had already been made on the house, now it was just a formality of evicting the tenants and the deed would be done. No wonder the old bird had strained her heart muscle. I put the letter back on the table.

'Cunts by name, cunts by nature,' I said.

'If anything happens to Nan, I will personally make sure that those bastards pay for it.' I knew he meant it as well. He wasn't the best to cross at any time, but something like this, well, it was scary.

'Geordie mate, don't talk like that. Let's wait and see what the Doc's got to say.' I made the tea and sat down. The atmosphere was tense and I didn't want to speak unless Geordie spoke first. After a tedious ten minutes that seemed more like an hour, the doctor came through into the kitchen. We both stared at him. He appeared grave and I feared the worst.

'What? What is it Doc?' asked Geordie nervously.

'Don't worry, she's going to be alright ... for the moment at least. I'm not sure whether it's angina or a mild heart attack. I've given her a shot and she's feeling a lot better, but nevertheless, I've called an ambulance. It's going to take about an hour to get here. We'll take her to the hospital in Aberdeen and do some tests. I've insisted that she recuperates in a convalescence home for three or four weeks. She took a lot of convincing. What she needs is quiet and absolutely no stress.'

'Those bastards, they've done this to her!' growled Geordie shoving the letter in the doctor's direction. He took the letter and read it.

'Yes, she told me about this, it could certainly have brought on the attack but I believe she's been stressed for some time and this was the straw that broke the camels back, so to speak.'

'Stressed for some time! What do you mean "stressed for some time", I'm here to help her?' said Geordie incredulously.

'You're the reason that she's stressed Allan. She worries about you all the time, whether you'll ever get a job, whether you'll ever get a girl, if you'll go off on another bender, how you'll look after yourself when she's gone. You are the biggest cause of her stress, Allan!' The doctor pointed at him with his finger. I saw Geordie's eyes narrow, not a good sign. I stood up between Geordie and the doctor's finger. Luckily, Geordie was diverted.

'Oh what a crock of shit Doc! That's not true, you've only been in there five minutes what would you know about it?' He was wounded and hurt.

'No you're wrong Allan. I do know about it, I call around about once a fortnight to check on your Nan. She's confided in me but promised that I should never tell you. Well, sometimes it's necessary to break a confidence if the end justifies the means. Let's face facts Allan, you've been here over seven years and you've not done an honest days work yet. If you'd got a job you could have bought this house for your Nan and that would be one less worry for her. She's not bothered about the house for her sake, she knows she hasn't got long left, she's worried about where you will live.

I've told her she has to stop worrying about you. I suggest you take a good look at yourself Allan and lift your game.' He put his coat on and Geordie stared at the table top averting the doctor's disapproving eyes.

'Well, I've said my piece, I've probably said too much already but I feel it had to be said. I'll come back when the ambulance arrives and have a word with the paramedics. I suggest you get an overnight bag ready for your Nan. She'll need pyjamas, dressing gown, slippers, a couple of clean sets of clothes for the convalescence home and toothbrush, toothpaste etcetera. Can I rely on you to sort that out, Allan?' Geordie didn't look at him but with a hint of sarcasm replied,

'Aye, I think I can manage that. I'll go with her in the ambulance and stay over.'

'No, definitely not, she must not have any more stress. You'll be more useful here, I think you'll agree?' Geordie nodded reluctantly.

'Good, right, I'll bid you good day then.' The doctor made his way out of the house, I followed and closed the door quietly behind, leaving Geordie to his solemnity. I chased the doctor up the gravel path towards the gate. The doctor spoke first.

'I'm sorry about that, but I do feel it needed to be said. Maybe I was a bit harsh but ...'

'Don't worry about it Doc, I think you're probably right. He could do with a reality check, although he does do a bit around the place you know, he's not a total cabbage.' He didn't reply. 'How long have you been here doctor?' I inquired.

'In Dinkiad Bay?' I nodded. 'Over ten years, and before that five years in Aberdeen.'

'How much would you say a house like this would be worth?' I said, turning and studying the small two-up-two-down cottage.

'If you'd asked me that question five years ago, I would have said about thirty thousand, but now, well you could easily double that, sixty, sixty-five thousand. There's a lot of wealthy people in Edinburgh and Aberdeen who think there's nothing better than finding a tiny little fishing village like this and buying a holiday house. "Weekend Whiners" they're known as around here. They expect all the facilities they get in a big city but at half the price. I'm not sure whether it's greed or one-upmanship that drives them, but whatever it is, it's pushed the house prices through the roof. The locals can barely afford to buy them on the wages they get around here. It's a real problem. Why do you ask? Don't tell me that you're a friendly benefactor who's going to solve Allan's problems for him?'

'No ... no, it's just an idea I've had, that's all. Okay, well thanks again Doc and sorry about ... well you know, what happened earlier. Next time I'll wait for an answer before I barge through a closed door.'

'Good, good ... yes ... well I think the matters forgotten ... erm ... goodbye then Mister ...' he paused for me to fill in the blanks.

'Harding, Will Harding.' He held out his hand and I shook it. For a fraction of a second he scanned my eyes searching for signs of character. Could I be trusted, that's what he was thinking. The doctor turned and headed off down the street. I watched him for a moment and then went back inside. Geordie was still sat in the same position as when I'd left him.

'Cuppa?' I asked.

'No. If I drink another cup, I'll be pissing tea. Top cupboard, left hand side,' he instructed. I went to the cupboard and opened the door and pulled down a large bottle of single malt whisky that had barely been touched.

'How long have you had this?' I was intrigued. Geordie momentarily pulled a puzzled expression.

'I don't know, six months, maybe a year, why?'

'That's not bad for a dipsomaniac. I'm quite impressed.' I grabbed two small tumblers from the cupboard and cleaned the dust out with my finger. I placed the glasses on the table and twisted the top off the whisky bottle. The amber liquid splashed like molten gold into the tiny receptacles. Geordie picked his up and threw it down his neck. It barely touched the side—what a waste of good malt. He slapped the glass back on the table.

'Twist,' he ordered. I refilled the glass. This time, he briefly cradled it in his large claws like it was a precious jewel before he knocked it back again in one hit. 'Twist,' I obliged and got the same result. 'Twist,' I poured again.

'Stick,' I said. I wasn't going to allow him to get plastered. I sat down next to him.

'What am I going to do Billy? This is her home, they can't just kick her out like that. She's been here over sixty years. It's wrong, it's fucking wrong! But I know those maggots; solicitors and lawyers are all the fucking same. They wrap you up in jargon until you can't breathe and then throw you down the well. There's nothing I can do, I'll have to find us a flat or something … what a fucking mess!' He was visibly distressed and spun the whisky glass round and round in his hands as though he was ringing blood out of a cloth. I decided to make my move. I sometimes wonder now, whether I was doing it for my benefit or for Geordie and his Nan; I'm still not sure.

'There is a way out of this.' I said the words slowly and paused to make sure he had heard me correctly. His eyes widened and a glimmer of hope flashed across them.

'What Billy? What is it?'

'Well, there's a two hundred grand cheque with your name on it waiting for you out there.' I nodded in the general direction of the outside world and lifted my glass and had a gentle nip of the malt. I savoured the flavour and enjoyed the burning sensation as it slid down my throat. Geordie said nothing, as though not comprehending what I'd said.

'The reunion tour? It's easy. Here's how it will work. Tomorrow we get up, you collect your gear and we set off for Aberdeen. We go visit your Nan in hospital. Explain the situation and tell her that there's nothing to worry about. Then we go see the solicitors. We make them an offer on the house. Whatever they've been offered already we throw in an extra five grand. People are greedy, they'll take it. I'll even leave a cheque as a deposit. It'll take a month or so for all the paperwork to be sorted so that gives us a bit of breathing space. We head down to London, meet up with Robbo and Flaky, get the tour contract inspected by a music lawyer. If everything's above board we sign the contract and then start rehearsals. We do the tour and in eight weeks it's done. We take the money, say thank you very much and we'll be sat back around this table before you can say "geriatric rock star". Your Nan will be back, you'll own the house and you'll still have well over one hundred grand in the bank. It's as easy as falling down the stairs.' I finished with a flourish and a big smile on my face. Geordie's initial expression of hope fell off his face like a climber off the side of a mountain. 'What is it Geordie?'

'I can't do it,' he mumbled. He took another shot of whisky and took the bottle from my grip. 'I told you before, it's a non-starter.' I'd tried my best, and to be honest I'd just about lost patience. I mean, how hard was it to do? It wasn't like signing up for the Army and spending three years in Iraq; it wasn't going to Bosnia, it wasn't infiltrating the Russian Mafia, it wasn't working down an asbestos mine. No, it was playing rock stars for a couple of months. Having every whim catered for. All our meals provided, hotels and room service, our favourite drinks always at hand, all expenses paid and just to throw a bit of icing on the cake, a big sack full of money at the end of it. I was wasting my time on the man, not only would he not help himself but he wouldn't accept help from anyone else either. One last try,

'Why not Geordie? It's not fucking rocket science, it's playing a few songs and getting a lot of money for it; money you need. You know you take life too seriously, it's not that precious what we did, it was just music. Fuck me! In twenty, thirty years we'll just be a name in an A to Z rock almanac. In a hundred years we probably won't even be that. It will be like we never existed. Lighten up Geordie, stop punishing yourself for what happened in the past, it wasn't your fault you know ...' He cut me off as he mumbled something I couldn't comprehend. 'Sorry, what was that?'

'I'm ... I'm scared,' he repeated softly. I almost laughed but managed to hold it back. I remembered what my Dad used to tell me, "never mock a man's fears". I was quite taken aback really, I'd never known Geordie to be scared of anyone or anything, apart from people with prosthetic limbs.

'Bloody hell Geordie, is that all! Why didn't you say! Of course you'll be a little bit scared, I will, we all will. It's only natural, I mean we haven't played together for ten years, we're bound to be a little rusty, but we've got two weeks in the rehearsal rooms to knock everything back into shape. And once we've done the first couple of gigs we'll be as right as rain. It'll be like putting on an old shoe. Anyway, I saw the way you

119

played this morning, you've lost nothing man, if anything you've got even ...'

'No, I don't mean scared of playing ...' Now I was confused.

'Well ... what then? What are you scared of Geordie?' He lifted his eyes from the table and downed another shot of whisky. In a quiet, calm voice he replied,

'Myself ... I'm scared of myself.' I wasn't much the wiser. I stared at him with the same gormless, confused expression. 'I'm scared of what might happen, or more precisely I'm scared of history repeating itself, which, it has a tendency to do in this family. I'm scared that I'll start drinking again, that I'll get sucked back into the drugs. I'm scared that I'll become a violent, unpredictable monster. I'm scared that I'll fall into the abyss—again, and this time there'll be no-one there to pull me out. That's why I can't do it. That's the only reason.' He fidgeted with his glass like a nervous schoolboy. I smiled at him.

'You big daft prat! Is that it? Is that what all this has been about? Why the fuck didn't you say that from the start? Listen to me, I'm going to make sure that history doesn't repeat itself. We aren't kids anymore, we've all grown up a lot. There's no way that I'm going to let you go off the rails, if you do I'll whack you in the head just to let you know. I'm going to watch out for you this time, trust me ... what do you say? Are we gonna do it or what?' He stared at me with big wide glistening eyes.

'Do you really believe that?'

'Yes, I do. You're different now. You've been through the wringer and you've come out the other side. Now what about a toast to the Shooting Tsars?' I refilled our glasses and we both lifted them in unison.

'The Shooting Tsars,' I said.

'Aye, the Shooting Tsars. One last time, let's show the bastards eh?' We necked off the malt and refilled for an action replay.

\#

The ambulance arrived fifteen minutes later than it was due. The doctor reappeared to chaperone proceedings much to the annoyance of the qualified Paramedics. Geordie had collected all his Nan's gear as requested and hovered behind the Paramedics as they wheeled his Nan into the back of the ambulance.

'Now don't you worry about a thing Nan, everything's going to be all right. I've got everything under control, I'll sort everything. You just concentrate on getting some rest and getting better. You'll be back home before you know it.' His Nan offered a weak reply.

'Good boy Allan, I know I can rely on you.' She had been sedated but still offered encouragement to her Grandson. They lifted her into the back of the ambulance and Geordie put her bag down beside her and grabbed her hand. Her eyes were closed.

'Nan, I'll be in to see you tomorrow, now you just rest up do you hear?' Her eyes opened momentarily and she nodded her head. With one last big effort she raised her head a little and beckoned me over,

'Billy, Billy come here?' I walked over and she grabbed my arm. I could feel her shaky, bony fingers through my shirt sleeve.

'What is it Iris?' I asked softly.

'Remember what I said now, you will keep your promise won't you?' I briefly wondered what the hell she was on about and nodded falsely,

'Yes Iris, of course, I promise, you can trust me.' She released her grip and fell back onto her stretcher, breathing heavily, eyes closed. I noticed a tear roll down her wrinkled cheek and into the crinkly skin of her neck. I was brushed aside by one of the Paramedics who quickly slammed the doors shut. He was obviously in far more of a hurry to get back to Aberdeen and knock off than he was to come here in the first place. Just another job I suppose. We watched the ambulance depart. I didn't know it then, but that was the last time I was to ever see Geordie's Nan. As the flashing lights slowly disappeared, her words came echoing back, "Watch out for him like a true friend would". A cold biting wind was starting to gain strength as it skimmed across the grey North Sea. I saw Geordie shiver beneath his shirt as he stared down an empty street, the ambulance long out of view. I walked up to him and put my arm around his big wide shoulders,

'C'mon mate, let's go inside.' We walked silently back to the warmth of the house and sat at the table. There was a flatness about the place now, it was almost as though this house of bricks and mortar knew it had lost its curator and mourned the fact. Geordie looked like a wet weekend and said nothing. I felt stifled, claustrophobic, I craved my own space and suddenly missed my hermitage in Whitstone and the familiar, comforting Yorkshire Dales. I decided we needed to get out of the house for a while.

'C'mon, let's go down the pub,' I suggested.

'Nah, don't really fancy it. I'm not into having another heavy session.' Geordie must have got the blues bad. I'd never known him knock back an invitation to drink.

'C'mon, we need a change of scenery. It's nearly five now, we'll have a couple of quiet pints and by six they'll be serving food. I don't know about you but I'm bloody famished. No heavy sessions, I promise. Anyway we have a big day tomorrow so we'll need an early night and early start.'

'Aye, c'mon then, it can't be any worse than being here.'

#

We were greeted by Stereo Stan as we walked into the pub.

'Here's trouble, I say here's trouble!' followed by a hearty laugh. We both nodded at Stan behind the bar.

'Two pints of bitter please,' I ordered. Stan took on a grave appearance.

'er … sorry to hear about your Nan, Geordie, sorry to hear about your Nan. How's it looking?'

'Thanks Stan,' he replied, 'too early to tell yet. They've taken her to Aberdeen for observation and tests. Then they're going to put her in a rest home for a few weeks, just as a pick me up really. But yeah, I think she's going to be fine.'

'Ooh, I don't know about that Geordie, once they go in those rest homes the only way out is in a box, I say, in a box.' Nice one Stan. I stood shaking my head in disbelief. Geordie stared at him coldly. Luckily, Margaret came out from the kitchen to take control of matters.

'Bloody hell Stan! What do you want to go and say a thing like that for? Can't you see Allan's upset? You big oaf, now go do something useful like collecting the glasses, I'll serve these gentlemen.' She whipped him on the back of the head with a tea towel as he went past. He cowered and let out an "Ouch!"

'Sorry Geordie, sorry Geordie, I didn't mean anything by it, I was just, I was just ...'

'Don't worry Stan,' said Geordie, 'I know you didn't mean it.' Stan wandered off around the pub, suitably chastised, as Margaret took over the duties of pint pulling. Geordie let out a big sigh.

'I'm gonna take a dump.' He said and walked off towards the toilets.

'Yeah, thanks for telling me that.' I called after him. Margaret continued pulling. She hadn't made eye contact with me yet. I felt it my duty to break the ice and put her at ease.

'Ah Margaret, I didn't recognise you with your clothes on.' She pursed her lips and gave me a withering glare. I tried again, 'I didn't realise the NHS was in such a perilous state that they'd started charging customers in kind!'

'Oh I see, a fucking smart arse eh?' she hissed, as she passed me the first pint, just as Stan returned with a handful of empties. He had already forgotten his previous rebuke and was bristling with nervous energy, a sure sign that he'd thought of something funny to say.

'Eh, Will, my missus told me about your little faux pas, eh, eh, at the surgery, eh, eh,' he insisted on winking at me. 'I hope you didn't see anything you shouldn't have, did you hear that, Ha! Ha! Didn't see anything you shouldn't have, eh!' I matched his false laugh with my own.

'Ha! Ha! No, unfortunately not Stan.' I could see Margaret biting the inside of her lip while steadfastly staring at the rising, frothing liquid in the glass. 'No, Margaret was taking her medicine like a good girl. A bitter pill to swallow but I think she managed it.' Stan threw his head back in a loud guffaw,

'Ho, ho! Bitter pill to swallow, oh, I like that, yes very good, bitter pill to swallow, did you hear that Margaret, did you hear that?' Margaret appeared a little less jolly than her husband.

'Yes, I heard. Will is quite a wit, isn't he.' She spat the words out with venom. Stan wandered off again to collect more glasses, chuckling away to himself.

'Sorry Margaret, I couldn't help myself,' I apologised. She put the second pint down on the bar and leaned across to me.

'Listen dickhead, this is a fucking small town, if anything ever gets out I'll be tarred and feathered, so less of the wisecracks eh!' I glanced down at her cavernous cleavage, an action that didn't go unnoticed.

'Okay Margaret, fair enough. My lips are sealed. I've told no-one and as far as I'm concerned it's forgotten. Anyway, I'll be leaving tomorrow and probably won't be back for quite a while. '

'You mean that?' she asked in a suspicious tone.

'Yep. Cross my heart and hope to die,' I even did the actions. 'Let me buy you a drink, it's been a stressful day for all of us. What will you have?' Her face visibly brightened as her relief dissipated.

'Oh, well thanks, I'll have a rum and coke.' I handed her a tenner and I watched her womanly figure reach up and eject a stream of rum into a small tumbler. She turned back to the bar as I sipped on my pint. She suddenly had a wicked grin on her face. 'So ...' she began, 'did you like what you saw?' *Bugger me, she has some brass, I'll give her that!*

'Very impressive. If it had been a diving competition I would have given it a 9.5 I think.'

'Only a 9.5?' she replied with exaggerated disappointment. 'I'll need to lift my game then. Maybe next time you're up here you can re-evaluate my performance on a more … intimate level?'

'Maybe I can.' Stan returned to the bar and cut the conversation short, still chortling over my previous, not very funny, remark.

'Ho! Ho! Bitter pill to swallow, bitter pill to swallow.' Poor old bugger—if only he knew the truth, the rest of his hair would fall out. Geordie reappeared, patting his stomach,

'Ah! I feel better for that.' Genteel, refined civility—you can't beat it.

We ordered a meal and Geordie challenged me to a game of pool, I agreed and he walked over to the table to rack up the balls. I remembered I still had something to do and it would be easier with Geordie out of earshot.

'Margaret, there is a favour I'd like to ask of you?'

'You can't contain yourself can you, I'm sorry love but I've had enough frights for one day.' She thought I was asking for a bit of light relief, I could have done with it but had more important things on my mind.

'No, no, it's nothing like that.' She dropped her busty barmaid act and became serious.

'What is it?'

'Well, you know Geordie's Nan is going to be out of action for a few weeks, well by the time she gets back here Geordie is probably going to be on tour.' She raised her eyebrows in surprise and smiled broadly,

'So, you've finally got the big lummox motivated enough to do something with the rest of his life?'

'Not really. It's a case of Hobson's choice.' She seemed a little puzzled but I didn't elaborate on the matter. If I left you some money

125

could you make sure she gets a lunch and dinner once a day?' I pulled a large wad out of my inside pocket and began to count off the notes.

'Of course dear, I'd be delighted. I'll take it around personally and make sure she's alright. Not a problem at all.' I counted off a three hundred pounds and handed it over just as Stan returned. Stan spotted the cash and made a dart for it but Margaret was too quick.

'What's all this then eh? What's all this?' he joked.

'It's for Iris. We're going to make sure she gets a couple of good meals each day while Allan's away.' She rolled the wad of notes into a tube and slid it between her cleavage in classic barmaid style.

'Bloody hell, it'll be safe down there Will, I say it'll be safe down there.' I wasn't as sure. I wrote down my mobile on the back of a beer mat and handed it to Margaret.

'If you ever need to get hold of me or Geordie for any reason, you can call me on this. Geordie doesn't own a mobile, in fact I'm not sure he knows what a mobile is.' Margaret took the beer mat and pinned it to the notice board behind the bar. 'I'd prefer you didn't mention the money thing to Geordie just at the moment, he'll only get uppity and start ranting on about charity. I'll tell him tomorrow.' They both agreed and Stan winked at me while tapping his nose,

'Say no more Will, say no more.' I didn't.

14: BIG COUNTRY

I woke tired but cheerful at about six in the morning. I opened a window as the bedroom reeked of farts, stale beer and BO. I blamed it all on Geordie. Mind you, the bedroom was hardly big enough for one grown man never mind one grown man and a brick shithouse, so it was hardly surprising the place stunk.

I made us both an unhealthy breakfast of bacon, eggs, fried tomatoes, mushrooms, sausage, buttered toast, fried bread and about a gallon of strong tea. Well, we did need to use up the perishables before we left; waste not want not.

Geordie packed a small holdall full of the essentials required for three weeks away; two pairs of socks, a pair of black jeans, a blue denim shirt, a brush (that hardly had any spikes protruding due to the amount of hair wrapped around it) and two pairs of jocks. I suppose I should have been thankful for small mercies. I remembered the days when he only used to pack one pair of jocks for a six-month tour. You certainly couldn't accuse the man of being a fashion junkie.

We accomplished the usual house leaving duties and locked up behind us as we braved the cold, austere, Scottish morning and walked towards the jetty where my car was parked. The little fleet of fishing boats were long gone even though it was just past eight. I opened the boot of the car for Geordie to throw his bag into.

'What's this?' he asked in a bemused fashion.

'It's a car, what do you think it is?' I replied.

'A fucking Mondeo! A red one at that, what are you? Some sort of dog food sales rep.' He threw his bag into the boot with a certain amount of disdain. This was classic Geordie; he wasn't happy unless there was some sort of discord, some sort of friction to keep his mind occupied while he waited for more interesting things to appear on his horizon. I knew his little game and could play it as well as him.

'Oh, well pardon me, I'm sooo sorry that a Mondeo is beneath you. We can always take your car if you like? Oh what's that? You can't fucking drive! Well knock me down with a white dog turd!' Geordie opened the passenger door and climbed in, muttering to himself. I slammed the boot shut and got in the car.

'Well, it's hardly fucking rock and roll is it,' he continued.

'No it's not, but then again, at the moment, neither are we.' He still grumbled away wittering on about Rod Stewart not being seen dead in one of these things and that it was the sort of car that Bono would drive. I tried to ignore him, but in reality, I was quite pleased with his behaviour; it showed he wasn't in a depressed state about the events of the previous twenty-four hours.

We hit the road and soon left Dinkiad Bay behind us. Geordie messed around with the radio incessantly, picking up nothing but white noise and the motor sound from the windscreen wipers. He was already annoying me and we'd only been in the car ten minutes—it was going to be at least fourteen hours before we got to London! I lit a cigarette as this thought reverberated in my head.

'Oh that's nice,' he said winding his window down, 'not content to kill yourself, you also want to take me with you. Haven't you heard of passive smoking?'

'Haven't you heard of passive whining? You don't think I can spend fourteen hours in a car with you and not have a smoke do you?'

Eventually the adolescent behaviour subsided as Geordie managed to pick up a Glasgow talk-back programme on the radio. He continued a running commentary on the whole event. He criticised and abused everybody who called in but he saved his most savage attacks for the host, a one Michael Carmichael. Most talk-back shows were slightly right of centre but this one was slightly right of Hitler. Geordie hated all politicians and political pundits with a passion—I think what he really craved was a glorious and bloody revolution. 'Have you heard this little right wing fuck? Here he is, on a couple of hundred grand a year, spouting off about what people on the dole should be doing. Why doesn't he try a couple of years on the dole, the filthy maggot. Ex-public schoolboy—silver spooned bastard! I thought we'd got rid of all these bastards years ago? Conceited, arrogant prick, have you heard him? Work for the dole, pick yourself up by the bootstraps, what a royal prick he is. I'd like to pick him up by his bootstraps and wrap them around his fucking testicles.' At least his abusive, cynical monologue broke the monotony of the drive.

#

Time passed quickly, surprisingly, and we were soon in Aberdeen searching for the solicitors' office.

'What's the address on that thing?' I asked nodding at the letter from the solicitors that Geordie gripped in his giant mitten as though he was brandishing Chamberlain's famous "Peace In Our Time" note.

'57A and B Lithgow Street. I'll give you directions, I know this place like the back of my hand.' He may have known his way around the city like the back of his hand but being a non-driver he was completely useless. He didn't seem to understand simple concepts like one-way systems, traffic lights and turning right when you're in the left hand lane of a three lane road. After a few arguments and numerous insults we eventually found our way to the street in question. It was in a well to do and leafy suburb on the outskirts of the city. We crawled along until we spotted a row of large, stone, Victorian townhouses set back from the road. I could make out the large gold letters on a plaque outside one of the houses. "Cooper, Unsworth, Noble and Tilburg - Partners in Law". I parked up and turned the engine off. I stared across at Geordie, who was grinning.

'I wonder why they don't abbreviate it. Cunt pil has a nice ring to it, don't you think,' smirked Geordie.

'That would be an initialism or an acronym, not an abbreviation.' Geordie huffed and glared at me disdainfully.

'You know Billy boy, there's only one thing worse than a smart arse and that's being sat next to one in a car.'

'Yeah whatever. Okay Geordie, let's do this the easy way. We go in there, act polite and courteous and conduct ourselves in a civil and professional manner. We put in an offer and see whether they'll accept it.' Geordie peered at me in true innocence.

'Well of course, it goes without saying, etiquette and decorum, not a problem for me, I just hope you can wing it.'

#

We were sat in the opulent office of Mr Lachlan Cooper, drinking tea daintily from china cups. Geordie had already had an altercation with one of the younger partners in the reception of the building. The unsuspecting solicitor had told Geordie that he should have made an appointment first and that no-one was available to see him. A stream of abuse followed, along with threats of anal penetration by a size fourteen cowboy boot. Luckily Mr Cooper had emerged and calmed the situation. We were both taken aback by Mr Cooper's appearance; he was a small, stout man in his mid-sixties who sported a handlebar moustache, which was patently a public health hazard. He wore an immaculate tweed jacket and matching pants with tartan socks pulled up to his knees. He was bald apart from a few well manicured strands and horn-rimmed glasses hung precariously from the end of his bulbous, ruddy nose; he completed his appearance with a large red polka-dot bow tie. He looked like he'd just come from a grouse shooting party at Balmoral Castle—maybe he had.

'I do apologise for my colleague. He's young and keen, maybe a bit too keen, and can appear rash, maybe even a trifle arrogant at times. I hope you'll accept my apologies.'

'Not a problem at all Mr Cooper, it's forgotten already,' I replied.

'Good, good ...' he leaned back in a large, red leather, reclining chair and steepled his fingers together, narrowing his eyes as he contemplated us both. The room was timber lined and down one side was a vast bookcase that was full of expensive and sombre looking tomes. Hanging from the wall on the other side of the room were elegantly framed lithographs of old steam engines and iron suspension bridges from a bygone era. These caught Geordie's attention.

'Do you mind if I have a look at your pictures Mr Cooper?' he inquired.

'No, not at all. Be my guest. Are you interested in the age of steam or the industrial revolution Mr Kincaid?'

'Aye, too right I am. History was the only subject I was good at in school, especially the industrial revolution. I think it comes from being born in Glasgow. There were so many things that reminded you of that age when I was a kid. The cranes, the ships, oh yeah I love all this stuff.' He wandered off and began studying the pictures intently. I placed my cup and saucer down on Mr Coopers unnecessarily large desk.

'Now what can we do for you Mr Harding?' asked Mr Cooper. I explained the situation in detail. I showed him the letter that Geordie's Nan had received, explained how long she'd lived there, her age and her condition and how the shock had given her a mild heart attack. I told him I was willing to put down a deposit on the house and sign any forms necessary. When Geordie was at the far end of the room studying the lithographs I decided to play my joker. I motioned towards Geordie and stuck a finger to the side of my head and twisted it round and round, indicating madness.

'Allan, Mr Kincaid, well he's not quite a full shilling. They'll probably put him in a psychiatric home if he loses the house. He's been diagnosed with SDGS.'

'Really!' Mr Cooper exclaimed, quite astonished, 'I didn't realise, I mean he seems pretty normal apart from maybe his attire.' I studied the old man in his tweed shooting suite and polka-dot dickie-bow tie and resisted a smile. He continued, 'Dear, dear, poor old chap. What exactly is SDGS by the way?'

'SDGS stands for symbiotic delusionary grandeur syndrome,' I lied convincingly. 'Basically, it's when you believe you're someone you're not. Some people may think they're Superman or Batman, others, famous figures from history, but Allan's version is more subtle.' He bent his head and moved closer toward me, intrigued by my tale. 'Yes, Allan actually believes that he used to be in a famous group from the early nineties. He thinks he's the bass player and the imaginary band he was in sold millions of records all over the world. He's very convincing.' Mr Cooper was hooked.

'How absolutely astounding! Quite amazing. You mean, it's a form of schizophrenia?'

'That's exactly what it is—although most schizophrenics change between characters, whereas with this form of the condition they just live in the one character all the time. They are so convincing they can actually live quite normally in society, a problem only arises when the veracity of their belief is threatened or questioned, then they can become violent and detached. They do actually believe in who they are. Can you imagine what it must feel like to be told you're not really the person you thought you were? That you're not Napoleon, you're not Joan of Arc, or in Allan's case you're not the world famous Geordie from seminal nineties rock Gods the Shooting Tsars'. I glanced over at Geordie who was still engrossed in the pictures.

'Geordie?' Mr Cooper asked looking puzzled.

'Geordie, that's Allan's nickname in his imaginary band.'

132

'Ah, I see, strange nickname for a Scotsman.'

'Hmm, that's as maybe, however, you can see why it's important that we get this house, to keep Geordie in his safe little world out of harm's way.'

'You mean there's no treatment of any kind?'

'Oh yes there's treatment all right, drugs! But it's virtually impossible to get the patient to take the drugs. They don't think there's a problem you see. Imagine if a man in a white coat walked in here right now and said, "Come on now Mr Cooper, time to take your medicine, you think you're a Solicitor again". Well what would you do? You'd think the guy in the white coat was crazy, wouldn't you?'

'Well, yes, yes, of course, I can see the dilemma. Well let's see what we can do. We need to sort this business out in the best possible way.'

#

Thirty minutes later the deal was done. I wrote a cheque as a deposit on the house and Geordie, who was delighted, signed some paperwork.

'This is fucking amazing!' he yelled grabbing me in a rib busting bear hug and shaking the bemused Mr Cooper's hand until the poor fellows arm nearly fell off.

'Well, the rest of the paperwork will take a few weeks to sort out, so let's set a date of thirty days from now till settlement shall we?'

'Yeah, whatever!' roared Geordie, 'this is great, wait till I tell Nan, this will make her fucking day, no it will make her fucking life, no more paying rent, yahoo!'

'Easy big fella,' I signalled for him to tone it down a bit as we were in a solicitors office after all. He shook Mr Cooper's hand again.

'Thanks a lot, you don't know what this means to me, this is great, great news.'

'I think you should really be thanking Mr Harding, without him I'm not sure that any of this would have happened.'

'Who? Oh you mean Billy boy, you're right there. He's a not a bad lad for a Sassenach bastard and a Yorkie at that.' How touching.

'Come on, we better make tracks, we've got a lot of driving to do today,' I said as we headed towards the door.

'So, Allan, I suppose you'll be heading to the bank to sort a mortgage out will you?' quizzed Mr Cooper as he held the door open for us.

'Mortgage!' replied Geordie taken aback. 'No way, I'll be paying cash for the house.' Mr Cooper seemed taken aback. He glanced at me and then back at Geordie.

'Paying cash, that's an awful lot of money to come up with Allan.'

'No problem,' said Geordie cockily, 'you see Mr Cooper, the band's reforming and we're doing a UK tour. At the end we each get paid two hundred grand each, so you see, I'll have plenty of money to pay for the house, pay Will back and still have enough left over for a bag of chips and a can of Tizer.' Geordie turned and marched triumphantly out of the office. Mr Cooper smiled at me and winked. I motioned with my finger, indicating yes, he was completely nuts.

'Oh well, good luck Allan, maybe I'll see you on "Top of the Pops" soon?' Mr Cooper shouted after him while winking again at me. Geordie stopped dead in his tracks and turned to face him,

'Top of the Pops, you gotta be joking, I wouldnae be seen dead on that pile of shite. Anyway, we haven't got a record deal, nor do we want one.' He turned and carried on walking.

'Quite amazing, very convincing,' Mr Cooper whispered to me while covering his mouth with his hand. 'And of course there's no way to disprove it. No record deal means there can be no records. It's almost foolproof, an elaborate fantasy world that lives side by side with reality. Truly amazing.' Mr Cooper was fascinated.

'Aye, poor bugger. There but for the grace of God and all that ...'

'Yes, you're quite right Mr Harding, quite right.'

'Well, I best be on my way. Thanks again Mr Cooper.' I shook his hand.

'Not at all, it's been a pleasure doing business with you. Oh, by the way Mr Harding, I hope you don't mind me asking, but what line of business are you in?'

'Me, didn't I say, I'm in the same band as Geordie.'

15: ON THE ROAD AGAIN

It was just past noon and I was standing outside the main hospital in Aberdeen. I'd just had a bollocking from a male staff nurse. Apparently, it's not a good idea to use a mobile phone in geriatrics. Well how the hell was I to know that mobile phones can interfere with heart machines! I had left Geordie in the ward with his Nan. I didn't go in, I felt it would have been a bit intrusive. Also, I needed to make a few calls, that I should have made the previous day, but Geordie had been stuck to me like a limpet. I didn't want him to hear any of my calls otherwise he'd detect my economy with the truth. First, I needed to speak with Robbo and see if he'd managed to talk Flaky into agreeing to do the tour. If he hadn't, everything I'd worked towards would be in tatters. I phoned his studio but only got an answering machine that directed me to his mobile. I tried that and after a few whistles and pops, he answered.

'Hey Robbo, it's me Will. Any luck with Flaky?'

'Yeah man, it's all cool, he took a bit of convincing but I think the two hundred G's sealed it for him.'

'Oh, that's great news, well done Robbo.' I let out an audible sigh of relief.

'What about you? Did you find the big Glaswegian twat?' he asked.

'Yes, I've got Geordie, got him by the short and curlies actually.'

'Nice work man, nice work. Has he ...' there was a brief pause, 'has he mellowed over the years?'

'Mellowed,' I replied thoughtfully, 'erm ... mellowed is not the first word that springs to mind.'

'Oh fuck.'

'Yes, "oh fuck" indeed. I tell you what Robbo, we are definitely going to earn that money. Anyway, listen up, me and Geordie are heading to London now but we won't get there until later tonight. Can you book us all into a hotel and text me the address?'

'Yeah, no worries.'

'Oh, and Robbo we have no gear.'

'Don't worry man, I'm on my way right now to score some.'

'Not that sort of gear you moron! I meant musical gear. Can you organise all that? We'll need a bass guitar and bass amp and acoustic. And we'll need all the other shit too—leads, mics, the whole shooting match.' Robbo's collection of musical equipment was immense.

'Don't worry Will, I'm onto it.'

'Good man. Okay, I'll see you tonight at some point.'

'Ten-four. Hey Will, before you go, have you told Geordie about Chas yet?' There was a crackle and hiss and the phone went dead. No I hadn't. That was a problem I'd face when I had to. I pulled out a cigarette and lit it. It was all going good so far, maybe a little too good. I wondered who or what was going to come along and piss on my strawberries.

I rang Chas's mobile number, but again was redirected. What was it with the world these days? You could no longer contact people without having to listen or speak to about three or four machines in between. I rang the alternate number and a woman's voice with a strong cockney accent answered the phone.

'Dupont Enterprises, how may I help you?' Not a very enterprising name, I thought.

'Hi, is Chas there please?'

'No I'm sorry he's going to be out of the office all day, have you tried his mobile?'

137

'Yes, I've tried his mobile, that's how I got this number. Is there any way I can get in touch with him, it's pretty important.'

'Not unless you go to France,'

'Pardon?'

'He's got some business in France and he's taken the Chunnel across. He won't be back in London until late tonight.' Business my arse, he'd gone on a shopping trip I bet.

'Okay, well can you take a message and make sure he gets it tonight.'

'I'll try.'

'Tell him Will called and that I've got all the boys on board and we'll be in London by tonight. Tell him to call me ASAP.' The girl took the message and I hung up. I threw my cigarette into a nearby ashtray just as Geordie appeared from the large glass sliding doors of the hospital. He appeared concerned.

'Well how is she?' I inquired gently.

'I'm not sure. She looks tired. She kept falling asleep while I was talking to her.'

'So? I have the same problem.' He ignored my fatuous comment.

'I told her about the house. I thought she'd be over the moon, but she just said, "Oh that's wonderful news Allan" but like she didn't really care.'

'Hey, come on, give the woman a break, she's just suffered a bloody heart attack and you want her to be doing backflips when she hears a bit of good news.' I could see him pondering something as we walked back to the car.

'It's not just that. When I first walked in she was asleep but after a few minutes she opened her eyes and said, "Oh Hamish, I'm glad you're here, I think I'm ready to go now." What does that mean?'

'Well, do you look like your Granddad?' I asked helpfully.

'Hardly, not considering he's been dead seven years!'

'No, I meant did you look like him when he was alive?'

138

'No. Nothing like him. How could she confuse me with him?'

'Well she's an old lady, mate, you know, they get confused.' I recalled Iris's comments from the day before, about Hamish waiting for her, but didn't have the heart to relate those words to Geordie.

#

We cut across the country and got onto the M6 below the Lake district. This part of the motorway was pretty good. We could chew up the miles before we hit Manchester, from there on in it would be a nightmare. Geordie was quiet and I could feel him brooding on events.

We drove on and managed to pass Manchester with only about a dozen roadworks on the way to slow us up. We stopped off at a service station and fed ourselves before continuing. We chit chatted away talking about the bands that we were likely to be touring with. We knew them all, The Green Circles, The Stoned Crows and Divina. The rock and roll world is a small place when you achieve a certain amount of success. We had either supported each one or they had supported us during our rise to the top. We had all come out of the same furnace—the post-Madchester music scene that had risen so far and so fast before dying away, almost prematurely. A clutch of bands, including ourselves, had risen from the ashes and forged a new, powerful, musical vanguard.

'I think the Green Circles could have been a great band,' mused Geordie.

'What are you talking about … they were a great band.'

'No. They never quite made it in my eyes. Don't get me wrong they were good, very good but they never transcended that gulf between good and great. In the early days they promised so much. I remember that first album of theirs; it scared the shit out of me.'

'Why?' I asked.

'Because they very nearly stole our clothes. The chord structures, the way they could effortlessly change key without making it seem trite or predictable. Their songs were formulaic but not in a tedious way, more of

139

a hypnotic way. And Connie had such a strong stage presence, he was much better than you, he was a real showman.'

'Thanks a lot, pal!' Connie was the frontman of the Green Circles and I had to agree that he was a far better frontman than I ever was. I liked to think of myself as a minimalist sort of raconteur. Mind you, Connie only sang, so it gave him a lot more freedom on stage, but it wasn't just that. He was wild and unpredictable. He was a diminutive figure, barely passing five and a half feet and sported a huge afro. Half West Indian, half Scouser, he would prowl the stage like a caged lion before unleashing a dance frenzy that made him look like Joe Cocker on electric shock treatment. He would jump from the top of speaker stacks, some as high as ten feet and land like a mountain cat before rolling and doing somersaults and cartwheels. He could have been an acrobat. He had a great voice as well, with a range and depth that put me to shame. During a couple of their slower songs he would stand rooted to the stage, a giant white spotlight on him, the band would edge out into the darkness to magnify the effect. His eyes would glaze over, sweat would pour off his forehead and he would hold the mic stand as though it was the stem of a rare and delicate flower. His voice would power out through the crowd. Then his eyes would close and tears would flood down his face as he sang. I'm not one for sentimentality, but that part of the performance always brought a lump to my throat. He gave it his all and the crowd responded.

'Oh, no disrespect to you,' consoled Geordie, fearing he may have wounded me with his previous comment, 'but Connie was one in a million. So what happened to The Green Circles in the end?'

'I'm not sure really, I think they had their time and that was it. You know what it's like. There are very few bands that can sustain a career past five years. If you can't continually reinvent yourself the market moves on and you get left behind playing the dives and working men's clubs …'

'Or sad fucking reunion tours,' Geordie sniggered.

140

'Well it may be sad, but it's just bought you a house!'

'Aye, nevertheless, it's still a bit sad. So much promise, by so few, for so many and what became of it all ...'

'Oh spare me the Winston Churchill's will you. It's just music Geordie, it's not religion, it's not war, it's not life and death. It's just ephemeral music for bored kids.' Geordie stared aghast at me.

'If I thought for one moment that you meant that, I'd punch you so hard that you'd be sucking hospital food through a straw for years.' He was right, I didn't mean it, but at least I got a bite.

'Easy boy, just out fishing, testing the bait.' He threw me a disdainful glance and picked up a newspaper and began to flick through the pages. I pulled out another cigarette and tried to stretch out my legs.

#

We were now heading down the M1 and making good progress. A large petrol tanker suddenly pulled out in front of me without indicating and I had to take preventative action by swerving into the outside lane. As I overtook the tanker, Geordie let his window down.

'You fucking arsehole!' he bellowed following it up with the finger as a sudden blast of cold air filled the car.

'For God's sake Geordie! Wind the window up. What's the point of that? Do you think he can even see you let alone hear you?'

'Oh he'll hear me alright. Drop in behind the bastard and we'll follow him into the next service station.' I began to wonder, for the first time, if getting the band back together had been a good idea. Thankfully, Geordie pushed his seat back, stretched out and closed his eyes. He shuffled around for a few seconds, then lifted his right arse cheek and let out a rip-snorter of a fart before finding his comfort zone.

'Charming—I don't think.'

'Sorry. Wake me when we get to that hole in the ground they call London.' I turned up the heater and put my headlights on. What did the next few months hold, I wondered. I felt tired and a little drained.

16: LONDON CALLING

It was nearly six-thirty before we hit the outskirts of London. We had been on the road for nearly thirteen hours—I was flagging. I needed a clean hotel room, a hot shower, a good meal, a glass of red and a long sleep. I peered at the quietly snoring giant next to me. A smile crossed my face and I got a sudden pang of guilt. I hadn't been a good friend. Friendships are very rarely on equal terms, usually one person takes more than they give. Geordie always took more, in fact he often took too much, like a vampire sucking the lifeblood from your veins. But so what, that's what the term friend means, for better or for worse, with the good and with the bad, and in Geordie's case, with the ugly as well. I suddenly remembered the speed in my jacket pocket and decided a little taster would revive me. The trouble was, my jacket was on the back seat and I didn't want to disturb Geordie. I knew he'd want a good snort if he saw my illicit stash and I wanted to keep him off the drugs altogether, if at all possible. I waited until the traffic came to a halt and then swung my left arm around my seat and tried to reach for my jacket. No good—it was too far away. I pushed myself back into the seat as far as I could and tried again. I kept turning my head to cast an eye over Geordie and the stationary traffic in front. I was starting to feel a pain in my bicep and shoulder but I persisted and managed to grip the bottom of the jacket with my fingertips—I nearly had my prize. A large deafening blast from a car horn behind me made me jump erratically and I lost the grip on the jacket. The car that had previously been in front of me by a few metres, was now disappearing out of sight. More horns began to blare. I rushed the car into gear and managed to stall, sending myself and Geordie jerking forward. The impatience behind me grew, as Geordie let out a groan but continued sleeping. I restarted the car and sped off way too fast. The car in front had come to a sudden stop and I slapped on my brakes way too hard. The wheels locked and almost instantaneously the automatic braking system kicked in, creating a deafening rumble. I was convinced I was going to ram the vehicle in front but luckily I came to an ungainly stop, mere centimetres away from the bumper of the car in front.

'Shit!' I cursed myself and felt embarrassed and wanted the road to swallow me up but it would not oblige. I could feel eyes from the car in front and the car behind bearing into my head. I could imagine they'd be saying what I would be saying if I were in their shoes."What a cockhead,!" I lit a cigarette to ease my nerves. We trundled slowly along and I thought I saw a snail overtake on the right. A moment later we were parked up again. I decided to try for my tonic anew. I reached behind and managed to grab the corner of my jacket and pull it towards me, I was nearly there, my arm began to ache. I reached into my pocket and felt for my little envelope. I began to feel the numbing sensation of pins and needles running down my arm as my over overstretching began to cut off the blood supply. A quick glance forward. Traffic still motionless. I grasped my package and retrieved it from its hideaway, but it was too late. My pins and needles had taken a turn for the worse and turned into a sudden cramp attack. An agonising pain spread from my bicep to my shoulder and into the nerves of my neck.

'Aargh! Shite!' The pain was intense and I thought I was having a heart attack. The cigarette fell from my mouth and landed in the crevice between my legs. 'Bugger.' I grasped for the cigarette and lifted my bum off the seat, which in turn let the cigarette roll further back. Just at that point I noticed the car in front move off. The buffoon in the car behind me let loose on his horn again. "PHWERP-PHWERP-PHWERP.' That was it! My normally calm and logical persona momentarily departed. I located the cigarette, picked it up, and in doing so managed to burn the top of my thumb. I stuck my head out of the window and shouted at the driver behind me.

'GO GET FU ...!'

'PHWERP-PHWERP' went the horn. I was contemplating getting out, but the pain in my neck had returned with a vengeance thanks to my shouting. I regained my senses, sat back down, closed the window and set off. Geordie was still fast asleep. Luckily, I had managed to hold onto my envelope of white powder. With one hand on the wheel and fag in mouth, I tentatively peeled back the folds of the package. I removed the cigarette from my mouth, wetted a finger and dabbed it into the fine, creamy powder. I raised the white splodge to my mouth and was just about to rub it around my gums when a loud, booming voice took me by surprise.

'JUST SAY "NO!" DON'T DO DRUGS!' It was Geordie. I swung around to see his big toothless grin, staring at me, one eye opened the other closed.

'You bastard!' I yelled as I stuck the bitter grains into my mouth. 'I thought you were asleep.'

'Aye, I guess you did. That was quite a performance. I didn't know you'd taken up slapstick. Thought you'd have a clandestine meeting with Dr Speed eh? Well, pass it over here then.'

'No way, you promised that you were going to stay clean.'

'In actual fact *you* promised that you'd keep *me* straight. I never promised anything. Come on pass it over, just a wee snifter, promise.' I reluctantly gave in. I couldn't win. It was my own stupid fault. I handed him the package. He sat up sharply like a man with a mission and stuck his oversized finger into the drug. He carefully dabbed his tongue, swilled it around as though tasting a fine wine, grimaced a little and made a smacking sounds with his lips.

'Hmm, not bad, not bad at all.' He re-dabbed the packet taking a good clot onto his finger and repeated the process.

'Ah yes!' he said contentedly. 'Just the job.'

Ten minutes later, we were both talking non-stop. Before I'd finish a sentence, Geordie would cut in to make a point. Before he'd finished making his point, I would recapture the conversation and go off at a tangent to make yet another point. I felt a rush of energy and optimism—the buzz had hit me good.

'You know that's damn fine Billy you've got there Billy. Where'd you get it from? I thought you said you hadn't done any drugs for years?'

'I got it from some bloke who bummed a cigarette off me at a service station. A Scouser as a matter of fact.'

'Oh great, we've probably just consumed washing powder.'

#

We travelled along making our way into the crux of the huge city, chattering away like two excited teenagers.

'So here we are at the very heart of the Tory powerbase ...' sighed Geordie with an air of resigned disappointment.

'Bloody hell Geordie, you *have* been out of circulation!' I exclaimed. 'The Tories lost power in '96. It's new Labour and all that shit now.' I laughed at his apparent naiveté.

'Like I said, heart of the Tory powerbase. If that's the Labour party in power then I'm Paul McCartney's chiropractor.' I still hadn't told Geordie about Chas's role in all of this and I figured now was probably as good a time as any to broach the subject. The speed had put us both in a good mood and I thought I'd strike while the iron was hot.

'Geordie, there's something I need to tell you. Now, you promise you won't get angry?' He glanced at me and smiled.

'I couldn't ever get angry at you Billy Boy, you know that.' He slapped me on the thigh a little too hard.

'Well,' I continued, 'if you had asked me at the time I would have told you, but you didn't ask … so I didn't tell you … if you get my drift.'

'You're waffling Billy. What is it?'

'Okay … well.. this tour is being organised and funded by Dupont Enterprises … they are the tour promoter.' At first, my statement didn't seem to register with Geordie, but slowly the words I had uttered entered his consciousness. He turned to stare at me. His good humour had gone and I realised that I'd probably made a mistake. Calmly but forcefully, he asked,

'You mean Dupont Enterprises … as in Chas Dupont Enterprises?' I nodded, there was no turning back now. 'That's right. Chas—this is his tour, it's his baby.' There was silence and I became intensely aware of my surroundings. The traffic was moving steadily and the rain was getting heavier. All around, the busy world of London went about its night-time routine. Traffic lights and traffic jams. People milling everywhere like an uncoordinated army of ants. Lights, neon-lights, flashing lights, flickering lights, red, yellow, orange, blue, green. Horns, alarms, engines, rubber on wet tarmac. Shops, sales, adverts, 20% off, newspaper headlines, billboards, McDonalds, KFC, Subway, Coca-Cola. A consumerist's paradise. I sensed the nervous energy of a city that never stopped, high on drugs, alcohol, sex, money, life. I hated it, but at the same time had to admire its draw and power. I would take a little sip of its elixir and let it make me younger for a while—but *only* for a while. My thoughts had become lucid and real, sharp and cognisant. Time had slowed down.

I turned my head to meet Geordie's menacing stare that was burning into my head. It was like a flashback in slow motion of some bad splatter movie. Before I realised what was happening, Geordie yanked hard on the hand-brake. I suddenly saw the orderly stream of traffic turn into a writhing, spinning serpent. I fought with the steering wheel in vain, for it was obeying its only true master—the wheels, which were screaming and struggling in torment. I wondered if Caesar had been fed

147

yet and knew he'd be missing me. Lights dazzled me, horns deafened me. I couldn't talk, or shout or scream. I don't know how, I don't know why, but the car came to a shuddering halt hard against a kerb outside a cinema. I gazed up to see posters promoting the latest Shrek movie. I wished I was in there now, tucking into a jumbo sized box of butter popcorn. I switched off the engine, lay my head on the steering wheel and breathed a sigh of relief. My heart pounded with such a ferocity that I thought it was going to bruise my chest. Geordie was up and out of the car, leaving the door wide open. He paced up and down the pavement outside the cinema, head down, occasionally shaking it from side to side. The slow motion flashback ended as abruptly as it had started. I realised the car was now facing in the opposite direction to the way we'd been travelling. Not only that, but we had crossed four lanes of traffic to get to our new position. I'm not sure whether we'd done a 180 or a 540 degree spin. Whatever we'd done, it was a miracle that we had managed to avoid any other object. I gazed at the traffic continuing on its way, our perilous pirouettes now nothing more than a fading memory to the disappearing witnesses. I leaned across the passenger seat and shouted through the open door.

'Geordie, get in the car!' The rain was heavy and a cold wind blew spray into my face. Geordie continued his pacing, like a man possessed by some unfathomable mathematical calculation. My relief had now turned to anger. What a stupid, dangerous irresponsible act he had just committed. We could both be dead, not only us but other innocent people as well. Maybe a family; mam, dad and two teenage kids on their way for a Big Mac. Maybe a mother and her newborn baby on their way home after visiting a doting grandmother. Unknown faces and lives put at risk by this big, stupid, ugly, mentally disturbed oaf. It wasn't just a reckless act, it was also arrogant and selfish. He didn't mind putting his or my life at risk, but he hadn't for one moment, not one second, given a flying pig-fuck about how he had jeopardised the lives of others. It was conceited and egotistical, and I hated him for that. I slammed the door

148

shut and made my mind up to drive away, to leave the madness behind me. *Why am I getting this band back together? What exactly am I after? Recompense, acknowledgement, kudos, revenge?* I wasn't sure anymore. I started the car and made to pull away. I stopped—I couldn't do it. I remembered the promise I'd made to his Nan and cursed myself for my impatience. I glanced over and watched the big old fool still pacing up and down the pavement, hands deep inside his huge olive green overcoat, muttering to himself. Then I noticed something else. A group of four lads were making their way along the pavement, laughing and joking. They were oblivious to Geordie at first, probably making their way to the local for a few jars. But once they came within a few feet of him, their attention focused on this huge, wild man, the abominable Scotsman. They slowed down and began making a few comments to each other as they got closer, followed by a few laughs and sniggers. I slowly opened my door and lifted my head above the roof of the car. If the lads had any sense they'd keep their mouths shut and their feet moving. But they didn't. One of them must have made a humorous comment because they all burst out laughing only a few feet from the pacing madman.

'Oh no …' I whispered under my breath, 'let it go Geordie, let it go my son,' I urged, willing my thoughts into his head.

'Oi! Fuckface! What are you laughing at?' Too late. Geordie had snapped out of his reverie and marched up to the group. Their laughter suddenly stopped. Now confronting them was a lithe, wild-eyed, toothless giant. Life wasn't quite as funny as it had been a minute ago. The four lads stopped dead in their tracks and then took a few tentative steps back.

'I said, what are you turd sucking gobshites laughing at?' Geordie roared. His hands, now removed from his pockets, were a menacing pair of sledgehammers. He towered over his quarry. I prayed to some unknown God. One of the group, nervously, stepped forward, arms open in an unthreatening gesture.

'It was … just a joke, a joke that's all, a joke that Sammy made,' the youth stammered, indicating towards one of his friends. Geordie's eyes narrowed and he leant forward toward the youth.

'Oh, is that right,' he replied in a soft calm tone, 'well, don't be shy, let's hear it then.'

'Wh … what?' responded the youth, taken aback by the request. The others shuffled nervously behind him, edging a few steps further back.

'I said, let's hear it then, I like a good joke. I mean, it must be real funny because it had you and your fuckwit mates in stitches. Now let's hear it,' he ordered, menacingly with lips peeled back. Time to act.

'Geordie, get in the car right now!' I yelled at him. The youths seemed surprised and a little relieved that someone else was witnessing their trial. But Geordie was unmoved. Without looking at me, he held a palm up in my direction.

'I won't be a minute, I'll just hear this joke and I'll be with yer … now,' he addressed the youths again, 'the joke, I'm getting a tad impatient.' The leader of the group cleared his voice nervously.

'This horse … this horse goes into a … into a pub and orders a drink. The barman serves the horse and asks, "What's with the long face?" That's the joke.' The youth took a step back as he finished. There was deadly silence. It was an old joke and not a particularly funny one. I began to edge around the car without making any sudden moves as though I was stalking an antelope. Geordie's eyes changed from narrow angry slits to one of surprise.

'Haha! What's with the long face, haha!' He began to let out a large and long belly laugh. The sense of relief from the youths was palpable. They joined in nervously laughing along with Geordie, the joke teller laughing the loudest and glancing around at his pals for moral support. They gave it, first with sniggers and then with great big, false, laughs. They were faking it, but Geordie was genuinely laughing hard.

150

Seemingly, the joke had never made it as far as Dinkiad Bay, probably got turned back at the Scottish border. Geordie turned to me, still laughing.

'Did ya hear that, "what's with the long face". That's a cracker, oh I must remember that, did ya hear that Billy?'

'Yeah, I heard it Geordie, very amusing. Now please get back in the car, I want to get to this sodding hotel tonight.'

'Aye okay, ya right. Alright boys,' he turned to the group who were still nervously chortling away, 'on ya way, thanks for that, that's right cheered me up. Very good, very good.' The youths didn't waste any time hanging around. They didn't run, but they certainly did the fastest walk this side of the Olympic Games. I stood by the passenger door and motioned for Geordie to get in. He manoeuvred his large frame into the car. I bent down to face him,

'If you ever pull a stunt like that again I'll stick you on a bus to Dinkiad Bay faster than you can say "What's with the long face?" And I'll promise that you'll never see me again, and, the contract on your Nan's house will be ripped up.' I spat out the words with restrained anger, eyeballing Geordie without once blinking. Geordie, averted my gaze like a chastised puppy. 'Do I make myself clear?'

'Aye, crystal.' he replied sheepishly.

'Good!' I shouted and slammed the door in his face. I climbed back into the driver's seat and before we set off, I stared across at him,

'We've got some talking to do.' I let him have it with both barrels. 'Right, you big dumb oaf, any more ridiculous behaviour and you're out!' I yelled. I mellowed a little and continued. 'Listen Geordie, I know you've never trusted Chas, but it's all going to be above board; there'll be no dodgy deals; no-one's going to get ripped off this time, promise; I'm going to get the contract checked out by a top lawyer and the merest skerrick of impropriety and I for one will be back up the M1 quicker than you can say "Geoffrey Boycott" and that's a promise.' I looked across at him as I lit a cigarette. 'You really need to grow up, take responsibility for your life and your actions. It isn't my, or anybody else's job, to look after you, you're not a child. I know you had a pretty horrendous childhood, but you're not alone there—you and about half of the world. It doesn't mean you can absolve yourself from all responsibility for the rest of your life, it isn't a get out clause. Either get some counselling or get over it and move on. The best way to get even in life is to lead a good one, make the best of it, grab each day. Don't let old grievances and festering bitterness steal away the hours, because if you let them, they certainly will.' I felt like a headmaster admonishing a naughty schoolboy but it had to be said. By the time I had finished my lecture we were at the hotel. I parked up and turned the engine off. I was waiting for Geordie to give some sort of acknowledgement of my words, but he just sat there sporting an expression of bemusement.

'You know a good lawyer do you?' His tone was critical.

'What? Lawyer … oh yes, bumped into him at a service station. Turns out he's a really big fan of the band.'

'You seem to spend an inordinate amount of time hanging around service stations. Is there something you'd like to tell me? Anyway, it's hardly a ringing endorsement is it; bumping into a lawyer coming out of the crapper at the Little Chef.'

'Never mind about the lawyer, did you *hear* what I've been saying?' I was hoping for some sign of redemption from him, just something, anything, the smallest sign to signal that, yes, he understood he had to grow up and be responsible.

'Aye, I hear, roger over and out.' It was said without conviction and I decided to drop the matter, it was like pushing shit up a hill. As he disappeared through the revolving doors he said resignedly,

'Probably for the best anyway.'

'What's probably for the best?' I asked as I followed him through the doors into the hotel reception.

'Chas,' he said, 'it makes things a lot easier.' He walked off leaving me to ponder his words. I caught up with him at the soft drinks machine as he tried to fit what appeared to be a foreign coin into the slot.

152

'And what exactly does that mean?' I demanded.

'Oh, nothing, nothing at all,' he replied nonchalantly. 'You havnae got a pound coin I could borrow have yer?'

17: HOTEL CALIFORNIA

Thirty minutes later I was ensconced in my hotel room getting a long, hot, relaxing shower. Robbo had booked four single rooms all adjacent to each other, which I was eternally grateful for. The last thing I wanted to do was share a room with Geordie. We hadn't yet caught up with Robbo and Flaky; the receptionist had told us that they both went out together earlier and hadn't yet returned.

I reflected on the day and felt a tad contrite at my berating of Geordie but unnerved about his final comment in regards to Chas. I got out of the shower and lay on my bed with a towel wrapped around me, sucking on an expensive continental beer and watching a soft porn video on the hotel TV. It was eight thirty and I was feeling relaxed for the first time in days. I'd arranged with Geordie that we'd find a good curry house once Robbo and Flaky returned; this seemed to brighten his mood. I had a couple of calls to make, one to the lawyer John Peterson and the other to Fiona and decided to get on with them before Geordie came barging in. I hadn't told Geordie about Fiona, I knew he'd only take the piss and start asking how big her tits were. I rang John Peterson on his mobile and told him of the intended tour and arranged a meeting with him for the next morning at eleven. He sounded extremely excited by the news and wanted to know more details but I told him I'd divulge all the facts tomorrow. I hung up and was about to ring Fiona when I heard an angry rap on what I assumed was the door of the adjoining room, Geordie's room. My heart began to race a little faster as I unconsciously held my breath. There was a brief pause and I breathed out and began pressing the digits on my mobile. Before I got to press the call button, the angry rap came again. Then voices, normal volume at first, but then rising and rising until I could hear the aggressive boom of a Scottish accent.

'Oh, for Christ's sake,' I cursed as I sprung from the bed. I tightened the towel around my waist and tentatively opened my door. I peered down the corridor to see a tall, well dressed and well groomed man, in a heated discussion with Geordie who was sporting nothing bar a pair of shabby, off white, "Y" fronts.

'It really is quite reckless and dangerous behaviour Sir!' exclaimed the man.

'Aye, well like I said, it was an accident. If you idiots had a moveable stand this would never have happened.' This only seemed to further infuriate the man, whom by his demeanour, I assumed to be the Hotel Manager.

'REALLY SIR! All articles and furnishings are in a specific spot and they are not there to be rearranged willy-nilly by guests. If you had bothered to call down to housekeeping I'm sure we could have accommodated your request. As it is, you narrowly missed one of our Trainee Chefs who just so happened to be in the alleyway below emptying one of the bins. If that TV had hit him it wouldn't be me stood here now Sir, it would be the London Constabulary!' The man was turning red with rage and I decided I better intervene before he started pointing his finger at Geordie, which would only escalate the situation.

'Aye, well I don't particularly like being talked to in that manner by a pompous, upper-class, tw ...'

'Geordie, what's going on?' I interrupted before the war of words got out of hand.

'Its Basil Fawlty here!' he pointed at the Hotel Manager with his thumb while turning to me.

'Are you the manager?' I asked the man,

'Yes Sir, and you are?'

155

'Mr Harding, I'm Geordie's friend. Now what seems to be the problem?' The manager seemed to breathe a sigh of relief that he'd now found someone that he could communicate with.

'Your friend here, Sir,' he nodded towards Geordie, 'has managed to eject our expensive and extremely heavy TV from his window into the alleyway fifteen stories below, narrowly missing one of our Trainee Chefs.'

'Is this right Geordie?'

'No, it's not, I didn't eject it, what do you think I am, some sort of ageing rock star. The thing slipped, it was an accident, as I've been trying to explain to this puffed up meringue!' I could see the manager take extreme umbrage at the insult.

'OKAY GEORDIE! That's enough, get back in the room and I'll sort this out.' He turned and walked back into his room shouting out while he went,

'Aye, well don't let that imbecile bamboozle you, it was only a fucking cheap TV ...' I gently grabbed the manager's arm and led him down the corridor until we were stood outside my door. He noticed for the first time that I was only wearing a towel around my waist and straightened himself as he peered down at me with suspicion and a touch of disdain.

'I'm sorry about Geordie, he's a little sensitive ...' I explained.

'Hmm, amongst other things,' the manager replied haughtily.

'I'm sure if he said it was an accident, it was an accident. I've been his friend a long time and I've never known him to do anything stupid or reckless.' If I'd been Pinocchio, my nose would have grown ever so slightly. 'Now, how much was the TV worth?'

'Well, it's not just the TV Sir, I mean it's the irresponsible act, I really should ask him to leave ...'

'Would two hundred cover it?' I knew I was paying over the odds for the TV but I really didn't want to start crawling around London searching for another hotel room.

'Well, yes, I'm sure that would cover the replacement cost, but it's not just that ...' I turned and walked back into my room as the manager kept on protesting. I reached into my coat and pulled out my trusty wad of rolled up notes. I peeled off two hundred and handed it to the manager, who paused and then quickly took the money and inserted it into his breast pocket.

'As I was saying, it's not just about the money. I have a Trainee Chef downstairs who is in a state of shock ...' I peeled off another hundred and handed it over.

'Offer him our sympathies and tell him it was an unfortunate accident and maybe this will soothe his nerves.' The manager repeated the exercise by grabbing the notes and carefully sliding them into his breast pocket. I peeled off another hundred, 'and this is to cover your time and effort.' I winked at him and he seemed placated. Well, who wouldn't be, with four hundred quid in their pocket for a shitty TV.

'Well, thank you Sir for your graciousness and understanding. I think I can overlook the matter on this occasion, as long as you can assure me that nothing like this will occur again during your stay.'

'I guarantee it, you won't even know we're here.'

'Well, in that case ... have a pleasant evening Sir.' He turned and walked back down the corridor, pausing at Geordie's room. I followed behind. He tapped on the open door and Geordie appeared a few seconds later with toothbrush in mouth and white froth splattered around his beard.

'I'd just like to say that the matter has been sorted out amicably Sir,' he said politely, addressing Geordie.

'Aye, okay, well I accept your apology, no hard feelings eh?' Geordie, ever the diplomat, stuck out his hand. It was not the answer the manager was expecting but he realised it was all he was going to get and decided to cut his losses while he was still ahead.

'Hmm, yes ... quite,' he grabbed Geordie's hand tentatively and they both shook for a few seconds, before Geordie relinquished his grip and walked back to the bathroom. The manager stared down at his hand with disgust as it was now covered in sticky toothpaste residue. He pulled a pristine white hanky from his trouser pocket and wiped the offending appendage. He turned and walked past me, nodding respectfully, but with his lips curled in obvious distaste. Geordie was now gargling in the background.

'Have a good evening,' I offered him on his way past. He was part way out of the door when Geordie's pleasant dulcet tones rang out.

'Oi, pal, I don't suppose there's any chance of a replacement TV is there?' The manager merely huffed and went on his way. I shut the door behind him and walked into the bathroom to confront Geordie. He stood facing the mirror as he flossed his broken teeth. He eyed me in the reflection appearing totally unconcerned.

'That's just cost me four hundred bloody quid!' I exclaimed. 'What the hell happened?' He pulled the floss from his mouth and put his foot on the pedal of a flip top bin, raising its lid. He dropped the offending floss towards the bin, it missed and fell delicately to the floor—he didn't notice.

'Well, like I was trying to explain to that overpaid show pony, it was an accident.'

'Oh yeah, go on, I'm listening.' He snapped off a fresh piece of floss and began his account while prying relics of old food from his teeth.

'I was just about to get in the bath when I realised it was time for Coronation Street … I never miss an episode. Now you can see by the position of the bath and the sideboard the TV was previously sat on,' he nodded in the mirror for me to inspect the now barren sideboard that sat parallel to the bathroom door, 'that I was never going to be able to see the TV from the bath. So, I placed the TV on the windowsill, the lead just stretched, so it wasn't a problem.' I walked back into the room and looked at the windowsill that had seated the TV. The ledge was only a few inches wide and woefully inadequate to carry a TV. Two things puzzled me; firstly the glass in the window was still intact and secondly, the socket on the wall wasn't damaged. Surely when the TV fell, it would have smashed the window and ripped the socket from the wall or at least left its plug behind? I walked back into the bathroom where Geordie was still carrying out his disgusting ablutions.

'And?' I probed,

'And what?'

'And the TV was sat on the windowsill ... and then what?'

'Oh, yes, well it just sort of fell ... and that's that,' he concluded confidently.

'Hmm, it just fell ...' I scratched my head in an exaggerated fashion. 'How come the window's not broken?' Geordie stared at his reflection and then threw me an annoyed glance.

'Because it was open. You know how I hate the stuffiness of hotel rooms.' I recalled his phobia—on the unlucky occasions that I had to share a room with him, while on tour, I had often woken with a stiff neck as an icy breeze travelled by my bed.

'Hmm ... and how come the power lead didn't stop it from falling, or how come there's no damage to the wall socket?' Geordie shifted nervously and would not make eye contact with me. I knew he was hiding some idiocy that he had undertaken, if you can get more idiotic than balancing a heavy, twenty inch wide object on a five inch wide windowsill, while the window is open, fifteen floors up, while sat in the bath watching a soap opera. I waited. 'Well?' I badgered impatiently.

'Well, I needed to dry my hair ...' he said sheepishly. In a flash it all fell into place.

'Aha, eureka, I have it!' Geordie seemed abashed as I continued with a dramatic flourish. 'So let's recap. Idiot wants a bath but that would coincide with his favourite sad bastard soap opera, and on inspection, the idiot detects that the watching of said show from the confines of his bath would not be possible due to the position of bath and TV. Idiot stops to think. Two options spring to mind: either move the bath or move the TV. Of course any normal person would have watched the soap opera first and then got a bath, but the idiot is not a normal person ... he's an idiot! So, back to the idiot's dilemma; move the bath or move the TV? For once the idiot actually gets it right, he decides to move the TV, after all there's no point taking the mountain to Mohammed. Idiot precariously balances TV on window ledge, knowing full well the window is open. Does this ring any alarm bells in the idiots head? No, of course not. Idiot has a bath and watches favourite TV show ... for sad bastards ... probably has a wank over Bet Lynch at the same time ... who knows? Show finishes, idiot gets out of bath and decides to dry his long, hippy hair. Idiot finds hair dryer and looks to plug it in. "Aha!" he says to himself, "I'll plug it in here," and with that he pulls the TV's power lead from the wall and sticks in the plug of the hairdryer. Probably in the time it takes a heavy TV to fall fifteen stories, the idiot maybe got an inkling that something was not quite right ... or maybe he didn't ... because he is an idiot. Maybe it's only when a bang on the door, from a justifiably incensed Hotel Manager, does the idiot realise that something's amiss.' It was a good piece of detective work and I was pretty sure it was close to the mark. 'I therefore put it to you, Allan Kincaid, that this is, in fact, the real sequence of events that led to the fateful demise of the TV—am I correct?' Geordie pulled on a vest and eyed me suspiciously.

'Have you been spying on me?'

'For God's sake Geordie ...' I was lost for words.

'Two things,' he began in a most indignant fashion. 'Bet Lynch hasn't been in the show for donkey's years, and, I NEVER, EVER, wank in the bath ... the shower yes, but the bath, never!'

'Oh, I'm glad we've clarified that.'

'Yep. All's well that ends well, eh? Like I said, it was an accident.' He finished dressing without a care in the world and walked over to the bar fridge and grabbed a couple of beers. He twisted the tops off them both and handed me one. I took a long slug of beer and let out a deep sigh. Geordie ambled back into the bathroom, picked up a scabby brush and began pulling it through his hair. I sat down on his bed wearily, when a glint from the ruffled bed sheets caught my eye. I gingerly pulled back the sheets to reveal a gun—a gun that was only ever seen in Westerns. I carefully picked it up and examined it. The gun was heavy and cold. I casually sauntered into the bathroom where Geordie was grimacing as he came to terms with a particularly taxing knot of hair. I leant against the door with the firearm behind my back.

'So,' I began in a friendly manner, smiling at Geordie via the mirror, 'anything else you want to discuss?' Geordie stopped tugging at his tangled mop and eyed me warily.

'Not really, why?'

'Nothing you'd like to get off your chest, come clean about; you know, anything at all?' He busied himself with his hair but still observed me coolly.

'No, absolutely fuck all, why?'

'THEN WHAT IN HELL'S NAME IS THIS!' I roared as I produced the gun.

'It's a gun, what do you think it is—half a pound of chopped liver?' I waggled it in his direction making sure the barrel was pointing downwards.

'YES! I can see it's a gun, the question is, what are you doing with a gun—are you insane? Sorry, stupid question, of course you're insane, but even madmen know not to wander around London carrying illegal firearms.' He stopped brushing his hair and turned to face me.

'Listen, don't get your knickers all bunched up—it's not even loaded.'

'You just don't get it do you? You're not in touch with reality.' I was exasperated and Geordie's casual, offhand manner was only exacerbating my condition. I tried a different tack. 'So, the little chat we had in the car was a waste of time eh?'

'You mean your little chat, I can't remember saying much.'

'In less than a few hours, you very nearly caused a multi-vehicle pile up, you've thrown a TV out of your window, you've abused the

Hotel Manager, and now, you leave a deadly weapon lying around your room! Not bad going.'

'Yeah, and I wasn't even trying,' he glanced at me and laughed, 'anyway, don't call it a deadly weapon, it's a Colt 45; there is a difference you know—a gun can be any old piece of shit, a Colt is a work of art.' I was getting nowhere fast and decided to bring the situation to a close.

'Oh, I do beg your pardon,' I said calmly. 'It's a gun! They kill people!' I said, a little less calmly. I placed the gun on the bathroom dresser. 'Get rid of it by tomorrow morning otherwise I'll be looking for a new bass player and when you return to Dinkiad Bay you'll be sleeping in a tent.'

'That's a cheap shot ... ha! ha! ha! Get it? Cheap shot?' I glowered at him. For once, his gormless smirk evaporated. 'Hmm, you mean it don't you?'

'Yes, I mean it alright. This is my world you're in now and there's no place for guns. I don't care how or where, but it better be gone by tomorrow—okay?' He nodded silently. I swallowed the rest of my beer in two large gulps and slammed the bottle down next to the gun. 'Right, if you don't mind, I'd like a little time to get dressed. I'll see you later.' I turned and headed for the door.

'Hey Billy?' I stopped and studied him.

'What?'

'I'm a bit short, any chance of a loan? I want to pay my own way. London is an expensive place and my dole money is all gone. You know I'm good for it ... well when the tour's over ... I mean.'

'How much?' I asked resignedly.

'Oh, I reckon four hundred should do ... but don't worry, if I need more I'll let you know.'

'Thanks, but don't think I'm not keeping a tab on this. You owe me ten quid for the food and drinks I bought you on the way down here. Twenty grand for the deposit on your Nan's house. Three hundred I gave to Margaret to provide your Nan with meals. Four hundred to sort out the TV debacle and another four hundred now.' I peeled off the notes and handed them over.

'You never told me about the three hundred to Margaret? I'm not a bloody charity case you know,' he replied in a huffy manner as he grabbed my cash and stuck it in his pocket.

'Oh, and one pound for the drinks machine downstairs.'

'And people say the Scottish are tight—they have nothing on the Yorkshire man.'

#

I spent the next hour trying to relax and reassure myself that I'd made the right decision in agreeing to do the reunion tour. The problem was I wasn't doing a very good job of it. I could logically argue the case but the niggling doubt in the pit of my stomach would not decamp. My introspection was eventually broken by a loud rap on my door.

'Hang on!' I shouted. I stared at myself in the mirror and repositioned a piece of hair off to the side to mask my receding hairline and then immediately asked myself what was the point. I peeked through the peephole in the door and three convexed, ugly, gawping, faces stared back at me; Robbo, Geordie and one I didn't instantly recognise, until it dawned on me that it must be Flaky. I opened the door.

'Haha! Come in you set of bastards!' There was much hugging, handshaking, non-stop talking and big guffaws as we all reacquainted our friendships.

'Flaky mate, I hardly recognised you ... you look, sort of ...' I was trying to find the right words without making it sound offensive but Geordie helped me out.

'Like a fucking ageing geography teacher!' It was true—Flaky had aged. Always tall, skinny and angular, his short-cropped hair had receded to the middle of his crown, accentuating his sharp features. His dress of grey jacket, trousers and shoes and a faded green shirt gave him the demeanour of a new age university lecturer. Not that this was a bad

163

thing, it was just completely different to the last image that I'd had of him a decade ago. His skin was tight and full of colour, his deep brown eyes sparkled and despite his rake like physique he appeared fit and full of vim and vigour.

'You look great man, what drugs are you on?' I joked.

'No drugs anymore Will, only vitamins. I'm a bit of fitness freak these days; I do marathons and the occasional triathlon. I try to keep as fit as I can, I mean, none of us are getting any younger.' He slapped me on the back as Geordie went to my bar fridge and pulled out four beers. He handed them out and everyone accepted apart from Flaky much to Geordie's incredulity,

'Not for me thanks Geordie, is there a bottled water in there?'

Robbo hadn't changed much from the last time I saw him the previous summer. He was, as ever, the cool ageing rock star through and through. The latest labelled street clothes, the long sideburns, the Beatles mop top. Unlike Flaky, his skin was sallow and puffy and his slight pot belly was testament to his nocturnal world of takeaway curries, six-packs and pot induced munchies. We sat around talking and laughing for a good hour before we headed out for the long awaited curry.

#

We all piled into a black cab and Robbo directed the taxi driver toward some rundown hamlet, a good half hours drive from our hotel. Robbo was still a frequent visitor to London and knew all the best eateries. During the ride, we continued our disjointed conversations, all talking at once, interrupting one another, laughing like clowns and relating our experiences since we'd last been together.

'Flaky how did Robbo convince you to do the tour? I thought you'd adamantly refused when he first asked you?' I inquired.

'Yes, that's right I wasn't interested. I have a great new life and I didn't want to jeopardise it by getting back into touring again. But my wife, Gillian, eventually persuaded me to do it. She said it was only a couple of months and it would do me good ... you know ... sort of heal old wounds and bring some closure. Plus, two hundred grand will pay off my mortgage!'

He went on to tell us of his deep sense of loss and hopelessness after the Tsars had split. He had floundered around for six months doing nothing but getting drunk every day. He finally woke up one morning and looked at himself in the mirror. What he saw staring back was not a pretty sight. He was emaciated, haggard and devoid of any energy. He had creditors chasing him wherever he went. No friends, no girlfriend, no future. He decided there and then to change. He went cold turkey on the booze and fags and took up running. When he received the tax bill, which we all got for unpaid taxes on our earnings, it wiped him out. He had to sell his London flat and all his possessions to clear the bill. But he wasn't going to wallow in self-pity. He took stock of his life and saw the light and decided to follow it. He went back to University and got a degree in psychology. It was a hard struggle, studying and trying to do part time work to pay the bills, all the while being recognised as the ex-rock star. Eventually, he graduated and landed a job with the National Health Service. It wasn't long before he was doing work for the Prison Service with disturbed inmates and then specifically, with young offenders.

He became animated and empowered when he told us of his day to day work with troubled and underprivileged youths. He helped set up a "Young Offenders" centre, a kind of half-way house for the kids who'd been released from prison.

He'd married Gillian five years ago and had two beautiful sons, Jason and Julian aged two and three, but he said he was also part of a much larger family—a comment I didn't fully understand. He didn't regret his time in the Tsars but he now had a new vocation.

'You know, being rich and famous is one thing; having to deal with the public and their expectations, but being skint and famous is much worse. Every loudmouth is ready to have a pop at you. The British seem to love nothing better than seeing a former successful person on the skids.'

'Aye, yer not wrong there Flaky. It's the tall poppy syndrome,' concurred Geordie.

'I don't think you can tar everybody with the same brush. I recently came across an old fan who was overjoyed to see me and was asking if we'd ever reform. You've just got to take each person as they come,' I replied, thinking of my recent encounter with the lawyer.

'Yes, you're right Will. It's most uncharitable of me. Not everyone's the same.'

#

We tumbled out of the cab and into a side street with Robbo leading the way towards an uninspired looking building that was lit up by a flickering, red neon light that spelt out the words "Tandoori Dreams". I hoped the food was a little more adventurous than the name. Before we entered I pulled Geordie aside.

'Have you got rid of it yet?' I asked quietly, referring to the gun.

'Yep. Done and dusted,' he replied without looking at me.

'Good. We'll forget about the matter then.'

The aromatic smell of curry, herbs and spices assaulted my senses and I felt my tummy rumble and my mouth begin to salivate at the anticipated delicacies. We walked into the restaurant and were immediately greeted by an elderly Indian gentleman dressed in a deep purple waiter's suit.

'Aha! Mr Robbo, my very, very good friend. How are you today?' The man was pleased to see one of his regular customers.

'Ranjit, I'm very well, but more importantly, how are you?'

'Oh, Mr Robbo, I have been plagued with a very bad case of the gout, the doctors can do nothing for me, what is it you call them, "fucking quacks". I tend to agree with you, but thank God, at present I am in much relief of the condition.'

166

'Ah, Ranjit, you need to keep off the red wine and fine food.'

'This is not the case Mr Robbo. I live a very austere life and have very few extravagances. Now, please introduce me to your party?'

'Ranjit, this ugly bunch are my old bandmates. You remember me telling you about the Shooting Tsars? Well here they are.' Robbo turned and introduced us all, one by one, to Ranjit, who politely shook our hands and repeated our names suffixed with, "It's a very great honour to meet you." He led us to a table at the rear of the restaurant and took our drinks order. It was fairly quiet for a Saturday night and apart from a sprinkling of couples and three bored looking waiters we had the place to ourselves. The setting was conducive to a more detailed conversation on our respective lives and once our drinks had arrived the dialogue began in earnest.

Ten years had passed since we'd been a group, the hair had thinned and greyed, the skin had sagged, the bellies had expanded, but underneath we were still apparently the same. I told them all about my life of reclusive domesticity; my love of the Dales, the walking, the solitude; I also let them know that over the past couple of weeks I had begun to feel an inkling of melancholia, as though I were missing the final piece of the jigsaw. I told them of Fiona and got some slaps on the back for it, although I insisted the relationship (if you could call it that) was at a very early stage. Predictably, Geordie inquired as to the size of her breasts—which I ignored. I recounted my near-death experience on top of Inglegor, my conversation with Chas and how it all seemed connected, as though it was meant to be. Flaky jumped in at this point to agree that indeed it was all connected. Apart from being a psychologist, he was also an amateur astrologer and believed the planets had an effect on everything we did.

We tucked into our starters of shish kebabs and onion bhajis while all continually questioning each other and relating snippets from the past. When the mains arrived, Robbo began, in his languid, unruffled way, to tell us of his life since the Tsars demise.

167

'When we came out of that courtroom after the Judge's verdict, I was completely numb. I took it for granted that we'd win, but to be honest, I was quite relieved the whole thing was over in a way. I'd had enough; I know the rest of you felt the same. I mean, let's be honest, we could hardly stand being in the same room as each other.' We all exchanged ashamed glances with one another. Robbo continued, nodding at Flaky and Geordie,

'You two hadn't spoken to each other for six months. When we'd finished recording "Bloom", I knew it was the best thing we'd ever done but I also knew it was to be our swansong. We were finished, spent, wasted; we were burnt out physically, mentally and emotionally. Not that I lay the blame at anyone's door in particular, not even Chas. We'd worked non-stop for five years and we were worn out. Okay, we signed a duff deal, we were stitched up, but to be honest, losing the court case was merely the straw that broke the camels back. Sometimes I think it was meant to be; if we'd carried on we'd have just been going through the motions, the music would have suffered and we'd have faded into obscurity, that's if we hadn't ended up killing each other first.' He was right. I'd almost forgotten the finer details of the break up and on the rare occasions I did think about those days I always blamed Chas and GMC. For the first time I realised that maybe the problem was ourselves; we were our own worst enemy. Robbo continued.

'I just wanted to run away and feel sorry for myself, which I guess I did for about a year or so. Despite the court costs and the tax bill and the fact we hadn't released anything for twelve months I was quite well set up financially. You see, I'd been passing a proportion of my income to Dave my brother—you all remember Dave?' We all nodded in between mouthfuls of curry. 'Dave, as you know, was, is, a stockbroker, a bloody good one at that. He invested my money really well and I was financially comfortable, for a few years at least. So for about a year all I did was drink, smoke dope and hide away.

Then I met Julie, my wife, who really turned things around for me. She was working for the same stockbroking firm as Dave, that's how I met her. We fell in love and it was during our honeymoon she really laid into me about being a self-pitying bastard. Trust a woman to hit you with the truth on your honeymoon. Anyway, to cut a long story short, I realised she was right and I needed to get my shit together. Julie helped me exorcise my demons and I started to think about what I really wanted to do with the rest of my life. It didn't take much working out. For five years I'd ate, slept and breathed the Tsars. That was all I knew. There was no way I was going to go back to being a clerk in an insurance company. I decided that what really fired me, what inspired me, what made me get out of bed in the morning was music and whatever I did I knew I had to be involved in it.' He stopped and took a long satisfying drink of his beer, grimaced, thumped his chest with his fist and let out a small belch. 'Excuse me. Knowing what you want to do is ninety percent of the battle I reckon, the rest is easy after that. I bought a large mobile 16 track recording studio on the cheap, placed a few adverts in trade and music magazines and before I knew it I had bands queuing up to record.

At first I would travel anywhere in the country, set up the studio and sleep in the van. After a while, a couple of the record companies heard some of my work and started using my services. I managed to save enough during this time to buy an old church and convert it into a 24 track recording studio. I spent twelve months scouring the country searching for the right equipment. You see, I wanted the studio to be an authentic valve studio, like they used to have in the sixties. I wanted to do away with all the digital crap that they use today. So that's what I did. It was a risky move that could easily have backfired but it didn't.' He scooped a large spoonful of curry into his mouth, chewed momentarily and carried on with his tale.

'I wanted to create a niche market. You know, recreate that amazing sixties atmosphere, which I'd use as a selling point. Not only that but it also ensured that the only people who would be willing to use the studio were proper musicians, people who could play and could sing. All the fakes and record company puppets wouldn't come within a country mile of a studio that couldn't iron out their flaws or auto-tune their voice or program the drums. It wasn't long before I was choosing my own customers. If I liked the band or artist I would work with them, if I didn't like them I'd tell them that I was fully booked for the next two years.' He leaned back in his chair looking quite satisfied with himself. Flaky nodded attentively. 'But, I may have made one silly mistake ...' we all pricked up our ears. 'From day one I made it quite clear that I would never do any work for GMC or their roster of artists.'

'Haha! Nice one Robbo,' laughed Geordie.

'Hmm, maybe not the wisest choice, Robbo. You know what those bastards are capable of,' I added. GMC were the biggest and most powerful record company in the world and they hadn't achieved that status by being benevolent and altruistic. They were ruthless, merciless and unrelenting. They got what they wanted and if they couldn't get it, they made damn well sure that no-one else got it. They had scores of subsidiaries dressed up as mock independents; they had fingers in the pies of many recording studios, trade magazines, publishing houses and legal practices. Basically, their influence had seeped into every area of the music business and beyond. No-one did anything without GMC knowing about it. They really were the musical Mafia.

'As it turned out, GMC weren't initially concerned with what I was up to. I mean why would they—a tuppence-ha'penny recording studio, big deal. But then a few of their big stars and a few of the new acts they'd signed wanted to use me and the studio for their next albums. I told them politely to shove it where the sun don't shine. While ever they were signed to GMC I wouldn't be available to work with them.' He paused for effect.

'Anyway, about four months ago me and Julie decided to go to our villa in Spain for a fortnight. When we got to Manchester Airport there had been a rolling strike called by the Air Traffic Controllers. We were going to be delayed twenty four hours so we set off back home. We'd probably only been gone three hours in all, but when we returned the studio had been broken into. This wasn't a smash and grab by kids, this was professional; the alarm system had been disabled and the lock on the door had been drilled and removed; there was virtually no damage to the door whatsoever; whoever did it knew what they were doing.' There was a collective audible gasp followed by a few, "fucking hells", "I don't believe it" and "villa in Spain? You bourgeois bastard" from Geordie. Robbo raised his hand to halt our exclamations.

'The first thing I did was to check the safe. I've got over fifty G's in cash in there ...' Geordie cut him off.

'Fifty grand! Where in hell did you get that sort of money from?' he asked, astounded at the amount.

'Well record companies always pay me the full invoice amount—by direct deposit into my bank account. But, all the unsigned bands, who are paying for recording out of their own money—well, they like to pay cash to avoid the VAT. Over the years it's accumulated. I can't put it into the bank otherwise the tax man will be onto me.'

'Fair enough,' we all mumbled in unison.

'But here's the strange thing—not one penny was missing; in fact, nothing had had been taken. All my master tapes had been rifled through but not one single thing was missing. I've got over half a million quid's worth of equipment in that studio and not so much as a plectrum, guitar string or drum stick was out of place—bizarre eh?' We all slowed our eating and exchanged cryptic glances as Robbo continued.

'But that's not the end of it; then there was the case of the invisible band.'

'What do you mean?' asked Flaky who appeared concerned at the way the conversation was going.

'In hindsight I should have twigged straight away, but I didn't. The band's name was "Marie Celeste". They'd booked six months studio time to work on their first album and I had cleared my diary of any other

171

commitments. Anyway, the band didn't show for the first week, which didn't really concern me at first. I know what bands are like, especially bands that have just been signed up—they're too busy playing rock stars, buying new equipment and sourcing their drugs to worry about something as trivial as recording their first album. And besides that, their so-called manager kept ringing me up to reassure me that they would eventually materialise and that I'd still get paid for the time. The first month passes and still no sign of them and it starts to drag into the second month and I begin to get a little suspicious—it just didn't feel right. So, I rang around a few of my industry contacts and asked if they'd heard of this band from North London called "Marie Celeste" or of their manager, a guy calling himself "Bart YC Punk". Nobody had heard of either of them.'

'Bart YC Punk!' I yelled, throwing myself back in the chair, 'and with a name like that you didn't get suspicious for a good month?'

'Well, I assumed that he was some sort of gangster rapper or punk death metal artist ...' I interrupted again.

'Oh yeah, gangster rapper, death metal, what was the band's name again "Marie Celeste", hardly the name you'd associate with gun-toting rappers is it?'

'Okay smart arse, I take your point. Anyway, when I finally rang the manager's mobile to see what was going on, the number was dead. By this time I'd lost two months studio time and no-one to pay for it. It wasn't until later that I realised that Bart YC Punk was an anagram.' We all stopped chewing and glanced at each other as we tried to mentally reconfigure the letters of "Bart YC Punk". Geordie was the first cab off the rank and laughed.

'Aw, shit mate, you were stitched up good and proper.'

'What is it? What does it mean?' nagged Flaky.

'Bankruptcy, that's what it means,' replied Geordie.

'Then the text messages started. I ignored them at first, just thinking they were from a crackpot or someone having a laugh but now

I'm not so sure.' I suspected Robbo was being paranoid and wasn't totally convinced by his conspiracy theories.

'What sort of text messages?' I asked.

'Things like, "if you want it, here it is come and get it" and "you can't always get what you want", and what was the last one,' he screwed his eyes up in strained concentration, 'oh yeah, that was it, "money, money, money, always funny," all very strange.'

'Well you must know the number of your texter, have you contacted him or her?' probed Flaky.

'I've tried ringing it a few times but it just rings and rings. Whoever it is obviously doesn't want to talk to me. I've also replied to their texts telling them to piss off but all I get back is a sarcastic "ooh, touchy touchy" or "can give it out but can't take it eh?" so I've given up now, I just delete them.'

'It all seems like coincidence to me Robbo,' I said. 'Shit happens sometimes and when it occurs in quick succession there's a tendency to attach meaning to it where there is none. It's not GMC's style. If they wanted you out of business they'd have burnt you down or worse, without a second thought. Why go to the bother of fake bands and break-ins where nothing's taken or damaged; and as for the text messages, well, that's just someone having a wind up.' Robbo chewed on a chapatti and nodded.

'Yeah, maybe.'

'Well why not ask the psychologist?' interjected Geordie with a smirk on his face. We all turned to Flaky who put his hand over his mouth and coughed.

'I think you need a criminologist not a psychologist,' protested Flaky.

'They do psychological profiling in murder cases these days, I've seen it on the box. Why not have a bash and use that expensive university educated brain to come up with a theory,' mocked Geordie.

Flaky had a drink of water, put his glass back on the table and cleared his throat.

'Okay then, I'll give it a go.' He pulled an expensive looking ballpoint from his jacket pocket and grabbed a napkin, which he carefully folded in half. 'Right, let's get things in chronological order. Now, what event happened first?' Robbo sat back and began to pick food from his teeth.

'The break in, like I said, that was last December, early December.'

'Okay, and did you still go away for two weeks to Spain?'

'Yeah, we delayed it a couple of days until the police came around.'

'Police? You never mentioned police?' Robbo shrugged his shoulders.

'I didn't think it important.'

'And what did they have to say?'

'Nothing much. You know what the coppers are like, they couldn't find their arse with both hands. They just said it was a professional break-in. No fingerprints were left behind and as nothing had been stolen they weren't particularly concerned.' Flaky scribbled on the back of the napkin and nodded.

'When did you get back from Spain?'

'Just before Christmas.'

'And what happened next?'

'Well, in early January I got a call from this character "Bart YC Punk". He wanted six months recording from March through until the end of August. I told him no way, initially, as I had three bands booked in during that time, but he offered me one hundred and fifty grand; well I wasn't going to knock back that sort of dough, so I agreed.'

'Right, and they never turned up. What did this Bart Punk sound like?' Robbo struggled for a moment and then tentatively offered a reply.

'Well, now I come to think of it, that was another thing that was a bit off—he didn't sound like music biz, I picked that immediately—more sort of like a copper, you know, sort of stiff and proper, meat and two veg, a bit like you Flaky, no offence.' Flaky scribbled something else down while muttering,

'Yes, yes, very funny,' before continuing his probing. 'And when did you receive the first text message?'

'Hmm … let me think, not long ago,' Robbo scratched his head, 'I suppose it would have been about two weeks ago now.'

'I see, and anything else untoward?'

'No, not really,' replied Robbo.

Flaky nodded and leaned back in his chair studying his notes. It seemed this dramatic investigation was drawing to a close; a wild goose chase if ever I'd seen one. I ordered another round of drinks and relaxed back into my chair. Geordie stirred the pot again.

'Go ahead Miss Marple, what's the conclusion of your rapier like investigations?' Flaky caressed the napkin that contained his notes as though in deep contemplation.

'Well, on first look there doesn't seem to be any correlation between events. The phone calls, as Will pointed out, could be just a prank by someone … more annoying than sinister. As for the mystery band and this character Bart Punk, well, the obvious assumption is that it could be a rival recording studio who is trying to put you out of business or at the very least, steal some of your business.' Robbo screwed his nose up as though doubting the plausibility of the last supposition. 'But the really strange one, and may I say, the most sinister is the break in.' Flaky was now really getting into the swing of it and finished with a flourish as though he were some legendary QC at the Old Bailey. 'Why would someone expertly break into your studios and take nothing. Presumably they were not after any monetary gain. The only thing disturbed were your master tapes. This would lead me to suspect that at some stage you have held onto someone's master tape in lieu of payment; although, this does not sit too well, as it brings us back to the professional way in which the premises were entered; not your usual means of entry by some disgruntled, destitute musicians. So in summing up; I would say the first two events are of no consequence and the last event is still under a cloud of some ambiguity.' Flaky sat back with a smug smile on his face. Geordie began to clap very slowly.

'Well done Hercule Poirot. After all that and we're still none the wiser.' Robbo reached forward and took the last onion bhaji and began to slowly bite into it.

'Hmm ... you may be right about the calls, it may be some dickhead who thinks it's funny. As for a rival trying to put me out of business, I don't really think so. I've never had any run-ins with any other recording studio. As I said before, my studio is unique in the fact that it's a recreation of a sixties setup—it's a niche market. I think there's only one other in the country and that's in London, so I hardly think that they're going to try and knobble a competitor in Sheffield. And, I can honestly say that I've never had any problems with any of my customers—everyone's always paid up and I certainly would never hold someone's master tape as ransom anyway. No, I'm sorry Flaky but you're way off the mark.' Flaky narrowed his eyes and rubbed his chin as he leant across the table.

'Now, are you sure there's absolutely nothing else out of the ordinary that's happened recently; anything at all—think really hard.' Robbo sucked on his beer and shook his head.

'No nothing, just the same old same old.' A thought suddenly occurred to me that sent a slight tingle down my spine.

'Well that's not quite true is it Robbo?' Everyone stopped what they were doing and stared at me.

'What do you mean?' he asked.

'You got a call from me about the reunion tour—hardly an everyday occurrence.' There was silence as everyone digested the implications.

18: MELTING POT

I had a fitful nights sleep. I dreamt that a large yeti shaped creature was dangling me by my foot from the top of a skyscraper. I remember the fear I felt as I swung back and forth screaming helplessly at the ant-like people a hundred stories below. He eventually let me drop and I fell like a lead turd toward the onrushing concrete below. I somehow managed to tell myself it was only a dream and woke up before I hit the pavement. I cursed Geordie and went back to sleep.

I awoke again, this time to a gentle but persistent tapping on my door. I was confused and extremely tired as I went to the door and asked who it was.

'It's me Flaky, open up.' I unlocked the door and let in a tracksuit clad Flaky.

'Bloody hell Flaky, what time is it?'

'It's ten past seven,' he replied. I wiped sleep from my eyes and scratched my testicles through my jocks as I stared at his apparel.

'Don't tell me you're going for a run at this time?' I asked incredulously.

'No, I've just got back. I hit the streets at six. Go every day, if I miss I get withdrawal symptoms. Best time of the day is the morning—I love it.' The guy wasn't even breathing heavily. I slumped back on my bed and blinked at the ceiling, still trying to come round.

'Well that's great Flaky, I'm very pleased for you, but did you have to wake me to tell me all this? He seemed a bit disappointed at my response.

'No, I guess not ... sorry, I didn't think, I just wanted to see if you were ready for breakfast yet, I've tried the others but I can't wake them.' I felt like a bit of a shit, the guy was excited, we hadn't seen each other for a decade and all he wanted was a bit of company for breakfast.

'Okay, listen give me half an hour to get showered and dressed and come back for me and we'll head down to the restaurant.' He smiled and seemed relieved. I stood and patted him on the back as I opened the door to show him out.

'You really are into this fitness lark aren't you?'

'You should try it Will, it gives you so much energy and positive vibes, it's the best thing I've ever done,' he paused and looked at me seriously as though he was ready to impart some very grave matter but stopped short, smiled and said, 'I'll see you in half.' With that he was gone.

'Silly old bastard.' I muttered under my breath. I stared longingly at the bed but bypassed it on my way to the shower. I freshened up and dressed and lay on the bed watching the breakfast news. I still hadn't called Fiona. The longer I left it the more reluctant I was to get in touch. I was full of self-doubt. My feelings of elation a few days ago now seemed juvenile and premature. *For God's sake, all I'd done was have a good chin wag with the local barmaid, she'd get idiots like me chatting her up all the time. Then there was the fact that she has three kids.* The whole thing now seemed like a bad idea. There was another gentle knock on my door. *That will be Flaky ready for his brekky. I'll phone Fiona later.*

\#

'So you see, I'd really prefer that there be no drugs on the tour and that alcohol is kept to a minimum, and I'd rather not play on a Sunday,' stated Flaky in a schoolmasterly tone.

178

'No, there'll be absolutely no drugs I can guarantee that and I don't think any of us are big drinkers anymore, maybe a couple of beers and the odd glass of red but that's about it. As for playing on Sundays, well, that's really out of my hands Flaky; we'll all have to follow the tour schedule,' I replied knowing full well that what I had just said was complete bullshit.

'Hmm ... well, two out of three isn't bad.' He smiled and got up from his chair.

'I'm back for a refill, some more cereal and OJ for me, can I get you anything?'

'No. I'm fine with this coffee at the moment, I may get some bacon and eggs later, once I've come round.'

'Bacon and eggs, tut tut! Clogs the arteries. Eating the flesh of a dead animal is not the wisest health choice.' He wagged his finger at me and smiled. I returned a feeble grin that turned into a grimace once he'd turned his back and headed off over to the breakfast counter.

My head was reeling and I had to think quickly. Flaky had just spent the last ten minutes telling me a little bit extra about his life, a little bit that he conveniently left out from the previous night's discussions, although thinking back he had dropped a few big clues, something about seeing the light and being part of a larger family. Not only was he a vegetarian, a fitness health freak, a psychologist and a frigging astrologist but he was also a "Born Again Christian" to boot! He despised drugs of any sort; he believed drink was evil if imbibed just for the sake of it, (he'd turned a blind eye to last nights little session, he'd informed me) and he believed in the way of the Lord. He confided that Robbo was well aware of his religious conversion and was surprised that he hadn't mentioned it to me before now; so was I, the twat! He said that he had not wanted to tell me last night as he didn't want it to come as too much of a shock—bollocks! He wasn't game to make such an announcement in front of Geordie, that was his real reason. Geordie was a hater, a malcontent, a cynic, a spoiler and these were just his good points; he generally had it in for most of the world, but he paid particular attention to politicians and religious zealots. Flaky was telling me now, so I could be the one to break the news gently to Geordie. If Robbo knew, why in hell's name hadn't he told me before this! I'd sort that little prick out later, first of all I had to think fast to come up with a strategy to minimise the possible collateral damage.

This wasn't just a spanner in the works, this was the electric drill, jackhammer, lawnmower and chainsaw thrown into the mix. Something else bothered me nearly as much as Flaky's sudden revelations; his manner; I'd overlooked it last night but this morning it was unmistakable. He had become arrogant, superior and opinionated in the way that only people who have found God could. There was no room for debate or logical discussion; it was faith against secular rationalism. There was no way I could tell Geordie. I felt out of kilter and hung-over. I took a large gulp of coffee and reached into my pocket for my little parcel of energy. I looked around. The restaurant was still fairly quiet, a couple of business types, a middle aged couple, me and John the Baptist, who was now in discussion with some poor old businessman at the breakfast counter. He was probably trying to convert him. I dabbed, sucked and then folded my little parcel away, making a mental note that there wasn't much of the white powder left. I got up and went outside for a smoke.

It was grey and drizzling and the London streets were already bumper to bumper. The stench of petrol and diesel fumes mixed with my own cigarette smoke sent me into a reverie for a moment. I felt the unmistakable kick of the amphetamine begin to work. I immediately felt an improvement in my spirits and my brain began to rev up into top gear. What was the way out of this? Maybe Geordie would understand, maybe he'd matured? Maybe they could both live with each other's foibles? No! No chance, not on tour, not when we were going to spend eight weeks in each other's pockets. Even if they started off okay, it wouldn't be long before there were serious ructions. There was no way that I was going to play referee between Billy Graham and the Abominable Snowman. No,

180

the best thing to do was to keep the news from Geordie for as long as possible. I threw my cigarette into the gutter and got a disgusted glare from a young upwardly mobile businesswoman, she looked at me as though I'd just asked her for a rim job. I turned and went back inside. Flaky was sat down happily tucking into his second serve of muesli.

'Listen Flaky,' I began, he looked up at me as he chewed away, 'I appreciate and understand your beliefs and convictions and good luck to you is all I can say—I wish I had something in my life that I could believe in ...' he tried to intervene.

'Well there is ...'

'Let me finish,'

'Sorry,'

'Like I said, I'm very pleased for you, even if I don't necessarily share your beliefs. However, I'm not sure that everyone in the band will be as accepting as me ...'

He stopped eating,

'Geordie?'

'Yes, Geordie. You remember his attitude to people with any sort of beliefs.'

'Yes, I was hoping that he may have mellowed, maybe even matured. I'm sure if I counselled him I'd be able to make some progress. I was just hoping you could test the waters first.'

'I don't think that's a very good idea. I haven't seen anything yet to suggest that he's mellowed or matured. I really think the best idea is to play possum, you know, just keep this information to yourself. It doesn't make you any less of a person, any less of a Christian.' He stared at me disdainfully. 'Well then, what do you say?'

'Well, I don't like hiding my beliefs and if he asks, I'll have to tell him the truth.'

'Of course, but he'll never ask, just don't bang on about it that's all, and maybe go easy on the vegetarian and health craze thing as well.' I feared I may have overplayed my hand.

'Listen Will, I am who I am, and I don't intend to hide away under a rock for eight weeks just because an overgrown child can't accept other peoples life choices.'

'Okay, well don't say you weren't warned and but don't expect me to play umpire because I won't.' I stood to get myself some breakfast.

'Sorry, Will, I'm just a little tense that's all. We'll do it your way, I won't preach, not that I do, but I aren't hiding.'

'Good. I want this tour to be hassle free and enjoyable. Can I get you any bacon and eggs?'

#

I was back in my room speeding. It was eight thirty and Robbo and Geordie were still unconscious. Flaky had gone off to find some Christian bookshop that he had the address for. No booze, no drugs, no work on Sunday, he must be off his fucking rocker! I assessed the situation as I lay on my bed watching another rerun of a crap soft porn movie. On one hand I had an unhinged, psychologically damaged, intolerant and insensitive ogre with a tendency to violence and on the other I had a virtuous, arrogant do-gooder, bible basher with too much energy and an opinionated, superior manner. Oil and water; and in the middle, me—me and Robbo … the bastard! I had a good mind to wake him up and give him a piece of my mind for not informing me of Flaky's conversion, but it was too risky with Geordie next door. I'd deal with him later. My mobile rang and I answered; it was Chas.

'Will, well done! I knew you'd make the right choice, how are you and the rest of the boys?'

'Good Chas, we're all good and you?'

'Couldn't be better Will, couldn't be better. Now listen Will, we've got a pretty hectic schedule so let's get down to business. You and the boys need to come into my office and sign the contract today, I need the legal side wrapped up ASAP. Then tomorrow I need you all down at Bell rehearsal rooms in East London, do you know it?'

'No I don't, but Robbo will.'

'Don't worry I'll give you instructions how to get there. You need to be at the studios by 11 am sharp, all the other acts will be there ... DON'T BE LATE! We'll have a bit of a get together and I'll outline the itinerary. Now you've brought all your gear with you haven't you?'

'Yes I think so, Robbo threw everything into his van, although I haven't double checked.'

'Will! Don't fuck me around, no assuming, no "I think so". This is big money and a serious event. Get your shit together. ' This was the Chas of old, managing, lecturing, laying down the law.

'Okay Chas, keep your hair on. Anyway, if you think we're all going to trot into your office and sign a contract without first getting it looked over by a lawyer then you're off your trolley; once bitten twice shy.' He immediately changed his tone, replying in a slightly miffed, haughty fashion.

'Will, that is your prerogative but it's only going to cost you money and waste your time. But if that's what you want, fine. Remember that these are standard contracts for all the acts, they're all exactly the same, they've been drawn up by a top music lawyer and hold no surprises.'

'All the same, I'll be getting it checked out.'

'As you wish, but you must bring the signed document with you tomorrow otherwise it will jeopardise your position on the tour. Oh, and one last thing, you know I said you'd be headlining ...'

'Yes ...' I replied warily.

'Well, there's been a change of plan. Some of the other bands kicked up a bit of a stink, so I've decided that we'll mix it up a bit, you know, we'll rotate the headline act for the first half dozen gigs. Once we find out who is the biggest draw-card then they will become the headline act.'

'You mean you lied to me?'

'Will, c'mon, you know I don't like that word. It wasn't a lie at the time. I'm caught between a rock and a hard place here—help me out.'

'Alright Chas, I'm fine with that. Let the cream rise to the surface eh?'

'Exactly, I knew you'd understand.' Chas gave me his office address and we hung up. Once again his story didn't add up. First he'd insisted the contracts had to be signed today, then he said tomorrow. He'd said they were standard contracts but had been specially drawn up by a top lawyer. The sign of a bad liar—always changing their story. As for not headlining every gig at the start, well, I wasn't too concerned, in fact I took it as a bit of a challenge.

I finally plucked up the courage and called Fiona. It rang a few times before the familiar click of an answering machine kicked in. I listened to the soft sexy tones of Fiona's voice and imagined her long flowing hair, her full soft lips and her sweet scent. I was lost for a moment and could feel the familiar rise of an unnecessary erection. I realised the beep for me to speak had passed quite a few seconds ago and here I was breathing heavily into the phone, every lascivious breath being captured by the machine.

'Hi … erm … it's me … that is, it's me, Will. Fiona, I was just thinking about you … I mean I was thinking about you, to ring you, I didn't mean I was thinking about you sexually … not that I don't find you sexually attractive, of course I do … is that a double negative … I'm sorry, I'm rambling … erm what am I trying to say … I want you … no I didn't mean that, I take that back, what I meant was, I want to see you again soon, yes that's what I meant. I'm not sure what's happening yet. Did I say I was in London? Probably not; I got Geordie, thanks to you. Yeah, no change there really. Well, that's it, erm … I'll call you after tomorrow, no, I mean tomorrow not after tomorrow; we've got our first rehearsal; anyway best go, I need to sort myself out … no that came out wrong, I didn't mean sort myself out like … well you know sexually, no definitely not; I meant I had to get the others up; when I say the others I

184

mean, Robbo and Geordie, there's no-one else in the room with me, well I had Flaky in here earlier; I mean I had his presence, his company; anyway he's gone to find a Christian bookshop. I'll speak to you later ... if you like ... okay ... bye ... bye.' What a fucking car crash! If there was ever a way to put a woman off, it was to leave a message for them sounding like a drooling, insane sex-pest. I considered ringing back and apologising for my ridiculous message but I didn't trust myself not to dig myself deeper into the shit.

Thanks to the speed, the soft porn on the TV and the thought of Fiona, my cock felt like a barge pole bulging against my jeans. I considered having a wank but decided that I had far more important matters to address than paying a visit to Sister Palmer. There were a lot of things on my mind; Robbo's tale from the previous evening; my suspicions about Chas; had Robbo brought all the gear; God's latest moonbeam; collecting the contracts; meeting up with John Peterson by 11 am. No, a quick self-abuse session was definitely out of the question. *I have to concentrate and remain focused, concentrate and remain focused, yes, definitely focused.*

#

After I finished my wank I went and banged on Geordie's door and in turn, Robbo's. There was no sound from Geordie's room but a few guttural grunts emanated from Robbo's abode. I banged again.

'Come on Robbo, open up I need to speak to you, it's nearly nine.' From behind the door I could hear muttered cursing and stumbling. This would be like the crack of dawn for Robbo, poor bugger.

'Hang on a bloody minute, just wait ... ARRGH! Shit the bed, bastard thing ...' the door opened and a dishevelled and grumpy Robbo confronted me. He was wearing a pair of tight budgie smugglers and was holding his foot while sporting a pained expression.

'What's wrong with you?' I asked,

'I stubbed my bastard toe on the bastard bed ...'

'Oh, is that all.' I walked in and shut the door behind me.

'Listen Robbo, how much gear did you bring down with you?'

'Well I've got about 12 ounce of weed, a few grams of coke and a bag of speed, why? Do you want to score some?'

'No I don't! I meant musical gear you tart, what the hell are you doing with all that shit? I thought we agreed that this was to be a clean tour?' I stormed, exasperated that we had fallen at the first hurdle. He appeared puzzled.

'I never agreed to anything of the sort. I think you must be getting me mixed up with Mother Teresa. Anyway, it's only a small amount really, between us all that is. This is what I'd usually do in a month to six weeks. You'll be thanking me when we hit a brick wall and need to oil the wheels a little.' I couldn't stay angry with him considering I had on my person a wrap of speed. He walked over to his bum-bag and pulled out a spliff and lit up, sitting back down on the bed. He inhaled deeply and offered it to me; I shook my head.

'Ah, that's better.' He slumped back into the pillow and took another drag. He looked like shit and I told him so.

'Robbo mate,'

'What?'

'You look like shit.'

'Yeah? Well I smoke, I drink, I do drugs and eat crap ... what's your excuse?' he replied, unperturbed by my comments.

'So what about gear, musical gear, what have you got?' I persisted.

'Don't fret man, it's all taken care of. I came down in the Merc van. I've got everything we'll ever need. All we need to do is visit a music shop to get spare strings, plectrums, skins etc. Maybe we should do that this morning.' I signalled a sigh of relief. At least that was one less thing to worry about.

'Yeah, you can take Geordie and get provisions for all of us. I have to pick up the contracts from Chas's office and take them to a lawyer.' He took another drag on the spliff and re-offered it to me. The room was already heavy with the thick smoke. I was tempted but declined. I had to keep sharp.

'What about Flaky?' Robbo inquired dreamily. I suddenly remembered the very large bone that I had to pick with him. I put my ear to the wall that adjoined Geordie's room and I thought I could hear the faint sound of snoring. I saw Robbo eyeing me suspiciously.

'Yes, well I was meaning to ask you about that?' I began in a friendly manner.

'Ask me about what?' Robbo seemed perplexed.

'About Billy Graham!' I hissed as loud as I dare. Robbo still looked confused.

'Billy Graham? What the fuck are you on about man?' Then the penny dropped. 'Oh, yeah, ah, you mean Flaky …'

'Yes, Sir Francis Of bleeding Assisi; if I'd have known that he'd been *saved* I'd have had second thoughts about this whole venture. Why didn't you tell me he was a Born Again Christian? You must have realised that would be a red rag to a bull for Geordie, you know how intolerant he is of anyone with beliefs?' He took another drag and his worried expression disappeared.

'I was hoping Geordie had mellowed. Anyway, what's the big deal? Flaky's into God, so what, if that's his bag, so be it. It doesn't worry me, I mean he does go on about it a bit but I just block it out and ignore him. Geordie will be alright, they may have a few bust ups but so what, Geordie will have a bust up with anyone, whether they're a God-botherer or not.'

'That's not the point. What if there's a bust up and Flaky walks out? I can bet that Chas will have some clause in the contract about completing the tour in full otherwise there'll be penalties.'

'So we lose a bit of money—it's not the end of the world.' He took another drag and laughed as he blew the smoke out.

'Yeah, well if we don't get paid I'm out of pocket big time because I've paid a twenty percent deposit on Geordie's house in lieu of tour monies.' His gormless expression didn't change.

'Yeah, you said last night, I thought it was a bit insane.' He laughed again, totally unconcerned at my predicament.

'You're right, I must be mad. Mind you, I may not have followed through on such a rash decision had I been made aware of Flaky's conversion.'

'Look, what's the worst that can happen ...' His disregard was now beginning to piss me off.

'I'll tell you what can happen. We don't finish the tour, we don't get paid. Geordie loses his house and he comes and lives with you!' Suddenly Robbo's manner changed. He sat up and dropped his roach into a half drunk cup of cold coffee.

'Now hang on a mo, there's no way that can happen, if he lives with anyone it would have to be you, I mean you have no ties; my Missus wouldn't wear that at all.'

'Well too bad because I ain't wet nursing him.' He stood and walked unsteadily over to the kettle and flicked it on. He emptied a sachet of coffee into a cup and turned to face me.

'Shit, what are we gonna do?' At last he saw the possible consequences.

'Geordie's not to find out. I've asked Flaky to lay off the religion thing and also to take it easy on the vegetarianism and health stuff. He's agreed that he'll wind his neck in a bit but he can't guarantee anything. We'll just have to monitor the situation. I suggest that we subtly try to keep them as far apart as possible without it becoming obvious. I'll take care of Geordie, you sort Flaky out.' He seemed slightly relieved.

'Yeah, okay that's a good idea. The less time they spend together the better. I mean they never used to get on too well at the best of times.'

'There's going to be tough times ahead when we're stuck on the tour bus but I suggest we just keep space between them.' The kettle clicked and Robbo poured the steaming water into his cup. He suddenly appeared wide awake.

19: NEW BOOTS AND PANTIES

I caught a taxi to West London and located the offices of "Dupont Enterprises". They weren't particularly impressive. An uninspired, mid-seventies design of concrete, glass and bland bricks. There were two people in reception; a young, dizzy looking receptionist whom I assumed I had talked to the day before and an older woman with beady eyes and horn rimmed glasses, who typed away furiously in the far corner. I was puzzled to see that she was still using a typewriter. Hadn't the whole of the western world converted to computers?

'Yes, can I help you?' asked the young looking woman in a bored cockney voice.

'Yes, I'm Will Harding I've come to collect a draft copy of a contract for the Shooting Tsars … is Chas in?'

'Na, Mr Dupont is out on business, but if you'd like to leave a message I'll make sure that he gets it.'

'No, that's fine, I'll just collect the contract.'

'What contract is that exactly?' She asked while chewing gum and staring at me blankly.

'The contract for the Shooting Tsars,' she still looked blank. 'The reunion tour, of nineties bands, you know …' her eyes jumped into life with recognition.

'Ah, you mean the "We Thought You Were Dead" tour.' She laughed like a drain at her own comment and threw the older woman a look, who was also sniggering away like a closet hyena.

'Yes, that's right, the "We Thought You Were Dead Tour". A tour that will earn me in eight weeks what you'd earn in ten years'. The girl stopped laughing and cocked her head to one side and turned her mouth up. The older woman peered over the top of her glasses and down her nose at me before issuing a loud "TUT" and returned to her typing. The girl fumbled about below her desk and pulled out a package of large brown envelopes held together with an elastic band. She flicked through them before pulling one from the sheaf.

'Will Harding, Shooting Tsars. Is that you?' she asked.

'Yes, it is, that is who I just told you I was a few moments ago.' She gave me a dirty glance, which I admittedly deserved, and handed me the envelope.

'Mr Dupont said that it's essential that you bring the signed contract with you tomorrow to the rehearsal rooms.'

'Yes, thanks, I know.' I turned and began to make my way out. I heard the young woman state in a loud voice to her colleague, that I was patently intended to hear,

'Well I certainly won't be going to see a bunch of old has-beens anyway …'

'No love,' her colleague replied, 'they were crap first time around why would anyone want to see them now when they're old, bald and still crap.' They both cackled like demented geese as I made my way out of the building.

#

It was nearly 11 am by the time I reached John Peterson's offices. They were located down a quaint and tidy looking laneway, away from the hustle and bustle of the metropolis, yet still right in its heart. The building was in stark contrast to Dupont Enterprises building of mind-numbing blandness. It sat in a row of large Victorian brick terraces that had recently been sandblasted and re-pointed. An impressive wrought iron railing fence ran the length of the street demarcating public from

191

private. I walked up five well worn stone steps and pressed a buzzer. A silky female voice answered.

'Peterson Lawyers, may I help you.' I stared at the large blue door as I answered.

'Yes, it's Will Harding, I have an appointment with John Peterson.'

'Hello Mr Harding, we're expecting you, please come in.' There was a buzz and a click and the door was suddenly ajar. I walked into a small but plush reception area. A young attractive woman with a fiery red bob, a very short skirt and knee length boots met me and introduced herself as Kelly. She led me up a wide staircase that turned back on itself so when we reached the first floor I was back facing the small laneway of a few moments before. She led me straight on, to a large red leather covered door directly ahead. She opened it for me and I walked in. As I passed her, I felt her warmth and her youth and smelt her freshness and vitality. I felt a slight pang of envy to think that some young, testosterone fuelled rock ape would be getting his sweaty paws on such a precious beauty. I cursed my age, and my body, and my receding hairline. I was nearly forty, yet already, such summer fruits were out of my grasp. I walked into a large oblong office with one huge window that ran the length of the room giving a most magnificent view of the city.

'Aha, Will, great to see you! Come in and take a seat.' John appeared from the far end of the room. Behind him was a floor to ceiling bookshelf on which sat expensive books sporting gold leaf on the leather bound spines. I handed him the envelope containing the contract. He carefully put it down on a modest but tasteful looking desk.

'You've met Kelly I take it?' he asked as he shook my hand warmly.

'Yes,' I replied quietly as I turned to smile at the young woman. She returned the smile in the way only young women can to older men, a sort of "I know I have to be polite to you, but you make my flesh crawl you disgusting old sex pest, and if I were as old and decrepit as you the last thing on my mind would be sex; I'd be more worried about topping up my private health insurance … you creep." Then again, maybe I read too much into these things.

'Tea and biscuits Mr Harding?' Kelly inquired politely. 'Or would you prefer coffee?'

'No, tea will be fine thanks.'

'Earl Grey, black or green?' she continued.

'Earl Grey would be nice.' She turned to leave.

'Oh Kelly?'

'Yes Mr Peterson?'

'Absolutely no calls, okay, I'll be with Mr Williams for a good part of the day.'

'Very good.' She replied and with that she was gone, leaving her heavenly alluring scent behind her as she disappeared out of the door.

'Come sit, sit,' beckoned John with a huge grin on his face. I sat down on a large Chesterfield which faced out onto the city—John sat down opposite. I smiled at him but felt a slight uneasiness. I didn't know this guy from Adam. He was obviously very successful and Oxford educated to boot and it didn't sit easily with my working class upbringing. After all, traditionally, we should have been enemies.

'Wonderful girl Kelly, don't know where I'd be without her,' he gestured. I thought I'd break the ice with a little smut.

'Coming up those stairs I could almost see …' I was going to say "what she had for breakfast" but luckily John interceded at just the right time.

'Yes, she's my stepdaughter.'

'Ah! Yes, I was going to say I could almost see a family resemblance but of course that can't be if she's your Stepdaughter.' I think he had offered me a lifeline and I was grateful to him. John was a tall, extremely thin man with pointed features and short curly blond hair. He wore suits, which were expensive but not flash, and when he took his jacket off he rolled up his shirt sleeves, as if to say "right, let's get down to business". I had to concede, the guy had class, nothing was fake; there was no façade at work here; this was the real thing, a solid business built on skill, talent and a deep knowledge and understanding of how the world worked.

'So, tell me all about it, I can't believe the Tsars are back together. I'm extremely excited about this—start from the beginning, I want to hear absolutely everything.' I related my tale and slowly relaxed into his company. The tea and biscuits arrived and John sat opened mouthed as I told the story of how we got back together. Occasionally he'd laugh, only to say "I can't believe it". I told him of all my concerns, including Chas, Geordie's erratic behaviour, Flaky's religious conversion and Robbo's mysterious episodes. He listened intently. As I talked I glanced around the room. Framed artwork from artists he had represented over the years adorned the walls, but centre stage on the far wall, was the largest frame that held a poster that seemed vaguely familiar. As I continued talking my eyes returned to it once again. I stopped talking and laughed. I realised it was a poster promoting the Tsars first album "From the Cradle to the Rave".

'Where did you get that from?' I asked breaking off from my storytelling.

'The Hammersmith Palais 1992. I got all your autographs apart from Geordie's.' I laughed again.

'How come you didn't get Geordie's?'

'I think Geordie was actually attempting to perform some sort of medical examination on …' he paused, 'how can I put this politely, erm, a rather large member of the opposite sex. I really didn't think it appropriate to interrupt.'

'That figures.' I laughed. I thought back to those early tours and all the hangers on and groupies. It wasn't unusual for someone to be having a shag or getting a blowjob in the dressing room. Everyone became blasé about it after a while and it was no more conspicuous than re-stringing your guitar or doing interviews with the music press, although I suppose to the outsider it must have been an eye opener. John picked up the envelope from the table and pulled out the contracts and had a quick scan of the contents.

'Hmm … looks like standard contracts but I will need to go over them carefully to make sure there's no hidden nasties in there.' He carefully replaced the documents into the envelope and continued.

'So, on one hand you're looking forward to the tour but on the flip side of the coin there's a certain amount of trepidation?' I ignored his mixed metaphors.

'Basically, yes! The music is no problem, that's what I'm looking forward to. That's what it's all about. But for that hour or so on stage you have to go through twenty three hours of shite.'

'Well, you can't deny it's good money. It'll be over before you know it.' He leaned forward towards me peering thoughtfully down at the carpet. 'Do you have any plans to make this reunion permanent, maybe resurrect your recording career?'

'Not a snowball's chance in hell. After this, that's it, no-more, never again.' He raised his head and fixed me in the eye.

'Have you given much thought to why all this is happening?' he asked pointedly.

'Well at first I thought it was just chance. If I hadn't answered the call from Chas I would have been down in Cornwall for two weeks and it would have been too late for us to join the tour. But now I'm not so sure; not after the things Robbo told us all last night. I've got a sneaking suspicion that Chas might be behind some of the strange happenings; but for the life of me I can't think why.' John stood and walked to the far end of the office and opened a drawer where he removed a couple of glasses and a bottle of whisky. He returned to his seat and placed them on the little table that separated our seats and poured us both a very generous glass of whisky.

'You're probably aware that most tours make a loss?' I nodded my confirmation as I sipped on the malt. 'I mean, if you're the Rolling

195

Stones or U2 and are playing to a hundred thousand people every night it's very profitable, but medium sized venues around the UK ... well, that's a different matter,' he now paused to take a sip of whisky, 'you've got to ask yourself the question "why?". It's not like you have a new album to promote. If Chas is really funding all this he's taking a big risk. Even if all the gigs are sellouts, he'll do well to break even, maybe at a push make a small profit. If the gigs aren't sellouts—well, he stands to take a heavy loss.' All good points and ones I hadn't as yet given much thought to.

'Well John, the way I see it, Chas and whoever can run around and play whatever silly little games they want; if you tell me the contract is bona fide we'll do the tour, take the cash and say au revoir. But, I do want to make sure that we don't get ripped off, so look out for anything irregular.' He nodded solemnly.

'So, we won't be seeing a new Tsars album anytime soon?'

'No. We won't be re-signing with Chas or GMC or anyone else for that matter. This is a one-off and that's that. ' He stood up and walked over to the window and stared at the panoramic view.

'You know there is another way?' he said cryptically, still admiring the view.

'I'm listening.'

'This is the 21st century. A world of MP3's, internet, web pages, blogs, downloads, I-pods. The computer age is expanding at an exponential rate that has left even the most exaggerated predictions of a few years ago for dead. Some see this as a bad thing; the rise of the machine; all those science fiction stories from the fifties and sixties coming to fruition; others, like myself, see it as empowerment, emancipation for the masses.' It was a nice speech but I didn't have a clue where he was going with it.

'Who needs record companies and agents, publicists and managers? Who needs to spend three million on a video or be made to sit down and write a hit single to sell a forthcoming album. Those days will soon be gone Will.' He turned and looked at me.

'You wouldn't have thought that I used to be a punk rocker would you?' He was dead right there. 'I'm as straight as a slide rule now, to look at, that is. But underneath this conservative shirt and tie I'm still a punk.' I was entertained by his ideas and I was enjoying his fine malt and the pleasant surroundings but I hoped he'd get to the bloody point soon.

'DIY! Do it yourself. That's what punk was about when it first started, before it got ambushed and emulsified by the big boys. Anyone with a guitar could start a band, or their own fanzine or run their own club. Who needed the big corporations anyway, just go out and do it.'

But it was bound to fail because it *did* need money. Money to record and pay for vinyl and covers and artwork and pay to get the music into the shops; and who owned all that? The usual suspects, your GMC's of the world. So what started out as a brave new world soon became the safe old world.' He walked back to the table and lifted the whisky bottle.

Refill?' he asked politely. I polished off the drop in my glass and nodded.

'I don't disagree with anything you've said John, but if you don't mind me asking, where is all this leading?'

'You said you still enjoy the music side, right?' I nodded, 'Well, why would you let the Chas Dupont's and the GMC's of this world stop you from doing what you love and what you're bloody good at. You write a song today, record it tomorrow and upload it onto your own website the day after. You already have an army of fans out there, a ready made audience.' I narrowed my eyes as I comprehended what he was saying.

'You sell your own music, via your own web page. You have a database of all your fans; when you have new material or decide to tour, you email them all. Everything is purchasable from your website; tickets, songs, T-shirts, memorabilia the whole shooting match. The money goes directly to you; no middle men, no managers taking 20%, no draconian contracts stating how, where and when. This is the new punk!' He was really firing on all cylinders now and I was beginning to be swept away by the idea myself.

'You can even set up your own publishing company to collect royalties. As it happens, I am a bit of an expert on music publishing and can explain everything in fine detail at a later stage should you wish to go down this path.' The idea excited me. We could be our own cottage industry. Even if the others weren't interested, I could go solo. Once I had my head around websites and mailing lists and publishing I'd be good to go. Then there was the old barn that I'd been meaning to convert for the last ten years. It would make a great recording studio— Robbo could help design and build it. The idea was definitely growing on me. Making music on my terms without the vampires and bullshit artists—it was perfect.

'Okay, well that's enough of my "Brave New World", but I hope you give it some thought. Now, I will need about an hour to go through this contract and then how about I take you to lunch? That is if you haven't got anything else planned?'

'No, no plans, but I think it should be me that treats you to lunch.' I stood up and held my hand out once again. 'It's lucky I bumped into you when I did,' I said.

'It was I who bumped into you,' he laughed. 'Very serendipitous indeed.'

'Okay, well I'll get out of your hair for a while and let you get on with studying the contract. Where should I meet you for lunch?'

'There's a fantastic little Italian place on the corner of this street. Turn left as you leave the building, a five minute walk. It's called "Bello Italiano". I'll get Kelly to ring ahead and book us a table. It can get awfully busy.'

#

I strolled around the boutique shops that populated the area looking at nothing in particular as my mind grappled with John's idea. I kept trying to look for a downside but I really couldn't see one. After an hour had passed I made my way to the restaurant and went inside where I saw John sat in a far corner. A waiter escorted me over and we ordered a chilled bottle of pinot grigio.

'So how did you go?' I asked, referring to the contract. John puckered his lips and seemed a trifle concerned—I feared the worst.

'Well as I suspected, it's an off the shelf contract that has been modified to suit. There's the usual requirement by both parties to honour their commitments. Dupont Enterprises to provide accommodation, transport, meals, per diems etc, etc. On completion of the tour, the band, that's you and the others, to receive eight hundred thousand pounds less any expenses incurred over and above the aforementioned expenses. Dupont enterprises can cancel the tour at any time but are obliged to pay in full regardless of how many gigs have been completed.' John still seemed a little perturbed.

'But?' I asked apprehensively.

'If for any reason you fail to fulfil your obligations, ie you miss a gig, then Dupont Enterprises (at their discretion) can impose penalties of up to twenty five percent of your total tour fee; in other words two hundred thousand pounds. I've seen penalty clauses in these sorts of contracts before but nothing as severe as this. And also, most curiously, there's a little clause in there that states that even if you are given a day off, by the management, ie Dupont Enterprises, you must still attend the gig and be available.' The waiter arrived and handed us both a menu and then poured us each a glass of wine. I sipped on the wine as John continued.

'But apart from that there's nothing too untoward in there. The only thing that's concerning me, and please be aware that I want you to do this tour probably more than anyone else in the world, is that it's all so rushed. This Chas fellow would have had to have booked the gigs well in advance, at least six months ago. And then he has to organise publicity, ticket sales, hotels, transport, a road crew, merchandise. Either the man's a complete buffoon who is going to lose a lot of money or he's prepared everything well in advance.'

'Well Chas is a lot of things but he's no buffoon and he's certainly averse to losing money.' I replied thoughtfully.

'Well then it must be the latter. He must have planned this months and months ago and if that is the case how was he so sure that he could get the Tsars onboard? That is if you are onboard?'

'Hmm,' I pondered.

We ordered our food and went over the subject a few more times until our meals arrived at which point we changed the subject and began talking about our families and interests while indulging in seafood pasta and ordering a further bottle of wine.

I liked John, he was a good man and after being surrounded by so many wankers when I was in the Tsars, it was refreshing. It was a welcome change to have a conversation with an intelligent and refined man.

We returned to the subject of setting up our own website and being in control of everything we did, which made me feel exhilarated and happy. John even said I should keep a tour diary that could be published on the website as a "blog", whatever that was. And then we talked about the upcoming tour, Chas and the contract, which made me feel anxious and a little fearful. We finished off with a large cognac as I pulled a pen from my pocket and tore the top off my cigarette packet.

'So John, I know entertainment lawyers don't come cheap, so send your bill to this address,' I said scribbling on the piece of cardboard before handing it to him. He grabbed it from me, gave it a quick perusal and slipped it into his back trouser pocket.

'Nonsense,' he replied, 'I don't want paying. Remember I'm your biggest fan, this is a fantasy come true for me.' I tried to intervene.

'No John, come on …'

'No Will, I won't hear of it. All I ask of you, is that if you do the tour, maybe you could get me on the guest list for one of the London shows, maybe even backstage.'

'Of course, it would be a pleasure.' He beamed like he'd just won the lottery.

'Now, you have my business card, I urge you to call me any time of day or night if you have any concerns or anything untoward happens—I mean it. And at some point we will need to get together to discuss the finer machinations of publishing, that's if you decide to go DIY.'

'Okay, no problem. You could always come up to my place in the Dales for a weekend. We could discuss it over a good long walk and a few refreshing ales in my local.'

'What a splendid idea, I'm afraid I may take you up on that. It would be great to get away from the city for a while.'

We finally left the quiet hubbub of the restaurant, satiated and a little merry and re-entered the noisy clamour of the street. We shook hands again.

'Well, I think I may finish early today. I can't be looking at contracts after over imbibing. Well, good luck with everything Will and keep in touch. Remember I have a lot of influential contacts, all you need to do is call.'

'Thanks John, I will, I'll be in touch about the guest pass.'

'That would be marvellous Will, thank you. Now take care and I'll speak to you soon.'

'And you,' I said as I turned to walk away. He called after me,

'Oh Will, I forgot to ask,' he dropped his head and rubbed the underside of his chin.

'Yes, what is it?'

'Do you still have a copy of your old recording contract? The GMC one?' It was a strange request and I was a bit taken aback.

'Well, yes, somewhere, I'd have to dig it out, why?'

201

'Would it be possible for you to scan it and email me a copy?' I was puzzled but didn't see any harm in it.

'I suppose so, but why?' I persisted. He smiled widely showing off a set of immaculate white teeth.

'Don't worry it's nothing to worry about. Just wanted to check a few things out that's all.'

'Okay, next time I'm home I'll have a look for it.' I bade him farewell again and began to walk up the narrow lane back towards the tube station.

'Oh and Will!' he shouted after me for the last time, 'good luck!'

#

When I got back to the hotel I rounded the boys up and we sat in my room as I went through the contract with them. I let the boys know the importance of not missing a gig.

'What's all that about? Why would he put in such a clause?' asked Flaky.

'I'm not sure,' I replied. 'The only thing I can think of is it's his way to catch us out and reduce our money. If the tour bombs he can cut his costs by telling one of the bands that they won't be playing on a certain night … he could use any excuse, like we're behind schedule and there isn't enough time for all four bands to play. Then, if that band doesn't show up at the gig—bingo, he can legitimately reduce their tour money by twenty five percent. Oh, and lastly, we're not guaranteed to be headlining …'

There was much consternation and cursing of Chas but I told the boys to play the bastard at his own game. Give nothing away and play it cool. Whatever happens we must all be available to play at every gig. That was the golden rule. They all agreed and we cracked open a bottle of champagne stolen from Flaky's bar fridge. We discussed whether we should inform the other bands that we'd be performing with about the clause and decided against it at present. Not because we were bastards but we didn't see any point in starting the rumour mill on a hunch of what might happen. We finished the champers and headed out into the night to find another good curry house.

20: DOGS OF STRAW

I deliberately rose early so I could have some breakfast in peace, forgetting that Flaky, the religious and health nutjob, would already have been up for a good hour or more. Sure enough, there he was sitting in the hotel dining room masticating dried prunes and porridge as I casually sauntered in at six fifteen.

'Hey Will, over here!' he waved to get my attention. I reluctantly went over.

'Morning Flaky, how are you?'

'Top of the world Will, top of the world. I'm really looking forward to getting behind the kit today. It's been a long time so I may be a bit rusty around the edges.'

'You'll be fine mate, it'll be like falling off a bike,' I encouraged. I began to make my way over to the breakfast bar but was pulled back by Flaky.

'Will, I need to speak to you about Robbo.' He stared up at me with his big doughy eyes, all concerned and sincere.

'Well I'm just going to get some brekky,' I made to leave again. He grabbed my hand which I instinctively pulled away, naturally repulsed by another man's touch so early in the morning. He seemed a trifle surprised at my reaction.

'I'll be brief,' he said. I relented and sat down.

'What, what is it? Go on then, what?' I said grumpily.

'Well, I spent most of the day with Robbo yesterday while you were sorting out the contracts and I must say I was very concerned to see the amount of drugs he takes.'

'He's a big boy Flaky, he's been doing drugs since before we formed the band. I can't see how it's done him much harm yet. I think he's a moderate user.'

'Moderate user!' he exclaimed releasing a half chewed dried prune onto his chin. 'Moderate user,' he repeated.

'Well I'm glad we both agree,' I said, standing to get my food. He grabbed my hand once more. That was it, I couldn't help myself.

'Don't fucking do that!' I shouted pulling the offended appendage away.

'Don't do what?' he yelled back. I noticed a couple of business types who were previously busy reading their papers, glare at us with disdain.

'Don't touch my hand okay!' I explained in a forced whisper.

'Well pardon me, I didn't realise you were so homophobic.'

'What are you on about? I'm not homophobic.'

'Well it seems to me that if you're afraid of another man's touch it could be an indication of repressed sexual tendencies towards your own gender.'

'Bollocks!'

I went and collected a plate and stacked it up as high as I could with bacon, sausage and fried eggs along with a large mug of coffee and a glass of orange juice. I returned to the table where Flaky was gently sipping on some herbal tea. I banged my king sized tray down in front of him. I saw his mouth curl and his head shake but I ignored him and tucked into my carnivores delight.

'At least eight spliffs, three snorts of what was either speed or coke and a couple of tablets that he took, which, when I asked what they were, he replied "male contraceptive pills". It's not funny Will!' I couldn't help chortling when I thought of poor old Robbo spending a whole day with Flaky—served the dope-head right.

'I think he's got a serious habit and after this tour we need to get him into rehab.'

'Oh back off Flaky, it's hardly Sid Vicious stuff is it. I mean, he's not shooting up heroin; a few spliffs and a bit of whizz isn't a big deal. He's been doing that level of shit for the last fifteen years, he's never escalated, he knows what his limits are, it's purely recreational,' I mumbled through a mouthful of bacon and egg.

'Hmm, maybe you're right, but all the same it can't be doing him any good.'

I spent the next fifteen minutes listening to Flaky's nagging and scolding and instead of enjoying my breakfast and relaxing slowly into a new day I ended up with indigestion and a spinning head. As he waffled on and on I slowly switched off. I stared at him blankly as words tumbled out of his mouth like lava spewing forth from an angry volcano. My eyes glazed over and slowly his head turned into that of a giant rat, his voice became a high pitched squeak and it wasn't until he barked a question that I was finally brought back to reality.

'Well, are we agreed? Well, well, do you agree? Well, do you?' I didn't have a fucking clue what he was on about but I agreed anyway just to shut the bastard up.

'Yes.'

'Good. Right, I'm heading back to my room to do a Yoga work out and then I'm going to ring my wife. I think we should be prompt for the rehearsal we don't want to appear slovenly, not on the first day. According to Robbo the rehearsal rooms are about forty minutes away, so what do you say that I round everyone up at about 10 am?'

'Yeah, sounds good Flaky.' With that he was gone, thank God. I went back to my room and laid down, tired, bloated and pissed off. I had a little speed and within ten minutes I was back on top of things. I gave my Mother a call and gave her an update on proceedings and checked on the well being of Caesar. I was really missing the old dog. She said he was fine and told me to give Fiona a call as she'd been asking after me.

'She's been asking about me?'

'That's what I said, are you going deaf with all that rock and roll?' I had to tread carefully, Mother was good at picking up anything untoward but luckily I knew how to play her like a fiddle.

'She didn't say anything, erm, unusual then?'

'No of course not why would she?' she replied indignantly.

'Oh, no reason.'

'Will, what have you done? Tell me, I know you've done something, I hope you haven't ruined your chance of happiness!' She's onto me; damn that fiddle!

'It's nothing, really. I just got a bit tongue tied on her answering machine that's all, and I suppose it may have sounded a bit funny when she played it back.'

'Funny?' she asked suspiciously, 'funny Haha, or funny peculiar?'

'Erm, I suppose peculiar.'

'You suppose peculiar? But you're not sure?' Mother had definitely missed her vocation—MI6 would have been proud of her.

'Well, maybe more creepy, than peculiar,' I replied foolishly.

'Creepy, creepy! What do you mean by creepy?' It took me ten minutes to explain myself and convince Mother that I was not a sex pest; her own son; how could she think such a thing. After I hung up I decided to bite the bullet and call Fiona again. I prayed it wasn't the answering machine. I would be surprised if she even wanted to speak to me after my last call. The phone rang four times and then a click as the answering machine kicked in, 'Hello you've called Fiona, I'm sorry ...'

'Oh for fuck's sake,' I said disappointedly. I was about to hang up when I heard her voice.

'Ah, so this is my nuisance caller. I wondered when you'd call back.'

'Hey, Fiona, how ya doing? Yeah, I'm sorry about that other call, I sort of got all tongue tied and everything came out wrong and ...'

'Don't worry, I found it very amusing.'

'Oh good, you didn't think it was weird then.'

'Noooo! Well just a little!' We both laughed and I felt a lot more relaxed. The trouble with speed, is that you never want to shut up talking and before I knew it we'd been on the phone for nearly an hour.

'Listen Will, I love talking to you but I really need to start getting the kids ready for school and kinder ...'

'Shit, I'm sorry, I just got carried away ... it's just so nice to speak to you.' I meant it and she sounded pleased.

'Aw, that's very sweet. Why don't you give me a call tonight and we can talk as long as you like.'

'Okay, that sounds great, what time?'

'Anytime from seven thirty onwards after I've got the kids to bed and read them books.' We said our goodbyes and I lay back on my bed feeling pleased with myself, confident, assured and happy—it didn't last long.

Within ten minutes all hell had broken loose. There was a ruckus emanating from down the hallway, or to be more precise, from Geordie's room—where else? By the time I arrived, to quell the racket, there was a petty argument raging between Geordie and Flaky; what was it about I wondered? Religion, drugs, vegetarianism, politics the environment? No—none of the aforementioned—it was about apples and beer! Geordie had managed to give Flaky a swollen eye by throwing an apple at him, accidentally, or so he said. Apparently, Flaky had requested some fruit in return for some beers that Geordie had purloined from Flaky's bar fridge the previous evening. Geordie had obliged by launching a large Granny Smith at Flaky who managed to catch it with his right eye socket.

As Flaky sat nursing a stinging eye, Robbo walked in with a monster spliff hanging out of his mouth. This set Flaky off on another "anti-drugs" rant. I must concede, he did have a point, after all, it was only eight thirty in the morning. Robbo, for once, lost his cool and told Flaky to wind his scrawny neck in, which in turn, prompted another heated argument.

Meanwhile, Geordie was in the bathroom, happily drying his hair with an electric hairdryer and wet shaving at the same time. Never one to miss out on a good stoush, he kept the fires burning by lobbing a few verbal grenades into the mix. His missiles were mostly aimed at Flaky, but with great aplomb, he also managed to slander the Pope, defame Prince Charles and question the parentage of Oliver Cromwell—how his mind worked was an unfathomable mystery. Unfortunately, unaccustomed as he was to the dark art of multi-tasking, he soon forgot which hand was which. This resulted in him attempting to shave his beard with a hot hairdryer and dry his hair with a safety razor. The dual surprise of singeing his left cheek and witnessing a large chunk of forelock dislodge itself from his gargantuan sized head, made him release the hairdryer into the sink full of water. Electricity's immutable relationship with the laws of physics immediately took hold. There was a loud crackle followed by an even louder bang. Geordie stumbled out of the bathroom like a shell-shocked soldier from the WWI trenches. Hair standing on end, eyes vacant and bulging, he looked like a giant porcupine that had just been informed there was a new tax on pointy things.

'What the f ... f ... fuck was that?' he stammered. At least it ended the drugs debate between Flaky and Robbo, and for that I was thankful.

'Well done Geordie—nice circuit breaker.'

#

We managed to get to the hotel's underground car park at about eleven. Already an hour behind schedule. The bickering had never stopped and I was caught in the middle trying to play peacemaker and police officer. The musical gear was packed into the back of Robbo's

209

Mercedes van. All three of them were still arguing and bitching as Geordie tried the passenger side door.

'It's locked you idiot!' shouted Robbo as he fumbled for his keys. There was a clunk and the door swung open.

'Oh, I see, locked is it,' sneered Geordie sarcastically. Robbo momentarily appeared concerned before returning to his normal indifferent poise.

'Well nothings been nicked has it, so we're all right,' Robbo stated confidently.

'Well how do you know? Have you checked the back?' asked Flaky in a concerned manner. Robbo went to pull open the back doors but Flaky beat him to it.

'I can't believe you'd be so stupid as to leave it unlocked!' screeched Flaky. 'I've got an expensive drum kit in here, that's a lot of money.'

'Flaky, you've had that drum kit for over twenty years, it's worth jack shit. No thief worth his salt would bother with that heap of crap,' replied Robbo as he stuck his head in the back of the van and surveyed the contents. 'Two Marshall stacks, Vox AC30, six electrics, two bass, two acoustics, effects pedals and boards, mixing desk, tape deck, trunk of odds and sods. Oh and yes, one fucked up, knackered Ludwig drum kit. Yep, seems like everything's here.' Robbo pushed Flaky out of the way as he slammed the doors shut.

'That kit is a classic, it's a collectable, it's vintage,' whined Flaky unable drop the issue.

'Oh aye, it's vintage alright, fucking obsolete and for good reason,' said Geordie, always ready to rattle the cage.

'Come on let's just get in and get going shall we,' I muttered. I was sick of their sniping and wanted to get to the studios. Geordie snorted and jumped into the front of the van, I climbed in next to him and Robbo strapped himself into the driver's seat. Flaky stood indignantly outside holding onto the passenger door. There was only room for two passengers in the front.

'Oh, that's right, self, self, self. First you leave the van unlocked putting all our gear at risk,' moaned Flaky.

'All my gear,' interjected Robbo.

'And then you two decide, without any consultation may I add, that you are going to sit up front.'

'Oh fuck off and get in the back Flaky, you sound like an old hen,' chided Geordie.

'First in best dressed,' I offered him in consolation. Robbo fired the engine, which echoed around the underground chamber.

'C'mon Flaky, there's a comfortable bench seat in the back.' Robbo encouraged.

'No, I refuse to budge. This has got to be decided democratically, not by bully boy tactics. I'm making a stand now otherwise I'm going to be treated like a second class citizen for the rest of the tour.' He was adamant. I was about to offer up my seat to keep the peace, as I knew Geordie wouldn't, when Robbo turned to us.

'Hang on a minute, I wasn't the last to get something out of the van.' He stared at Geordie. 'You asked me for the keys yesterday to come and get the bass remember, you wanted to put new strings on it.' Geordie went silent and thought for a moment. What it mattered—I did not know, but this lot were not the type to let things lie. A smile spread across Geordie's face.

'Aye, that's right and I passed the keys onto Flaky who wanted to put a new skin on his snare. He was the one who left the van unlocked!' We all turned to Flaky, who suddenly turned crimson.

'I'll get in the back then, I'm sure it's very comfortable.'

\#

We got to Bell Rehearsal Rooms only two hours late and were still the first ones there. The manager of the rooms, Mick, told us that

211

Chas had rung ahead to say he was caught in traffic. Mick could only be described as an ageing hippy. He looked a bit like David Crosby from Crosby, Stills and Nash fame, except he talked with a strong Brummie accent, wore a calliper and brandished a walking stick. Robbo obviously knew him quite well the way they did the high fives and back slaps.

'Hey man, good to see you again, it's been a while now, how have you been?' exclaimed Mick.

'Hey, right on man, right on, yeah it's been what, oh let me see, I came down here to get some demo tapes for that bunch of toilet seat sniffers "HUG", what, about twelve, eighteen months ago?'

'Shit! Is it that long ago, wow, tempus fugit man, tempus fugit! What happened to Hug?'

'First album flopped, record company dropped them quicker than a hot turd and now they're all doing shit jobs paying off the advance.' Robbo pulled out a pre-rolled spliff from his shirt pocket and sparked up. Flaky shook his head.

'You guys want a guided tour while we're waiting for Chas?' Mick asked looking at the rest of us.

'Yeah, that would be good.' I replied. Mick led the way, hobbling off in front. Geordie was never backward in coming forward and inevitably, curiosity got the better of him.

'Hey Mick, how'd you get the gammy leg?'

'Motorbike accident in seventy two.' It sounded impressive. It conjured up mental images of a young, carefree hippie travelling the Californian highways on a Harley with a bronzed, golden haired beach babe riding pillion while Steppen Wolf's "Born To Be Wild" played in the background. I could almost picture Peter Fonda and Jack Nicholson flanking Mick as they gunned their engines down a drug induced highway to hell.

'Bluddy came off me moped just outside Woolies in Birmingham when a daft old biddy stepped out in front of me, I swerved and went into the back of a hamburger stall. They took two inches out of my femur and put six pins in my hip.' How easily illusions are shattered.

Mick showed us around six large professional rehearsal rooms. Each one was the size of a small dance hall with its own stage, large PA, lights, mixing desk, bar fridge and mirrored walls. There was also a viewing area at the back of each room where onlookers could sit and watch, which could only be entered from the outside of the room.

'Which one is ours?' asked Geordie.

'Whichever you like, they're all exactly the same and seeing as you're the first to turn up, you get first pick.' said Mick.

'Okay, we'll take studio one,' continued Geordie triumphantly as though he'd scored some coup over the other acts. As we walked back to reception, we passed a large, wide stairway that led to a mezzanine floor.

'What's up there?' asked Geordie.

'That's room 101,' replied Mick enthusiastically. 'That's where the big boys play. Mind you, they pay for it—3k a day it costs, but it is the bee's bollocks.' I pondered for a few seconds whether bees actually had testicles or not.

'Can we have a look?' badgered Geordie.

'Sure.' said Mick. We all trooped upstairs and entered through two large doors into a room that was enormous. It would have been three times the size of the other rehearsal rooms.

'Fucking what!' exclaimed Geordie, obviously impressed.

'Hmm, pretty cool isn't it?' nodded Robbo who had evidently seen the room before. 'Acoustic wall tiles, large bass arrestors at the back to eat up the boom, tiled sweet spot over there to get a bit out of the vocals, it's even got its own light show. You see that piano over there,' Robbo pointed at the far wall where a large black shiny grand piano stood, 'that is only the piano that Paul McCartney sang "Let It Be" on.' We were all suitably impressed. Geordie went across and lovingly stroked the black shiny wood. Robbo continued his appraisement. 'Yep, this is state of the art, you can record albums in here, live. Best rehearsal room in the world they reckon and I'm inclined to believe them. Hug insisted rehearsing here. I told them they were wasting their money the other rooms would suit them just fine, but they just laughed and said the record company was paying for it. Yeah, sure—the record company's paying for it—my arse! I told them it would come out of any future royalties. Those bastards wouldn't give you the steam off their shit, they make it appear like it's their money, that's why they appear so generous and extravagant, it's easy to be like that when you know it's someone else's dough your blowing. But did they listen? Did they hell as like.' Without saying anything there was a common acknowledgement in the truth of Robbo's words. We all ambled back down the stairs where Mick was standing with a brew in his hand.

'So who's been up there recently?' asked Flaky. Mick bent closer towards him, staring intently into Flaky's face.

'Let me think now,' he rubbed his chin while chasing his memories, 'ah, yes, we had U2 in there six months back and before that we had Paul Weller and before him it was Van Morrison …'

'That'd be right,' snorted Geordie, 'U bloody 2!'

'And what's wrong with U2 may I ask?' challenged Flaky.

'Have you got a spare hour? I'll tell you what's wrong with them …' Flaky and Geordie entered into a heated argument about the merits or not, of U2. Mick continued his recollections to no-one in particular.

'… and before that was it REM or was it the Stones?' I wandered off with Robbo towards the lift that led to the underground car park. The voices of Mick, Geordie and Flaky became faint as the lift doors thankfully shut and Robbo handed me the remaining length of his spliff.

'Thanks, I need this.' I took a long toke and felt my tensions begin to ease.

'It's not going to be easy man, it's not going to be easy at all,' conceded Robbo. I nodded in agreement.

#

An hour later, we were all set up in studio one. There was still no sign of Chas or any of the other bands and I was beginning to wonder if the whole thing was an elaborate hoax by some disgruntled figure from our past. I quickly tried to think of people that we'd previously offended but instantly gave up as the imaginary list soon tailed off into infinity.

Mick set up the mixing desk while the rest of us set up our gear and individually sound checked. I felt nervous. *What if we're shit? What if we've lost it? What if we'd never had it?* Behind me Flaky was doing one drum roll after another before stopping to adjust his hi-hat and snare. He sounded quite tight and I was pleasantly surprised. I pulled out four sheets of paper containing a setlist that I'd worked on the previous night. It was the cream of our three albums and ten singles. Not all my personal favourites, but it was what the public would easily recognise.

'Okay boys,' I handed them out expecting argument and confrontation. They all stopped what they were doing and studied the list. In the past, setlists had always been a source of argument. There were a few raised eyebrows but much to my relief no-one said anything. We were ready. I taped my setlist to the floor and stared down in trepidation. Mick raised his thumb to signal he was good to go. I counted us in, turning to face the other three.

'A one, two, three, four.' The hi-hat burst into life and Geordie began his melodic run on the bass as Robbo stroked crystal clear open chords on his guitar. I opened my mouth and the words came easily, clearly, naturally.

#

The set took just over an hour. There were no breaks, no disputes, no bickering. It may have been a long time since we were last together as a band but it sounded like we'd never been apart. It felt good, better than good, it felt liberating and exciting. As the last chord of the last song died away, I turned around to face the band with a satisfied

215

smile on my face. They all smiled back. Mick gave us a rousing cheer and ecstatic hand clap.

'Fooking great boys, fooking great!'

'Shit, that was good!' I exclaimed.

'That was better than good Billy boy, that was the tops!' corrected Geordie. Robbo sat on his amp and pulled out another pre-rolled joint from his shirt pocket, lit it, inhaled deeply and handed it on to me.

'Yep, man, that was sweet. Not much rust on this old bike.' I took a drag and passed it onto Geordie who quickly disappeared in a blue haze.

'I can't believe that I could remember all the songs. I've been listening to the old CDs but still, it all came back as though I'd never been away.' Flaky was clearly impressed with his own performance.

'Okay space cadets, let's do it all again, this time for real!'

Half way through the set I noticed a couple of figures enter the viewing area at the back of the room. The lights were down and it was hard to make out who they were. I turned to face my band once again. Geordie was stood legs akimbo, head back and eyes closed, his trademark stance. Robbo was bobbing and weaving, fingers like slivers of silk up and down the neck of his guitar. Flaky, hunched over, head swaying from side to side in time with his beats. As the last notes of "Quadro" faded and before we launched into the next song, the door burst open and someone marched in, clapping and shouting "more, more". As the figure came closer to the stage, I assessed his appearance. Early fifties, five and a half feet tall, grey curly hair, white trainers, tight jeans, lived in jacket with patches on the elbows, John Lennon style spectacles with thick glass, behind which sat a pair of sapphire blue eyes, sharp and glassy.

'Chas Dupont has entered the building!' I boomed through the microphone.

'Oh boys, boys, you haven't changed a bit, maybe a few wrinkles, an extra few pounds, the odd fleck of grey, but still the same shit hot musicians from all those years ago. Geez, you sound so tight! I didn't

216

expect you to be this good after all this time.' He made his way to the stage and jumped up, trying to show that he was still young and sprightly himself, unfortunately his foot caught the edge of the stage and he managed to land with a loud thump on one of his knees. He let out a muted, "Oh fuck" before rising slowly and holding out his hand to me.

'Will, you look marvellous, how's it been?' I shook his hand, cautiously and without much enthusiasm.

'Yeah good Chas, very good.'

'Robbo my son, I hear you're one of the best producers going around.' Chas had always been an expert schmoozer—the trick was not to believe it too much. Robbo shook his hand with about as much ebullience as I had shown.

'Flaky, you look as fit as a butchers dog, what are you on Prozac? Viagra? Botox? What's your secret?' Flaky laughed a little, almost embarrassed.

'No, no drugs Chas. I'm totally clean, have been for years, that's why I look good. What you put in is what you get out.' He threw Robbo a superior glance and shook hands with Chas, showing a little more gusto than Robbo and me. There was a pregnant pause as Chas turned lastly to Geordie, who was sitting on his amp staring down at his bass, which was cradled in his large arms like a small child. He had a mean look on his face; not a good sign. Chas seemed a little nervous but held his hand out nonetheless.

'And of course, Allan, me old mucker, how have you been my big Scottish warrior?' A couple of seconds passed but it felt like an eternity. I held my breath and I could see Robbo and Flaky both tense up as well. In what seemed like slow motion, Geordie, slowly and gracefully began to rise from his amp. His body began to extend—legs that went on forever, arms, torso, head, a forest of wild straggly hair all expanding upwards and outwards. He looked like a giant octopus that had been rudely awoken from slumber. He towered over Chas by a good twelve inches, more like fifteen with his cowboy heels. Chas gawped nervously

217

upwards. It didn't look good and I stepped forward slightly just in case I had to intervene.

'Let's put the past behind us hey Allan?' A bead of sweat appeared on Chas's forehead and I noticed his fingers trembling slightly. I felt a tinge of sympathy for the old larrikin. 'Let bygones be bygones eh?' Whatever Chas had or hadn't done in the past I couldn't stand public humiliations. Geordie finally spoke.

'What? Shake hands with a low-down, dirty, double-dealing, backstabbing, soft-soaping, shandy drinking, lying, knock-kneed, pigeon toed, spineless, rubber lipped, forked tongued, lizard eyed, wire haired, floppy eared, short-arsed, limp dicked, cock-smoking, arse licking, brown nosing, two-faced, turncoat, pig wanker, Judas SHIT TURD LIKE YOU!' There was silence. A couple more beads of sweat appeared on Chas's brow. The tension in the air was conspicuous; if it could have been tapped into, it would have kept the national grid going for days.

'C'mon Geordie, don't sugar coat it—tell Chas what you really think,' I said, trying to diffuse the situation. I thought I could discern Chas's heart pounding on his chest, pleading to get out. I glanced at Geordie then back at Chas and then back at Geordie again; it was like the stand off at the OK Corral. Almost imperceptibly at first, the corner of Geordie's mouth began to curl, not down but up, and within a few seconds there was definitely the beginning of a grin. I sensed Chas breathe a sigh of relief as he too began a cautious smile. Then the moment, the defining moment, like Armstrong's first step on the moon or maybe more like the bullet from the grassy knoll, Geordie reached out and grabbed Chas's outstretched hand of friendship. I began to breathe again. Robbo reached into his shirt pocket and pulled out yet another spliff and sparked up. I was beginning to have my suspicions about that shirt pocket—did it in fact conceal a miniature troop of dope monkeys constantly rolling spliffs for their master? Flaky rubbed his hands together and did some neck exercises. Chas laughed, Geordie laughed, we all laughed. Nervously at first, then louder and more uncontrolled. It was infectious and the more we laughed the harder we laughed. Fuck knows what we were all laughing at. Chas laughed so hard that he fell onto one knee and then both knees while his hand was still attached to Geordies. Tears were streaming down his face. I stared at Geordie who was no longer laughing but grimacing. I looked back at Chas, whose tears of laughter, I realised, were actually tears of pain. Geordie was crushing the life out of his hand.

'Fucking hell Geordie!' I yelled. 'Let him go you dickhead!' Geordie relinquished his grip and Chas slumped onto his back holding the offending appendage in the air like a fleshy Excalibur.

'Oh,' he moaned, 'I think you've broken my hand.'

'It's not broken,' declared Geordie. 'I can feel when the bones begin to break and if I had wanted to break your hand I would have. Stop whining like a wuss, it's only pain.'

'You need help Geordie—you've got issues,' said Flaky. Chas slowly sat up.

'I guess I deserved that, for letting you boys down. I know you think I knew about the options deal that GMC held over you, but as God is my witness, I didn't. Maybe I should have, if I had done my homework and done my job correctly I should have known. If I'm guilty of anything it's incompetence, and for that, yes I deserve your scorn, your criticism, even Geordie's violence, but I don't deserve your hate, no-one deserves that.' It was quite a touching little speech and I actually believed him and by the look on Robbo's and Flaky's faces, they did too. Not so Geordie, who looked on impassively as he tenderly rubbed down his bass with a soft cloth. Chas rose to his feet, dusted off his pants, adjusted his spectacles, patted down his hair and waggled his hand.

'Allan?' The big fellow ignored him and continued his tender exertions. 'Allan, does this make us equal now?' Geordie stopped his cleaning and eyeballed Chas suspiciously.

'Well?' Chas asked softly.

'Aye, okay. The slates clean. But don't expect us to be bosom buddies. If you keep out of my way I'll keep out of yours.' Geordie always knew how to bury the hatchet, usually deep in the back of his antagonist's head.

'That's fair enough. A cordial working relationship is all I ask. Shake on it?' Chas held his hand out once again. I'll give him his dues, he had some nerve, either that or he'd recently had a lobotomy. Geordie shook his hand quickly and let it go this time.

'Right, anyone fancy a pint and a pickled egg?' shouted Robbo.

'That's the most sensible thing you've said all day,' agreed Geordie.

#

By the time we got back to the rehearsal rooms in the late afternoon there was an unholy commotion raging and for once it was nice to stand on the sidelines and watch as a dispassionate spectator. Mick later told me how it all started. Apparently, the Green Circles (the four Scousers) had turned up not long after we'd all left for the pub. Mick had told them to set up wherever they wanted, apart from studio one where we were. This they did. Unbeknownst to Mick they set up in Room 101, the aircraft hanger. Ten minutes later, the Stoned Crows turned up. Lead singer, Paul Effingham (Effy), immediately upset the apple cart by throwing a "tortured artist style" tantrum at Mick and the Scousers, insisting that they, the Stoned Crows had been "bigger" than the Green Circles and therefore they should have the biggest room. This didn't go down particularly well with the four Liverpool lads, who point blank refused to budge. The Crows decided to take matters into they're own hands by first setting up in the same room as the Circles and then by trying to forcibly eject the alleged cuckoos. Not very sensible behaviour from fully grown men who were fast racing toward middle age—but if my lot were anything to go by it was par for the course.

Although outgunned five to four, the Green Circles were more than a match for the southern boys. One Crow was thrown down the stairs resulting in a badly bruised arm. Not far behind, followed the Crows bass drum, which, after descending the stairs at high speed, managed to career off into an onrushing Mick, skittling him like a ten-pin.

The ensuing fight descended down the stairs and into the reception area like an old "wild west saloon" brawl scene. By the time we arrived, Paul Effingham was trying to protect himself from a very short bald man, who was swinging a microphone stand around his head. The microphone's heavy metal base would have inflicted serious injury to anyone it connected with. I suddenly realised the short bald man was "Connie" and I wondered what had happened to his famous afro hairdo.

Elsewhere, someone else was having his head rammed against a drinks machine, which I perceived, they were not enjoying one little bit. The soft-drinks machine graciously spilt a random selection of its contents. Coke, 7-Up and Fanta cascaded around the floor. Bodies began to trip and roll on the cans; arses went up and tits came down. Fizzy drink spewed forth in frothy jets, spraying anyone who was stupid enough to be within spitting distance of the melee. I leant against a wall next to Robbo, well out of harm's way. Flaky was a little closer and managed to get a spray of coke in his face—the nearest thing he'd ever get to doing drugs again.

Geordie meanwhile, had taken up position at the top of the stairs and sat down to watch the proceedings, with obvious merriment. Suddenly, Chas appeared from nowhere; he seemed a little bewildered at first, but once he'd perceived the situation and taken in what was happening, he ran into Mick's office and returned with a large, old fashioned, schoolyard bell and began ringing it furiously while screaming,

'Enough, that's it, enough! Do you hear me!'

Slowly but surely, the altercation came to a stuttering end. One Crow lay on the floor, moaning lowly as he held his arm up in pain.

221

Three men emerged from a scuffle on the floor. The soft drinks machine banger and bangee stopped their madness and the whirring sound of the gyrating mic stand slowly came to a halt.

They stood and lay there, dripping in soft drink—a couple with bloody noses, some with ruffled hair and all with puffed up red faces due to their exertions. Debris from what used to be a bass drum lay next to a mangled Rickenbacker guitar. A coke can did its last dying waltz, spinning around and around sending a fine spray into the air before settling in a corner to expire. The bell stopped ringing. There was silence for a few seconds. This was rudely broken by the sound of a "ping" as the lift doors opened and a soft, sexy, refined, female voice captured everyone's attention.

'Hello boys, not fighting over me already are you?' All eyes turned to witness a Goddess step gracefully from the lift; long jet black hair, porcelain skin, tall, well toned thighs, buttocks that could crack walnuts, ruby red lips and almond shaped twinkling brown eyes—Divina had entered our world!

21: I HOPE YOU HAD THE TIME OF YOUR LIFE

When tempers had calmed down and the Stoned Crows and Green Circles had reluctantly shaken hands, Chas informed them that neither band would be rehearsing in Room 101 due to the cost; that was only for the "really" big stars he informed them, much to Effy's indignation.

Chas led us all into a conference room off from reception where there was a row of chairs lined out in front of a large projector screen. As we all trooped in there was still some ongoing cursing and argy-bargy between the Circles and the Crows. We were ushered into our seats by Chas who was pleading for quiet. A young, scruffy looking man appeared at Chas's side. He was short and fat and sported a long pony tail and equally long goatee. His demeanour could only be described as teenage sullen, although he must have been thirty, if he was a day.

'Okay boys, boys, and girl, or should I say Lady,' Chas began. A chorus of "oo's" went up and everyone turned to stare at Divina, who shuffled uncomfortably in her chair and appeared a trifle embarrassed— Chas continued.

'Right, this is going to take about an hour. I'm going to run through the tour schedule, the contracts, the rules and regulations. Please don't interrupt, you can ask as many questions as you like at the end. Now I am the promoter and tour manager and Jez,' he turned towards the sullen looking man, 'Jez is assistant Tour Manager and he's also my right hand man. When I'm not around, Jez is head honcho.' It didn't take long for the pompous Effy to pipe up.

'What experience has he had? I don't recognise him? I'd prefer to use my own crew.' Chas seemed impatient and took his glasses off as he rubbed his eyes. He took a handkerchief out of his pocket and began to clean his glasses with barely disguised annoyance.

'Jez, would you be so kind as to give us a quick rundown of your resume for the last ten years?' requested Chas impatiently. Jez shuffled forward and in a gruff northern accent he began;

'94, guitar roadie for the Stones world tour. '96 guitar roadie for Oasis, Black Sabbath and Fleetwood Mac. '97 and '98 Tour manager for Elvis Costello, Van Morrison, Joe Strummer, the Pogues and Lindisfarne. '99, Tour Manager Ocean Colour Scene, Oasis, Supernaturals, 2000 ...' Chas interrupted,

'Thanks Jez, I think the point's been made.' Effy looked a little deflated but didn't know when to shut up.

'All I was saying was that I haven't seen him around the traps for the last ten years!'

'Well that's hardly surprising considering you've been playing bingo halls and pubs while Jez has been frequenting the biggest stadiums around the world,' declared Chas smugly.

'Well maybe we should take a vote on it, you know a sort of referendum.' Effy didn't get any further with his pointless whining—Chas exploded.

'Now listen here and listen good,' he screeched, 'let's get this straight, right now! This tour is not a fucking democracy, it's not a vehicle for over-inflated egos and pompous arseholes. It's a dictatorship and I'm Mussolini, right! You do what I say, when I say and don't question me. If you don't like it pack up your gear right now and sod off and I'll forward you the bill for your rehearsal, accommodation and meal costs.' He was red in the face and shaking with anger. The Tsars had witnessed these blow outs many times before in the past. At first they'd been disconcerting and quite intimidating, but it didn't take us long to realise that Chas's bark was worse than his bite. Of course the other groups didn't realise this and sat quietly like reprimanded schoolboys in front of the headmaster. Effy stared back in defiance but said nothing. Chas calmed down as a quiet fell over the room. Geordie stretched out his legs and yawned, unimpressed with Chas's show of authority.

'Right let's move on. Jez, lights please and we'll roll the film.' Jez turned the lights off and flicked a switch on a projector. A clapperboard came down and so began thirty minutes of animated instruction. Chas was the main star of course. He stood centre stage as he ran through the cities and concert halls and arenas we were to play. He discussed our remuneration, and that we'd all be paid no later than one month after completion of the tour. The money would be paid to each act, not individuals, how each act split the money up was up to them. He explained accommodation, riders, meal allowances and transport. Riders were extremely important to bands—they were a perk of the job. They consisted of everything a band wanted backstage such as what type of food and drinks to be supplied. Some artists even specified certain hand creams, aromatherapy oils and a personal masseuse to be available. Chas then went through the "publicity" itinerary, which stipulated which artist was to do what on each day. There was at least sixty press, radio and TV interviews scheduled and undoubtedly the list would grow bigger as the tour began. I noticed with some relief the Tsars had been spared the ignominy of appearing on TV chat shows. This had been left to the Circles, the Crows and Divina. It was probably a good call as the Tsars had never been comfortable or particularly photogenic under studio lights and there was always a chance that Geordie would go "off script". Instead we were handed a few radio interviews and the usual music press. He laid out the rotation policy of which bands were going to open the shows and which were going to headline. The timetable was written in stone. Chas had evidently done his homework and I must admit I had a sneaking respect for his attention to detail. I also knew the reason why. He was doing this tour on a budget. He wasn't certain how it would go, that's why he was cutting his cloth to suit. If the wheels fell off and the tour was a disaster he or his backers were going to be out of pocket big time, the last thing he needed on top of that was a runaway budget. He'd worked everything out to the last penny, as far as one could, and I didn't blame him, I'd have done the same. I'd never been one for the extravagant trappings of rock and roll stardom.

At the height of our fame we were offered and encouraged by the record company to travel everywhere by limousine, to stop in the penthouse suites of the best hotels, to frequent the trendiest and most expensive nightclubs. We tried it for a while but it wasn't us, it made us feel like fakes. We were soon back to staying at mid-price hotels and spending the night in a local pub chatting with fans. Our only concession to luxury was a top of the range tour bus driven by our roadie who chauffeured us around wherever we wanted to go.

Just as everyone was getting bored, Chas dropped in his penalty clause. For each non-appearance by any act, regardless of reason, they would forfeit twenty five percent of their total remuneration. This was a big clause, but as I glanced around the room no-one else seemed to comprehend the full intent, apart from Robbo, who gave me a knowing glance.

Chas's presentation finally ended and he spent 10 minutes answering questions. He picked up a large bundle of papers from the desk and walked around handing a copy to everyone whilst hectoring us all.

'Okay, here is the itinerary, which is basically what you've just seen up on screen. This is the most important item of the tour. You MUST carry this with you at all times. It has dates, times, cities, hotels, addresses, telephone numbers. It lists what time the coach will be departing and who will be doing the publicity for that day. If your name is on there to do publicity, whether that be TV, radio or press, then DO NOT get on the tour bus. There will be a hire car that will be dropped off for you at the hotel. Follow the directions on the itinerary to the

LETTER! This tour is going to run like clockwork, like a well oiled machine.'

'Fuck me, it's the cliché kid,' Geordie whispered to me from behind his hand.

'If this tour is going to be a success then the itinerary is our bible. You are each personally responsible for knowing, where, when and what you are doing each day. Do I make myself clear.' A few of the jokers from the Green Circles all replied in unison,

'Yes Mr Dupont.' Chas ignored them but it resulted in a few chuckles.

'Right, finally, I hope you've all got your signed, witnessed and dated contracts with you, if you haven't, you won't be going on this tour. If you could all hand them over to Jez and he will get photocopies for you. And one member from each band needs to also hand their driving licence over as well. That person will be the nominated driver for the hire car on publicity days. No-one else can drive apart from that driver, understand? This does not apply to Divina as she will have a driver provided.'

'How come she gets a fucking driver?' questioned Effy appearing aggrieved.

'Because she doesn't have a licence, okay?' stated Chas forcefully. Jez walked around the room collecting the contracts and the licences from each nominated driver. Flaky volunteered himself to be our allotted driver, which I was thankful for at the time but would soon live to regret it.

#

It had now been nine days solid rehearsal since that first infamous meeting and eleven days and nights in all since I'd arrived in London. I was on edge. I missed my solitude, the peace and quiet and the sparkling fresh air of Whitstone and most of all my old dog Caesar. The weather was glorious, unusual for springtime in England and I lamented the fact that I could have been out walking the dales and moors of Yorkshire instead of being cooped up with a bunch of reprobates. But the first part was nearly over. We'd been booked in for fourteen days but we were ready. We'd been ready since about day three and knew our twenty song setlist back to front and blindfold. To relieve the monotony of going over the same setlist again and again, we'd started to play through some of the Bloom session songs. They sounded as crisp and as sharp as the day we recorded them. There was some debate as to whether we should include a few in the set but decided against it.

Chas insisted we stick to the game plan of fourteen days solid rehearsal. We weren't kids learning the ropes, we were all accomplished musicians and the ten years apart had not diminished that. Rehearsing the old songs was like slipping into a pair of warm, familiar slippers, it was easy. We usually made it to the rooms by about 11 am each day and practised until 2 pm, then broke for lunch. We resumed about and went until 5:30 pm before finishing for the day and hitting the town for a decent meal and a few drinks. Flaky would usually head off back to the hotel about 7 pm and the rest of us would dig out some real pubs and settle down for the evening. This was the usual routine. Occasionally some or all of the Green Circles would join us if we happened to finish at the same time. There was Connie their diminutive lead singer, Paddy their scrawny and wizened looking bass player, Ricky their overweight drummer with no neck, who was odd to say the least and lastly, Billy Hughes, a wonderful and inventive guitar player and also full time fence. They were all good lads, but they were always up to something. Connie was never off his mobile phone, speaking in some weird gang lingo that could only be to do with drugs or stolen goods. When he hung up he would always whisper something to Billy, who would say nothing but just nod enigmatically before retiring to a corner to converse on his mobile. Paddy, despite his decrepit look was a lively and amusing raconteur and did amazing impressions of unknown people. They rehearsed roughly the same time as us and we struck up a good friendship. Connie and Geordie got on especially well as they both had something in common—they both hated the Stoned Crows, in particular Effy. Connie was still as fit and agile as all those years ago when he used to perform his gymnastics on stage. When I quizzed him about his prowess he recalled his early life, brought up in the back streets of Liverpool. He'd ran away to the circus when he was thirteen, lied about his age and learnt all his routines there. When he wasn't doing dodgy deals, Connie would entertain the whole pub. His signature performance was to do a handstand on a table with a pint of beer balanced on each foot. Occasionally he'd do a cartwheel across the bar and backflip onto the floor just to break things up a bit. Whatever he did, he'd always receive huge cheers from the whole pub and people would buy drinks for him all night. He was also a contortionist and could stick his head right under his arse. Of course he got the usual question about whether he'd ever sucked himself off, to which he always replied, "Well, what would you do?" I eventually asked him what had happened to his huge afro.

'Playing a gig one night in Southampton, got an electric shock from the mic. It gave me a right belt. All my hair completely fell out, right there and then on stage.' I wasn't sure if the story was true or not, but if it was it would have been a sight to behold.

The constant eating out and late night drinking sessions had taken its toll on me. I weighed myself on the scales and had already packed on two kilo's and I'd developed love handles around my midriff for the first time. It also took me a good hour, three cups of coffee, six cigarettes and a dab of speed in the morning to get me going. It didn't seem to have any effect on either Robbo or Geordie though. I was willing to do the hard yards to build friendships with the Circles as we'd be on tour with them for over eight weeks. I knew we'd all get along fine, even the malevolent Geordie was happy in the Circles company. The Stoned Crows were another story though. I'm not one to harshly criticise my fellow musicians but in the case of the Stoned Crows I'll make an exception. Geordie was right after all, maybe he was a good judge of character. To put it bluntly, they were a bunch of wankers who were so far up themselves that they should have been locked up for self-abuse. Not only that, their music had not aged well. I made a point of slipping into the viewing areas at the back of the rehearsal rooms while each band (or artist in Divina's case) rehearsed. Divina was magnificent, ethereal, mesmerizing and powerful. It was impossible not to dance when you listened to her music. The Circles were shit hot; tight, infectious, lucid and uplifting. They were as fresh and exciting today as they had been ten years ago. Then there were the Stoned Crows; bloated, tedious, predictable and hackneyed. No substance—scratch below the surface and ... a vacuous waste of space.

Everyone could hear it and see it apart from themselves. They strutted around the rehearsal rooms as though they owned the place, barking orders at poor old Mick and whining like a 747 on the runway. The PA was crap, the lights didn't work, the stage was too small, the acoustics were rubbish; you name it and the Crows, in particular Effy, would complain about it. Effy was an imposing figure. He was nearly as tall as Geordie but carried a lot more weight. Where Geordie was tough, sinewy and chiselled, Effy was a little pink and flabby. But he was a good actor. He played the hard guy, the cool guy, the mysterious artist and although everyone from the bands involved saw through the masquerade, I could see how the public had been fooled by it. The guy still wore leather trousers for God's sake and there were also a few other curiosities about him. He always looked immaculate, in fact too immaculate. I was once chatting to him by the coffee machine when I noticed how jet black his hair and eyebrows were, how well manicured everything was. His face was tight and he had full rubbery lips. At first I didn't twig, but then I realised. He dyed his hair, he'd had a face lift and I suspected he'd had botox injections in his lips. I told the rest of the group about my suspicions and they concurred with my observations. From then on Geordie always referred to Effy as "Botox Boy".

The first time the Crows began rehearsing we were all sat in the kitchen having a refreshment break. It sounded like amateur night at the local youth club.

'What in hells name is that unholy commotion?' queried Geordie looking momentarily bewildered.

'That's the Crows. Wait till they really get going,' sniggered Robbo, 'they'll have you reaching for the Paracetamol quicker than you can say Duran Duran.'

'You don't mean we've got to put up with that abuse for eight weeks do you?' asked Geordie. I nodded my head. He screwed his face up as though someone had just shat in his cup of tea—which, metaphorically they had. The din from across the corridor abruptly stopped and a few seconds later the door to the Crows room was rudely flung open and out stomped Effy.

'Mick?' he yelled angrily. 'Mick get your snivelling arse out here right now! Mick? Where the fuck are you?' Effy spotted us all in the kitchen and marched over. 'This place is the fucking pits. Nothing works, the feedback is terrible. I've rehearsed in better toilets than this.' Geordie lifted his right arse cheek off the chair and let out a long musical fart.

'Now what's that about a workman and his tool?' feigned Geordie with a smirk. Effy picked up the inference and edged towards Geordie just as a clearly cowed Mick came hobbling in.

'What's the matter Effy? You having problems again.' Effy's attention was immediately diverted to poor old Mick.

'Yeah, you could say that, you thick brummie tosser. The feedback is playing fucking havoc with our performance. I suggest you shuffle your short fat arse into the room and sort it out. How can you expect us to rehearse when we can't even hear ourselves?'

'Count your blessings pal,' muttered Geordie. Mick limped off into the Crows room as Effy rounded on Geordie.

'Listen here you northern scum, you should be grateful that you're even on this tour. We're the stars of this circus and you're just

231

coming along for the ride. Don't forget that we had three number ones in a row. Now there's not many bands achieve that, so don't be under any misapprehension—we are the headlining act—we are the draw card; so show some respect!' I was half expecting Geordie to flare up but he simply let out a large yawn.

'Stars of the circus eh? Aren't they usually the clowns? You're nothing but a novelty act for teenyboppers.'

'Oh fuck off Geordie you Jock wanker!' Effy turned and stomped off back into his room while shouting more orders at the hapless Mick.

'Chas will be hearing about this Mick, I'm telling you; it's a bloody disgrace!' The door slammed behind him and there was silence.

'Botox Boy seems a bit temperamental today,' laughed Robbo.

'Yeah, he must have broken his comb or something,' concurred Geordie.

'You know, I really don't like that man and I don't much care for his music either, but we really should all try and get along with everyone. We're going to be in each others company 24/7 and it would be in everyone's interest if there was a little bit of détente,' said Flaky sensibly.

'Flaky?'

'Yes Geordie?'

'Shut up!'

22: ALL I NEED IS THE AIR THAT I BREATHE

We were due on stage in a few minutes. Flaky was busy throwing up in the toilets, Robbo had disappeared into the festival crowd to try and score some skunk and Geordie was last seen in the donna kebab tent arguing with Effy from the Stoned Crows about the various attributes of glam rockers Slade and T-Rex. As for myself, I sat nervously in the oversized trailer that was our temporary home, wondering what I had let myself in for. We were on the Isle of Wight, a strange place at the best of times but even stranger when the first open air festival of the summer was hosted here. It was freezing and pissing down with rain.

We had all arrived twenty four hours ago via the ferry. It had been a nightmare journey with the roughest seas I'd ever witnessed. The ferry was buffeted from all quarters and I was convinced that my number was up. Waves the size of New York tower blocks appeared beyond every window. Flaky had been so seasick that I was convinced that one more violent barf would see him relinquish his internal organs onto the floor. He was a shade of green that is rarely seen in nature and is usually reserved for cartoon characters. Geordie was pissed before he even got on the ferry and slept the entire journey like a newborn babe. Robbo found a quiet corner and smoked himself into another world.

This was the first day of a three day festival that would headline with REM on the final night—we would be long gone by then. I'm not sure how or why Chas had managed to get his bunch of resurrects onto this gig but he had. It was an imprudent decision to start the tour off at a festival as that meant we couldn't do a sound-check. We should have been allowed to get four or five gigs under our belt at smaller venues before we did any festivals, but it was what it was. All Chas's acts were under strict instructions not to exceed forty five minutes on stage and absolutely no encores apart from the Stoned Crows, who were to be the last of his bands on before the main headline acts took over for the rest of the night; we were basically fillers to pad out the festival until the latest and greatest took the stage. I was puzzled by Chas's decision to let the Crows headline our particular ensemble. I had always suspected Chas's musical nous. He was a great bullshitter and manager, but when it came down to the fine art of musical understanding and appreciation, he was like a whale out of water. He'd heard us all at the rehearsal rooms for the past few weeks, surely he must have realised that out of all the groups, the Stoned Crows were—how can I put it—shite! But if he wanted to kick off the first gig of the "Resurrection" tour with his worst band on last, so be it.

Divina had been the first act on. She tried her hardest but came off stage to a muted reception. Poor girl, my heart went out to her. Despite her regal and cool persona I'm sure she was disappointed with her reception and performance. It wasn't her fault. The sound was horrible, the swirling wind carrying the high notes off into some distant land, leaving a bass wobble. Divina's theatrical and gymnastic stage routine was lost on such a huge platform and in the daylight. The crowd hadn't come here to watch a bunch of old has-beens in the freezing cold, they'd come for sunshine, summer fun, and the bright new things of British pop: Gandhi's Sandal, Marathonic and The Amazing BJ's. In the meantime however they were going to have to put up with the old farts. Chas was running around like a headless chicken trying to organise everyone so we didn't blow the schedule.

'Fucking hell Will, where's the rest of the boys? You're on in five minutes, do you hear, five fucking minutes and there's only you here. I thought you were reliable, responsible. For God's sake!' Chas was

234

chewing gum furiously while pacing up and down the trailer. I threw him a resigned glance.

'I'm not their mother, Chas. They know the score. I'm sure they'll be here on time.'

'ON TIME! On frigging time! It is time, two minutes to go!' Chas put his head in his hands and let out a whimper. I lit a cigarette, took a deep drag and reflected on the previous month's events.

#

After we'd finished our rehearsals in London, we had four weeks off before the tour started. Robbo and Flaky had headed off home and Geordie went back to Scotland to visit his Nan in the convalescence home. I went straight down to Cornwall to catch up with my Mother and re-bond with my hound but most importantly, to spend time with Fiona. It was a majestic fortnight. The cold fresh spring weather had matured into a warm, flower scented summer, full of dragonflies, dancing butterflies and wilfully employed blackbirds. The sun smiled down benignly on the little fishing village of Pugstow and its citizens responded in kind with a busy optimism as they set about a new day.

I called on Fiona and we organised a day trip to Torquay for the kids. Child restraints and seats were hurriedly fitted to my trusty Mondeo. Backpacks were filled, sandwiches made, picnic accessories packed, nappies changed, perambulators collapsed and after what seemed like an eternity we headed off on our trip. The kids had the time of their life on the various rides, roller-coasters, swings and water slides. Seeing the laughter and joy on their faces touched something in me that I'd never felt before. I was getting immense enjoyment and satisfaction out of giving someone else happiness. This was a first for me and I wondered what I'd missed out on all my life. The kids ran and fell, shrieked and cried, squealed in excitement and laughed like clowns. Fiona was also having a ball. As the kids went around and around on a pirate's ship we sat on a bench and ate ice cream. She smiled at me and the hurt in her

235

eyes that I'd noticed on our first meeting, momentarily vanished. I wanted her—not just physically, but mentally and emotionally. We talked openly about her life and mine, two contrasting paths. One of self-absorbed, comfortable isolation, the other of sacrifice, loss, hardship and unconditional love.

We left the rides behind and found a quiet little beach where we set up our picnic. The kids played happily in the sand, building castles and filling buckets up with sea water and eating sandy peanut butter sandwiches. I popped the cork on a chilled bottle of white wine and filled two glasses. We lay back on the blanket and gazed into the turquoise sky.

'What do you want Will? What do you want from life?' Always a tough question and I struggled for an answer.

'Erm, I don't know … happiness I suppose, I'm not sure. I don't really think about it. Why, what do you want?' Fiona rolled onto her side supporting her head with her hand. Her eyes suddenly fired into life and she spoke with an urgency and conviction I hadn't heard from her before.

'I'll tell you what I want; I want my kids to be happy and healthy. I want to be able to spend quality time with them like this. I want them to grow up confident, to have empathy for others, to grab life, to live life.' Her red lips sucked on the edge of her wine glass, gently sipping the sweet liquid into her mouth. She rolled onto her back once more.

'Well, they're very commendable ideals. But what about something for you?' She let out a laugh,

'Haha, me? I don't want anything apart from the things I want for my kids.'

'Nothing?' I rolled onto my front so my head was positioned slightly above hers.

'Well,' she paused, almost embarrassed, 'it would be nice to have a man, a good man. Not just for the sex …' she let out another laugh, 'although God knows that would be very nice to have, but maybe a father for my kids, a lover and friend for me. Yes, that would be nice.' Her eyes

236

glazed over and the sadness returned. I assumed she was either thinking of her late husband or the fact that the chances of her dreams coming true were very slim. I dropped my head and positioned my lips above hers. I could smell the wine and feel the warmth of her sweet breath. Her bosom rose and fell like the swell of the ocean. Her eyes met mine. Our lips almost touched when I sensed I was being watched. I looked to my left; stood in a row, appearing very concerned, were Mitchell, Callum and Joe.

'Are you going to be our new Dad?' asked the eldest Joe, in a plaintive voice.

'Well, I erm … I don't know.' I responded in my usual confident and definitive manner.

'Joe!' scolded his Mother, 'what a question to ask, that's very rude!' Joe was defiant,

'Well I hope you are, I want you to be my Dad and so do Mitch and Callum!' With that he stomped off with his bucket and spade in hand followed by his younger siblings. I rolled off Fiona and we both laughed. I reflected on the idea of fatherhood once again; perhaps it was not for me, I was irresponsible, I was too self-centred, the change would be too much, I was too old … but then again?

'That's kids for you,' giggled Fiona, 'they always ask the curly ones, straight in there—no messing around.'

'Well it's an interesting question,' I said teasingly.

'Oh yeah, like you're going to chuck it all in to become a father to someone else's kids.' She laughed sarcastically and I was shocked to find myself wounded by her tone and her comments. Was it so ridiculous? Was I so shallow that the idea of being a parent was laughable?

'What's that supposed to mean?' I asked churlishly. She immediately detected my fragile ego and sat up.

'Oh, sorry Will, I didn't mean it like that, it did sound rather callous didn't it.'

'Well, what exactly did you mean then? You don't think I'm father material? You think I'm selfish and immature?'

'No, no, no! That's not what I meant. I meant that you have a career, you have a life, why would any man in their right mind throw it all in to take care of someone else's kids. That's what I meant. I'm sure you'd make a fantastic father, if and when you meet the right woman and settle down. It's just I don't think you'd be happy if you were a surrogate father, that's all I meant. I'm sorry if I hurt you, that's the last thing that I wanted to do.' She touched my arm and stared in to my eyes. I relented and smiled.

'And how do you know that I haven't already met the right woman?' Now she seemed wounded and stared out into the blue ocean.

'Don't tease Will, that's not very kind. I know what I am to you but you don't have to rub my nose in it.' I was confused—what the hell was she on about?

'Sorry? What do you mean?' She turned on me.

'Look we are both grown ups. You want to fuck me and I want to fuck you. But we have to play these games first. You have to pretend to like me and my kids and take us out and spoil us rotten and I have to pretend to be demure and innocent. But we both know that when the sex is over you'll be gone and I'll still be here. It's a fling, a meaningless fling, that's all, so don't pretend it's anything different. I may only be a barmaid but I'm not thick you know.' She gripped her knees and pulled them tightly into her chest. I was dumbstruck. I stood up and brushed the sand from my legs. I glanced down at her but she continued staring, glassy eyed, out to sea.

'I wasn't teasing and I'm not after a quick meaningless fuck,' I said slowly and calmly. I picked up a football and walked down the beach to where the trinity of innocence were nonchalantly battering, a long ago deceased crab, into oblivion.

'Okay, who wants a game of footy?' I challenged.

'Meeeeeeee!' they all cried together.

238

I pulled up outside Fiona's home and began to unload the car. Fiona got the kids out of their seat belts and took them inside. Despite the long day, which was now rapidly coming to an end, they all chatted away incessantly; arguing, accusing, sympathising, laughing. Fiona took them upstairs and ran a bath. I washed up the picnic utensils in her small kitchen and made us both a cup of coffee. We had hardly said a word to one another since the altercation on the beach and I had contented myself with entertaining the kids. We played football, we threw the Frisbee, we sang songs and nursery rhymes on the way home. I taught them some old ones and they taught me some new ones. We laughed a lot.

I heard Fiona's footsteps descend the stairs and the cackle of children's laughter from the bathroom. I handed her a coffee and she thanked me.

'I need a smoke,' I said. She nodded. It was still a warm night and I went out into the fenced in back garden. I sat down with my coffee and lit a cigarette. She followed and sat adjacent to me with a small gap between us. I let out a deep sigh.

'It's not that bad is it?' she asked. I laughed.

'No, there's no bad about it. I've had a fantastic day, I'm just sad it's coming to an end.'

'Did you mean what you said earlier?' She studied me intently. I blew out the smoke high into the air and watched as it slowly dissolved into the sky.

'Yes.'

'Okay, well I apologise for being so miserable but I've got to know the truth. I have my kids at stake and I'm not going to enter into a relationship with someone who is going to suddenly disappear out of the kids' lives again.' I wasn't one hundred percent sure, but I wanted to sound completely committed.

'Give me a go and I promise I won't let you down,' I stated emphatically. She grabbed my hand and narrowed her eyes.

'Okay, I will … after the tour.'

'Why after the tour?' I asked.

'Well, let's call it a cooling off period. I fell for you the instant you first walked through the pub door, but at the moment what I want comes second. The wellbeing of my children comes first. If you still feel the same way about me after the tour then we'll give it a go.' My heart soared and I laughed inside but on the exterior I remained calm. I nodded my head in agreement.

'Okay, it's a deal.' I leant over and our lips touched, lightly at first and then with greater passion. Her breathing intensified along with my own. She pulled away.

'Sorry …' I said, feeling I may have rushed things.

'No it's quite alright. I mean, I want to but …'

'But what?' I asked.

'Not yet. Again, let's wait until after your tour. You'll be like a kid in a sweet shop. What I'm saying is, if you've got any whoring to do, get it out of your system on tour. Do it before we've committed to each other. I won't ever ask you about it, but if we do end up giving it a go I will expect total commitment, mentally and physically if you know what I mean.' I realised it was useless arguing so I just nodded and said,

'Okay, you win.' She smiled, pecked me on the cheek and headed back into the house.

'I best get these kids dry and into their PJ's.'

#

I spent the whole of the last week with Fiona and her children. I slept on the couch, frustrated but happy. Each day, the bond between us all grew stronger and each day I began to question whether I had what it takes to be a family man. Don't get me wrong, I was loving every minute of it, the tears, the tantrums, the mess, the noise. I breathed it all in and

240

flourished in the organised chaos. But deep down I worried about what might happen. What if I came into Fiona's and the kids' lives, gave them love and respect and security and then woke up one day and thought "Nah, this is not for me" and left them high and dry. I couldn't convince myself that I wouldn't do it, however improbable it seemed. The closer I got to them the sadder I became.

#

It was my last day before heading back to Yorkshire and we were taking a slow walk along the beach. I had Mitch on my shoulders, the other two had wandered off up ahead, picking up shells and occasionally throwing the ball for an exuberant Caesar.

'Will?' she called my name softly and her hand found mine.

'What?'

'I know what you're thinking you know,' I couldn't believe that she did and humoured her.

'Oh yeah, am I that transparent?'

'It's perfectly natural that you should feel this way. You're questioning yourself whether you'd be able to stay the distance aren't you?' Damn! How could she possibly have picked up on that. The woman must be a bloody mind reader.

'Maybe a little bit. The last thing I'd ever do is intentionally hurt you or the kids.'

'I know that. You're a good man. If it were the other way around I'd be doing the same. That's why this tour will do you good. It will give you time to think about everything. It's all happened very fast and it will be good for us both to take a breather. You'll find the answer sooner or later. You'll know whether you can or can't do it. It will come to you when you least expect it.' I felt like crying and gripped the tiny legs of Mitch tightly to my chest and walked on in silence.

#

Of course, I got the Spanish inquisition from my Mother every night.

'How was it all going? What did I think of her? What did I think of the kids? Did they like me? Was I in love? What were our plans?' My answers were non-committal and infuriated her but I didn't divulge any of my inner turmoil. In the two weeks I'd spent with Fiona and the kids I hadn't once thought about the upcoming tour, I guess that told me something.

#

My reverie was broken by a frantic Chas,

'Oh my God, that's it you're due on; get out there Will, you'll have to d … d … do it s … s … solo!' Chas was distraught and cleaned his spectacles in an agitated manner. 'This is n … not the sort of st … st … start we wanted, is it.'

'No, I guess not,' I replied calmly. I picked up my guitar just as I heard an announcement come across the PA.

'Okay ravers, next up is one of the greatest bands of the century. They haven't played together for ten years, but today, especially for you, they've reformed.' There was a low-key cheer from the meagre crowd. 'Please give a rousing reception for nineties seminal superstars the SHOOTING TSARS!' A little over the top, but I guess that was the guy's job.

'Did that twat just say seminal?' boomed Geordie as he entered the trailer, hastily stuffing the last greasy remnants of a donna kebab down his throat as he grabbed his bass.

'Aye, it was definitely seminal,' reiterated a happy looking Robbo following behind.

'Where's Kermit?'

'He's still in the toilets chucking, I think.' I replied.

'No, no, I'm here.' Flaky staggered through the door next. Gone was his many shades of green, replaced by a ghostly white. Chas suddenly became animated.

'Quick, quick, get out there, now, for God's sake.'

'No need for blasphemy,' moaned Flaky without much conviction. We all ambled quietly and efficiently out of the trailer and headed towards the back of the stage.

23: THE ONLY WAY IS UP

The lift took us to the fourth floor and I followed Divina out and along the corridor. It had seemed like a good idea at the time, as many ideas do; but now in the cold glare of the hotel lighting, I was having second thoughts. I wasn't sure why I was here; it had all happened so quickly—no, that's a lie—I knew exactly why I was here—sex! The trouble was, after my initial sense of rapture and exuberance at being propositioned by one of the most beautiful women on the planet I was now feeling decidedly nervous and had suddenly become tongue tied.

I trailed behind Divina silently like a little lap dog as the porcelain Goddess led the way to her hotel room. I should have felt elated, euphoric. I should have had a horn on as big as the obelisk—but I didn't. There she was, right in front of me. Leather thigh boots gripping her long tanned silky legs. A tight white dress clinging to the most perfect buttocks in the business. It was not hard to make out the black 'G' string under the thin white material, not an act of naiveté but one of deliberate torment. Even with her back to me I could see her pert breasts jig up and down slightly as she strode purposefully ahead, her long jet black hair swaying from side to side. She stopped at a door and swiped her key card, there was a buzz and the door sprung ajar. She held it open for me, as though I was the lady, and smiled in a superior fashion as I stumbled through, catching her sweet fruity perfume on the way.

The room was lit by a couple of lamps and was neat and tidy. A light was on in the bathroom and I could see my reflection in the mirror.

It wasn't a majestic sight by any means. Dishevelled hair, old jeans, a tour T-shirt and a pair of scruffy old Nike trainers. My only concession to fashion was an expensive cream coloured jacket that had been given to me the night before by a Welsh stalker. She came up behind me and whispered softly,

'Are you okay?'

'Yeah, sure, I feel great,' my confident response was paper thin and only heightened my unease.

'Good,' she responded, 'fancy a little something?' She walked over to her bedside drawers and fumbled around before pulling out a little plastic bag. I walked over to her.

'What is it?' I asked.

'Oh, just a little something to keep us both going.' I recalled the conversation we'd just had in the taxi, about how she was a very demanding woman, about her unconventional desires, about the flame within her that burnt like a furnace until it was satiated. I thought about myself, shagless for years. I had a sudden mental image of a soft cuddly lamb about to be pounced on by a fearsome tiger. She held out the pill, which I took and slipped into my mouth—she followed suit. Trouble was, I couldn't swallow it. With the combination of speed and alcohol I'd had earlier, and my current trepidation, my mouth was as dry as a desert river bed.

'Right, I'm going to shower. Help yourself to a drink or if you prefer I have some good blow in my handbag.' With that she turned and walked off elegantly into the bathroom and closed the door.

'Thanks,' I called after her. I heard the shower taps turn and the cascading volley of water noisily hitting the base. I decided against the blow, it would slow me down and it certainly wouldn't assist in my sexual performance. I wondered why I was so intimidated. It was the thought of the unknown. What had she meant by "unconventional desires", that was the killer for me. I'd never been particularly adventurous or curious in the sexuality stakes and I now reckoned I might have bitten off more than I

245

could chew. I grabbed a beer from the fridge and twisted the cap off. I took a large slug washing the little pill down my throat. Sighing, I lit a smoke and sat down on the edge of the bed. My old friend nicotine got to work and I felt myself begin to relax. *Hey, what's the worst that could possibly happen, maybe we don't hit it off, maybe I can't perform, maybe she tells the rest of the people on tour about my failure, maybe she even announces it on stage in Leeds, my hometown, maybe it gets into the papers. I'll be the laughing stock of the country!* I jumped up from the bed with my heart beating madly. *Calm down you idiot!* I could hear her singing a lilting lullaby in the shower. Such a sweet, innocent voice. *Unconventional desires?* I took another swig of beer and inhaled the tobacco deeply before sitting back down. *Okay pal, take a chill pill. It's just sex, that's all. It's perfectly normal. You're a man and she's a woman and you'll do what comes naturally. As simple as that.* I looked around for an ashtray and noticed one poking out from under the bed, half hidden by the valance. A partially smoked joint rested forlornly in its midst. I bent down to retrieve the ashtray and noticed it was sat upon a pile of magazines. I pulled them out to have a quick browse, maybe it would help me forget about my impending challenge. On top was "Country Home". I read the banners. "Top Five Things To Do At Royal Ascot", "Every Home Should Have A Herb Garden", "10 Slow Cooker Recipes". I was beginning to feel more relaxed now and cursed my previous nervousness. For God's sake, most men would give their right testicle to be in my position. A beautiful woman in the bathroom, good beer, free hotel, on tour, no worries, a bucket load of money coming my way. *Damn, I'm a lucky bastard!* I took another swig of beer and was considering reading the article on herb gardens but decided to have a quick flick through the other magazines. I shuffled "Country Home" to the bottom. My heart skipped a beat as I read the next magazines title, "Secret Lust". It was a fetish magazine, not your usual top-of-the-shelf porn from the local newsagent—this was subscription only. I skimmed through the pages; S & M, bondage, role play, fetish, rubber, latex. *Good grief! Surely that's illegal … no, no, that's not humanly possible … Jesus, that has got to hurt ... there's no way that would ever fit ... what the hell is she intending to do with that thing ... that guy won't walk straight for a week!* I quickly threw the magazines back under the bed without looking at any more and wished I'd perused the article on herbs. I considered myself a man of the world but what I'd just seen was an eye-opener. My heart began to race again and I began to hyperventilate. *That's it, I'm out of here!* I searched for a pen and piece of paper. The least I could do was leave her a note apologising. I liked to watch a soft porn film as much as the next man, but this was way out of my league. I mean each to their own and as John Lennon sang, "Whatever Gets You Thru the Night, it's Alright" and I agree with that philosophy, but this was not for me. I was a missionary man, meat and two veg ... hell, I considered having sex standing up in the in the shower as kinky. Ten minutes was about my record and I wasn't particularly bothered about changing it. I heard the shower taps turn and the hiss of the water die away. *Shit!* I opened a drawer next to the TV and found a pad of hotel notepaper and a pen. I sat down and began to write.

"Dear Divina ..." I stopped. What would I say? "Sorry that I left, but you scare me to death" no, too harsh. "Much as I like you I don't think I'm ready for a relationship ..." no, she made it quite clear that tonight was about one thing only—sex. Okay, what about "Sorry I had to leave but I've got a sudden bout of diarrhoea." Yes, that got me out of jail, no-one could argue with that, not even someone who had a fire burning below.

I picked up the pen and began to write. I'd just finished the word "bout" when I heard the click of the bathroom door. I jumped to my feet and turned around. I'd just have to lie to her face to face now, God damn it! She stood by the bathroom door in a long white bathrobe. Her inky, tousled hair, fell down around her shoulders. Her high cheek bones were flushed and her soft full lips were as deep red as an aged shiraz. She leant against the door frame as wafts of steam billowed out behind her, making her appear like some angelic apparition. She was captivating and I was suddenly entranced again. I forgot all my previous aberrations. How could I walk away from someone as beautiful as this.

'What's that you're writing?' she asked, staring at the pen in my hand and the notepad on the table.

'Writing, writing …' I stuttered, 'erm, oh nothing … just some ideas for lyrics.'

'Read them to me,' she requested.

'What!' I exclaimed, alarmed at the prospect.

'Read them to me; surely you're not embarrassed?' she laughed. She reached back into the bathroom and pulled out a towel and began slowly caressing her hair. I turned and picked up the note. I read the words silently to myself first and then carefully folded the piece of paper and slipped it into my back pocket. I turned back to face her.

'Well?' she persisted 'I'm waiting.' I cleared my throat.

'Nothing can bring meaning, to this world I'm visiting, from the bowels of hell to the angelic cloisters, where purity dwells.' It was the worst thing I had ever come up with. 'And that's as far as I got.' She stopped drying her hair and stared at me in bewilderment.

'That's fucking terrible,' she stated matter-of-factly.

'You're right, it's complete rubbish.' She walked over and kissed me on the cheek. I could smell her soft scent and feel her fresh breath. I suddenly felt a faint twinge from down below and decided I wanted to get on with it. All those stupid thoughts I'd had about the perverted sex I thought she was after. Here she was, demure, wrapped in a bathrobe, sweet and innocent.

'I'll just get a quick shower then,' I suggested.

'Yes, I'll be waiting for you—I'm going to give you something special.' I smiled awkwardly as I shut the bathroom door behind me. I looked at myself in the mirror as I slowly peeled my clothes off. *What did she mean, something special? Why did she have to say that!* I peered down at my flaccid penis, which hung dejected, like a fallen acorn and I was less than convinced that a mighty oak would shoot forth anytime soon. I turned the shower on and stepped under the water like a man sentenced to death. *What is wrong with me? Why can't I act normal?* I felt a sense of impending doom. I spent as long as I could in the shower, probably fifteen minutes, delaying the inevitable. I dried slowly and sullenly. I realised I didn't have any fresh undies or for that matter any fresh anything. I didn't even have a toothbrush. I squeezed some toothpaste onto my finger and improvised, gargling vigorously afterwards. I glanced in the mirror and grabbed my pecker. *C'mon you bastard, don't let me down, puff yourself up a bit, at least look the part. I don't ask much of you for God's sake!* It was no good, even with a few firm strokes my old todger wasn't playing ball. I think he'd gone into hibernation.

I was beginning to get performance anxiety. I could hear soft music coming from the bedroom and footsteps busily treading a path back and forth, for what purpose I did not know. There was nothing for it but to take a deep breath and get out there. With a towel wrapped around my waist and stomach sucked in I opened the door and strode purposefully out. A strange and foreboding figure suddenly appeared in front of me whilst letting out a large catlike "meow". It scared the living bejeezus out of me and I leapt backwards jagging my big toenail into the corner of the bathroom door. I hopped around the room like a demented Flamingo on a trampoline and became unceremoniously disrobed as the towel fell to the floor. My old pecker didn't know what to do—he wasn't sure whether to come out fighting or dive for cover. He chose the latter, shrinking in size by half as my testicles also made a tactical retreat upwards. I fell in a heap on the floor as blood flowed from my gouged toe. I peered up to see Divina staring down at me with a bemused smile. She was dressed in a leather catsuit with matching cat ears and mask.

'You certainly know how to make an entrance—this could be an entertaining evening!'

#

I sat on a chair feeling naked, which was hardly surprising, because I was naked. Divina gently bathed my bloodied toe and applied some antiseptic cream to it. She curbed the bleeding and applied a large band aid. I nonchalantly rested my forearm across my upper thigh to hide my confused genitalia. The only thing throbbing around here was my bloody big toe. Divina stood up in front of me.

'Feeling better?' she asked kindly.

'Yes thanks, a lot better.' I stared at her. Yep, I was definitely in a hotel room with a feline impersonator. She walked to the bed whereupon sat a small suitcase. She grabbed something from it, turned and threw it to me.

'Here, catch.' It landed at my feet. I picked it up and studied it. *Oh no, for fuck's sake, please no.* It was a costume. A pale, bluey-grey all in one cotton jump suit, a pair of navy blue underpants, gloves, booties, a cape and to round it all off, a pair of plastic ears. *Fuck me sideways!* Divina pulled out a riding crop from her suitcase and strode purposefully over to me.

'Come on, go get changed,' she ordered as she let out a wristy flick with her riding crop that caught me squarely on the end of my John Thomas. I instinctively recoiled with the sudden infliction of pain. 'And don't be long,' she commanded as I trudged once more to the bathroom with my costume under one arm and shut the door behind me. I gingerly climbed into the jump suit, my big toe still throbbing, and then donned the rest of the outfit. I examined myself in the mirror.

'What a complete and utter twat you look,' I said to myself in a low whisper. The suit was meant for a bigger man and it hung loosely from my medium frame. The underpants were way too big and as for the booties, well, whoever they were made for had size fourteen feet. I tried to think of sex and Divina but there was no stirring from below. My schlong had left town in a hurry and taken his two mates with him—cowardly bastards! In the final act of humiliation I put on my plastic ears.

I opened the bathroom door and slunk, like a whipped dog, into the bedroom. Divina was busy at the bloody suitcase again pulling out all sorts of malevolent looking sex toys and laying them out on the bed. There was a massive black dildo that must have been a foot long if it was an inch, with a girth that made my eyes water. There was a nasty looking pink vibrator with latex spikes on it, a butt plug, a love egg, leather straps, a blindfold, an Arab strap and an industrial sized tube of KY jelly with pump action dispensing arm. Also, rather worryingly, there were a couple of metallic objects that I didn't recognise, but I'm certain they belonged in a Victorian blacksmiths not a modern hotel bedroom.

'Okay lover boy ... ready for action?'

#

I heard movement, the opening of a door and a click followed by the distinctive sound of water cascading down from a shower rose. I drifted off again. Sweet soft singing awoke me a second time and I gently opened my eyes to the bright light shining through the bedroom window. I let out a long yawn accompanied with an achy stretch. The bathroom door opened and Divina walked out, fully dressed in leggings, ballet shoes and a clingy sports top.

'Morning sleepy head,' she said.

'Morning,' I groaned back. I watched her as she filled the kettle with water and flicked the switch.

'Coffee?'

'Yes please,' I replied. She pulled out two cups and picked up a sachet of coffee and tore it open before pouring it into one of the cups.

'It's only instant I'm afraid,' she said repeating the process for the second cup.

'That's fine.' She disappeared back into the bathroom and returned with her toiletries bag. She pulled a large and small suitcase from out of the wardrobe, quickly unzipped the larger one and deposited the toiletry bag inside before re-zipping it up. The smaller one I

251

recognised from the night before. She tipped both of them onto their wheels and yanked out their respective handles. She looked immaculate. *How can that be, so early in the morning?*. She poured the boiling water into the cups, placed mine on a saucer and carried it over to me. I sat up and propped a pillow up behind my head. She handed me the cup and I breathed in its deep rejuvenating vapour.

'Ah, that smells good, instant or not.' Divina sat down on the edge of the bed and smiled at me. I sipped the coffee and smiled back. She leant forward. I thought she was going to kiss me on the lips but instead she kissed me on the forehead, like a kindly mother would do when dropping off her son for his first day at school. I smelt her warmth and femininity, which for some reason, made me feel safe and relaxed. She leant back.

'Thanks for last night,' she said.

'No problem. Thank you,' I replied.

'You were sweet.' With that she got up, pulled her hair back into a tight ponytail took a couple of sips of her coffee and grabbed her key card.

'You better get a wriggle on. Only forty minutes before the coach leaves. Don't be upsetting Chas before the day's begun.'

'No, it's our turn for the bleeding promotion and publicity. The hire car's being dropped off here at the hotel.'

'What time are you supposed to leave?'

'The itinerary says the same time as the coach, but Chas will be on the coach, so he'll never know will he.'

'Ooh, you be careful. Remember the well oiled machine. Right, I'm off to get some breakfast. See you at the gig.' I watched her struggle to get both suitcases out of the door before it finally slammed shut behind her.

Sweet? What the hell is that supposed to mean. I don't want sweet, definitely not sweet. Why couldn't she have said I was magnificent or fantastic or that I was a Tiger. I'd have even settled for a "not bad"—but not sweet.

As I sat sipping my coffee I recalled the events of the previous night. At first I smiled to myself but then a sinister realisation came to fruition. *Well that's it, I can never have sex again. Nothing can ever compare to what happened with Divina. She's set the benchmark, a benchmark that will live forever. I'm doomed, doomed. I'm going to be celibate for the rest of my life*

I finished my coffee, had a brisk shower and quickly dressed. I had a quick scan around the rooms to make sure nothing had been left behind when I noticed something pink protruding from underneath the bed. I bent down and pulled it out.

'Oh twat,' I cursed. 'What am I supposed to do with this?' It was the vicious looking pink vibrator with the spikes. I couldn't leave it behind otherwise it would be tittle-tattle for the cleaners. I decided I'd stick it in my my suitcase and give it back to Divina at the next hotel. I picked it up and stuffed it into my jacket pocket and left the room.

24: BABY YOU CAN DRIVE MY CAR

I stood outside my hotel room fumbling for my key card. I heard a noise and threw a glance down the corridor to see a middle aged woman in hotel uniform wheeling a breakfast trolley my way. I found my card and ran it through the slot but I had it the wrong way round and there was a ten second time delay before I could retry. By this time the trolley lady was upon me.

'Good morning Sir,' she offered smiling politely.

'Morning. Nice day for it,' I replied. I tried the key card again and it gave me the green light. The handle clicked and I gave it a downward twist, unwittingly releasing the pink vibrator from my jacket pocket onto the floor at the same time. It rolled a few inches along the corridor before finally wedging itself neatly under the front wheel of the breakfast trolley, thereby bringing the trolley to an abrupt halt, which, in turn, jettisoned a spurt of cold coffee from a resting coffee cup. I made a hasty grab for the offending prosthesis but the astute room service lady got there before me.

'Here you go Sir ...' her sentence trailed off as it suddenly became apparent what the object was. Her grip changed from a full on grasp to a tentative fingertip purchase; her polite smile changed to one of faint disgust.

'Ahem, I can explain ...' I started. She dropped the item into my outstretched palm and wiped her hands on her pinafore.

'No need Sir. Each to their own.'

'But it's not mine, you don't understand,' I implored.

'Of course not Sir, that's what they all say. Good day.' She muttered something under her breath about "perverts" and made off down the corridor. No doubt the story would circulate quicker than a hotel fire once she returned downstairs. I entered my room and dropped the bothersome vibrator into the bottom of my bag and began packing up.

#

As the lift descended I studied the day's itinerary. The Tsars were booked in at the commercial and BBC radio stations in Manchester, Sheffield and lastly Leeds and also had to get to the venue and sound check by five thirty. It was a hectic schedule in terms of travel and ultimately tedious and dreary. We were all supposed to take a turn in the interview stakes but I knew it would end up being Robbo and me doing it all. Geordie couldn't be trusted to keep a civil tongue in his head and I was worried that Flaky might use the occasion to spout on about his religious conversion. If it had just been me and Robbo in the car it wouldn't have been too bad, but as Flaky was the nominated driver he also had to come along and because the three of us were going, Geordie insisted that he travel with us also. I grabbed a quick bite of breakfast from the restaurant and then made my way to the reception. I saw Chas speaking animatedly into his mobile. I wandered over. He hung up as I neared. He appeared agitated and anxious.

'Hey Chas, what's wrong? You seem a little stressed.'

'Traction Will, I can't get no traction.'

'What do you mean, traction?'

'We're getting no press,' he replied.

'Yes we are. There was a piece in the NME and Melody Maker last week about the tour.'

'I don't mean the bloody music press, they're no good, they barely sell over 100,000 copies a week between them, plus they're not our

255

demographic. No disrespect Will, but your fans are thirty-forty-somethings, they don't buy music papers anymore, they all read the tabloids and we've barely been mentioned. I tell you Will, we need traction otherwise we will be out of pocket big time. The crowds aren't turning up because they don't know about the tour.' I was a little puzzled.

'What's all this "we" business?'

'Pardon?'

'You said "we will be out of pocket". I won't, the bands won't, it's all in the contract. We get paid no matter.' It was a little callous but I was trying to catch him out. He stared at me blankly as the cogs revolved in his head.

'I meant "we" as in the royal "we". I will be out of pocket big time.' I knew he was lying. This whole thing wasn't being financed by him alone as he'd been making out. He definitely had backers and the hastily concluded phone call was probably them airing their concerns at the small crowds so far.

'Anyway Will,' he said, quickly changing topic, 'you know your lot are doing the radio stations today? The hire car should be here any minute. Make a good job of it, try and sell the bloody thing will you.'

'We'll do our best, Chas.' He glanced at his watch nervously and then noticed the tour bus pull up outside the hotel.

'Right, good, good. Well, I better go round up the rest of them and get them onto the bus. Traction Will, traction is what I need.' I watched him as he wandered off, deep in thought.

I hung around reception for a few minutes waiting for the hire car to arrive. I watched my motley crew suspiciously. They were all flopped on the same large couch together near the hotel doorway, bags and suitcases at the ready. Flaky was reading a copy of National Geographic, Robbo was reading The Sun and Geordie was reading Viz. *Fuck me, the three wise monkeys.* Divina appeared from an alcove pulling her suitcases behind her. She spotted me as she made her way to the hotel entrance, sending a big beaming smile in my direction.

'Just waiting for the hire car to be dropped off,' I explained as she neared. She put her suitcases down and readjusted her ponytail. I looked over my shoulder at the three stooges who had stopped reading their literature and were all staring at me and Divina with stupid lopsided grins. I lowered my voice.

'Hey, Divina, I have something of yours, you left it behind in the bedroom,' I said discreetly.

'Oh, what is it?' she asked smiling benevolently.

'Erm, not here. I will catch up with you at the hotel tonight,' I explained quietly. She tilted her head to one side and narrowed her eyes inquisitively.

'Okay. Well have a safe journey.' She stroked my face gently. 'You're so sweet.' She grabbed the handles of her suitcases and walked towards the doors. Before she exited, she swung her head around quickly,

'Catcha later … lover boy,' she said loudly and with a wink she was gone. I winced—not good, not good at all. I was hoping and praying the triumvirate of fools hadn't heard her, but of course they had. I stared at them as Geordie turned to Robbo and Flaky.

'Lover boy eh?' he said with a chuckle as the other two grinned.

'More like a fucking bovver boy if you ask me,' replied Robbo as they all returned to their reading matter.

#

We were on the motorway and doing a top speed of 55mph. There were grannies in electric wheelchairs overtaking us on the right hand side. I was in the back with Geordie and Robbo was in the front passenger seat with Flaky at the wheel.

'For fuck's sake Flaky, put your foot down, the gigs tonight not next fucking week,' yelled Geordie. His scorn was incessant, but for once I had empathy for him. Flaky was becoming a real pain in the arse; his self-righteous piety was enough to make the Pope puke. If people smoked he moaned; if they drank he moaned; too much swearing and he

257

moaned; there wasn't much one could do without it coming under the critical eye of God's chosen one. Robbo turned the music up again.

'Robbo, for Pete's sake turn it down! I can't concentrate with the volume that loud!' Flaky shouted, clearly annoyed.

'You're a rock and roll drummer in one of the loudest rock 'n roll bands in the world and you're asking me to turn down the car stereo! You're fucking warped man, warped!' Even the normally laid back Robbo was losing his cool.

'Put your foot down Flaky otherwise I'll stick my boot right through the back of your seat!' continued Geordie.

'Oh very good, very good. You know it's a sign of insecurity and lack of self-worth that leads to threats of violence.'

'Oh is that right, well this is no threat it's a fully funded commitment!' Geordie boomed. Flaky complied slightly by raising his top speed to 60 mph.

'Whoa! Hang on, I cannae handle the G-force.' Geordie was pulling on his cheeks and flapping them in and out causing spittle to fly from his gaping mouth. Robbo turned around laughing loudly. 'No, we cannae make it captain, she's gonna break up, we've never been past warp speed two before; a don't know how much more of this she can take!' I began to chuckle even though I was in danger of being covered in spittle. I saw Flaky look in his rearview mirror to witness Geordie's performance.

'Okay you reprobates, you've asked for it,' shouted Flaky. He hit the accelerator and we slowly climbed to a top speed of 65 mph.

We drove on for a good hour talking about everything and nothing. I saw a sign for services in 1 mile.

'Hey, Flaky, pull in at the next services will you, I'm dying for a smoke.'

'Dying being the operative word,' he retorted smugly.

'Aye and I'm bursting for a piss,' added Geordie. We pulled in and parked up. I glanced at my watch.

'We'll meet back here in twenty minutes right,' I said. 'It's going to be a push to make it to Manchester on time at this rate.'

'Aye, well if we didn't have Mr Magoo here driving, we may be on schedule,' Geordie moaned. I lit up a smoke and watched wearily as they all headed off towards the services, Geordie and Flaky bickering as they went, Robbo silent as he lit up a spliff.

I finished my cigarette and headed off into the services where I bought myself a Cornish pasty. As I turned to leave I saw Flaky sat down at a table in a salad bar. He was just starting on a large bowl of fresh salad. I wandered over to him.

'Flaky, give me the keys, I'm heading back to the car.'

'No probs, here,' he fumbled in his jacket pocket and passed me the keys. I took them and glanced at my watch again.

'Don't be too long, eh?' He was in the process of masticating a particularly large piece of tomato. He nodded and I left him behind and headed back to the car where Robbo and Geordie were already waiting, leaning lethargically on the bonnet.

'Where's sanctimonious Sam?' asked Geordie.

'He's tucking into a big salad,' I said. I pushed the button on the keys and the doors clunked. We were just about to get in when Geordie said,

'Hey Billy Boy, give me the keys, I want to drive.'

'No way!'

'Aw, c'mon Billy, play the game, why not?'

'Because one, you are not insured to drive this car; two, you can't drive and three I don't want to listen to Flaky wittering on, all the way up to Manchester.'

'I can drive, I just haven't passed my test yet,' he implored.

'Well that's another reason; learners aren't allowed to drive on the motorway.'

'Yeah well, that's a stupid rule. How can you learn to drive on a motorway if you're not allowed to drive on a motorway. That's a double paradox or something. C'mon Billy, it will be good experience for me,' he pleaded. I stared at Robbo.

'What do you think Robbo?'

'Well,' he paused considering the matter, 'I don't suppose he can do too much damage. I mean it's a straight road, no junctions, no traffic lights, no roundabouts. Even he can't fuck that up, can he?' I wasn't so sure but relented and threw Geordie the keys.

'Nice one Billy boy!' he yelled, immediately jumping into the driver's side and readjusting the seat. I got in the back.

'But listen Geordie, *no fucking around*, no speeding, no overtaking, keep in the left hand lane and once we're off the motorway you pull over and Flaky drives, okay?'

'Yeah no problem, you can trust me!' he replied beaming from ear to ear.

'Trust; I wouldn't trust you to wipe your own arse properly. And another thing, if you see any cop cars just act normal, alright?'

'That's an oxymoron,' replied Geordie blithely.

'Yeah, well in your case, I think we can drop the oxy.' I looked out of the rearview mirror and saw Flaky heading our way. 'Okay Flaky's on his way, ear muffs at the ready, batten down the hatches—incoming verbal assault imminent.'

After five excruciating minutes of admonition from Flaky we finally hopped out of the motorway services, heads lurching back and forth like demented turkeys. I kept a close eye on Geordie, I could tell he was nervous and I began to question his assertion that indeed he could drive. He changed gear with a crunch. Flaky sat staring out of the side window cradling an enormous sulk. Robbo unzipped his jacket and pulled out two magazines.

'What did you buy?' I asked.

'Recording Magazine and UK's Hottest MILF's,' he replied holding them up. Evidently, Robbo's two passions in life. I grabbed the MILF mag and relaxed back into my seat.

'Pornographic filth,' mumbled Flaky. We made it onto the slipway without too much fuss and Geordie accelerated away. He pushed the car up to seventy, still in third gear and paid no attention to the traffic that he was about to merge into. I glanced over my shoulder and saw a continuous stream of heavy goods wagons in the right hand lane. There was no way through without dropping back. Geordie kept accelerating, still in third gear. The engine screamed. There was space of about a car and half's length between two large petrol tankers, somehow Geordie managed to swerve the car into this spot, more by luck than intention. The tanker behind us blasted its horn, our car kept moving rightwards into the next lane.

'I told you this was a bad idea!' yelled Flaky not missing an opportunity to berate us all. There was another car in the middle lane that we were destined to collide with but luckily for all concerned the driver of that vehicle hit the brakes sending his car swerving off towards the central reservation. We continued our diagonal route across the motorway moving into the outside lane just as a car, doing at least 100 mph, came screaming up behind us. It was a top of the range Jaguar and had a little flag flapping madly on the bonnet. The Jaguar blared its horn, flashed its lights and Geordie swerved erratically back into the middle lane. He was still in third. By now, Flaky was gripping the back of Geordie's seat, his knuckles white, his face even whiter. The Jaguar went zooming past, horn still blaring, lights still flashing. Geordie wound down his window and gave the two fingered salute in violent fashion.

'Go fuck yourself, you wanker!' He yelled. It was then that I recognised the flag on the car's bonnet. It was the Royal Ensign. Staring open mouthed, out of the Jaguar's passenger window, was the unmistakable face of Princess Anne.

#

Robbo lit a massive spliff, took a few tokes and handed it over to me. We'd been sat in silence for the last twenty minutes.

'Oh just great,' started up Flaky. 'Not only have I had my life put at risk by your reckless actions, but you've managed to offend a member of the Royal Family and now you're poisoning me with that noxious weed.' He wound his window down slightly and stuck his nose into the gap. He was not a happy camper. Robbo began flicking through his recording magazine.

'Hey Flaky, there's an article here about Mark Knopfler ... you're a big fan of his, aren't you?' Flaky looked around sulkily.

'Yes I am actually. He's a great guitarist and songwriter. I love Dire Straits. What does it say?'

'It says that he's teaming up with Chris Rea to form a super-group.'

'Really, that sounds interesting, I love Chris Rea as well.'

'Yeah, they're going to be call diarrhoea.' Everyone, bar Flaky, burst out laughing.

'Oh yes, very funny I don't think. Why don't you lot grow up!' Flaky was not the least bit amused and sank into his seat like a man who'd been sentenced to life imprisonment.

'Ah, c'mon Flaky, just a bit of humour to break up the monotony, what's wrong with you?' laughed Robbo. The journey ground on.

#

At last we saw the sign for the Manchester exit. I informed Geordie to keep in the left hand lane as the turnoff was only one mile ahead. Robbo lit another spliff and handed it to me.

'Hey what about me?' questioned Geordie. Robbo pulled it back and in an act of foolishness passed the monster spliff to Geordie.

'Yes that's right, illegal driving, illegal drugs, why not combine them at the same time, yes that's right, any more laws you can break? I'm sure you could think of some if you put your collective heads together,' Flaky chastised. Geordie had always been greedy with the dope and his head momentarily disappeared in a haze of thick blue smoke. I saw the sign for our turnoff, stating "400 Yards Ahead". At this point Geordie decided to overtake a coach directly ahead of us. He tried dropping gears from fifth to fourth to accelerate past but managed to hit third sending us all shooting forwards. The engine protested loudly. He was now struggling to get past the coach.

'Geordie mate, I'd drop back if I were you, we're going to miss our turnoff if you're not careful,' I advised.

'Don't worry. I'll blow this bastard off and then drop back to the inside lane.' He had the accelerator down to the floor, the engine screeched in agony and I noticed two red lights appear on the dashboard. Something was amiss. For some reason I glanced behind me nervously and spotted a motorway police patrol car speeding up the outside lane. *Shit!* I didn't tell Geordie. It appeared they were going somewhere in a hurry, but as they drew level with our vehicle they slowed down to the same speed. I saw the sign again, "Turnoff 200 Yards". I stared out at the cop car that was now travelling alongside. Both front seat occupants turned and looked our way. Geordie edged past the coach, stuck the spliff back in his mouth and peered out of his window at the police.

'Hello boys!' He waved, big toothless grin, monster spliff and all.

'Geordie, the turnoff is just about now!' I stated concertedly. We had missed it. The coach followed the left lane and began to depart from us. The police were still riding shotgun.

'Oh fuck! Yeah, why didn't you tell me earlier!' cried Geordie. He swung the car violently to the left, cutting across the diverging lanes, crossing the chevrons and managing to take out a dozen or so speed cones along the way.

'Fucking great driving man!' laughed Robbo.

'Thanks,' smiled Geordie.

'Ahem, excuse me! I don't like to bother you three musketeers, but I think you've just managed to attract the attention of the police,' stated Flaky in an arrogant "told you so" manner. We all glanced behind and saw the familiar blue flashing lights and the distant wail of the siren.

263

'Don't worry, I'll outrun the bastards!' shouted Geordie, suddenly bristling with excitement.

'Geordie, just pull over mate, the game is up.' I pleaded.

'Ah, at last a voice of reason!' Flaky was now lapping this up. I think he was actually quite pleased that we'd been spotted; all his protestations would now be justified.

'No fucking chance, they won't catch me without a fight!' Geordie attempted to push the accelerator even further down into the floor but it was already flat out. The police car was gaining, its headlights flashing on and off and above the siren I could make out the words, "PULL OVER TO THE SIDE. PLEASE STOP YOUR VEHICLE" emanating from the police Cars PA.

'Ah get fucked you pig bastards!' screamed Geordie. It appeared some demonic spirit now possessed him. He had one last attempt to find fourth gear but only managed to hit second. The car had had enough; there was a loud bang from the engine and a sudden burst of blue smoke hit the windscreen.

'Aw! Would you sodding believe it, Japanese crap!' yelled Geordie.

'Korean crap, actually,' corrected Robbo. The car hissed and spat and began to slow. The smell of burning oil was very strong and I worried the car may burst into flames at any moment.

'Maybe we can fight them off!' shouted Geordie as he manoeuvred the broken car onto the hard shoulder.

'You just don't know when to stop, do you?' cried an incredulous Flaky.

'No mate, it's time to face the music. I'd get rid of that spliff as well if I were you,' I said looking over my shoulder as the police car pulled in behind us. Two cops emerged from their respective sides and I watched as they neared our vehicle. Geordie unscrewed the top off a coke bottle and dropped the spliff into it, not before taking one last drag.

'What a waste,' bemoaned Robbo sadly. The younger copper pulled out his notebook as he stood at the back of the car noting the number plate; the older one made his way to Geordie's door, his stripes indicating he was a sergeant. He tapped on the window and Geordie reluctantly wound it down a few inches. Smoke still billowed out from the engine and the policeman coughed as he bent forward,

'Nearly missed the turn-off back there Sir,' he stated caustically.

'Aye, they don't give you enough warning, the bastards,' agreed Geordie.

'Looks like she's in a bad way,' the policeman nodded towards the engine, 'hire car is it Sir?'

'Aye, I would nay be driving it if it were mine, Japanese crap,'

'Korean crap,' said Robbo again. The young copper, a spotty faced juvenile of lanky frame and limited intelligence, came around to his superior's side.

'It's not stolen Sir, it's a hire car; hired to one Chas Dupont with a named driver of Mr Steel.'

'Well done constable,' praised the sergeant. 'And you would be Mr Steel, I take it?' the sergeant directed his question at Geordie.

'No. I'm Kincaid, Allan Kincaid,' he replied nonchalantly.

'I see, so you're not the registered driver then?' This wasn't going too badly, I thought to myself, we might even get off with a caution.

'Ahem,' coughed Flaky trying to get the officers attention. The sergeant stared quizzically into the back at a slightly sweaty faced Flaky.

'You wish to say something Sir?' invited the sergeant calmly and slowly.

'Yes, er, yes; I'm actually Mr Steel; well that is … I was Mr Steel, but now I'm a Mr Whittington …' we all turned and stared in disbelief at him; 'You see, I changed my name by deed poll some years ago, but I overlooked updating my driver's licence. So I am Mr Steel but also Mr Whittington … if you see what I mean?' The sergeant didn't move, but

265

the eyes in his head slowly swivelled around, eyeballing us all with intense mistrust.

'That wouldn't be Dick, would it Sir? Asked the sergeant.

'No it's the truth officer, I swear!' exclaimed Flaky.

'I meant Dick, as in Dick Whittington Sir; you know, the bells and all that.'

'I think you're getting him confused with Quasimodo sergeant. Although I must admit there is a striking resemblance,' sniggered Geordie unhelpfully.

'I think I know my Whittington from my Quasimodo. The sound of Bow Bells calling him back to become Lord Mayor of London,' the sergeant paused for a while as though in deep thought, 'I think there may have even been a cat in there as well,' he added carefully.

'Aye well, where there's a pussy there's usually a Dick,' added Geordie. Robbo tried unsuccessfully to restrain a laugh. The Sergeant's patience finally ran out.

'Okay you set of fucking smart arses, get out of the fucking car right now!' he barked. As we exited the car I noticed the smoke from the engine had begun to subside, which was not good, as the smell of burnt oil had been masking the smell of dope. Flaky didn't know when to shut up and tried to smooth things over.

'Of course Geordie, that's Allan, erm, Mr Kincaid, is only a learner so it can be quite intimidating driving on the motorway for the first time …' he tailed off as he realised what he'd just said. We all glared at him hatefully. The sergeant picked up on his little faux pas straight away.

'So, I take it Mr Kincaid, that not only are you not registered to drive this hire car but you are also on a provisional licence; are you aware that's it's illegal for a learner to drive a hire car and also to drive on the motorway?'

'No officer I wasn't aware of that but it doesnae matter yer see?'

'Oh and why's that Sir?'

266

'Cos I don't actually have a provisional licence yet.' Wonderful, the fuckwit twins had landed us right in it.

'I see,' said the sergeant smiling wryly. 'Would you all mind lining up alongside the car please. Now I'd like to see some ID from all of you.' Flaky had left his door open and the strong odour of dope drifted out.

'Hmm, that smells familiar,' the sergeant said, nose twitching like a Beagle. We all produced various pieces of ID apart from Geordie who didn't have anything. The younger copper checked them all as the sergeant slowly walked around the car examining inside and out with his beady eyes. His old instincts telling him he was onto something.

'And where's your ID sunshine?' the young copper addressed Geordie.

'I don't have any, SUNSHINE!' snarled Geordie. I prayed he'd keep his cool. The young copper smirked,

'Looks like you're coming to the station then.'

'Oh actually I do have some ID ...' Geordie offered hopefully. He reached deep into his overcoat and pulled out a card and handed it to the copper, who twitched and began to study it. The sergeant circumnavigated the car and returned to the line up.

'You boys wouldn't have been smoking any of that wacky backy now would you?' Flaky told the truth.

'No, definitely not Sir, I wouldn't touch the stuff; apart from it being illegal it's extremely toxic to the system.' The sergeant studied the card in the Constable's hand.

'Constable, a Library card for Dinkiad Bay does not constitute legitimate ID!' he yelled. The young copper appeared embarrassed and slightly hurt and twitched his head again, this time more violently. The sergeant turned to us all.

'I have reason to suspect that there may be illegal drugs within the confines of your car and I am therefore going to instigate a search. Now you can save us a lot of time by showing us where it is.' No one said a word.

'Okay constable, start in the boot.' The constable went to the back of the car and opened the boot; his head disappeared inside.

'You can't do that!' accused Robbo, who was clearly aware of the correct procedure.

'Yes I can, I have "just cause", which means I can stop and search.'

'Bullshit, you need a warrant!' argued Robbo.

'No I don't.'

'Yes you do! You didn't stop us on suspicion, you stopped us because of a traffic infringement, therefore you cannot search the vehicle without a warrant!' A full blown argument was now under way. The younger copper reappeared at his superior's side, clutching something in his hand. Everyone was now occupied with the ensuing quarrel.

'Oh, you seem to know the law pretty well eh? Well I'm telling you, I am well within my jurisdiction to stop and search if I have just cause …'

'Well, you're wasting your time because it'll get laughed out of court.'

'Is that an admission of guilt sir!' thundered the sergeant. I knew we were digging ourselves in deeper and suspected the constable had already discovered Robbo's illegal stash.

'Sir!' the constable tried to get his Sergeant's attention. He was ignored as the bickering raged on.

'Oh nice try, you fascist pig!' Geordie decided that this was too good not to join in. 'Shouldn't you be out catching rapists and murderers, instead of bullying law abiding citizens like our good selves?'

'Now look here smart arse …' the sergeant was becoming increasingly agitated.

'Sir!' the constable tried again but to no avail.

'Oh, starting to get aggressive now are we?' chided Geordie, which was a bit rich coming from him. 'What next? The rubber cosh in the ribs, electrodes on the testicles?'

'I've just about had enough of you lot, I knew you were trouble when I first saw you. Thirty years on the force gives you a sixth sense about these things!'

'Sir!' shouted the constable.

'What is it constable!' screamed the sergeant, resenting the intrusion into his tirade. The constable handed him a large, silver, Colt 45—Geordie's Colt 45—the Colt 45 that he'd sworn he'd disposed of. The sergeant took the gun in his hand before he realised what it was. When he looked down to examine the offending object he threw his arms up in shock and juggled with the gun, spinning it round and round before it finally fell onto the road. Everyone, apart from Geordie and me jumped back.

'Ah, yer big jesses, it's not even loaded,' derided Geordie

'Geordie, what the fuck!' I yelled at him.

'Sorry Billy boy, but I couldn't do it.' The sergeant, immediately withdrew his radio and called for backup.

'Zero Oscar Ten Four,'

'Come in Zero Oscar ten Four,' the radio crackled back.

'Request immediate assistance. Apprehended four IC1 males heading northbound at junction 57 M1. Illegal firearm discovered in S and S. Repeat, request immediate assistance.'

'On its way, zero, oscar, ten, four,' replied the radio. Now we *were* in the shit. The sergeant pulled a handkerchief from his pocket.

'Okay you lot back up against the car, don't fucking move.' He bent down and picked up the gun with his handkerchief. I heard the distant sound of many sirens approaching.

'This is a bit like "Butch Cassidy and the Sundance Kid" isn't it?' stated Geordie quite cheerfully.

'Great film, but not a good ending,' mused Robbo. The flashing lights approached rapidly; the sirens deafening. Four police cars blocked the motorway bringing traffic to an abrupt halt. Through the police cars emerged two vans that accelerated towards us. The vans dramatically screeched to a halt and out jumped eight armed police officers, four with machine guns and four with handguns.

'Oh fucking great,' muttered Robbo, 'Looks like the Rapid Response Unit. This should be interesting.'

'Okay, get on the ground, DO IT NOW!' ordered one of the armed officers. Flaky dropped like a sack of shit. The rest of us, slowly, tentatively made our way down to terra firma as you do when you're older and stiffer than you wish to be.

'Hands on the back of your heads, DO IT NOW!' We all obliged. Another van turned up, less frenetic this time but I could hear the sound of barking dogs. Out jumped another two coppers who flung open the back doors of the van. They both struggled for a few seconds before emerging with a couple of large nasty looking Dobermans; I thought of Caesar and wished I was with him walking in the Dales. One of the handlers struggled with an over enthusiastic dog. He yanked hard on the lead hoping to subdue the hound but it roundly turned on him and sunk its vicious looking canines into the fleshy part of his forearm, at which point he let go of the lead.

'Aargh! You bastard! he screamed at the dog. The dog bounded off and leapt onto one of the armed policemen, knocking him flying. As the man hit the ground, there was a large bang as his firearm was accidentally discharged.

'Firearm discharged! Firearm discharged! Officer down, officer down!' Screamed a hysterical voice from somewhere.

'Get this fucking thing off me!' yelled the disarmed copper. The Doberman had a firm grip on him and was not about to let go any time soon. Pandemonium ensued and anything could have happened. Luckily, the original sergeant took charge of the situation.

'Put those fucking guns away!' He yelled, 'Rapid response unit, more trouble than they're worth. Someone get that bloody dog back in the van. And constable, get up off the ground!' I glanced to my left and saw the young constable who was also laid prostrate on the ground next to us.

'When they said "on the ground" they were referring to the suspects NOT YOU!' shouted the sergeant. We were ordered to stand, handcuffed and searched. The only thing they found was Robbo's little stash of blow which they didn't seem particularly interested in.

'Do you realise the paperwork you've caused me now a firearm has been discharged. I'll be knee deep in forms and statements and investigations for a fucking month!' he screeched at us. The dog squad and one of the Rapid Response Teams had already departed the scene. The young constable was sent to continue his search in the boot while the older sergeant took down our details.

'And make sure you give all the luggage a good search!' shouted the sergeant to his understudy. 'Okay, you boys are going to have to come with me to the station, where you have some explaining to do.'

'Sergeant, we've got a very important gig in Leeds tonight and we can't miss it otherwise we could be penalised very heavily. We're the rock band the "Shooting Tsars", you may have heard of us?' pleaded Flaky.

'Nah, can't say that I have. As far as I'm concerned they stopped making good music the night the King of rock and roll died.'

'Fuck me, I didn't realise Shakin' Stevens was dead?' said Robbo.

'I'm talking about Elvis you smartarse,' spat the sergeant.

'You know he had a heart attack while sat on the crapper?' added Robbo tactfully. The sergeant pursed his lips as though trying to restrain himself.

'Sir,' the young copper returned with a few small plastic bags, containing white powder.

'Well done constable. A proper little chemical factory aren't we?' The sergeant sniggered in Robbo's face.

'Personal use,' he replied in a bored manner, 'only enough for personal use, not enough to be charged with dealing.'

'We'll see about that won't we,' said the sergeant. I took it that neither of them particularly liked each other—I had a sixth sense for these things.

'Sir, I've found this!' The constable held up a leather bound "Good News Bible".

'Yes constable, it's a Bible. As far as I'm aware there's no law against being in possession of a Bible.' The constable twitched twice and went back to the boot, muttering something about fundamental terrorists.

'Well said sergeant,' said Flaky, 'that happens to be mine. If more people read the Good News Bible maybe the world would be a better place to live in—what do you think Sir?'

'Oh, shut up you cretin,' he responded. I noticed Geordie eyeing Flaky suspiciously. The constable returned a few seconds later holding my suitcase.

'Sir, a large suitcase?'

'Yes constable I can see it's a suitcase, just open it and search it will you—and stop giving me a running commentary on everything you do.' The constable twitched three times and began to unzip my case.

'I heard a strange noise was coming from it Sir,' he continued sulkily.

'What sort of strange noise?' the sergeant asked as an afterthought as he busily scribbled in his notepad.

'Ah, that will be my electric toothbrush sergeant. It's very temperamental,' I explained.

'It's definitely not a toothbrush Sir,' continued the constable. He retracted his hand from my suitcase and stood there on the hard shoulder of the motorway holding up a pink spiky vibrator. All eyes turned to me.

'Yes, I do believe that is mine,' I confessed. 'I was planning to smoke it later.'

25: CUM ON FEEL THE NOIZE

We were all questioned at the police station, an old Victorian building that should have been condemned forty years ago. No charges were brought against Flaky or myself, but Robbo was charged with possession of a small quantity of class A drugs and Geordie was charged with driving without a licence, driving a vehicle without insurance, reckless driving and possession of an unlicensed firearm. The sergeant rued the fact there was no law in place for insulting members of the Royal Family, otherwise we *all* would have been charged accordingly.

I rang Chas and expected a rocket up the arse but he listened intently as I recalled the chain of events that had led to our incarceration. He seemed to become overly excited, as if inspired by the day's proceedings. I told him that we'd need to find bail for Robbo and Geordie and that if he wanted us at the show tonight he had better get his arse down here quick.

After a couple of hours they released Flaky and me with a caution, for what, I'm not sure. They carted Robbo and Geordie off to the Magistrates court. We followed by taxi. Flaky, didn't say a word the whole journey, I sensed he was slightly pissed off, and he brooded like a withdrawn teenager. By the time we arrived at the courts Chas was already waiting outside. He paced up and down on the pavement like a caged tiger. I knew we'd blown it and was expecting a typical Chas bollocking. We alighted from the taxi as the paddy wagon that transported the criminals disappeared around the back of the Magistrates court.

'Chas, thanks for coming. Sorry about all this, it … it just happened. We missed the radio interviews as you will have gathered,' I offered apologetically. He looked me straight in the eye through his oversized spectacles.

'Don't worry about the radio interviews. That's small fry.' He wore a mischievous grin and grabbed me in a big hug. He let me go and then gave Flaky a big hearty slap on the back before breaking out into a little jig, laughing like a boiling kettle as he did so. I was perplexed and glanced at Flaky who in turn raised an eyebrow in bemusement.

'I knew I could rely on you boys, I knew you wouldn't let me down.' I still didn't understand.

'Chas, you're not making any sense!' I exclaimed. He suddenly froze and looked up and down the high street like a nervous chicken that was being stalked by a fox. He peered at his watch.

'3 pm—it should be breaking about now. Another half hour and it will be pandemonium out here.' Flaky and I surveyed the street trying to spot Chas's imaginary predators but saw nothing untoward.

'What should be breaking and why will it be pandemonium?' I asked, still baffled by his behaviour. Chas appeared a little impatient with me.

'Will, when you rang me two hours ago what do you think was the first thing I did when I hung up?'

'Curse us all and then divert your journey from Leeds to Manchester?'

'No, no, no,' he laughed patronisingly. 'I got on the dog and bone and rang every media contact I know and gave them all an exclusive about your little misadventure, embellishing it a little bit along the way, not that it needed much embellishment. This story will now be breaking on the 3 pm news and newspaper editors around the country will be scrambling to get it into their late night editions. By the time we get out of court there should be a throng of journalists, TV cameramen and radio guys ready to get a few sound-bites. Our unwitting saviours. Come on, they'll be here soon, let's get inside. I've brought my chequebook to bail those two clowns out.'

#

Chas was right—by the time we emerged from court there were some media waiting for us, not quite a throng and not quite pandemonium but free publicity nonetheless. A TV crew rushed up to Flaky and a reporter stuck a microphone under his nose.

'Can we get a quick interview?' asked the reporter.

'Yes of course,' replied Flaky politely.

'And your name is?'

'I'm Flaky, I'm the drummer in the Shooting Tsars.'

'Okay, Flaky, is it true that you caused a major incident on the M6 earlier today?'

'Well no, not really, it's a storm in a teacup actually ...' he didn't get any further because Geordie, never one to miss an opportunity to air his grievances, pushed Flaky aside.

'Aye, the coppers were the storm and we were the tea cup!' The reporter immediately saw more sensationalist potential in Geordie than Flaky and excitedly directed his questions towards him.

'And your name is?'

'Geordie, I'm the bass player in the Shooting Tsars.'

'Okay, Geordie, what happened?'

'I'll tell you exactly what happened! We were busily minding our own business travelling up the M6 towards Manchester to do some radio interviews before the gig in Leeds tonight. We were doing nothing wrong, travelling at slightly under the speed limit, all was good. I manoeuvred cautiously into the outside lane to overtake a wagon and all of a sudden a fucking Jaguar comes screaming up our arse blaring its horn and flashing its lights—completely reckless! Must have been doing at least 120—130 mph. It was carrying Princess Anne and that's when it all started.'

'Are you sure it was Princess Anne?'

'Oh aye, you couldnae mistake a face like that.'

'And what happened next?' By now the rest of the media were being drawn to this wild looking behemoth with the Scottish brogue.

'I politely moved back into the middle lane once I'd passed the wagon,' continued Geordie really getting into the flow of things. 'And then I noticed our turnoff at which point I indicated left and moved smoothly across into the exit lane. Unfortunately, there were some stray bollards that had been knocked over by some clown and our car hit them and that must have caused damage to the engine and then next thing I know there's flashing lights and sirens and the coppers are trying to force us into the side barrier. Well, being a law abiding citizen I stopped the car in a timely manner, pulled on the handbrake and put my hazards on to alert other road users—that's when the engine exploded. For some reason best known to themselves, the cops thought it was a gun going off, panicked, and called the Rapid Response Unit. The next thing we know there's armed police, machine guns and vicious dogs bearing down on us. We were handcuffed, thrown to the ground and had guns stuck into the back of our heads. I really thought I was going to be assassinated by my own police Force. You hear about these things in third world countries run by dictatorships, but you don't expect it to happen to you as you casually saunter up the M6. Anyway, out of nowhere there's a sudden volley of machine gun fire. I didn't see what happened as my face was planted firmly into the Tarmac. We were then forcibly picked up and thrown into the back of a Black Maria.' Flaky tried to intervene.

'Can I just interrupt for a moment ...' Everyone ignored him.

'There's been allegations that you were found with drugs, a gun and a sex toy—can you confirm or deny these allegations?' A reporter shouted.

'Salacious and inaccurate accusations, nothing more. Clearly, invented by the police to cover up their own brutality and incompetence and smear the good name of four innocent men. Instead of hounding law abiding, hard working, honest musicians like ourselves, why aren't the police charging Princess Anne's driver with obliterating the speed limit? It's one rule for them and one rule for the rest of us.' Another reporter jumped in yelling a question.

'Geordie, are you inferring the Royal Family have immunity from the common law of the land?'

'I couldnae have said it better myself. The Royals and the police both have immunity from the law. Is this a modern 21st century democracy or is it still some sort of feudalistic serfdom? An aristocracy run by a few privileged inbreds, kept in power by a corrupt police force. If I'd been to Eton or Oxford, I'm sure I'd still be going about my lawful business unhindered by the cruel tyranny of our boys in blue. But as I'm working class and Scottish, I do not have the same human rights ... to the Establishment I am nothing more than a faceless number to be used and abused at will. I believe it's time the honest, hardworking people of this country stood up in unison and put an end to this archaic neo-fascist regime. United we stand divided we fall—all for one and one for all—power to the people!' Geordie thrust his arm into the air with fist clenched. The media throng were in raptures—Geordie was pure gold dust to them. The questions kept coming for the next twenty minutes, most of them answered by Geordie, much to the delight of Chas. Finally, after checking his watch, Chas reluctantly intervened.

'Okay Ladies and Gents, we really must wrap it up there. The Shooting Tsars really must get back on the road as they have an important gig tonight at the Leeds Arena. It's part of the "Resurrection Tour". I have a press release here for you all detailing future tour dates and if any of you want to cover the gigs then please give me a call and I will get you in on the guest list and a backstage pass should you wish to do any further interviews with the boys.'

'Can we get some photos of the group together before you go?' shouted a photographer.

'Of course, of course. Boys over here please.' We lined up dutifully and cameras whirred and clicked for the next thirty seconds as Chas handed out his press release.

#

Twenty minutes later were on the M62 heading towards Leeds. I was in the front with Chas, the others in the back. There was a mood of bonhomie and good natured ribbing amongst us all—apart from Flaky looked mildly annoyed. Chas called Jez on his mobile to make sure there were no issues at the venue.

'Good, good. Yep, we should be there in about an hour depending on the traffic. Okay, so everything's under control. And do you know how ticket sales are going? Really, really, that's amazing! Yes, well something has happened. I'll explain when I get there. Okay, good work Jez. Catch ya soon,' he ended the call and looked across at me.

'YES, YES, YES!' he screamed. 'We've nearly sold out. This morning we'd sold two thousand tickets; barely a third of the capacity and that was after six weeks of costly advertising. Now there's only a few hundred tickets left! Jez said that it was just after three o'clock that it all started kicking off. The ticket office was inundated with calls reserving tickets. This is it! We've cracked it, I knew I could rely on you boys. All publicity is good publicity,' he stated. 'But in your case, bad publicity is the best publicity. I'm gonna milk this for all it's worth. This is pure gold! You are now going to be portrayed as the bad boys of rock. You've come back from the past to show all these clean, goody two shoes, automatons what rock and roll is really about. It's about drugs, violence and sex crazed debauchery; you are the beasts of hell returned with a vengeance!' I didn't feel like a beast of hell with a vendetta, but nevertheless, the booming ticket sales was good news. 'You're going to make the Sex

Pistols look like fucking choir boys. The rest of this tour is going to be a raging success.' Flaky couldn't contain himself any longer.

'I don't think the sort of behaviour exhibited by certain members of this band today should be condoned let alone glorified. The kids out there need role models, not drug affected psychotics.'

'Bullshit!' yelled Chas. 'I'll tell you what the kids want, the same thing that kids of every generation have wanted, excitement, rebellion, someone to believe in even if they have nothing to say, that's what the kids want. They want a band that can buck the system, a band that says "fuck you" to society, a band that breaks the rules, they want Butch Cassidy and the Sundance Kid! Loveable rogues!'

'And you know what happened to them,' added Robbo.

'From now on you boys are headlining and if any of the others don't like it they can go fuck off.'

'Here, here,' applauded Geordie. Chas looked at his watch and turned on the radio.

'Shush now. I want to listen to the news.' We all listened intently as the news announcer went through the usual dull stories about government enquiries, policy u-turns and a bomb blast in the middle east. Chas was urging the announcer on.

'Come on you bastards, come on now, don't let me down.'

'And lastly,' the radio announcer continued, 'recently reformed rock band the Shooting Tsars were today involved in a bizarre police chase and an imbroglio with a member of the Royal Family. According to reports they were forced off the motorway by a speeding Royal cavalcade, which is believed to have been carrying Her Royal Highness, Princess Anne. They were pulled over by the police whereupon the Rapid Response Unit were called to deal with a suspected firearm. During the ensuing fracas a number of weapons were discharged, a police dog handler was bitten on the arm, and a small amount of class A drugs were seized along with a sex toy. All four band members were arrested, two later being charged with numerous offences and released on bail and another two released with a caution. The band's Tour Manager, Chas Dupont, said the band had been unfairly harassed and brutalised by the police and he hadn't yet decided whether he was going to launch a civil lawsuit against them for unlawful arrest. The Manchester Police declined to comment at this time and a spokesman for the Palace also declined our request for a comment. The band are due to play the Leeds Arena tonight as part of the nationwide "Resurrection" tour. And now to sport with Andrew Crudspoon.'

'You little beauty!' Screamed Chas. We all cheered apart from Flaky.

'Aw c'mon,' he cried, 'that is rubbish. This story has taken on a life of its own. The incident with Princess Anne, if it was her, was at least thirty minutes before the police pulled us over. This is all your fault Geordie, you've started a right brouhaha. And as for police brutality, I thought they were extremely measured considering the circumstances.' At that moment Flaky's phone rang.

'Hi love, no, no, of course not. It's not true … well parts of it are true but …' it was his wife Gillian. 'No, the sex toy was not mine … it was Will's … well how would I know what he was doing with it … no, of course not. Yes there was a small amount of drugs found … absolutely not! You know how I feel about drugs … yes, yes, of course. I'll call you tonight after the gig and I'll explain everything.' I looked at Robbo, Geordie and Chas who were all sat quietly smirking. It was mean of me, but I couldn't help but have a little chuckle, however, it didn't last long. My phone rang and I looked at the number. Shit—it was my Mother.

'Hi Mam, no, no, it's not true, well, most of it's not true. You know what the media are like …'

#

We were nearing Leeds and were all dying to get out of the car and as far away from Flaky as we could. His verbal tongue lashing from his wife had left him in a sour mood and his passive aggressive hectoring was driving everyone up the wall. First he started on Robbo and his drug habit. When he didn't get much of a response from him, he started on me.

'I firmly believe all this is laid at your door Will. If you hadn't have given the keys of the car to Geordie, much to my opposition, none of this would ever have happened. What were you thinking? Why would you do such a thing?' I didn't answer. I bit my tongue and let out a deep sigh. Flaky could suck the life out of any situation. Eventually he backed off when he realised he was not going to get a response from me. Unfortunately, he then went from passive aggressive to active aggressive and picked on Geordie.

'Anyway Geordie what in hell's name were you doing with that firearm and where did you get it from?'

'It's a gun, a Colt 45 actually and it's my talisman,' he said cheerily. 'I got it on our last tour of the States. I traded it for the "Cradle to the Rave" gold disc we received with a couple of New York rappers.'

'I always wondered where that gold disc went,' grumbled Robbo.

'Well, that just shows what a bloody idiot you really are,' continued Flaky. 'You smuggled an illegal gun out of America and back into the UK. Do you *realise* what would have happened to you if you had been found with a gun attempting to board a plane or get through customs?'

'Yep,' replied Geordie. 'I'd have been well and truly fucked. At least fifteen years in jail.'

'And yet, knowing the risks, you still went through with it? That is tactical stupidity and wilful ignorance. In psychology it's called "optimism bias" or the "ostrich effect"; the ability to consciously and deliberately overlook negative information in the false belief that it will never happen to "you". Classic risk-taking behaviour.'

'Well thank you Sigmund Freud, but there was no risk,' countered Geordie.

'Oh this is good, this is really good. I'd really like to sit down and have a long session with you. I've been assessing you since that first night in London. Shall I list the personality disorders that I've witnessed in your behaviour so far?'

'Aye, why not,' obliged Geordie.

'Okay, well where do I start? Right, first of all you have anti-social personality disorder, you are aggressive, violent and sadistic; then there's narcissistic personality disorder, the inability to take criticism but more than willing to dish it out ...'

'That's absolute bullshit,' snorted Geordie, who unwittingly confirmed Flaky's accusation.

'Ha see! Proof! You cannot take criticism.'

'Now listen here Flaky ...' Geordie interrupted.

'No you listen—I haven't finished yet. You also suffer from borderline personality disorder; risk taking, impulsive and erratic behaviour, explosive temper and mood swings. And lastly, schizotypal personality disorder, uncaring towards other people, lack of empathy, sympathy and having unusual thoughts ...'

'Ah fuck off pencil dick,' Geordie snapped, 'I don't give two shits what you think. Anyway what about you? You suffer from a superiority complex. Just because you've got a degree in psychology you think you're better than everyone else. Plus you suffer from PITFA syndrome.'

'I do not have a superiority complex!' shouted Flaky. 'And what in hells name is PITFA syndrome? I've never heard of it.'

'Pain in the fucking arse syndrome,' Geordie shouted back. 'You're an insufferable, pompous, tit!'

'I am not pompous. Will, am I pompous?'

'Well ...' I began, before being interrupted.

'See, even Will thinks you're a pompous tit ...'

'Hang on a minute, don't bring me into this,' I implored.

'Robbo, am I pompous?'

'Can everyone just chill man, just chill,' replied Robbo.

'Okay Geordie, give me one example of when I've been pompous,' demanded Flaky.

'I could give you a hundred. But one in particular, you changing your last name. "Oo look at me, I'm so famous, I can't handle it. I must change my name", only a pompous prig would do that.'

'Well ten years ago I was famous and it was intolerable everyone knowing who I was ...' Geordie cut him off.

'Bullshit, you were never that famous. *I* was famous due to my height and rakish good looks, everyone knew who Geordie was. Will was famous because he's got charisma and he's the lead singer. Robbo was famous because he's Daddy Cool, ace guitarist, but you, you were just the scrawny git who banged the drums. Anyway, as usual you didn't listen to what I said, which for the record, is another symptom of your superiority complex. I said that smuggling that gun involved no risk—well not for me anyway.'

'And what exactly do you mean by that?' yelled Flaky who was beginning to lose control.

'Quite simple really—I hid the gun in your suitcase.'

'You didn't!'

'Oh yes I did. And by the way, don't think that I haven't noticed your new found religious bent. I spotted it that first night in London. The way you talk, the way you walk, everything about you reeks of religious zealotry!'

'Poppycock! You can't stand it, just because I believe in something, whereas *you, you*, you believe in nothing! You're a hater and a flaming despot.'

'Boys, boys, calm down,' I tried to intervene but it had no effect.

'Listen wank features, I don't care what anyone believes in. My Nan has been a Presbyterian all her life and good for her. If she finds comfort and solace in that, well that's fine by me. But you strut around with an arrogance that only religious nut-jobs have—as if you have all the answers. Anyway, what particular denomination are you … Born Again Ninja? Six Minute Adventist? The Evangelical Order of Bald Badgers?'

'I'm a Born Again Christian if you must know!' Shouted Flaky who was now turning a beetroot red. 'And I don't preach. I have not said one thing to any of you that could be misconstrued as preaching.'

'Aye, you don't have to, it oozes out of you like shit out of a broken pipe.'

'Take that back!' screamed Flaky.

'Pigs arse I'll take it back!'

'I abhor violence, but if you don't take that back I may very well strike you!'

'Oh yeah, give it your best shot Popeye!' Flaky lurched across Robbo, who was unfortunately sat between the pair, and threw a punch which connected with Geordie's chin. There was silence. Geordie looked genuinely shocked and for a few seconds sat comprehending what had just happened. The silence didn't last long. Geordie reached across and grabbed Flaky by the throat and began to throttle him. Flaky responded by flailing his arms in all directions but only managed to whack Robbo in the head—an experience he didn't enjoy one little bit.

'Whoa man, uncool, like totally uncool!'

'Geordie,' I yelled, 'let go of him, you're strangling him!'

'Aye, that's the intention, the ferret faced fucker!' Chas turned to me and laughed.

'Haha, it's just like the old days eh?' There was now a full blown fracas in the car. Flaky was gasping for breath as his thrashing arms and legs became increasingly violent. I was trying to prise Geordie's giant mitt away from Flaky's neck and Robbo was trying to fend off Flaky's wayward arms.

'Holy shit!' roared Chas. 'Boys, boys, look at this.' We all stopped what we were doing and stared out of the car window. We'd arrived in Leeds and were slowly crawling up the road towards the venue. I couldn't believe my eyes. There was a queue half way around the block and all the

284

way down the main high street. Thousands of people waiting to get into the venue, which was still two hours away from opening its doors. The place was a-buzz and I felt the hairs stand up on the back of my neck. This was like our heyday.

'Fuck me blind,' exclaimed Geordie as he released his grip on Flaky's neck. 'Are they *our* fans?' Chas turned to him with a warm smile.

'They certainly are Geordie, me old China. The Shooting Tsars are definitely back.'

26: RIDERS ON THE STORM

The gig was an absolute blinder. By the time we took to the stage the place was completely full. The atmosphere was razor sharp, the raucous crowd transmuting their energy to us. The feeling of euphoria I experienced was ten times better than any drug I'd ever taken. After three encores, we finally departed and the crowd had truly got their monies worth. Backstage the place was buzzing with fans, old friends and journalists. Drugs and liquor were consumed in extra large quantities. By midnight I was feeling quite famished so checked out if anyone fancied a curry. Connie and Rick from the Green Circles were up for it as were Robbo and Geordie.

#

At the curry house, we ordered a mountain of food and beers and the feeding frenzy began. All was going swimmingly until a group of about eight rugged looking blokes walked in sporting England Rugby Union shirts. They sat down at a table opposite to us. They were in a loud and boisterous mood, but that didn't bother us as our group was also loud and boisterous. More beer flowed, vindaloos, masalas and plates of chapattis and dishes of rice were consumed. We all talked loudly and excitedly about the day's proceedings; the police chase, the hyped up news story; the gig we had just done. In hindsight, I suppose Connie inadvertently started the chain of events that brought the evening to a premature close. The man was a larrikin, a drug dealer and a fence, but he wasn't a trouble causer. Geordie and Robbo had put up a one hundred pound bet to say that Connie couldn't walk on his hands from one end of the table to the other. Connie accepted the bet with relish. I must admit, I thought he was going to make it. He managed to precariously weave a path through the obstacles on the table, his small sturdy frame teetering dangerously close to the edge. Rivulets of sweat flowed from his bald head and dropped in a steady stream onto the tablecloth. His bandmate, Rick, encouraged him on.

'Go on Connie soft lad, you can do it!' He yelled, fist-punching the air. The whole restaurant was now in attendance, crowding around the table, egging him on. He bypassed an oily plate of korma, manoeuvred past an onion bhaji and pirouetted around a dish of pilaf rice. He was less than three hand strides from completing his mission when a burly, blonde haired, rugby rock ape grabbed hold of his trouser leg and began to pour a pint of beer down it. A dark patch appeared all the way down Connie's leg and his crotch began to leak fluid. In a desperate attempt to see what was happening, he lifted his head and strained to look up. He wobbled, he tottered and his arms began to quiver. In doing so, he shifted his centre of balance and gravity takes no prisoners. There was an audible gasp and groan from the mesmerised audience. His bald, sweaty head made contact with a steaming hot plate of vindaloo and he skidded off the table at a rate of knots landing ungainly with his legs behind his ears in a most unsightly pose. Alas, poor Connie—I knew he fell. On the way down his flailing legs had managed to upturn numerous plates sending gloopy splodges of curry flying through the air and splattering many of his adoring audience. Connie looked up at the gawping, grinning faces.

'That's gotta be worth a ton, surely?'

'No fucking chance!' shouted Geordie and Robbo simultaneously. Connie got up and wiped himself down and his audience returned to their seats. A couple of waiters, who were less than impressed with the proceedings, appeared and began cleaning up the mess, shepherded by the elderly restaurant manager who barked orders and looked similarly miffed. Just as everything seemed to be calming down one of the rugby crew lit the blue touch paper.

'Hey Gupta?' he shouted to the waiter who was wiping the floor. The waiter ignored him. 'Hey Gupta, I'm fucking speaking to you.' The young waiter stopped his cleaning and looked at Boz.

'My name is James actually, you dickhead,' he hissed back in a Leeds accent.

'You're not going to let him speak to you like that are you Boz?' encouraged one of the rugby crew. Boz could not lose face now.

'Clean my fucking shoes you bastard and I'll forget you called me a dickhead,' ordered Boz. The manager tried to intervene.

'Okay, you boys have had your fun, now please finish up your food and pay your bill.' The rugby boys laughed and began mocking the old man in bad Indian accents as Boz kept on baiting the young waiter.

'Did you hear me or what? Clean my shoes you bastard!' The waiter took his cloth and bent down as though he was about to clean his aggressor's shoes. Our table fell silent—this had gone far enough. The waiter spat on the shoes and instead of rubbing the spittle in to aid the polishing, he stood and threw the cloth at Boz.

'Here, clean your own fucking shoes—dickhead!' There was silence around the room. Boz slowly rose from his chair as a chorus of "oos" emanated from his mates.

'What did you fucking say?'

'He said, "clean your own fucking shoes—dickhead." Are you deaf, daft or both.' It was the voice of Geordie. There was a chorus of dropped utensils on pottery as the whole rugby crew now stood aggressively to attention. The waiters and the manager edged slowly away. Connie and Rick pushed their chairs slightly back from the table. Robbo looked at me and I looked at Robbo.

'Here we fucking go,' I whispered in a resigned tone under my breath. Boz and his pals walked towards our table. They were all big lads, tall and wide and more importantly, there were eight of them and just the five of us. I felt a rush of adrenaline and looked around hoping to find a moderate, reasonable person, capable of diffusing a difficult situation—I saw none.

'Who the fuck do you think you're speaking to greaseball?' snarled Boz. Geordie was still seated, quietly eating his food. After what seemed like an eternity, but was no more than a couple of seconds, Geordie stopped chewing, picked up a napkin and delicately dabbed the edges of his mouth. The tension was building. I could feel my heart begin to pound as fight or flight kicked in. Geordie gently laid down his napkin and stood up. A flicker of surprise ran across the faces of the rugby gang as Geordie unwrapped his tall sinewy frame. I don't think they expected this bedraggled looking tramp to be so tall and imposing. There was silence. Geordie spoke in a firm but friendly voice.

'Now what I suggest is this; one—you apologise to me; two—you apologise to the waiters over there, and three—you sit down and quietly enjoy the rest of your meal.' Geordie sucked air through one of his few remaining front teeth, which made a gentle whistling sound. It unnerved the gang. Boz laughed, but it was an empty laugh. He looked over his shoulder, checking that his back up was still there. He turned back to Geordie and extended an arm and stuck his finger out at him. *Oh no Boz—not a good idea.* There was no going back now.

'You're fucking dead pal!' In one swift move Geordie grabbed the accusing finger and snapped it back. There was a cracking sound as the bone broke and a yell of pain from Boz. Still holding his finger, Geordie pulled it towards him and headbutted Boz on the bridge of the nose. Another cracking sound and an explosion of blood. I'm not sure exactly what happened next as someone kindly decided to crack a beer bottle over my head and everything became a little bit hazy. All I remember seeing was arms and legs, kicking and punching, the sound of breaking bones, the soft dull thud of yielding flesh being pummelled and a raging Scottish accent in full flight. I heard the distant sound of police sirens,

289

the scurrying of feet and then the icy touch of cold hard steel being roughly clamped around my wrists.

#

The police were bastards. They'd kept us locked up for over three hours and then released us at five in the morning without charge and without breakfast. In the space of twelve hours we'd been arrested twice—that was good going by anyone's standard. It was cold, windy and wet and I was tired, hungry and extremely thirsty. My head throbbed and I occasionally placed my fingertips tentatively on my temple to feel the swelling.

Our hotel was about fifteen minutes away. We walked up past Leeds Town Hall and then took a right turn through the financial centre. The traffic was sparse, the occasional taxi and the odd early bird. It was still too early for the buses. I stopped to light a cigarette as the others walked slowly and silently ahead. Geordie and Connie both looked unscathed—fucking typical considering they'd both started it all with their ridiculous bet. Robbo looked like a butchers shop window. He had a split lip, two black eyes and a lump the size of a golf ball on his forehead. Rick didn't seem too bad, although it was hard to tell, because he looked fucked even before the fight. I puffed on a cigarette and trudged disconsolately behind the others.

'Hey lads!' a voice shouted out. We all turned and looked behind us. A young bloke wearing a green parka, zipped up against the weather and carrying a large camera, came running up to us. He offered out his hand.

'My name's Steve Woolton. I'm a freelance photographer. Chas told me to come and get some shots of you all.'

'Oh yeah, pleased to meet you,' I said shaking his hand. 'But I don't think we're looking particularly photogenic at the moment.' The others had sauntered back to see what was going on. Steve stood and inspected us all.

'Bloody hell. Chas said you'd been in a bit of a fight. Came off second best did ya?'

'Don't you believe it,' countered Geordie, 'wait till you see the culprits.'

'Okay. Well full frontal shots aren't going to work, it'll scare the kiddies and grandmas. I've got an idea—why don't you all spread out in a line and just walk down the street and I'll get some photos from behind. Imagine you're at the OK Corral and you're walking into town to confront the baddies. You know, attitude, cocky swagger and all that.' No one was much feeling like a photo shoot but all we had to do was spread out and keep walking.

'Okay,' I said. 'But that's all. We aren't doing any re-shoots or fucking around with poses.'

'No, of course not.' We set off again in silence, slowly spreading out in staggered formation across the pavement.

'Yeah that looks great,' shouted Steve as his camera clicked away. The sun suddenly appeared low on the horizon in between two large office blocks and I looked up to witness thin needles of rain illuminated in a rainbow of colours. I thought of Flaky tucked up warm and safe in his hotel bed oblivious to the previous evening's turmoil and envied him with a passion.

'Okay lads, I've got some good shots here. Look in the music press this week and you may see yourselves, who knows, if they come out alright they may even make the tabloids.' Steve turned and jogged away. We all morosely walked on, not the least bit interested.

We arrived at the hotel and at first the concierge wasn't even going to let us in until we convinced him who we were. We were all about to make our way to our respective rooms when we noticed Chas in the bar waving us through.

'Boys, boys over here!' he called out. We all joined him and he ordered a round of whiskeys for us all. Just what I needed at five thirty in the morning. Chas was drunk and in an extraordinarily good mood.

291

'How come the bars still open,' I inquired.

'Oh, I bunged the manager a ton. Hey, did a photographer catch up with you?'

'Yeah, he got some shots from behind. How did you know we'd been locked up and released?'

'Contacts my son, contacts.' He took out a plastic bag of white powder, spilt a small amount onto the bar, took out a credit card and a fifty pound note and began chopping up the powder into a long white line.

'Who's for a bit of Charlie then?' he asked with a beam on his face. We all snorted a line including the barman and Chas ordered another round of drinks. I noticed that Geordie's antipathy towards Chas didn't extend to the bloke's stash.

'Here, look at these little beauties,' said Chas as he grabbed a swathe of newspapers that lay on the bar. I read the tabloid headlines with horror.

WE ARE NOT AMUSED

Aptly Named Ageing Rockers—The Shooting Tsars—Take on Royal Family and Our Boys In Blue

BACK   FROM   THE   PAST   WITH   A   BLAST
Communist party members, The Shooting Tsars, cause motorway carnage and threaten our democracy

SEX   &   DRUGS   &   ROCK   'N   ROLL!
All for one and one for all! Bad boys of rock, The Shooting Tsars, in Police shootout after insulting our Royal Family

The last headline had a montage of photos showing a pile of white powder, a gun, a vibrator and a picture of Geordie with his arm thrust into the air. I couldn't look at any more. I thought of my Mother and Fiona and even bloody Arthur and Ethel back in Whitstone.

'Aw God,' I groaned.

'What's wrong Will?' asked Chas, astounded at my reaction. 'This is fucking gold my son, pure fucking gold! I said we needed traction and fuck me rigid, have we got traction now!'

27: YAKETY YAK

Whoever had organised the itinerary for the tour (Chas), was a fuckwit! We'd zigzagged the country like drunken sailors in a rudderless rowing boat. From Leeds to Manchester, Manchester to Newcastle and today, back across the Pennines to Liverpool. The thought of another four hours drive in the company of my fellow comrades did not fill me with joy. The only bright side was that Chas had organised another hire car for us so we could arrive a couple of hours early to do some interviews. Robbo was driving, Geordie was trying to sleep off the mother of all hangovers in the front and I was stuck in the back with "the chosen one" who was busy scouring the political section of his paper.

The fight in the curry house had made the papers and once again the press had blown it out of all proportion. Then there was the photograph. Five of us, backs to camera, walking down a deserted Leeds street early in the morning with a slight rainbow in the distance. I must admit, it did look pretty cool. We looked dangerous and aloof, as though nothing could touch us. A few days ago Chas was having to beg to get interviews and a little publicity. Now his mobile never stopped ringing and we were doing around ten interviews a day between press, radio and TV. Despite the turnaround in our fortunes we all sat in moribund silence, the only sound was the gentle hum of the car engine and the occasional grunt from Geordie. It was grey and wet outside and I was tired, weary and bored, oh so bored. This was the crap part about being in a band on the road; hours and hours of driving, confined in a steel box, listening to drivel and petty arguments, smelling others body odours, nit picking and character assassinations. It was tedious—and when you finally reached your destination there would be sound-checks and hanging around while the sound guys fixed everything up. In between, it would be mindless interviews with spotty faced students, well meaning fanzine writers and pretentious music press journos, or worse still, the inane banter with clueless DJ's. Then back to the hotel and unpacking and showering and dressing. If you were lucky you may get an hour to yourself. Then back to the gig and the dressing room and all the other bands. More interviews, more waffle, more petty arguments about who'd stolen whose beer or ate so and so's sandwich. But as the night wore on the excitement and tension would build. Then it would be your turn to go onstage and you'd get butterflies in the stomach, the sudden bouts of self-doubt, the nervous jitters and the last minute rush to the toilet. You'd take to the stage to a huge roar and blast straight into your set. Then you were lost in another world where time accelerated, where every sense was heightened, where the adrenaline and euphoria took you higher and faster than any drug ever could. And before you knew it you'd be back in the dressing room, congratulating each other and grinning like idiots. You were on top of the world, speeding on nervous energy and adulation. And you'd want it to last and last so you'd drink more and take more drugs and party on till two, three, four in the morning, before you finally crashed, exhausted, into your hotel bed. Maybe you'd sleep, maybe you wouldn't. Maybe you'd done too many drugs and your heart and mind were racing, refusing to let your spent body recover. And if sleep finally did come, it would be short and empty. You'd wake feeling groggy, tired, ill. Your body ached, your head thumped, your tongue was furry, your throat was sore. You'd tentatively get showered and dressed and stagger downstairs for a breakfast that you could hardly stomach. Then you'd pack once again and wait in the reception for the tour bus to come and pick you up or for the hire car to arrive. Then you'd start all over again. The long tedious journey. Each town started to look the same, the roads just one long piece of never ending bitumen, the Happy Eaters, Macdonald's, KFC, motorway cafes. Everywhere you went, the same monotonous uniformity, the same ubiquitous blandness, ad infinitum, ad nausea. This was the life of a band on the road and I hated it. But for that few magical moments on stage, it was worth it.

#

We drove down the A1 from Newcastle and were soon back in the greatest of all counties—Yorkshire. We were doing a slight detour back to my house as I'd received a text from John Peterson the previous night asking if I'd found the copy of the Tsars original recording contract that he'd asked me for. I texted him back apologising and explaining I had totally forgotten about it and that I would get it to him ASAP. I was still not sure why he wanted to look at it, as it was long ago defunct but it was the least I could do for him considering he'd looked over the tour contract for us all those weeks ago.

As we drove down the long serpentine road into the somnolent village of Whitstone I suddenly got a mixture of emotions. I immediately felt happy and on a high but then came a rush of melancholia. It was only another couple of weeks on the road with the tour but I'd had enough and just wanted to get back to my old life. I wanted Fiona to be here. We could go for long walks and talk and stop off at rustic little pubs and have lunch. At the end of the day we could snuggle up on the sofa with Caesar snoring contentedly at our feet.

'Robbo, pull over,' I instructed. He pulled up outside the Beaconsfield Arms. 'This is my local and they still do dripping on bread sarnies! I'm famished.'

'Saturated fat, very healthy. No doubt washed down with a few pints of ale,' scolded Flaky.

'Sounds like nirvana to me,' replied Robbo. Geordie suddenly came to.

'Aye, I could do with a hair of the dog. Spanking idea Billy boy.' We all alighted and went into the pub. Its only patron was Arthur who was sat in his familiar place at a table near the window. We all walked over to him and he was somewhat surprised to see me.

'Ay up lad, as tha finished gallivanting off around the countryside? I wasn't expecting you back for another week or two.'

'No, I just need to pick something up from the house. Arthur, let me introduce you to the Shooting Tsars, this is Robbo, Flaky and Geordie.' They all shook hands and exchanged pleasantries. I went to the bar and ordered four pints of bitter and a glass of cordial for Flaky and eight rounds of dripping on bread and a salad sandwich for you know who. We all clustered around the little wooden table and gave Arthur a full account of our life on the road. He'd laugh and giggle as we recounted our adventures and occasionally break in with a, "well I never," or "I'll go 't foot of 'r stairs". He'd apparently missed the screaming headlines of a few days ago as he never mentioned anything. He and Ethel weren't the types to be glued to the national media and I was thankful for small mercies. I'd already had a long heated telephone call with my Mother about the motorway incident. What surprised me most all was the fact that she wasn't that bothered about the gun, drugs or insulting a member of the Royal Family but the fact that a sex thingy had been found. She couldn't bring herself to say the word "vibrator". I'd also called Fiona after plucking up the courage. I thought at the very least there would be cold, indifferent silence on the other end of the phone but she found the whole episode hilarious. I assured her that it wasn't in the least bit funny at the time.

We devoured our sandwiches like a pack of wolverines and washed it all down with another pint before jumping back into the car. I offered Arthur a lift back up the hill but he declined.

'Nay lad. Are Ethel's wallpapering front parlour. Best I keep out of her way for a couple of hours.' I laughed and said goodbye. Obviously, it had never entered his head that he could possibly be the one doing the wallpapering.

When we got to my house I gave Flaky and Geordie a quick guided tour and they were suitably impressed.

'Fuck me Billy boy, this is a bloody palatial mansion. Hey, Flaky, we're in the wrong business mate, we should have been songwriters, all those publishing royalties certainly pay the bills. We're just the dumb arse rhythm section.'

'I think for the first time this tour Geordie, I agree with you,' Flaky replied. I went into my office and rummaged around in the filing cabinet and finally found the old contract. It was pretty thick, about forty pages long. I pulled out the staple, turned the printer on, slid the document into the auto-feed and pressed scan to email and entered John Peterson's address. It was going to take a good ten minutes to scan so in the meantime I grabbed hold of Robbo and took him out the back.

'What's all this about Will?'

'I want your opinion and advice. Follow me.' I walked down the long garden and to the disused barn. 'Could this be turned into a studio and if so, for how much?' Robbo smiled and entered the barn, slowly feeling the walls and peering into the roof cavity.

'Well, it would take a bit of work. You'd need to get a damp course built into the stone walls and a waterproofed concrete floor. Probably need new slates on the roof. Windows, floating floor, at least two doorways. I'm no expert in building matters but I reckon it would cost you around forty G's to get it up to scratch and then there's the studio equipment. I mean you could spend another forty G's or over a million. What exactly are you after?'

'I'll tell you all about it in the car.'

Back inside I checked the scan had gone through, locked up the house and a few minutes later we made our way out of Whitstone heading towards the M6 and the home of the Diddy Men.

#

'So come on Will, why the sudden interest in a recording studio?' asked Robbo who had handed over driving duties to the dawdling Flaky, much to Geordies annoyance.

'Well, you know when I met John Peterson, for him to have a look at the tour contracts ...'

'Yeah, I remember ...'

'Well he mentioned an idea he had and I've been chewing it over ever since. I'm not much into this so-called digital age but he said that we could make music without a record company or manager and that we could do it on our terms. Basically we would have our own website and any music we made we could upload for sale from there. Plus everything else that is saleable, merchandise, DVD's, whatever. The beauty of it is that we could do it to our own timetable. We wouldn't do it the old way, you know, release a single, followed by an album and then a worldwide tour to back it up, followed by another six months recording the next album—I'm not into that at all. We'd record when we actually had something to record and when everyone's available. Maybe release EP's, four or five songs at a time. We would have complete artistic freedom to do whatever we wanted. As for touring, well we wouldn't do the long arduous tours that take a year to complete. We could do the festival season or maybe a few short tours, you know, two or three weeks max; or maybe we don't play live at all. It would be entirely up to us.'

'You know what, that sounds like a bloody good idea,' said Robbo who appeared deep in thought.

'Hmm, you maybe onto something there, Will,' added Flaky as he eyeballed me through the rearview mirror. 'I could still keep my job. The band would be like a hobby.'

'Hang on a mo ... you mean we could make music when we wanted, how we want it and sell it without any corporate vampire or cockney wide boy manager taking a massive cut?' Quizzed Geordie.

'That's right Geordie. As John Peterson said, it's the punk ethos—DIY. The only thing we would need help with is the publishing side of it, you know getting royalties from airplay and what not, but John said he was all over that and would gladly help us out.'

'And do you trust this Peterson guy? He's not just another fucking Chas Dupont in disguise is he?' asked Geordie in a suspicious tone.

'No. I trust him implicitly. He's a fan—a massive fan. He's already loaded and has a successful business. I genuinely believe he just wants to see us making music again and if he can be involved in any way, well, that's his pay off. Anyway, food for thought.' The car trundled on as everyone fell silent.

#

At last we arrived in Liverpool, home of the Beatles, Gerry and the Pacemakers, Echo and the Bunnymen, the La's, Cast and of course that quartet of rogues and rascals, the Green Circles. Under Chas's edict, we were the headline band for the rest of the tour but we'd graciously offered to step down a rung to let the Circles headline their hometown.

Chas was in and out of the dressing room relating reviews of our previous gigs, updating us on the total audience attendance so far and ushering in journalists for interviews. A few members of the Crows were mooching around eating burgers and kebabs. A couple of the roadies were playing pool. Robbo was having a snooze in a corner; Geordie was cleaning his bass guitar meticulously and Flaky was reciting a sanitised version of life on the road to his doting wife via his mobile. It was a typical scene of relaxed time wasting before the hectic night schedule. There was a sense of calm, almost tranquillity, the only person who spoilt the moment was Chas who seemed to have an unquenchable supply of nervous energy. I was restringing my guitar, minding my own business when Chas walked over with a spotty, nerdy looking youth in tow. I suspected he was from the University newspaper, they always appeared the same. My suspicions were confirmed.

'Will, let me introduce you to Dean Walker, he's the Music Editor of the Uni's weekly rag.' The youth gave Chas a supercilious glance when he used the term rag but stuck his long gangly arm out in my direction. I shook his hand.

'Let me say what an honour it is to meet you!' He exclaimed in a typical student accent that seemed to me to be entirely reserved for the middle classes.

'Pleased to meet you,' I replied politely.

'Will, Dean was wondering whether you had time to do a quick interview for the paper?'

'Yeah sure, why not.' No sooner were the words out of my mouth and Chas was off into a corner making love to his mobile phone. *Great, another pointless interview—the fifth one today. What can I say that I haven't said a thousand times before?*

'Take a seat,' I gestured to a chair opposite me and the youth sat down and pulled out a small dictaphone from his bag and clicked it on.

'Okay, so let's get straight into it. Ten years away from the biz— what made you decide to reform?' And so I spent the next twenty minutes repeating my story again. I finished restringing my guitar during the interview so the time wasn't completely wasted but now I was getting hungry and fancied a Chinese takeaway before the gig.

'Okay, I'm going to have to call it a day I have things to do. If you'll excuse me.' The student was crestfallen, his big dopey eyes bulged as he stammered,

'B ... b ... but I haven't done the twenty questions yet?' he pleaded.

'Pardon?'

'You know, it's sort of like a game, I ask you twenty questions and you answer them. It's the most popular piece in the paper, my readers would be devastated if I missed a week.'

'Well couldn't you just make it up or something?' I responded, quite annoyed at the selfish little prick.

'Make it up, make it up! Oh no, I could never do that. It would be totally unethical.'

'Fuck me mate, you're never going to hack it in Fleet Street.' I laughed at him, but relented and offered an olive branch in the form of Geordie.

'I tell you what,' I continued, 'I'll see if Geordie's willing to do it, okay? But that's the best I can do.' The student brightened immediately.

'Yeah, that would be awesome,' he replied beaming from ear to ear. Geordie had finished cleaning his guitar and had retreated to a far corner of the dressing room. He was now practising scales up and down the neck of his bass, with head thrown back and eyes closed. He was still courting a slight hangover and had been in a tetchy mood all day.

'Hey Geordie?' I bellowed. He opened one eye and squinted at me while his hand continued moving like a mechanical spider up and down his fretboard. He didn't answer. 'Fancy doing an interview? It'll only take ten minutes or so?' I waited. He stopped his practice, huffed loudly, placed his bass on its stand and walked over.

'Aye, okay. As long as it's not for one of those wishy-washy, right-on, left wing student rags though?' I turned and looked at the student apologetically and then back at Geordie.

'No! As if!'

I sneaked out of the fire exit door and sat on the fire escape grating casting my gaze over the great city. I lit up a ciggy and blew out soft blue smoke into the warm summer evening air. There was a buzz about this place, I could feel it. The hum of the traffic in the distance, the haze over the old buildings, the languid flow of the Mersey. The history, the stories, the music, the dirt and grime—I could almost taste it. I imagined a reckless and carefree bunch of teddy boys walking the alleyways below. Hair slicked back, leather pants, leather jackets and winkle pickers.

'Hey boys, where are we going?' shouts their leader. The other three yell back,

'To the toppermost Johnny?'

'To the toppermost of the what?' he bellows back.

'To the toppermost of the poppermost Johnny!' I can hear the opening bars of "Twist and Shout" as it floats in and out of the catacombs of my mind. I stay a while and soak it all in.

#

I finished my smoke and went back inside where the twenty question routine didn't seem to be going down particularly well with Scotland's number one neanderthal. I sat down opposite and began to tune my guitar listening with glee to the ensuing question and answer session, thanking God it wasn't me sitting in Geordie's place.

'Okay, not many to go now we're nearly half way there ...' the student was trying to placate Geordie who was clearly irritated.

'Nearly half-way, oh for fuck's sake! Okay, well get a move on laddie, I have more enjoyable things to do, like gauging my fucking eyes out with a rusty corkscrew.' The student laughed nervously and peered down at his list.

'Okay, what's your favourite colour?' Geordie leant back in his chair, folded his arms, let out a sigh and replied,

'Black.'

'Ah! Well, you see, black is not actually a colour, black and white are merely shades.' Geordie remained silent. 'So let's try that one again eh? What's your favourite colour?'

'Black.'

'Okay, maybe we'll move on.'

'Aye, I reckon that's one of your better ideas.'

'Question eleven, who's the person that you would least like to be trapped in a lift with?'

'Well until a few moments ago, that was without a shadow of a doubt, Bono, but all of a sudden a new blip has appeared on my radar.' The student grinned aimlessly, not picking up the inference.

'Bono? How can you not like Bono, he's a legend?'

'Next question!' yelled Geordie. The student gulped and returned to his sheet of pointless questions.

'Right, okay, erm … question twelve. What's your favourite drink?'

'Whisky, of course.'

'Right, yeah, erm, question thirteen, what's your favourite food?'

'Whisky, of course.'

'Okay …' the student was about to query Geordie on his last answer but decided against it and carried on.

'Question fourteen, what …'

'Listen pal,' Geordie interrupted, 'can you fucking count?' The Student cowered slightly.

'Well yes, of course I can …'

'Right, good! Do you think I can count?'

'Well yes, I suppose so.'

'Correct—you can count, I can count, so we can both count. So there's really no point in prefixing every fucking question with a number is there?'

'No I suppose not. Okay, question, I mean what day of the week were you born on?'

'Hmm, let me think … you know what, strange as this may seem, I can't recall. Silly of me really, I mean such a momentous occasion in my life and I can't remember what day of the week it was. Maybe I was preoccupied with squeezing my oversized head through an undersized birth canal. Of course, if I had known that in thirty odd years time I would be sat here doing an interview with you, then I may not have fucking bothered.' I spotted Flaky doing some sit ups in a corner and left the quiz show behind.

'Hey Flaky, how's the wife and kids?'

'They're all fine, yeah. Just missing their Dad and I'm missing them too. But not long to go now.' I could tell he was pretty cut up about being away from his family for so long and I felt a tinge of sorrow for him but also a hint of envy. Imagine having a wife and kids that you yearned for and who yearned for you, to be wanted and needed.

'What about you Will, ever thought about starting a family?'

'No, not really. You need to have sex with a woman to have kids …' I half joked.

'Well what about this Fiona? Is it serious, didn't you say she had kids?'

'Yeah she's got three young ones. They're great kids as well. I'd like to get more serious and I think she would but …' I paused.

'But what?'

'I'm not sure that I'd make a very good dad.' Flaky stopped doing his sit ups and sat up clutching his knees.

'Will, I can't think of anyone in the world who would make a better dad than you.' I was taken aback and was on my guard for a wind up, even though that wasn't Flaky's style.

'Yeah right,' I replied sarcastically.

'No I mean it. You're kind, generous and you're patient—far more patient than I am. I mean, if you can put up with me and Geordie for weeks on end then you can put up with anything.' We both laughed. He grabbed a towel and wiped the sweat from his brow.

'I'm not so sure Flaky. I'm a free spirit, a wanderer, a nomad, an artist who cannot be shackled by the constraints and routine of domesticity. I'm like a zephyr on the Serengeti, an unchained melody, a …' Flaky's hand came firmly down on my shoulder.

'Rubbish! You live a reclusive existence in a quiet, well to do, conservative little hamlet in the heart of Yorkshire. You're not a wanderer, stop kidding yourself, you're no Ernest Hemingway. You're steady, resolute, loyal, tenacious and you have empathy for your fellow man. You'd make a perfect Dad. Don't be scared of it, don't run from it. Embrace it and it will embrace you. You'll wonder what you've been missing all these years.' He patted me on the back and began to walk off.

'I'm back to the hotel for a shower and brush up. I'll see you back here later.' I pondered what he'd just said. I thought carefully about his words and suddenly felt a throb of excitement. Maybe it was time, maybe I could do it, maybe I could be a great dad—then again, maybe Flaky was full of shit!

I grabbed a beer from the rider and took a swig and walked back to where Geordie was still enduring his inquisition. I sat down on a table behind him and smiled sympathetically at the student, who was now sweating slightly. It was a warm night, but not that warm.

'Okay, nearly there, finally the last question, erm, question twenty,' Geordie squinted and stared malevolently into the student's eyes. 'What is your worst nightmare, I don't mean literally, you know when you've been asleep, but like you know, what's the thing that you absolutely dread happening the most ...'

'Yeah, I think I understand the question. Okay, my worst nightmare—ah yes, I have it. Being trapped in a lift with Bono and you, and to wile away the time, you ask Bono to play twenty questions, counting them out as you go.' The student wore a forced grin that could have shattered his face at any moment. He stood up, shook our hands while thanking both of us for our time and made a quick exit.

'Try to be nice Geordie—just once in a while,' I sighed, shaking my head at him.

'What yer talking about? I was *being* nice!'

#

I watched from the wings as the Stoned Crows took to the stage to a muted response and a few uncalled for boos from the small crowd. Effy was already pissed and stumbled around missing his cues. His tall, rather chubby frame, was swathed in a black leather jumpsuit, which belonged to another era. To wear an outfit like that, one had to be young and taut and carry an undefeated, audacious attitude. He was neither young, nor taut and his attitude was a shroud of self-pity.

Divina entered the stage to rapturous applause from the ever expanding crowd. She launched straight into one of her biggest hits, "Fascist Street", an unusually political lyric for an electronic dance queen. Her montage of Hitler and Mussolini and jackbooted Nazis goose-stepping into Poland, Austria and France on a huge backdrop behind her, gave her song context and the crowd responded in kind. She whipped them up into a frothing frenzy for forty minutes and then departed.

By the time we went on, the venue was bloated with people and the atmosphere was charged. We played a great set and I was sad to come off after only forty five minutes, but handing over top billing to the Green Circles had been the right thing to do. I tried to chill out backstage but the nervous energy I felt was like rocket fuel in my veins. As the Circles went on, the roar from the congregation was thunderous and it felt like the whole building was about to crumble.

When the Circles finally exited the stage after their third encore I was slowly coming down from my maximum high thanks to a few bottles of Heineken and numerous cigarettes. Chas was turbo-charged and went around congratulating everybody, turning on the charm and hugging people around the shoulders. Eventually the whole entourage moved en-mass into a private bar that at the back of the venue where we partied on. As night-time handed the baton over to daytime, I noticed Effy sat alone in a corner. Against my better judgement I went over and sat next to him.

'Hey Will, great gig man, you boys are hot. Won't be long before you're shooting back up those charts with new material.'

'Yeah, well, we'll see.' He had the aura of a broken man and as much as I despised self-pity and defeatism I felt a ripple of sympathy for him. Maybe after all these years, he finally realised that his band were extraordinarily average. 'What's wrong Effy? You seem a bit down?' I asked quietly as I sucked on a cigarette and took a swig of beer.

'Oh, it's this, you know, this tour. I mean it's okay for you guys, you're sounding great, I've heard you practice some of your new songs at sound-check and they sound brilliant. The press and TV are after you again, you just sound fresh and vibrant and full of fire. The kids are going fucking mad for you.' He dropped his head and spoke toward the ground while cradling a bottle of Jack Daniels (what else). 'Take us, we're crap, we've blown it. Probably our last chance and we've completely and totally fucking blown it.'

'C'mon Effy man! You're not that bad. You know there's a lot of kids out there who have come to see you. You'll get yourself back on top of things. A couple of new songs and a new record deal and you'll have all those sticky knickers being thrown at you again.' I tried to contradict him but he was right and my reassurances sounded hollow. He lifted his head, took a large swig of whiskey and patted me on the back laughing.

'Hey mate, you might be a good songwriter but you're a crap liar. No, we're finished. I've been pushing this band around the country for years, playing to fewer and fewer people, getting less and less publicity and losing more and more money. Do you know that we haven't written a new song in over five years. I couldn't believe it when Chas asked us to do this tour, I thought "Yes, we're back". But who was I kidding. We're just part of history now, not part of the future.' He stared disconsolately back down at the floor. I didn't have any answers for him. 'Do you know what I sometimes wish?' he continued. I shook my head. He stared at me with sad, glassy eyes. 'I sometimes wish that we'd never ever made it. That we'd never been signed up; that we'd never had number one singles and albums; that we'd never done sellout tours. I wish I had stayed an unknown. I've tasted the high life, I've drunk the Moet and eaten the caviar. I've had the pick of the worlds supermodels; I've had journalists hang off my every word. I've been ushered to the front of the queue, given the best seats, got into restaurants when they've been turning people away. I've driven fast cars, flown in helicopters. I've had the respect, that's what it is, respect. People respect success,' he laughed, 'but they don't respect failure. They want to bask in your shadow when you're on the up, but on the way down, they wouldn't cross the street to piss on you if you were on fire. Don't you feel the same? Don't you feel like the rest of your life is always going to be an anti-climax? We've had our bite of the cherry, tasted the highs and for the rest of our lives we'll have to endure has-been status. What's that quote from Shakespeare ...' he took another large gulp of whiskey. 'You know, the one that goes "It is better to have loved and lost than never loved at all," well I disagree.'

'Tennyson actually, but carry on ...' I cursed myself for being a smart arse.

'Tennyson, Shakespeare, whatever. Well whoever said it, it's bullshit. If you've never experienced it then you can never miss it.'

'Effy, there's nothing wrong with a has-been, in fact quite the opposite. Better a has-been than a could-have-been. You don't want to die wondering and you won't because you gave it a bash and you made it. You threw caution to the wind, probably gave up a safe comfortable job and you had a go. No-one can take that away from you.' By now Flaky and Geordie had sidled up and sat down quietly listening to the conversation. 'Anyway, I think your confusing success with fame. What you miss is the fame, but you have to realise that fame is only fleeting, it's ephemeral. Success is doing something well and being proud of it regardless of what the rest of the world thinks. If you can go out there on stage and play your heart out and give it your all and mean it, that's success. It doesn't matter if you're playing to one man and his dog or a hundred and fifty thousand at Glastonbury. Success isn't measured in how many albums you sell or gold discs you rack up, it's how you feel about yourself and what you do.

Do you know what my definition of success is?' He shook his head. 'Success for me is getting up in the morning knowing I'm going to spend the day doing something *I* enjoy, whether that's playing the guitar, writing songs, turning over the veggie patch or going on a twenty mile walk across the Dales with my dog. That's my definition of success.' Effy didn't seem convinced and continued drinking his whiskey. I tried a different approach.

'Did you know that originally we were called the "Shooting Stars"?'

'No,' he replied, appearing decidedly uninterested.

'Well we were—because that's what rock bands are—we follow the same trajectory as the arc of a shooting star. A brilliant projectile that bursts across the black night in an illuminating arc. Beautiful, mesmerising and impossible not to stare at and feel some sense of awe. But a shooting star only lasts a few seconds and then it's gone—burnt up in the earth's atmosphere. It's the same for rock 'n roll bands. We're not meant to last. We're here for a few brief moments to capture a time, to reflect an attitude and then we're gone—burnt up and burnt out. We rise, we burn bright and then we die. It's the normal cycle; there's no point regretting it, that's just the way it is.' Effy's eyes were wet and he nodded slowly. He stood up and wobbled slightly before finishing off his bottle of whisky.

'Yeah, I suppose you're right, although I'd still rather be snorting cocaine off a supermodels arse cheeks while getting a champagne enema.' He threw his empty bottle into a nearby bin and wobbled off through the crowd. 'Time to hit the town and do the rounds!' he shouted as his leather clad frame disappeared out of the door.

'Sad bastard,' said Geordie with a hint of sympathy.

28: ALL OVER NOW BABY BLUE

It was our second night playing Glasgow and the fact that we were back on Scottish soil had seen Geordie's spirits lift considerably. In fact, I hadn't seen him this happy since Margaret Thatcher fell down the steps of the Hague many moons ago. We were headlining again and were due on in thirty minutes once the roadies had done the stage change. Usual scenario; Flaky on the phone to his missus, Robbo smoking a giant spliff while tuning his guitar and Geordie and Connie partaking in a game of "tossing the Scouser"—yes that's right, "tossing the Scouser"—nothing sexual, may I add. It involved Geordie picking up the diminutive Connie by one leg and one arm and swinging him back and forth until he gained enough momentum to propel him high into the air. Connie, depending on the height he reached, would then put in a couple of backflips or half pikes, occasionally a triple somersault before landing back on the floor with the grace of a Puma. It had attracted a small but appreciative crowd who for some reason found it great entertainment. I, on the other hand, had become blasé about their circus capers; once you've seen one five foot four Scouser being lobbed through the air by a six-foot-six Scotsman, you've seen them all. I found sanctuary in the comfort of a reclining chair away from the madness and was busy trying to relax. My reverie was rudely shattered when my mobile began to ring. I was hoping it was Fiona as we hadn't chatted for a few days but when I saw the number I didn't recognise it. I was slightly puzzled as I was very particular about who I gave my number to.

'Hello?' I inquired tentatively.

'Will? Is that you?' A Scottish female voice and a worried one at that, sounded on the other end.

'Yes it's Will? Who's this?'

'It's me Margaret—you know, Margaret, from the Fisherman's Way,' I immediately thought she was a journalist from some fishing magazine. What the hell would a fishing magazine want with me? 'You gave me your number—remember?'

'I did?'

'Margaret from Dinkiad Bay?' she stressed the words as though trying to jog the memory of an elderly parent with Alzheimers. The cogs turned and meshed and I was soon back in control of my faculties. A sudden image of Margaret's large dangling breasts swinging freely in the doctor's surgery passed before my eyes.

'Ah! Margaret, yes of course, how are you?'

'I'm good Will, but listen, I have some bad news …' she paused. My heart began to race as my mind put two and two together; there was only one reason she'd be ringing me with bad news.

'Go on,' I responded.

'Is Allan there?'

'Yes, he's just in the middle of a Scouser throwing contest.'

'Well it's probably better that it comes from you anyway.' I found it a little odd that she never questioned my last remark. 'It's Iris … Geordie's Nan … she, she passed away earlier today. The doctor called to tell me a few minutes ago. Poor, poor Allan. He'll be devastated. He was so close to her.'

'Oh no … that's no good at all. How did she go?'

'Sounds like a heart attack. She'd been watching an omnibus edition of Eastenders …'

'Well that could explain a lot,' I said, immediately regretting my reply.

'It's not funny Will, this is serious.'

312

'Sorry. What needs to be done?'

'The doctor said that Allan will have to call in at the hospital to sign some papers and then there's the funeral to arrange.'

'Okay, well we've got a few days off after tonight, so that gives us time to sort things out. I'll drive Geordie over to the hospital tomorrow and then we'll go about organising the funeral. We'll probably be back in Dinkiad Bay by tomorrow evening.'

'Okay and please give our love to Allan and tell him that we're all thinking of him.'

'Will do Margaret, see you tomorrow.' I put my phone away. I stared across the room and watched the big fella as he hurled Connie a good two metres into the air. Connie did a somersault and landed sprightly on his toes before taking a bow to his audience. How was I to approach this? There was no easy way. We'd have to pull out of the gig, Geordie would be inconsolable. And what about Chas? He'd blow a fuse if we didn't play and there was also the small matter of the contract and the penalty clause. *Shit, what a mess.* I glanced around for support. Flaky was still on the phone, I caught his eye and gestured for him to come over.

'Oi! Robbo!' I yelled. Robbo sucked on his spliff and raised an eyebrow in my direction. 'Over here a minute.' I beckoned. He let out a plume of smoke and idled over carrying his guitar. I lit a cigarette and indicated for them both to sit. Flaky detected something amiss and bid farewell to his wife and hung up.

'What is it Will? What's the matter?'

'It's Geordie's Nan. She's carked it.' I said in a hushed whisper.

'What? You mean she's dead?' quizzed Flaky in disbelief.

'You're sharp Flaky I'll give you that, sharp as a razor,' mocked Robbo. Flaky threw him a lofty glare.

'Listen, I know what she meant to Geordie, she was his whole world. She saved his life, twice. This is gonna rip him apart; I'm not sure

313

how he'll handle it. I mean he's fucking unstable at the best of times, God knows what this will do to him.'

'Don't worry I'll take care of it,' said Flaky in a rather arrogant manner. 'I've had training in grief counselling. This needs to handled with tact, diplomacy and empathy. Leave it to me.' I wasn't at all convinced that Flaky was the best to handle it but I certainly didn't want to be the messenger of bad news.

'Okay Flaky, but take it easy. And you both realise we're going to have to cancel the gig?' Robbo and Flaky exchanged resigned glances with each other but nodded anyway.

'Easy come, easy go, eh. How much do we lose again?' asked Robbo.

'One quarter of the total, two hundred big ones,' I replied solemnly.

'Fuck me drunk!' exclaimed Flaky. It was the first profanity he had uttered all tour and it was a damned good one at that. Me and Robbo couldn't help but smile.

'Okay Flaky, do your stuff, we'll be right behind you. Then I better tell Chas about the gig.' Flaky got up and began to walk over towards Geordie with Robbo and me following a few steps behind.

'Now remember Flaky, break it gently, right?' Flaky stopped in his tracks and spun to face me. He put a firm hand on my shoulder and stared me in the eyes.

'Will, Will, my old friend, leave this to the expert. As I've told you, I've had training and plenty of experience in these situations.' I didn't take offence at his patronising manner—I was immune to it by now.

'Fair enough Flaky, but we're not talking about your run of the mill, average joe blow here, we're talking about Geordie—what was it you called him the other day—borderline psychotic, conflict driven, hostile embedded ...' For a moment a slight appearance of concern graced Flaky's face before he gave me a condescending pat on the back and a smug smile.

'Trust me Will, trust in God.' His words didn't fill me with confidence. I never trust anyone who says "trust me" and especially when they have God on their side. I shot a worried glance at Robbo who merely shrugged his shoulders. Flaky walked up to Geordie who was in the process of grabbing Connie by the arm and leg and readying him for another excursion into the air.

'Geordie!' Flaky shouted. Geordie ignored him and began his first of three swings back and forth that would give him the momentum to launch Connie skywards.

'Geordie, I have some news ...' Flaky persisted. The small crowd began to count.

'ONE!,' Geordie half turned to acknowledge Flaky.

'Can't you see I'm busy Flaky ... fuck off!'

'... TWO ...' shouted the crowd as Geordie gathered momentum. Connie grinned inanely and waved at me with his spare hand as he moved back and forth in a pendulous arc. I waved back sheepishly.

'Geordie, it's your Nan, she's dead!'

'... THREE ...' chanted the crowd. Unfortunately, Geordie comprehended Flaky's words right at the critical moment of release. Instead of sending Connie soaring upwards, he let go fractionally too soon and sent the pint-sized Scouser shooting off on a horizontal plane. Connie's inane grin was first replaced by one of mild astonishment, but, only for a second. A longer lasting look of complete bewilderment remained on his face throughout his flight across a long table of beer bottles and old takeaways. I've got to admit that he glided along that table with a certain amount of grace and elegance for someone in such an unexpected predicament, and moving at such alarming speed. Glass smashed and foil trays danced in the air. Whether by good fortune or just the vagaries of chance, there happened to be an office chair at the end of the table, which Connie was unceremoniously catapulted into. He clung on for dear life as the chair, which had been happily minding its own business a few seconds before, took off across the heavily polished floorboards in what can only be described as an un-motorised attempt at the land speed record. The chair, along with Connie, was now spinning wildly as it headed towards a closed door at the far end of the room. Against the laws of physics, the chair seemed to be gaining momentum. Round and round the chair spun. Connie's bald head was now gyrating around a fixed point with ever increasing violence. I could no longer ascertain his expression but I assumed it would not have been one of optimism. The chair sped, Connie spun and the large wooden door beckoned. When the moment of impact seemed inevitable, fate's mysterious hand dealt the last card. The door opened and in walked Effy. I'm not sure what, if anything, flashed across his mind in that final second before impact. Would he have had time to deduce that a madly revolving chair, hurtling at physics defying velocity while carrying a tiny Liverpudlian could cause serious injury? The back of the chair slammed into Effy's todger area and he was catapulted a few feet into the air in a toppling motion. It was like watching a Giant Redwood being felled. At this point Connie decided to relinquish his grip and he went spinning across the floor like a curling stone on a sheet of ice. Effy landed chin first with an alarming cracking sound followed by a loud expulsion of air. Meanwhile, Connie's rocket like trajectory came to a space shuttle exploding halt as he slammed into the wall and lay crumpled on the floor like a rag doll. I turned to Flaky.

'You've had training. Tact, diplomacy and empathy—trust in God—you wanker!'

#

When the ambulance had departed with Effy and Connie safely inside, we sat the big fella down and explained the situation. I told him we needed to go to the hospital in the morning and that he'd have to sign some papers and that we'd need to make arrangements for the funeral. He nodded as I talked but he wasn't listening. His eyes were gone, dead, distant. I didn't know where he was but I knew I couldn't reach him. I stood up and scanned the room for Chas but he was still nowhere to be seen. He had been absent during the Connie, Effy incident and he wasn't going to be pleased when he did show up. I was pretty certain that Effy's jaw was broken which would mean the end of the tour for the Stoned Crows. As for Connie, his left arm was at an unusual angle as he hobbled into the back of the ambulance so it didn't bode well for the Circles either.

'Look Geordie, we're going to cancel the gig tonight. I've had a word with Divina and she's willing to go on again in our place. Let's get you back to the hotel.' As Geordie stood up I saw Chas walk into the room sporting a cheery grin, oblivious to the fact that his "Resurrection Tour" had just about gone tits up.

'Chas!' I called and waved at him. He ambled over with hands stuck in his pockets.

'Hey, shouldn't you boys be getting ready to go onstage?' He glanced at his watch.

'We're not going onstage Chas,' Robbo replied. Chas's cheery demeanour was replaced with one of solemnity.

'Say what?'

'It's Geordie's Nan. She's passed away. Geordie's in no fit state to go on tonight,' I explained. Chas stared at the ground trying to comprehend what this meant.

'Well, I'm very sorry about your Nan Geordie; you have my condolences and all that, but you are all aware of the contract conditions if you don't play tonight. You will forfeit a quarter of your payment.' I'd expected him to blow up into a rage but I could almost read his mind. Yes it wouldn't look good on him if his headline band pulls the gig but the bonus is that he's two hundred grand better off. 'Well, we'll just have to get the Circles to go on again, can't let the fans down can we.'

317

'Yeah, well that's not going to happen either,' I said. Chas pushed his glasses up the bridge of his nose.

'And why not?'

'Connie's in hospital. He had an accident. Looks like his arms fucked.' Chas pursed his lips and paused.

'Okay, well, we'll have to put the Crows on again. Not ideal but we can't have Divina going on again, she's only just come off.'

'Well that's not going to happen either. Effy's also in hospital. Suspected broken jaw.' Now Chas exploded.

'What in the name of all fuckery has been going on here tonight!' he screamed. 'I've been gone for a couple of hours and the whole fucking shooting match has gone to shit! You lot need to get your sorry arses out there right now otherwise my name is fucking mud! I'm not going to let a bunch of retarded reprobates fuck my career! Do you hear me!'

'Chas, you can shout and bluster as much as you want but we're all together on this.'

'You're making a big mistake Will, a big, big mistake. You'll live to regret this. I swear to God that if you don't get out there right now I'm kicking you off the tour and that doesn't mean forfeiting twenty five percent, that's forfeiting one hundred percent of your payment!' Geordie reached out and grabbed Chas by the throat and lifted him off the ground.

'We'll do your fucking gig you weasel. But I'm warning you. I don't know exactly what you're up to but when I find out—I'm coming for you!' He let go and Chas fell to the floor gasping for breath.

#

We did the gig and gave it our all. I dedicated our song "Shooting Stars" to Iris Harris. It could have been a cheesy moment but it wasn't. Somehow it had got around the crowd that Geordie had lost his Nan and in-between songs they all chanted his name, "Geordie, Geordie". He remained to the side of the stage, out of the spotlight, rooted to the spot, casting a long demonic shadow across the stage. I kept checking him out to make sure he was alright; he never moved, he never blinked, he just stared straight ahead motionless and emotionless for the whole of the set. He never missed a beat or dropped a note. His playing was flawless and perfect, as it always was. When we finished our encores we came off backstage to a muted atmosphere. Most of the other members of the Crows and Circles had departed. Divina remained, also a fawning obsequious Chas.

'You boys were fantastic. I knew you wouldn't let me down. You were absolutely fucking awesome.' All four of us slumped down into chairs, sweaty and fatigued. Geordie picked up a full bottle of Johnny Walker, unscrewed the top and began to swallow the liquid.

'Now about that little misunderstanding earlier …' continued a creeping Chas. No-one spoke. We all just wearily watched Geordie as the brown liquid slowly disappeared.

'Of course I would never have kicked you off the tour. Your money was always safe, you boys know me.' Chas noted my look of contempt and gulped.

'Y … y … yes, well, I can see that maybe you need a bit of time for yourselves.'

'Yeah, why don't you just fuck off Chas!' said Divina who had pulled up a chair and joined our private circle. Chas realised he'd outstayed his welcome.

'Okay, well I'll be off then.' He combed a slice of hair over his bald patch, straightened his shirt and left the room. Geordie finished the bottle and hurled it at the far wall. It shattered and sent pieces of glass ricocheting across the floor. He rubbed his nose and motioned to Robbo who in turn peered at me. I nodded and Robbo pulled out a plastic bag full of coke and pulled up a nearby table. Flaky shook his head but said nothing. Robbo spilled out a large pile of white dust onto the table and began to carve it up with his credit card. He produced five long lines, took out a crisp fifty pound note and rolled it up. He passed the note to

319

Geordie who stood and bent his large frame over the white lines and snorted up two rows and sat back down.

'Greedy cunt,' muttered Robbo. The note was passed around and we all indulged apart from Flaky. Music blared from the hall's PA system and became more lucid as the coke kicked in.

'Alright wac!' The unmistakable twang of Connie's thick Liverpudlian accent rang out across the room. We all turned to witness Connie, with arm in sling, and Effy, with a white plaster on his chin, saunter over.

'Mind if we join you?' asked Connie with an irresistible grin.

'No, not at all,' replied Geordie. 'Broken arm?'

'Nah, dislocated shoulder. Bleedin' hurt though when they popped it back in. The sling's just for show.' Geordie laughed.

'And what about you Effy? You great big streak of piss.'

'Five stitches in the chin and one tooth removed.' He bared his teeth to show the missing molar. 'But the good news is ... I can still sing.'

'And that's the good news?' added Geordie caustically. We all had a snigger, even the long suffering Effy offered a painful smile. 'C'mon, sit yourselves down and have a whisky.'

'No thanks. We've been given strict orders from the doc, no booze tonight, we're both rattling with painkillers,' Connie replied.

'What about a snort of coke then?'

Yeah, why not. The doc said nothing about coke!'

'Robbo, get your stash out,' ordered Geordie.

'Fucking charming. You're pretty good at offering other people my gear.' Robbo pulled his little plastic bag out and threw it to Effy who caught it and set about assembling two lines. Geordie opened a fresh bottle of whisky and took another large gulp from it. The rest of us cradled beers.

'Geordie mate, take it easy on the whisky eh, we've got a lot of things to sort out tomorrow,' I regretted the words immediately. I may have been right but if he couldn't get wasted now, when could he. He'd

320

just lost the closest person in his life. To my surprise, he gazed at me and replied gently,

'Aye, I know. I'll get outa my brain tonight and then I'll be right.' I exchanged worried glances with the rest of the group. I heard footsteps approaching and noticed a tall well built woman heading towards us. She was in her early thirties and had long red hair that was pulled back quite severely into a ponytail. She was dressed in jeans and an army green three quarter length parka. Her eyes twinkled and she had a kindly face.

'Excuse me,' she began tentatively in a thick Glaswegian brogue, 'my name is Jackie O'Connor and I'm with the Herald. I was just wondering if I could get an interview. I saw the gig tonight and you were brilliant ...' I cut her off.

'Come on love, give us a break. You know what's happened tonight. Show a bit of respect.'

'No, I'm sorry, I don't know what you mean,' she replied in all sincerity.

'You lot never give up do you. You have no idea of privacy. You must get your nice juicy little story and suck up to the editor,' spat Divina. The woman seemed perplexed and hurt. 'Oh don't pull that "I don't know what you're talking about" look with me. Can't you see the man needs time to grieve,' Divina continued indicating toward Geordie.

'Look, I'm sorry, I had no idea. Please forgive me. I'll be on my way.' The reporter turned to walk away but Geordie called her back.

'Wait. Come back and share a drink with us. I must apologise for my friend's unwelcome behaviour. They must have forgotten that they're in bonnie old Scotland now and us Scottish will share a drink with anyone.' Jackie smiled.

'No, I shouldn't really. I don't want to intrude.'

'Away with yer! I don't want to sit here staring at their miserable mugs all night. It'll make a change to have a bonny face like yours to look at,' continued Geordie, suddenly playing the consummate host. He leaned forward towards Divina. 'No offence intended Divina, but when I said miserable mugs, I was referring to these five sad sacks not yourself of course.'

'No offence taken,' she smiled. Geordie stood up and grabbed another chair.

'Here, come and sit next to me Jackie. I'll give you the best interview you'll ever get. We can talk all night if you want. I'm sick of talking to this pack of pricks anyway. Jackie came over and sat next to Geordie and they began chatting away, both staring intently into each other's eyes. They were smitten with each other and witnessing the experience made me feel quite nauseous.

29: CARAVAN OF LOVE

I sat in the hotel's breakfast room trying to enjoy my bacon and eggs and mug of tea but the presence of Flaky was making this hard to achieve.

'So, the grieving process after a bereavement effects people in different ways and for differing lengths of time. Let me explain. The first part of grief is typically accompanied by sadness or loneliness as well as anxiety, pain, anger.'

'Oh great, that's all we need, a bit more Geordie anger,' I replied in a sarcastic tone. Flaky ignored me and carried on with his verbal dissertation.

'And there could be periods of shock, disbelief, denial and the desire to avoid personal invasion, ie intrusion. And of course there will be regret, guilt, remorse, the feeling that they should or could have done more.' I sat back and slurped on my tea.

'Are you deliberately trying to ruin my day?' Again I was ignored.

'Lastly, there could be social withdrawal. Hiding away, lack of social interaction. The inability to find pleasure in anything anymore, even a complete change in personality.'

'Well he was certainly finding pleasure in the whisky and coke last night not to mention getting more than friendly with that reporter.'

'This is what I'm saying. As far as I can ascertain, as a professional psychologist, he's in denial at the moment, maybe even shock.' I disliked people who name dropped their profession into conversations.

323

'Hardly surprising considering the way some fuckwit broke the news to him.' Flaky blanked me again and began to peel the skin off an orange. 'Well, in my considered opinion, as a professional singer songwriter of significant international standing, I'd say that we're all in shitters ditch.' I began tackling my last piece of bacon as Flaky slipped an orange segment into his mouth.

'Well, this is why I'm telling you all this. You're going to be with him for the next couple of days, so I'm just warning you what to expect.'

'Don't you think he should be accompanied by a professional psychologist who may be able to help him navigate through his Panama Canal of grief?' At last I got a bite.

'Panama Canal of grief? What's that rubbish?'

'Just being poetic ... after all, I am a poet.' Flaky huffed and pushed back in his chair.

'I don't think you're taking this matter seriously Will. We're talking about your friend's mental wellbeing here and you're making light of the matter.' I'd had enough.

'Look Flaky, I get it, okay. There will be a grieving process. We don't know when, where or how long, but Geordie will experience some negative emotions very shortly, which is a fucking paradox in itself. There may be a personality change ... here's hoping. It's not like he's the first person in the world to lose a loved one and quite frankly your advice has been as much use as a wank in a teacup. If I ever need psychological advice, which I probably will do after this tour ends, remind me not to come to you.' I placed my knife and fork on the plate and stood up to leave.

'Look Will, you're the only one that Geordie looks up to. You two always had a strong bond, even after ten years apart, nothing's changed. I see these things.'

'You see jack! Geordie doesn't look up to anyone. Right, if you've quite finished ...'

'Sit down,' he whispered, 'Geordie's here.' I glanced behind me and saw Geordie enter the room with Jackie the reporter at his side. They both wore giggly smiley faces, which for some reason irked me. They were holding hands and whispering to each other and both appeared as fresh as a pair of daisies.

'Hey! Geordie,' called out Flaky. Geordie glanced over.

'Flaky, Billy Boy, a very good morning to you both,' he smiled cheerily and made his way to the smorgasbord with Jackie in tow. I was confounded and by the look on Flaky's face, so was he.

'I don't think he's ever been that polite to me in all the years I've known him,' said Flaky.

'No, it's not normal for him to be courteous at any time of the day let alone in the morning. He's obviously trying to impress that Jackie woman. Don't worry, it won't last.'

'No, no, this is good.'

'It is?'

'Yes. His emotional attachment to Jackie and the positive sensations he's experiencing will counter balance the negative emotions.'

'Listen Flaky, I know Geordie and I can guarantee that this little romance will be over before they've finished breakfast. You know what a messy eater he is. Mix that in with his ability to find fault with absolutely anyone and one or the other will be looking to make their excuses and leave ASAP.' Geordie and Jackie sauntered over to our table.

'Do you mind if we join you?' Geordie asked cordially.

'Feel free,' Flaky replied. The lovebirds sat down.

'You both remember Jackie don't you?' inquired Geordie as he began to tuck into a fruit salad.

Sorry, but I've had a sudden onrush of chronic Alzheimer's overnight and I don't know anyone. Who are you again?'

'Oh very funny, Billy Boy. You know that sarcastic tongue of yours will bring you unstuck one day.' Flaky and I were both staring disbelievingly at Geordie's fruit salad as he carefully dabbed at a piece of watermelon with his fork.

'You seem surprisingly perky for someone who over imbibed in whisky and snow last night,' I stated. Geordie stuck the large piece of watermelon into his mouth and began to chew thoughtfully. Jackie popped a grape into her mouth and gave Geordie an impish grin.

'It's because I've turned over a new leaf. A brand new start. Yes, that's it for me. No more booze and definitely no more drugs. It's really bad for mind, body and spirit. From now on you can call me Mr Clean.'

'Well, that's great to hear Geordie. Well done!' exclaimed Flaky with a large beam.

'Aye, well you can only abuse your body for so long before you'll end up paying the price.' I realised I must have fallen through a wormhole somewhere and was now existing in a parallel universe. 'Yes, me and Jackie had a long chat last night and she's put me straight on a few things. No more booze or drugs and start looking after myself. Eat healthily, cut down on the red meat, reduce stress and avoid negative situations and negative people.' Yep, I was definitely on planet "What the fuck".

'Avoid negative people? So how exactly are you going to avoid yourself? That's going to be a little difficult don't you think?'

'There you go again William—negative energy. If you emit negative energy you'll attract negative energy,' he looked across at Jackie. 'You see what I mean Babycake? The sarcasm just oozes out of him like a lava flow of bad vibes.'

'Yes, I see what you mean Pumpkin,' replied Jackie as she threw me a stern look. Okay, this was getting out of hand; not only did they have sickening pet names for each other, but it appeared that Pumpkin had managed to convince Babycake that I was the sole cause of his miserable, self-absorbed, nihilistic existence—and the bastard had called me "William".

'Well good for you Geordie, that's all I can say,' joined in a sanctimonious Flaky.

'Thanks Flaky. I've got to say that you've been like a rock for me. I don't think I could have got through this tour without you.' I needed to leave immediately before I began vomiting profusely.

'You should take a leaf out of Geordie's book Will, and start afresh. It's never too late to make a new start.'

'Aye, you're not wrong there Flaky,' concurred Geordie, 'you could do with cutting down on the liquor and quitting the drugs William. You're only harming yourself. It's not big or clever you know.' All three now stared at me with disapproving eyes.

'Well, I'd love to join you all in your little self-congratulatory love-fest, but I've got practical things to attend to, like hiring a car to drive you, Mr Clean, over to Aberdeen and then Dinkiad Bay. Meet me at reception in one hour. Flaky, I'll see you in Sunderland in three days time.' I got up and walked away.

'Oh William, by the way, Jackie's coming with us, hope you don't mind,' Geordie shouted out after me.

'Great, that's just fucking dandy,' I muttered under my breath. The last thing I heard was Geordie saying something about me being in denial. Yes, there was definitely some weird space-time continuum thing going on. I was entering the lift just as Robbo was exiting. I pulled him to one side.

'Robbo mate how's it going?'

'Yeah man, cool, why?'

'Have you given up the drink?'

'Don't talk daft.'

'What about drugs, have you given up drugs?'

'Whoa man! You're spinning me out.' Robbo took a step back from me appearing very worried.

'Just answer the question?'

327

'No way Jose, I've just put down a monster reefer a few minutes ago. What's with the interrogation?' I grabbed hold of him and gave him a big hug and sighed.

'Thanks Robbo. Just wanted to check that I wasn't losing my mind.'

#

I exited the lift pulling my suitcase behind me. I saw Jackie waiting in a sumptuous chair in reception but I couldn't see Geordie.

'Hey Jackie, where's Geordie?'

'Oh, he's just nipped to the loo.'

'Ah, okay.' There was an awkward silence and I decided that a bit of small talk was in order. 'So, you work for the Herald then?' It was the best I had.

'That's right yes. Been there six years.'

'So you're not working today?'

'No. I booked a few of days off to be with Geordie. He asked, it wasn't my idea.'

'So what about the interview you did?'

'Oh, I emailed it through to my editor at six this morning. Just got a text back a few moments ago actually. Says that he loves the interview and that he's going to try to get it syndicated. He thinks the full interview would be perfect for the Sunday papers. It will be in the Herald tomorrow.' I was more than a little surprised.

'You're editor thinks it's great? You did interview Geordie, right?'

'Yes. Why do you seem so surprised?'

'Because Geordie is probably the worst interviewee of all time. He absolutely hates doing interviews and is as obnoxious as possible to the interviewer. I suppose he ranted on about Bono and Sting and the Labour and Tory Parties right? And of course the Royals.'

'Well he did mention Bono, but it wasn't a rant. He just said that he respected the man's work and that his heart was in the right place.' I couldn't believe my ears. Nothing made sense anymore. Then I had a lightbulb moment.

'And are you a U2 fan by any chance Jackie?' She looked over my shoulder and waved.

'Pumpkin!' she shouted, 'over here. Sorry, yes, I'm a massive U2 fan. I mean Bono really wears his heart on his sleeve. Don't get me wrong, I absolutely love your music but you're not very political are you? You don't really stand for anything.' By now Geordie had joined us. I wanted to like Jackie but she wasn't making it easy. Her supercilious manner and airy arrogance was beginning to annoy me.

'Well, if you actually listen to the lyrics I'd say that we make our position extremely clear on many fronts. Just because we don't pull stunts and join marches doesn't mean that we are apolitical.'

'What's all this about?' asked Geordie cheerily as he grabbed Jackie's hand. I was certain I could score a hit here with a bit of support from Geordie. He detested overtly political bands and artists as he let me and the rest of the world know at every opportunity.

'Jackie was just saying that although she loves our music she thinks that we could be more proactive in putting forward our beliefs and political views. What are your thoughts Geordie?' He grimaced slightly through half closed eyes.

'Well, she has a point. I mean we have a certain responsibility to fight the good fight and if we can influence the world for the better, then surely that's a good thing.'

'So you'd be happy to go on marches and demonstrations and pull a few publicity stunts would you?'

'Aye, why not—if it was for the right cause. You know I'd be one of the first behind those barricades if push came to shove.' Jackie smiled and pecked him on the cheek. I was now convinced the shock of his Nan's death had unleashed an alter-ego of breathtaking hypocrisy. With stops, it was going to be over four hours to Dinkiad Bay. The thought of four hours in a car with John and Yoko made me feel ill.

'Right, come on, let's get going,' I said eager to end the conversation. Geordie grabbed his and Jackie's bags and they followed me out of the hotel.

'We can continue this conversation in the car,' said Jackie.

'Splendid idea!' exhorted Geordie. God, give me strength

#

I dropped Geordie and Jackie off at the hospital in Aberdeen where, as next of kin, Geordie had to sign some papers. I took the opportunity to stretch my legs, have a smoke and unscramble my mind. The car journey so far had been dreadful. Anything Jackie said, Geordie wholeheartedly agreed with unbridled enthusiasm. Apart from making music, drinking alcohol and taking drugs, I had never seen Geordie be enthusiastic about anything. Now he was like a presidential hopeful at an election rally. I never thought I'd say this, but, I missed the old Geordie. And of course, old big gob, had to mention to Jackie the Tsars were thinking about reforming permanently and that we would manage all our own affairs and sell our music from our own website. Well, that set Jackie off. She expounded on her quite outstanding abilities with IT and how she was an expert in HTML, whatever that is, and how she could help us set up everything and she could be the site's Webmaster; by the time we'd arrived in Aberdeen, the pair of them had everything worked out down to the last detail; they made me sick.

It was a beautiful warm summer's day. Flowers were in bloom, the ground wore a verdant cape and trees flaunted their leafy finery and yet, I felt overwhelmed, depressed and just a little bit beaten. I took out my little parcel of pick me up that I'd scored from Robbo, dabbed my finger in it and rubbed it around my gums. The bitter taste made me pucker my lips and I lit another cigarette to mask the flavour. Ten minutes later I was feeling a lot better and was looking forward to arriving at Dinkiad Bay and having a few pints in the Fisherman's Way followed by a nourishing meal.

330

We were back in the car and things were not quite as bad as before. Mainly because I'd put Van Morrison CD quite loud to drown out the cooing of Pumpkin and Babycake. There was no sign of the "four stages of grief" that Flaky had warned me about. Maybe he had been right; the positives from Geordie's new relationship had cancelled out the negatives of his Nan's demise. Either way I was relieved. We'd been driving about thirty minutes when I saw the first signpost for Dinkiad Bay indicating we were less than thirty miles away. Not long past the sign the car began to make a most peculiar noise. It started as a long, high pitched wail that descended to a low grumble. I slowed down, turned the music off and tilted my head slightly to one side. The noise had ceased almost immediately I'd slowed the engine. I sped up again and the noise resumed. I slowed again. The noise now got louder and louder and sounded like the guttural mating call of an oversexed Walrus. The last thing I needed was for the car to breakdown. It slowly dawned on me the hideous noise wasn't coming from the engine at all but from the back seat. I peered in the rearview mirror to witness the screwed up face of Geordie taking a long, deep, silent breath and then slowly release a noise from hell. I assumed this was the first of the four stages of grief.

'I was okay until I saw the sign for Dinkiad Bay,' he blubbered, 'and that got me thinking about Nan.'

'Okay Pumpkin, it's okay. You need to let it all out,' comforted Jackie.

'Oh, I'm sorry for the noise but I can't help it,' he wailed.

'Don't you worry about the noise. Make as much noise as you like. Scream from the top of your lungs if you want—we don't mind about the noise—do we Will?'

'Well, if you could turn it down just a notch,' I replied. Jackie whacked me hard on the shoulder.

When I first saw him wailing like a babe I was overcome with a flood of sympathy. This soon passed and was replaced with mild annoyance, which in turn morphed into gritted teeth agony. The thirty miles to Dinkiad Bay should have taken about thirty five minutes but I had to stop the car on three occasions to release myself from that God awful sound and smoke a cigarette to soothe my tattered nerves. The protracted, torturous journey finally ended as we pulled up outside Nan's old house. Geordie suddenly fell silent and I let out a long deep sigh.

Inside, the house was warm and had a musty smell to it. Jackie put the kettle on and Geordie sat in despondent silence at the little kitchen table. I walked around the house and opened a few windows to let fresh air in. Back in the kitchen we sipped on black tea in silence. Jackie focused on me and raised an eyebrow—I got the message.

'Listen, Geordie, we really need to get to the undertakers today. I know you won't feel like it but we don't have a lot of time.' I said the words softly. Finally he raised his head and confronted me.

'Aye, c'mon then, let's do it.'

We locked up and all three of us ambled silently down the street. The sound of gulls screeched in the distance and a warm comforting smell of the sea was carried on a gentle breeze. The undertakers was only a couple of streets away and we were soon stood outside their door. I stared at the sign above, "Moody and Mingin Funeral Directors". It didn't bode well. Walking into their premises was like walking into a Dickens novel. In a dimly lit, stuffy room, decorated in deep red velvet curtains we were greeted by what surely must have been a relative of Uriah Heep. The elderly man was tall and spindly with hunched over shoulders. He had a few strands of grey hair that were brushed back across his head and seemed to be held down with some sort of grease. His long black coat was speckled with dandruff and he wore a black bow tie. As he spoke he peered over the top of his half-moon glasses at us. I wondered whether he was Moody or Mingin, maybe both.

'Ah, Allan, I've been expecting you. Let me first offer my most sincere condolences on the loss of your Nan. She was a wonderful testament to the strong, resolute, highland spirit and she will be deeply missed by everyone in our little community.'

'Aye, thanks Mr Moody. She was a real stoater. Her spirit will always be wi' me,' replied Geordie solemnly.

'Did your Nan discuss what arrangements she preferred in regard to her funeral, Allan?'

'Aye. She wanted a graveside funeral. No fuss, just a quick sermon from the Pastor and then a wake back at the house.'

'Very good. I shall make all the necessary arrangements. And the casket?'

'She said she wanted the cheapest coffin, just plain and simple ...' Geordie broke off and started snivelling again. Jackie put her arm around his shoulder and said,

'There, there, Pumpkin, it's alright.' It just didn't sit easy with me; someone calling Geordie, Pumpkin.

'She used to say, "may as well let the worms have a good feed on me". I used to laugh, but now it's gonna happen.' He broke into the high pitched wail that had accompanied us in the car. I needed a pint and fast.

'I can assure you Allan, all our caskets are built to the most rigorous standards and they'll still be intact long after you have passed.' I wondered how he knew. Did they dig a few coffins up every couple of years just to check their condition?

'An everlasting casket for an everlasting life, eh?' I tried lifting the oppressive atmosphere with a bit of light-heartedness. Mr Moody glowered at me.

'I don't think this is the time for levity, er, Mr ...'

'Harding, Will Harding. Sorry, it was inappropriate at such a grave time.' All three stared at me with suspicion—time to go.

'Right Geordie. I'll leave you and Jackie to it. I'm going for a few jars down the pub.' He abruptly stopped his wailing and I detected a flash of envy in his eyes.

'Well Geordie's off the booze now so he won't be joining you Will. I'll get us some provisions for dinner and we'll see you back at the house in a couple of hours.'

'Oh Babycake, I don't think a pint or two of beer is out of the question considering the situation.'

'No Geordie. For once I have to agree with Jackie. If you're on the wagon, you're on the wagon. Remember, a brand new start and all that. Anyway, I'll have one on your behalf. Okay, Mr Clean, I'll see you later.' Geordies top lip curled into a snarl and if looks could kill then Mr Moody would have been measuring me up for one of his everlasting coffins.

As I left the claustrophobic atmosphere of Moody and Mingin and returned to the late afternoon sun, I could feel the leaden weight of death evaporate into the air. I walked back towards the town centre and followed the alluring aroma of fine ale like a bloodhound on the scent of a fox. Inside the Fisherman's Way, Margaret was busy behind the bar polishing glasses and stacking them on a shelf behind her.

'Ah!' she cried. 'You're here at last. Where's Geordie?'

'He's still with Mr Moody. Anyway, he's off the booze so you may not see him tonight. Plus he's got a girlfriend that's turned him into a puppy dog.'

'You gotta be kidding me,'

'I kid you not. Pint of bitter please and a packet of smoky bacon.' Margaret began to pull the pint and I watched with increasing impatience as the amber brown nectar slowly slewed up the side of the glass. She placed the pint on the bar and I waited for a few seconds as the creamy head settled.

'So how was the journey,' asked Margaret as she passed me the crisps and collected my fiver. I picked the pint of beer up and put it to my lips. The smooth, silky liquid slid down my neck in one long easy drink. I slapped the pint back on the bar let out a long pleasurable "ah!" and wiped the froth off my top lip with the back of my hand.

'How was the journey, well I'll tell you how the journey was Margaret. If I said to you that I would rather be rogered up the freckle by a well endowed and over-enthusiastic rhinoceros, does that give you some idea of what it was like?'

'Oh dear. That bad eh?' she laughed as she pulled my second pint.

'Yes that bad. No, worse than bad. Far, far worse than bad. On a scale of badness, it would be off the scale.'

I had a few more pints and filled Margaret in on the details of Geordie's mental condition and then headed back to the house. There was a note on the kitchen table that read, *macaroni cheese in microwave – gone to bed – jackie/geordie*. I was thankful for the peace and quiet. I ate my dinner, washed up and then retired to bed myself.

The next day I kept out of the lovebirds way partly for their benefit but mainly for my own. I packed a small picnic, threw on my backpack and set off along the coastal path heading north. It was a gentle walk with barely a hill in sight, the complete opposite to what I was used to in the Dales. When I walked I forgot about everything for the first leg of the journey. It was my meditation. I stopped on some small dunes for lunch and chewed on my sandwich staring out at the grey north sea. It was a pleasant day with a refreshing salty breeze with the sun playing hide and seek behind large wispy clouds. There were small trawlers on the horizon and huge tankers and cargo ships nearer to shore, all appearing to be stationary but in reality moving at a steady pace. I finished lunch and continued walking, taking a slight detour to explore an old castle. I walked along the beach for a number of miles and then came across another small fishing village. I was feeling quite thirsty and decided to walk into the village and found a quiet pub with a beautiful beer garden. I sat outside basking in the sun. There was only one other patron, an old craggy looking man who sat quietly at a table reading his newspaper. After a few minutes he got up and left, leaving his newspaper behind. I went over and grabbed the paper; it was the Herald. I flicked through it quickly and came to a headline that read, "Renaissance Man", with a large photo of Geordie below it and the reporter's name alongside, "Jackie O'Connor". Oh my God, this was going to be good. I went and refilled my pint, went back outside, lit a cigarette and settled back down at my table and began to read the article. The opening paragraphs were a review of the Glasgow gig. Nothing spectacular there. Jackie had been generous in her review of all the artists, even the Stoned Crows came out of it smelling of roses. But now came the juicy part. I read on and continually shook my head in disbelief.

"Despite the outlandish headlines that have accompanied the Shooting Tsars, Resurrection Tour, in recent weeks by the tabloids, the truth, is a slightly different fish. I met up with Allan Kincaid, a.k.a. "Geordie", legendary bassist with the Tsars to separate fact from fiction. I was a little intimidated when the interview first began as Geordie is renowned for not giving interviews and on the rare occasions that he does it is typically not a pleasant experience for the interviewer. So it was with a little surprise and a great deal of pleasure that instead of finding an aggressive, turbulent agitator I instead came across a sensitive man, a thinking man, a gentleman, a renaissance man."

'What a load of bollocks,' I yelled to no-one. I kept reading.

"So Geordie, it's been ten years since the Tsars last played together, what's it like being back with the other boys?"

"Oh it's great, I'm loving every minute of it. There's no better feeling than being on stage with this band."

"And do you all still get along on a personal level?"

"Aye, we all get along fine. There's barely a cross word between us. A bit of ribbing here and there but that's about it."

"Now just for any readers who are not aware of the background of the Tsars can you give us a brief synopsis."

"Well we formed in the early nineties and within six months we had a record deal with GMC. Our first album was at number one for about eighteen weeks I think, plus a few number one singles. We began touring all over the country, playing bigger and bigger venues. And then we started on Europe and then Asia. Our next two albums went platinum. It was after the third album when we were touring the States that we realised our record company had signed us up to one of the most draconian and restrictive record contracts ever known. They were ripping us off and we weren't seeing much of the profits. We decided to axe our manager and try and get a fairer deal. GMC slapped an injunction on us that prohibited us from playing or recording together and took us to court. It took about six months for the case to come to court and another six or so months before a verdict was reached—which we won may I say—but GMC immediately appealed the decision. Another six months later the appeal was upheld and the record company won. We had to deliver them one more album. Well, that was never going to happen and we all just went our separate ways, just drifted apart."

"It's a terrible story and serves as a warning to other younger bands who are considering record deals to make sure they get the best advice from a professional music lawyer. How did you feel at the time about your record company, GMC and your ex-manager?"

"Oh, I wanted them all dead the same way as they killed the Tsars. I hated them all."

"How did you cope with that burning hatred?"

"I took to drink, drugs, violent behaviour. I sort of turned the anger in on myself. Instead of hurting them I was hurting me. It was a bad time. I think the others went through a similar experience."

"But in a bizarre twist of fate, it is actually your ex-manager who is the brains behind this Resurrection Tour, how do you reconcile your past feelings with working with him again?"

"I think you're being overly generous when you use the word brains. Look, I won't lie, the money's good and I need the money and I'm not the man I was ten years ago. I've mellowed, matured, grown up. I don't entertain anger or regret; they're negative emotions. I get along with Chas. I mean, we're never going to be bosom buddies or anything but at least we can be civil to each other."

"Moving on; is there any truth in the rumour that, although Will Harding is credited with being this amazing songwriter, in fact it is you who is actually the musical genius behind the band?"

"Well, yes, there is some truth to that. When I first hear some of the songs, they're sometimes a bit of a pig's ear, so I work on them and knock them into shape. But at the end of the day, you're wasting your time if you try polishing a turd and I've got to say it's very rare when Billy boy ever hands me a turd."

What a lovely turn of phrase and also what a humble and gracious man my old pal really was. I finished the dregs of my beer, put the newspaper in my backpack and set off on the return journey.

It was always this second part of the walk when my brain switched on and I began trawling over events. I thought about the interview. I wasn't annoyed with Geordie for what he said about knocking my songs into shape. There was an element of truth to it but his holier-than-thou attitude was beginning to grate. My mind once again turned to Chas. What was his game? Why now after ten years had he suddenly got back in touch? Could there be something in the tour contract that John Peterson had missed and we were all going to be ripped off again? There was something definitely missing but no matter how many times I regurgitated past events in my mind, I could not unlock the box that contained the truth.

I walked up the path to the house. It was early evening and I was feeling weary in a good way. The front door to the house was slightly ajar and I poked my head inside. Geordie was sat at the little kitchen table reading the Herald while picking at his teeth with a toothpick.

'Ah, well look who it is? None other than Saint Allan of Kincaid,' I announced loudly as I bundled in through the doorway. Geordie jumped from his chair and quickly folded the newspaper up and threw it onto the floor.

'Jesus H Christ, you nearly gave me a heart attack creeping up on me like that, you daft bastard!' he exclaimed. I walked over to the kitchen counter and switched the kettle on.

'Where's Jackie?' I asked with my back to him.

'She's gone to the shops to get something for tea. How was the walk?'

'Yeah good. Anything worthwhile in the paper?' He looked at me sheepishly.

'Nah, same old shite; death, destruction, lying politicians, diets and soap opera trivia.'

'Nothing about turd polishing or pigs ears then?' He stared at the ground.

'Look ... about that, it sounded a bit, sort of, well, you know ...'

'What? A bit arrogant, thankless, up-yourself?'

'Well, I wouldn't have used those exact same words, but ...' He seemed worried. I smiled.

'Don't worry you great big prannock. I'm not offended. It was probably the only sliver of truth in the whole story. Fucking "Renaissance Man" my arse,' there was a quiet pause, 'anyway, so when's the funeral?'

'Tomorrow, ten o'clock at the Kirk,' he said sadly, 'we're having the wake at the pub. Margaret's doing the food.' I stared at his big ugly face and felt a stab of sorrow.

'Look Geordie, I haven't said this before, but I'm really sorry about your Nan. I only met her that once but she was a great woman. I know you two were closer than close, what with everything that went on in your past. I know you've got Jackie now, but I'm always here if you need me, you do understand that?' The big fella answered me with a faint smile.

'Aye, of course I do, Billy. I've been doing a lot of thinking of late and although I'm gutted that Nan has passed away, I'm finally back in a good place. I get up in the morning now with purpose and something to believe in. I love playing in this band, it means everything to me. I've also

339

found Jackie, I've got a roof over my head and the future looks bright. It's amazing how the actions of one man can have such a profound effect on other people's lives. And that man Billy ... is you. You've created all of this.' I was genuinely touched by his comments and allowed myself a few moments of self-congratulatory smugness. *Yes, it is all down to me. I got the band back together, I found Geordie, I'm the glue.* It didn't last long before Commandant Paranoia stuck his two penneth in. *Wait ... is it really me? No it's not. It's Chas! He organised the tour, he contacted me, he cajoled me into doing this tour, this is not down to me at all ... it's all down to Chas!* I didn't air my thoughts to Geordie.

'Okay, right, well how about a few wee drams before Jackie gets back?' Geordie instantly brightened.

'That's the best idea I've heard in a long time!' he exclaimed as he reached for the whisky bottle at the back of the cupboard. I grabbed a pair of tumblers and Geordie poured out two extremely large measures. We clinked our glasses together.

'Here's to the Tsars,' I said.

'Aye, and sex and drugs and rock and roll. Long may she reign.'

30: JUST GIMME SOME TRUTH

The day after the funeral we dropped Jackie off at Aberdeen where she caught a train back to Glasgow. We continued by car to Sunderland where we met up with the rest of the entourage at the gig. We were due to headline but after our emotionally fraught sabbatical, we asked to go on second after the Crows. We played for forty minutes to another packed and enthusiastic crowd but I can honestly say we were merely going through the motions. I felt like I had cheated the fans out of their money and made a mental promise that I needed to lift my game for the remaining gigs.

The feeling backstage was pretty hollow, as though all the fun had gone out of the tour, before I reminded myself that it had never been fun anyway. Things began to brighten up somewhat when Connie disappeared for twenty minutes and arrived back with an excellent bag of speed that most of us indulged in. I began to loosen up and watched from the wings as the excellent Divina went out to perform. The crowd loved her, she grew in confidence with every performance and I knew her star had definitely risen again. I kept an eye on Geordie who seemed to be slowly slipping back into his old habits, for better or for worse. It seemed that without Jackie's calming and restraining influence he was returning to form.

By the time the Circles had come off stage I was relaxed and enjoying myself. The backstage gathering consisted of various musicians, journalists, drug dealers and other undesirables, but despite this, the atmosphere was light and carefree—there was a party in the offing.

I was talking with Connie and Robbo about the finer points of our respective live performances when I realised that I hadn't seen Geordie for quite a while. At first it was merely a factual realisation, an observation that raised nothing but mild inquisitiveness. I half listened to the conversation about the importance of a good sound engineer out front, but somewhere deep in the abyss of my mind, a thought had been born. It niggled away at me. I surveyed the room and the excitable throng. Geordie was never hard to miss due to his height and also wherever Geordie was there would usually be some sort of heated debate, raucous laughter or adolescent prank being performed—but not tonight. He was nowhere to be seen—hmm. Robbo noticed my preoccupation. He pulled out a ready made spliff from the top of his jacket and stuck it in my mouth before flicking his lighter and igniting it. I took a long draw and held onto the smoke. Robbo eased the spliff from my mouth and took a huge toke from it himself.

'Chill out man, he won't be far,' he said.

'Who ya talking about?' asked Connie in his thick Liverpudlian twang.

'Geordie. Will here, seems to feel some parental obligation towards him.'

'Don't worry man, I saw him heading off through that door over there with Chas about ten minutes ago. He can't be up to too much mischief can he?' said Connie pointing at a small inconspicuous doorway at the far end of the room. The narcotic smoke I had been holding onto was expelled in an involuntary gasp. I coughed loudly and Connie patted me on the back.

'What's wrong wac, go down the wrong 'ole did it?' Tears welled up in my eyes and through my gasping and coughing I managed to utter,

'With Chas? Oh fuck, that's not good.' Robbo nodded in stoned agreement. I walked through the crowd, turning down various offers and invitations and opened the door Connie had pointed out. It led into a little corridor with numerous rooms on the left hand side and a small kitchenette at the far end. As I shut the door behind me the music and chatter quickly diminished. I walked slowly down the corridor stopping at each door along the way and bending my ear towards it to try to detect any signs of life. As I approached the third door, I thought I heard talking. Yes, there were two distinct voices talking. Well, one was talking while the other seemed to be pleading. I gently opened the door and popped my head around. What I saw set my pulse racing as my heart thumped against my chest. Chas was sat on a sofa, arms outstretched in front of him, pleading with Geordie, who was holding a large silver Colt 45, its barrel resting gently on Chas's temple.

'For fuck's sake Geordie! What are you playing at?' I growled in alarm while quickly shutting the door behind me.

'Russian Roulette of course,' Geordie replied matter-of-factly.

'Oh Will, thank God you're here! Get me out of here please, I beg you,' implored Chas. I looked at the sorry figure that sat in front of me. His cheeks were wet with tears and there was a large dark patch between his legs, the stain spreading onto the tatty fabric of the pale green sofa.

'Geordie, put the gun down, stop playing silly buggers,' I instructed as calmly as I could.

'Oh I'm not playing Will. This is for real. You see I want the truth from this weasel slimeball. I've waited a long, long, time to get this opportunity and now I have it, neither you nor all the king's horses nor all the king's men are going to deprive me of it.' I suddenly had a flashback to when we Geordie and I had first arrived in London. As we'd walked up the hotel steps after the long drive from Scotland I recalled the conversation we'd had about Chas; Geordie's words reappeared from the past like an unpaid tax bill.

'Probably for the best anyway.'

'What's probably for the best?'

343

'Chas!' It makes things a lot easier.' It had unnerved me at the time but I had let it go, now I knew what he had meant.

'Okay here we go again Chas,' laughed Geordie. He cocked the gun with his oversized thumb and slowly squeezed the trigger.

'NO! STOP! GEORDIE DON'T DO IT! I yelled. But before the words had finished tumbling out of my mouth, the hammer on the gun had snapped back to its resting position with a silky "click".

'My God you're a lucky bastard,' mocked Geordie, before putting the gun to the side of his own temple and pulling the trigger. Another click. I gasped. Geordie gawped at me,

'Well, it's only fair isn't it. Got to give him a sporting chance.' The situation was bad, very bad. I thought about making a lunge for the gun but the coward in me overrode any illusions of bravery.

'Geordie, you need to tell me what this is all about?' I pleaded, still with a pretence of calmness.

'I liked John Lennon. Not just his music—I mean that was bloody great, but I liked him as a man, not that I knew him.' He spoke slowly as he casually spun the barrel on the gun. 'I think basically he was a truthful man, an honest man. I like that in a person,' added Geordie, pointing the gun in my direction. Chas appeared ashen and stared nervously at the threadbare carpet that covered the floor of the little room. 'I think he was a truth-seeker.'

'Geordie, you're making no sense?'

'Well, I know that everyone thinks I'm a bit of a buffoon, a loose cannon, unhinged and that's fine—I have a thick skin. But you see I'm also a bit of a thinker and over the last few days I've been doing a lot of thinking, and there are a few things that just don't add up. I think you first touched on it Will, when we first arrived in London, do you remember that first night at the curry house?'

I desperately tried to wind back the days and plethora of incidents to that first night but my brain was addled. There was a tap on the door and in walked Robbo. He stared at me, then Geordie, then the gun and lastly at Chas.

'Fuck me! Robert De Niro and Christopher Walken I presume? Who's who?' he smiled as he pulled a joint from his shirt pocket and sparked up.

'Ah, Robbo just in time,' continued Geordie, ignoring Robbo's "Deer Hunter" reference, 'I was just explaining to Will that I've been doing a lot of thinking lately and there're a few things puzzling me and I think Chas could help us out with a few answers.' Robbo grinned and expelled a long tube of blue smoke. He nodded at the gun.

'That's a bit, well … you know …' Geordie gazed at the gun with an impassive air.

'The gun? You think it's a bit Butch Cassidy and the Sundance Kid?'

'Just a bit,' concurred Robbo. I was getting tired of this farce. 'Geordie, put the gun down and get to the point.' He seemed annoyed but continued on his garrulous way.

'As I was saying, at the curry house Robbo told us of the run of unusual events that had befallen him; the mysterious rap band, the break in, the cryptic text messages. And Will added another; this tour—after all this time. Now obviously none of you bothered to think any more of it. Well I did and that's why I'm here, with me old mate Chas,' he thumped Chas on the back like a long lost friend, but with far more vigour than was necessary. Chas lurched forward and groaned. 'But first, as Mary Hopkins used to say, let's start at the very beginning, it a very good place to begin …'

'Mary Poppins,' Robbo corrected nonchalantly.

'What?' asked Geordie, slightly puzzled and a little annoyed at yet another interruption.

'You said Mary Hopkins. She was the first signing on the Apple label. "Those were the days my friend". Mary Poppins is who you're thinking of. The magical nanny, Julie Andrews.' Geordie pondered for a while before a grin spread across his face,

'Oh yeah, Mary Poppins. What did I say? Hopkins—Haha, what a wanker.'

'You're both wrong. It was the Sound Of Music,' muttered Chas still staring at the carpet.

'What?' Geordie snapped.

'It was the Sound of Music. The Von Trapps. Still Julie Andrews but it was definitely the Sound of Music.'

'It wasn't the Sound of Music, right! It was Mary Hopkins!' screamed Geordie.

'Poppins,' corrected Robbo.

'Yeah, Poppins! Mary bastard Poppins!'

'I'm sorry Allan but you're wrong! It was definitely the Sound of Music,' Chas had momentarily forgotten his perilous predicament and was now bristling with indignation at Geordie's and Robbo's musical faux pas.

'Hang on Geordie, I think Chas is right, now I come to think of it. It was the Sound of Music,' Robbo sucked on his spliff as though contemplating some immutable law of the universe. I, on the other hand, had had enough.

'Will you all shut the fuck up! What does it matter, whether it's Mary Poppins, Mary Hopkins, Anthony Hopkins or Peter Paul and fucking Mary! Just hurry up and explain what you're playing at Geordie!' Everyone stared at me as though I were clearly mad. There was a muted silence before Geordie began where he had left off some time ago.

'Okay, from the beginning; now Chas, did you know when you recommended we sign with GMC that we were being stitched up with probably one of the shittiest record deals in history?' Geordie spun the barrel on the gun again. I prayed this was a game of bluff and there were no bullets in the barrel.

'Look how many more times do I have to tell you! At the time I thought it was an okay deal. In hindsight, yes, it was a shitty deal, but a shitty deal is better than no deal. As for the three options, I assumed you understood what that meant—that you would possibly have to produce four albums not three. You can't blame me for your ignorance. And remember this, I did advise you to employ a dedicated entertainment lawyer to go through the contract, but oh no! You used Robbo's bloody brother to look through it.'

'Brother-in-law, actually,' corrected Robbo.

'Sorry, brother-in-law. How is he by the way?' apologised Chas.

'Yeah, he's going okay. Can be a bit of a dick at times, but who can't,' replied Robbo while throwing Geordie a knowing glance.

'Well, pass on my regards next time you see him,'

'Yeah. Will do,'

'Do you two fucking mind! I'm trying to do an interrogation here and you're playing Mr and Mrs,' growled Geordie. I decided to intervene.

'He has a point Geordie,' I said, referring to Chas's version of events, 'I do remember him advising us to use a good lawyer.'

'Okay well let's move on then. What do you know about the break in at Robbo's, the mysterious band that never showed up, the cryptic text messages and the real reason you organised this tour?' Geordie cocked the gun.

'Look I don't know anything about what happened to Robbo. And as for the tour, I just thought it was a good idea and a way to mend some fences. Everything I've ever done has been with good intent and I always put the interest of you boys above anything else.' Whoa! That was a bad hand to play at such a critical time. There was no way Geordie would buy that. Geordie impatiently leaned forward and put the gun to Chas's head and immediately pulled the trigger—"click". Chas began to shake. He stared at me with big round pleading eyes. I felt sorry for him and wanted to bring this episode to an end but I sensed Geordie's mood and he wasn't going to stop until he had the answers he wanted.

'Just gimme some truth,' whispered Geordie menacingly. He once again spun the barrel on the gun. 'That's the last spin Chas. From now on no more spinning of the barrel. So, that gives you a maximum of five chances left. Now, the truth.'

'I'm t-t-t-telling you the t-t-truth!' he screamed back.

'Okay, I'm sick of this. Will, Robbo, you may want to leave the room. No point us all getting splattered with blood.' I shot a glance at Robbo, who for the first time appeared concerned. Geordie put the gun to Chas's temple and cocked the trigger. Chas's face was contorted in agony as though bracing for imminent pain.

'Wait! Wait! Okay I'll tell you the truth just put the gun away,' sobbed Chas. Geordie lowered the gun. 'Has anyone got a drink?' Geordie pulled a small bottle of scotch out of his jacket and threw it to Chas, who unscrewed the cap and took a small gulp, grimacing as the fiery liquid scorched his throat.

'You've heard of Reed Lochlan?' began Chas. Geordie and I shook our heads.

'Yeah, I've heard of him. He's the head honcho at GMC isn't he?' answered Robbo coolly.

'Yeah that's right. The head honcho. He's the MD of GMC Europe, which makes him just about the biggest arse kicker in the music world. Ten years ago he was nothing more than a junior accountant. He's gone straight to the top and hasn't bothered who he's trampled on along the way. Anyway, about nine months ago I get a call from his secretary asking me, no, telling me to come in for a meeting with him. I thought he was going to offer me a job as a scout or something—I was a little nervous to say the least. The first thing he asks me after we've got the small talk over with is what I know about the Shooting Tsars "Bloom" sessions.' Chas stopped abruptly and eyed all three of us. Robbo and I shifted nervously in our seats as we exchanged glances with each other. Geordie didn't flinch, he just continued staring vindictively at Chas. 'Of course I pleaded ignorance; I knew nothing of the so called "Bloom" sessions. Then he tells me that he's been contacted by David Heidelberg who had in his possession a bootleg of his favourite British nineties rock band the Shooting Tsars. The bootleg was called "the Bloom sessions"; a bootleg of previously unreleased and unheard music. As GMC held all the rights to the Tsars music, Heidelberg rang Reed.' He stopped and took another swig of Scotch while scrutinizing us all guardedly. Geordie was a little perplexed and voiced his concerns.

'Who the fuck is David Heidelberg when he's at home?'

'You must have heard of David Heidelberg?' Robbo insisted. Geordie shook his head. 'Fuck me, even Dinkiad Bay must have newspapers and DVD players. David Heidelberg is only the biggest film producer of the decade, bigger than Spielberg or Scorsese. You must have seen or heard about his films?' Geordie shook his head again. Robbo sighed. 'Let's just say that he's "big". He has the Midas touch. Any film with his name on it is a blockbuster, seriously massive.' Chas took another swig of scotch before resuming his narrative.

'Well anyway, I finally convinced Reed that I knew nothing of the "Bloom" bootleg, which is the truth. He explained that Heidelberg was in the early development stage of his next movie. It is going to be a story about three young men who set out to discover the origins of hippie America, a sort of road movie-cum-history lesson. Anyway, to cut a long story short, Heidelberg decided the music from your "Bloom" session was exactly what he was after for his soundtrack to the movie, hence the call to Reed. Of course, Reed didn't reach the top by being a fuckwit, so he said he'd speak with his lawyers about a licensing deal; that's when he called me. I explained to him the history that GMC and you guys had and that you'd all dropped off the face of the earth, apart from Robbo that is. Reed made it quite clear that he was putting me in charge of finding this Bloom tape, by whatever means possible; he's not the sort of guy you say "no" to. Plus, I would obviously be rewarded for my efforts.'

'Obviously,' I echoed. Chas flung out his arms in mock surprise.

'Hey, I'm a businessman Will, and this is just business.'

349

'Aye, the amount of times I've heard that. I wonder how many millions of people are shafted every day in the name of business,' mused Geordie cynically. Chas ignored him.

'My first port of call was Robbo's studio to see if he had the master tape to the Bloom sessions, well not me personally you understand, let's just say GMC have on hand a small army of unsavoury but useful characters. Sorry about that Robbo, I hope there wasn't too much damage?' offered Chas apologetically. Robbo relit his spliff and heaved away.

'I'll send you the bill for a new lock,' he replied pithily. Chas winced as he leaned back into the sofa.

'Well, nothing turned up as you'd all be aware. So, my next idea was to try and find you two,' he said nodding in my and Geordie's direction, 'or Flaky. Three months later I still had nothing. Reed was becoming impatient so I came up with this plan.' He seemed to end prematurely. I recalled the day I'd returned to my house, after my fateful walk, when Caesar was excitedly sniffing around all the rooms, and then there was Geordie's home, suddenly on the market after fifty years. Surely these events weren't linked? I didn't air my suspicions in case it enflamed Geordie.

'What plan?' I asked.

'This,' he indicated with arms outstretched again, 'the tour.'

'You mean all this, the reunion tour and all the other bands is about you, GMC, trying to get your hands on some ancient recording session? It's a bit far-fetched Chas,' I added incredulously.

'It's more than far-fetched, it's like a bad episode of Scooby Doo,' Geordie sneered.

'You mean there was a good episode of Scooby Doo?' asked Robbo.

'Sorry boys, but it is true, gospel. It was a long shot but I had no choice.' I wasn't convinced by Chas's confession.

'How did you know we'd agree to the tour? How did you get my telephone number? Why didn't you just tell us the truth from the off? Plus, this tour could end up being a massive loss so how much exactly was this licensing deal with Heidelberg going to be worth?'

'You're always worrying about the detail Will. Getting your number was easy; I got one of GMC's computer geeks to hack into the telecom mainframe. I wasn't sure you would do the tour, in fact I was pretty sure you wouldn't but it's all I had. That's when I made the false booking at Robbo's studio hoping it would free him up to do the tour. I knew that if he was up for it then I was halfway there. Hope you didn't lose too much business, I'm sure the tour money has more than made up for it.'

'Yeah, thanks a bunch Chas, what would I have done without you.' Robbo drawled.

'As for telling you the truth from the outset, well, come on, really? What would have been your response if I had rung you up and said, "Hey Will, how's it going, can you forward the master-tape of the Bloom sessions to me, care of GMC, thanks, catch you later." Yeah, I'm sure you'd have been well up for that. As for the licensing deal, well that's hard to say but I'd estimate that we could all live the life of kings for the rest of our naturals. I mean, it's not only the licensing deal, it's about America; if you have a soundtrack to one of Heidelberg's films then you've cracked it; the back catalogue will be re-issued and then we put out some new product; tours, MTV, merchandise—it's going to be fucking huge! We're talking squillions!' Chas was getting a little carried away; his eyes were wide with excitement and beads of sweat dripped from his forehead. So much for fate, I thought of my ashtray and answering the call from Chas all those months ago. How naive I'd been to think fate had played a hand in it. Big business—they were after me and my band and they got us. Nothing could have stopped them. I felt like I'd been shafted again. But now, my brain had gone into overdrive and was converting information faster than an Intel processor. Chas took

351

another swig of whisky, appearing relieved that he'd finally unburdened himself of the truth, an act he was patently unused to. 'So, whaddya say boys? Get me the master-tape and I'll take it to Reed and we'll get this show on the road. Next year at this time we'll be all living in our private castles on some sun drenched Caribbean island.'

'Slight problem there Chas,' I replied cryptically. He eyeballed me suspiciously.

'Problem? What problem Will?'

'Well I'm rather fond of my little place in the Dales; Caribbean islands aren't really my scene.'

'Fuck the Caribbean then, you'll be able to buy the fucking Dales, Ilkley Moor and as many black pudding factories as you want,' Chas snapped back.

'Well, it's not just that. There is another small, teeny-weeny hitch.' Chas stood up and put his hands on his hips suddenly looking serious which was pretty hard to do when you have a large piss stain around your groin area.

'What?'

'Well, it's the tape; we don't have a copy, no-one does.' Chas's jaw dropped and for a moment he was lost for words. He laughed nervously.

'Haha, nice one Will. You nearly had me there,' he glanced across at Robbo and Geordie as he spoke, grinning hopefully.

'It's true Chas. We don't have a copy, no-one does,' confirmed Robbo. Chas stopped grinning.

'What, but how? What do you mean you don't have a copy? You must have the master-tape, how else, but, no, no, no, this isn't true, this can't be true.'

'You see Chas,' I explained, 'when we'd nearly finished recording and mastering "Bloom" there was a small fire in the control room. Nothing major but the mixing desk and tape machine were destroyed, along with our master tape. Fire Chief said it could have been a smouldering cigarette or faulty wiring.' Chas stared at me in disbelief.

'What about a backup? You must have surely had a backup?' I shook my head. 'Well how come David Heidelberg has a copy then? Explain that?'

'Well we made cassette copies for friends and ourselves at the end of recording and he must have somehow got his hands on one of them. But that's no good to anyone. I don't think the mighty David Heidelberg will want a crappy cassette quality recording as the soundtrack to his next blockbuster.' Chas stared at the ground for a few seconds.

'What's the chance of you boys getting back in the studio and re-recording it again?' it was a stupid question and Chas knew it.

'Do you really think, in your wildest dreams that we would ever work with GMC again?'

'No, of course not. I'm dead. Reed will kill me. I'm finished.' There was no fear or despondency in his voice, it was completely emotionless. He'd just seen his big chance come and go in a matter of seconds. I actually felt a trifle sorry for him, the conniving Cockney git.

'Well at least the tour has been a success after the initial false start—hasn't it?' I offered, hoping to cheer him up somewhat. He continued staring at the ground in a reverie.

'What? Oh yes, the tour; the tour will make a slight profit, and there's the product back in the charts again. Yes, yes, it's a success albeit a small success. It's hardly America, Heidelberg and a trillion squid though is it. Hmm ... never mind. That Caribbean island will have to wait, next time eh.' He snapped out of his gloomy thoughts, 'Well, if you boys will excuse me, I'd like to get back to the hotel and turn in. It's been quite a testing day.' He squinted down at the dark piss stain on his trousers. 'Hmm ... yes, quite. Okay, I'll see you lot tomorrow.' He moved towards the door, but Geordie beckoned him.

'Oi, Chas, almost forgot—what were the cryptic text messages for?' Chas cocked his head to one side like a sheepdog.

'I had nothing to do with it. What exactly did these messages say?' he asked inquisitively. I sensed he was telling the truth.

353

'Just song lyrics,' answered a slightly stoned Robbo.

'Such as?' persisted Chas.

'Oh, you know, things like …' I abruptly cut Robbo off.

'Just someone playing a prank. Trying to get a wind up out of Robbo,' I said. 'Anyway Chas, you better go before Geordie here, gets another case of the "Christopher Walken's." See you tomorrow.' I noticed a change in Chas's demeanour. He was alert again.

'Yes of course,' he made his way out of the door, 'oh, and by the way, you boys were fantastic tonight.'

'Thanks Chas. And please don't call it product, it's music, it's art.'

'You boys will never get it will you, it's just another commodity, like baked beans, just harder to sell, haha!' He laughed as he walked off. I shut the door behind him and put my finger to my lips to indicate to the others not to say anything. I listened for a few moments. I heard his footsteps disappear down the corridor and then the rush of noise from the backstage party as he opened the adjoining door. The noise dissipated again. I tentatively re-opened the door and scanned the passageway—it was clear. I turned and faced Geordie.

'I'll deal with you later,' I growled at him.

'You should be thanking me! At least we know the truth now,' he replied in all innocence.

'Shut the fuck up and both of you listen. Chas—he's onto it.' I sat down on a chair and lit a smoke.

'Onto what?' asked Robbo. 'I can't handle all this cloak and dagger shit. Just explain in simple layman's terms okay, and keep it short and sweet.'

'Robbo, give me your mobile?' I demanded.

'What? What for?'

'Just give me the fucking thing.' He reluctantly handed over his phone. I pressed a few buttons and came across the last text message from his mysterious caller. I hit the call button and waited. There was a click as an answering machine immediately took the call. A robotic voice said, "Please leave a message".

'It's Robbo, let's talk, call me,' I replied and hung up.

'Can someone please explain what is going on?' insisted Robbo.

'Cast your mind back to the "Bloom" sessions. We employed a sound engineer to do all the studio set up and tedious shit. He was a youngish, tall guy with bad skin.'

'Oh yeah, I remember that guy!' exclaimed Geordie. 'He was a fucking liability if I recall. His name was ... erm ... Deano! That's it, yeah Deano with the bad acne.'

'You're right Geordie, that was his name. Well done. Anyway, do you remember about a day or two before the fire he accidentally erased some overdub, it might have been Robbo's lead guitar, and you slapped him around the head, kicked him up the arse and sacked him?'

'Aye, yeah it's all coming back. I forgot about that. He deserved more than a boot up the arse. So you think this is the guy who has been texting Robbo?'

'Yep. And I bet you a penny to a pound of shit that he's got the Bloom master tape.' At that moment Robbo's phone rang. I put the phone on speaker and answered.

'Hello?'

'Is that Robbo?' a slow lethargic voice asked.

'Yep it's Robbo,' I lied.

'Do you know who this is and what I have of yours?'

'Well I'm guessing you are Deano and you have our Bloom master tape and you are going to blackmail us—am I warm?' There was a cough mixed in with a cackle that emanated from the phone's speaker. Geordie and Robbo both leaned in attentively.

'That's fucking cool man, you got it in one. So listen, the tape is yours for thirty G's.'

'Fuck off! We're not paying you thirty grand for something that legally belongs to us.'

'Hey listen man, technically it's not yours. It's GMC's remember? And anyway, I hear on the old musical grapevine that Heidelberg wants it as the soundtrack to his next film. So, thirty G's is a gift I'd say.' I gazed at the others who both shrugged their shoulders.

'Okay, it's a deal. But you'll have to give us a couple of days to get the money unless you'd take a cheque?'

'Haha. You're funny man, very funny. Two days or the deals off.'

'Okay. Two days time we'll be playing York. Text me the details of where and when you want us to meet.'

'Cool man, cool. By the way, any chance of getting on the guest list for that gig?' I hung up.

'Cheeky fucker!' I handed Robbo his phone. He still seemed a little confused.

'So how did he get hold of the tape?'

'Well, maybe that fire wasn't accidental. Maybe he snuck back and pinched the tape and started a small fire to cover his tracks.'

'Hang on a mo, there's some dodgy threads here. Why would he want our tape? Unless he could see into the future and see that in a decade it may be worth something.'

'He didn't steal the tape for monetary gain. He stole it for revenge. If I remember rightly we all treated him pretty shabbily during those sessions. And when we finally sacked him, I think Geordie sent him off with a size twelve up the arris—well that's when he probably snapped.'

'Okay Sherlock, well why doesn't he sell it back to GMC? He could get a lot more out of them than us?'

'Yes, that is a bit of a puzzle. I might ask him that when we meet him.'

'So what about Chas? You said he was "onto it", onto what?'

'Didn't you see how his whole demeanour changed when Geordie asked him about the cryptic messages? He went from being a broken man to someone who has just found out they've won the Lotto, but can't

356

quite remember where they've put the ticket. He smelt it.' Robbo finally appeared to understand. 'Can you get your hands on thirty thousand by tomorrow?' I asked him.

'Yeah, sure,' he replied nonchalantly as if I'd asked to borrow a tenner.

'I don't like it Billy boy; the whole thing stinks like a tramps jockstrap; I don't trust that cockney weasel, I don't trust GMC and I don't trust this Deano character.'

'Well how do you like this; we get our hands on that tape and take it to another record company; they licence it to Heidelberg, we make shit loads of money and stick one up GMC and Chas for that matter.' Geordie grinned.

'Yeah, I like that, I like that a lot.'

'Now about the gun,' I said seriously. His grin immediately disappeared. I rubbed my neck in an agitated way.

'What would Jackie say about this little incident, hmm?' He looked worried.

'Well there's no need for her to find out is there,' he replied nervously.

'Where did you get it from? I thought the police confiscated it?'

'Well, it was part of a pair. I picked this one up when we went back to Dinkiad Bay for Nan's funeral.' I let out a big sigh as I shook my head.

'I really thought you'd changed Geordie. What happened to the "Brand New Start" and all that crap?'

'Listen Billy, that was the last stupid thing I'll ever do. I just needed to get to the truth and it worked didn't it? Anyway, it was a blank bullet I put in the barrel. There was never any danger to anyone,' he beamed mischievously.

'If you pull any more stunts on this tour or even step out of line, I will be informing Babycake of your erratic, irresponsible and dangerous behaviour; do I make myself clear ... Pumpkin?' Geordie nodded contritely.

'Aye, understood.'

'Good. Now give me the gun,' I asked in an upbeat manner trying to lighten the mood.

'Aye, here yer go,' he said handing me the weapon. I was surprised at the weight of it but also the fine craftsmanship. I also felt something else, something I really didn't expect or want to feel, a sense of power. I held the gun, tentatively at first, but then dropped it to my side and quickly pulled it back up as though I was in a duel in some Western. I cocked the gun and pulled the trigger in one deft moment. I'm not sure what hurt most, the ringing in my ears or the sudden jarring of my hand, wrist and shoulder. I recoiled backwards, stumbling and falling to the floor. A strange smell—gunpowder? sulphur? I peered up and through a thin pale wisp of blue smoke and saw Geordie grinning.

'You could have had my fucking eye out with that ...' he sniggered.

31: WATCHING THE DETECTIVES

I woke feeling green around the gills—again. I opened my eyes tentatively and blinked as they adjusted to the filtered light that crept in through the vertical blinds. Another hotel room, another bed, another gig, another day. My heart suddenly began to race as I remembered that this wasn't just another day; it was the day of our assignation with Deano, the extortionist.

Robbo had made the round trip to Sheffield and back to York the previous day, collecting thirty thousand as he passed go. Geordie, Robbo and I had rendezvoused in the hotel bar that night to discuss possible pitfalls of the exchange but this had been a fruitless exercise as no sooner had we retired to a corner of the room clutching our beers than Flaky had shown up. There had been a unanimous consensus amongst the three of us that under no circumstances were we to tell Flaky of the situation. Things were weird enough without the self-righteous prick kicking up a fuss. Deano had texted Robbo with the details of where and when we were to meet him. Now the day had arrived. I felt a glug of adrenaline surge through my torpid body. Why was I nervous? I used the word extortionist but I was gilding the lily a little. It wasn't really extortion; he had something we wanted, we were willing to pay for it. Okay, there was some dispute over who were actually the legal owners, I mean, we recorded it, we paid for it and we were in dispute with our record company at the time, so as far as I was concerned it belonged to us. Obviously, Chas and GMC had a different outlook. They won the court case and could probably argue that when it was recorded we were still under contract to them; either way, it was a civil matter, not a criminal one so there was no need for my feelings of wrongdoing. Nevertheless, the emotion lingered like a stray dog outside a butchers shop.

I showered and dressed and at nine o'clock I gently knocked on Geordie's and Robbo's doors respectively. I heard movement and a creak as Geordie's large head protruded warily through the doorway. He eyed me suspiciously—I eyed him back impatiently. He had a quick look up and down the corridor before emerging fully from his room.

'Morning Billy boy,' he smiled broadly while scratching at his testicles through a pair of faded jeans. He had another quick furtive glance up and down the corridor, as though expecting some unknown assassin to suddenly materialise.

'What's your problem?' I asked sharply.

'Problem? There's no problem. Just keeping an eye open for anything untoward. Can't be too careful.'

'What are you on about?' I inquired resignedly. He looked over both shoulders again before pulling down twice on the skin beneath his right eye in a "mum's the word" gesture. Just what I didn't need; I was still feeling uneasy about the forthcoming rendezvous without the big oaf assuming the role of Inspector Clouseau. Robbo broke my train of thought as he emerged from his room toking on a joint—funny about that.

'Do you go to bed with one of those things in your mouth?' I questioned. He seemed bemused.

'Ooooh, touchy. You've been spending too much time with Flaky.'

'I've been spending too much time with all of you. Have either of you seen Flaky this morning?'

'Yeah, I saw him at breakfast. He said he was heading off to the gym and then the pool for a swim,' said Robbo.

'Good, the last thing we want is him stuffing everything up.'

'You're not wrong there Billy boy, he's an insufferable twat.'

'Okay Robbo, have you got the money.'

'Yeah, hang on a mo and I'll get it.' Robbo languidly ambled into his room closing the door behind him. He was back out in a jiffy with a Safeways carrier bag bursting at the seams with wads of fifty pound notes clearly visible through the flimsy white plastic. I was astounded.

'What the fuck's that?'

'What the fuck's what?' he answered in all innocence.

'THAT!' I shouted, pointing at the plastic bag.

'It's thirty grand, what the fuck do you think it is!' he replied in annoyance.

'Not the money you idiot, the bag, the bag you're carrying it in!' He stared naively at the bag straining in his hand.

'It's a carrier bag, a Safeway's carrier bag to be more precise,' he replied informatively.

'He's right you know,' backed up Geordie, 'it is a Safeway's bag.' The bell from the lift sounded and out walked a middle aged businessman with an attractive younger woman at his side. He obviously didn't like the look of the trio of buffoons standing in the corridor and carefully strode past eyeing us warily. I stood in front of Robbo to hide the money.

'Morning,' I offered in a friendly way. I got a terse "morning" back and a pleasant smile from the young woman. Geordie grinned like a gurner with an erection.

'Nice day for it,' he said winking at the businessman. The man turned away quickly and continued down the corridor.

'Dirty old bastard; screwing the secretary,' muttered Geordie, a little too loudly. The man spun sharply and bellowed indignantly,

'Actually, she's my Wife, not that it's any business of yours!'

'Yeah, of course she is mate, and I'm Tinker Bell and these two are Peter Pan and Captain Cook,' scoffed Geordie.

'Hook,' corrected Robbo. The man knew better than to get into an argument with a dishevelled bunch of ruffians and continued on his way with his alleged Wife in tow. When they had disappeared into their room I continued my interrogation of Robbo.

'Don't you think something more appropriate than a plastic bag would have been a better choice!' I shouted at him.

'Oh pardon me for doing a round trip of two hundred miles to collect thirty G's of MY money and having the audacity to put it in a plastic bag. What were you expecting? An attaché case of soft brushed leather, embossed with gold leaf and a titanium handcuff. You should be fucking grateful it's here at all!' I realised I was getting nowhere fast. It was like teaching a pig how to whistle; it wastes your time and annoys the shit out of the pig.

'Wait here!' I ordered, and went back into my room and located an old walking backpack at the bottom of my suitcase. As I came back out Geordie began to sing,

'OH, I'M A RAMBLER, I'M A RAMBLER, FROM MANCHESTER WAY ...'

'Aw, fuck off!' I yelled. I quickly transferred the cash into the backpack, zipped it up and slung it onto my back. I glanced at my watch, it read 10:30 am.

'Okay, we've got about thirty minutes before the drop off.' Geordie looked at his own watch.

'Shouldn't we synchronise watches?' he asked in an inquisitive manner.

'It's not mission fucking impossible you know,' I replied tersely. He seemed a little crestfallen.

'Okay, I was just saying ...'

'Come on let's get going.'

#

We left the hotel, crossed the busy road and made our way down the high street in the direction of the river and the "Oddfellows" public house. I noticed Robbo who was acting decidedly edgy, which was out of character for him. His head twitched from side to side as he scanned up and down the street. He was like an old dog with a tic in its neck.

'Right listen up you two. When we get there, Robbo, I want you to hang back and keep your eyes peeled and Geordie you can be my back up, just keep a few feet behind me when we make the exchange. Until then, just act normal.' I knew it was an oxymoron but I said it anyway.

'What do you mean by normal?' asked Geordie.

'You know, normal, just normal. Don't attract attention to yourself; that's all. We're just three blokes out for a quiet stroll.'

'Oh yeah, that's really normal. Three grown men out for a morning stroll together, you see that all the time.' I ignored Geordie's barb. I was beginning to feel a slow impending sense of doom. The sun was out, it was a mild summer's day, I was on tour, I should have been happy and carefree—but I wasn't and whichever way I looked at it I could only see the negatives. I was severely stressed. The tour, the gigs, Chas, Geordie, Flaky, now this dodgy exchange, it was all beginning to wear me down and my normally calm and relaxed persona had changed to one of bad tempered weariness. We stood at a crossing waiting for the little green man to entice us across. I observed our reflections in a shop window opposite. Me, with hunched shoulders and a worried frown; Geordie, unshaven, wild hair flowing in the breeze, olive green bomber jacket flapping loosely; Robbo, slight pot belly, head dancing from side to side like a scared rabbit. What a bloody sight! Try not to attract attention—even when we acted normal we still painted a sorry looking and conspicuous picture. We crossed to the other side of the road and continued with our ambling gait. Silence was the order of the day; the normal bickering, bitching and whining had temporarily ceased; another reason to make me nervous. I suddenly spotted two coppers about a fifty metres ahead walking towards us. Just two constables on their normal

363

beat, chit chatting idly to each other as they casually surveyed the humdrum of normal weekday activity. My heart began to race. Geordie was to my left and slightly behind. Robbo tailed further back like a tense poodle. *Best not say anything about the boys in blue, it will only raise everyone's anxiety levels.* I glanced across at Geordie who had a slight smile on his face. I think he was actually enjoying this clandestine cloak and dagger lark. He suddenly stuck his big head in front of me and with hand covering mouth, whispered loudly,

'Pigs, 12 O'clock!'

'Yes. I've seen them. Just act normal; don't catch their eye. We've done nothing wrong,' I said through gritted teeth.

'No, nothing wrong, but it would be pretty hard to explain what you're doing with thirty grand in your backpack.' He chortled away to himself—big bloody oaf. As the coppers neared I could see that they had not the slightest interest in us and were just going through the motions of showing a presence on the street. Ten feet away now. I averted my gaze and stared straight ahead. Five feet. Geordie began to whistle the theme tune from "The Bill". I suddenly sensed that they'd spied us and must have been wondering what an odd assortment we were. Of course Geordie couldn't keep his great big trap shut.

'Morning ossifers. Nice day for catching a few paedophiles eh?' Shit! I carried on walking as though nothing had happened. I didn't quicken my pace but wanted to put as much distance between us and the local constabulary as possible. I was expecting a shout or a call but nothing came. I decided to take an impromptu turn to my left and walked through a doorway into a shop to gather my thoughts. The other two followed.

'For fuck's sake Geordie! What the hell do you think you're playing at?' I yelled at him

'What? What have I done?' he peered down at me with all innocence. I was about to let him have it when I heard a well spoken female voice.

'Yes Gentlemen, can I help you?' I turned to see a well dressed and manicured woman in her early thirties. The owner or manager no doubt. I surveyed my surroundings and realised that I'd led us all into a ladies lingerie shop. Rows of knickers and bras hung from hangers. Mannequins, done up in lacy camisoles and silky stockings, adorned the shop window. Of all the shops in all the world.

'Well, actually … I … erm …' I struggled for words. 'I'm after something for my Fiancée.' I turned and looked at Robbo and Geordie who were both wearing silly grins.

'Not a problem Sir. Did you have anything particular in mind?'

'Well, erm, yes, something tasteful and classy,' I replied pensively.

'That's not what you said a minute ago,' Geordie's thick Scottish brogue interrupted, 'you said you wanted a pair of crotchless leather panties, a peek-a-boo bra and a nurses uniform—and don't forget the speculum and thermometer.' I felt my face redden and smiled sheepishly at the woman. Her face changed from one of helpfulness to a glare of sordid disgust.

'I'm sorry Sir, but we don't stock those sorts of items here. There's an adult shop two blocks back. Maybe if you were to enquire there, they could help you. Good day.' I turned and hurriedly exited the shop. I had a stealthy glance down the street to make sure the coppers were gone; they had. The two clowns followed me out and we all stood on the pavement blinking at each other, I with a face of thunder and Geordie and Robbo with childish smirks.

'You know what you are Geordie?' I yelled at him.

'A cunt?' he replied helpfully.

'CORRECT! With a capital C!'

We reached the pub without further incident and took up position on one of the many benches and tables outside. I took quick stock of my surroundings. The pub was situated on an intersection of a small lane. Directly across from us was the river that flowed back towards the heart of the city. Slightly to the left was an ancient, stone bridge that had bollards across its entrance to stop any motorised traffic from crossing. To the right, rows of three storey townhouses ran adjacent to the road. A couple of boats on the river, a few delivery trucks slowly navigating the tight narrow roads, cyclists, tourists, students—a busy hum. I studied the pub setting. There were a few people who were already having an early morning drink; a group of older men sporting trilbies and sipping on pints of bitter while discussing the racing form guide; a couple of young sweethearts cuddled up in a far corner; an American couple, the man talking loudly about the great architecture of York, his wife nodding approvingly; a man with broad shoulders in a black leather jacket and close cropped blonde hair, with his back to us, studiously reading his paper; a normal day, nothing untoward.

'Oh, smell that ...' Geordie stood up and stuck his nose in the air like a bloodhound on hunt day. 'Is there any better aroma on a warm summer's day than that of fine ale.' I had to agree, it was inviting, but we were here on business. 'Who's for a pint then? Your shout Robbo.' He continued.

'Bullshit, it's always my round, why don't you put your hand in your pocket for once?'

'Look, we're not here to drink. Let's get rid of this monkey on my back first, then we can have a wet, but not until then, okay?' Robbo began to roll a spliff. Geordie blew air out through his lips like a horse and sat back down. I looked at my watch, 10:55 am.

'He said he'd ring at eleven right?' I questioned Robbo anxiously. He nodded in agreement and lit his spliff, took a deep toke and slowly relaxed back into the wooden bench.

'Ah, that's better,' he sighed, 'Yep, eleven he said. What's the time now.'

'Five to.' I replied. Geordie checked his watch.

'I make it five past.' Robbo reluctantly checked his timepiece.

'I make it bang on eleven.'

366

'Told you we should have synchronised watches,' said Geordie smugly. Robbo's phone rang.

'Yep,' he answered, 'yep ... yep ... yep ...' I gestured towards him with my arms out-splayed as though to ask, "Who is it? Is it him?" He ignored me and continued on with his enlightening conversation, all the while nodding. 'Yep ... ahuh ... ahuh ... yep ... yep ... okay ... ahuh ... yep.' He ended his call and slipped his phone back into his jacket and drew heavily on his joint. My impatience got the better of me.

'Well!' I yelled. He blew out smoke, coughed a little and replied, 'That was him.'

'And ... what did he say?'

'He says he'll meet us on that bridge over there in five minutes,' said Robbo as pointed to a stone bridge not more than two hundred metres from us.

'How will we know it's him?' I inquired.

'He said he'll stop in the middle of the bridge and read a copy of the Daily Mirror.' It was like a scene from some bad, sub-titled, Czech film; I also didn't appreciate the way Robbo's joint had suddenly turned him into Mr Laid Back Relaxed. Gone were his nervous twitchings and startled rabbit eyes. Geordie was treating the whole thing as a joke, so once again it was left to me to keep my wits about me and be the sensible one. A few minutes passed as I stared intently at the bridge. Over came bikes ridden by students, tourists with cameras around their necks, a couple of young boys bouncing a football, business suits on mobiles, an old couple that shuffled unsteadily, a mother and two young children throwing something over the wall—presumably bread to unseen ducks below.

'Can you see him yet?' inquired Robbo.

'You can see just as much as I can!' I snapped angrily.

'No, my eyes are shot. Especially long distances; everything's a blur after about ten feet.'

'Yeah, my peepers are pretty poor as well,' agreed Geordie.

'Ever thought about wearing glasses?' I snarled condescendingly at them both.

'Can you imagine me with a pair of glasses on?' replied Geordie. I peered at him and had to chuckle slightly, the image of him wearing a pair of Elton John style glasses affixed to his large head was quite amusing. I returned my attention back to the bridge. A new figure appeared rising up as he traversed the crown of the road. Tall and skinny, bald or very short hair, long black coat, slim shades. He stopped in the middle of the bridge, looked around and casually leaned up against the low stone wall with his back to the river.

'This could be him,' I whispered. Robbo and Geordie both leant forward in unison, squinting like a pair of old perverts outside a schoolyard. The mysterious figure pulled something from his jacket and unfolded it in front of him. It was a newspaper.

'He's reading a paper,' I informed the myopic twins.

'Is it the Daily Mirror?' asked Robbo slowly.

'How the fuck would I know!' I growled back, 'I can only just make him out! Do you think I have bionic vision or something?'

'Keep your hair on, I was only asking.' It had to be him. I stood up.

'Come on Geordie, let's do it. Now remember Robbo, you stay here and keep an eye out for anything suspicious or untoward.'

'Like what?'

'I don't fucking know! Just anything unusual!' We set off at a steady pace and were soon heading towards our covert courier.

'Okay Geordie, just keep a few paces behind me and try and keep your big gob shut for once, we don't want to blow it.'

'Okay, you're the Captain, we'll sail this ship your way but don't blame me when we run aground.'

'Thanks for your vote of confidence.' We walked straight up to our target and stood in front of him.

'Deano?' I asked. A faint recollection came back. His face was pockmarked and bony and he was obviously older than I recalled. His cropped hair, narrow shoulders and spindly legs reminded me of a cartoon character. He wore Ray Bans and his narrow lips were frozen in a permanent wry smile. He carefully rolled his newspaper up and slipped it back into his long, black leather coat. He arched back and slowly removed his shades.

'Ah! Will Harding, singer songwriter extraordinaire, the main man of the Shooting Tsars. How the fuck are you?' he stuck out his hand. I ignored it and didn't move. He dropped his head to one side as though slightly disappointed but still kept his enigmatic smile. His attention now turned toward Geordie.

'And of course Allan Kincaid, A.K.A. Geordie. Legendary bass player, fighter, hell-raiser and all round bad boy. It's been a long time.'

'Not long enough,' growled Geordie. Deano threw his head back and laughed a long, hard, false, belly laugh.

'Oh you boys, you're a real set of wags.' I was becoming impatient. I hadn't gone through all this stress to be de-entertained by some really bad acting.

'Let's get down to business eh? Have you got the tape or not?' His face changed and he suddenly appeared serious.

'Have you got the money?' he asked. I nodded, 'Thirty G's?' I nodded again.

'It's in the bag,' I flicked the shoulder strap of the backpack to indicate my booty.

'Okay,' he said as he reached into his coat again and pulled out a tatty old Safeways carrier bag with the unmistakable outline of a reel-to-reel circular canister inside. I made a mental note to buy shares in whichever company made supermarket carrier bags. I unhitched my backpack and handed it to him as he passed the bag to me. He carefully unzipped the backpack and peered inside, his slimy grin returning once more.

369

'I take it there's no need for me to count it?' he asked.

'I take it there's no need for me to play it?' I replied nodding at the bag in my hand. He coughed and let out a cackling laugh. Geordie edged forward.

'And what's to stop me from breaking your face and throwing you in the river?'

'Leave it Geordie,' I ordered. Deano re-zipped the bag and threw it over his shoulder.

'Do you really think I'd be stupid enough to turn up here without back-up? I have a couple of associates who are watching our every move. Let's just say that they don't play by the rules.' He formed his hand into a pistol, pointed it in the air and said "bang". Geordie casually glanced around.

'I don't think so. You're a fake, looking at you is like reading a book, something about as interesting as a telephone directory, but a book just the same.' Deano's face hardened and he made an unconscious movement back and away from us.

'I said leave it Geordie. We agreed to the deal and we'll stick to it.'

'Anyway, I deserve this,' added Deano, patting the bag on his back. 'Remember the sessions? Six months of torture I had to endure with you lot, six long hard months of verbal abuse and intimidation, and then you Geordie, roughed me up and sacked me. I nearly had a nervous breakdown. I attribute that in no small way to working with you guys. So think of this as restitution. Anyway, if Heidelberg uses "Bloom" as the soundtrack to his next film, you boys will be swimming in money. So I really think thirty grand is a drop in the ocean don't you?' We said nothing, just stared straight at him.

'Okay Geordie we've got what we wanted, let's go.' I half turned but stopped. Something had been puzzling me and I wanted an answer. 'Oh by the way Deano, why did you sell the tape back to us instead of GMC?' He let out another false belly laugh.

'You really do think I am an idiot don't you?' he replied with incredulity. 'It's one thing to extort money out of a bunch of ageing, decrepit, balding, pot bellied has-beens like you, but GMC is a different kettle of fish,' his face went serious again, 'you don't fuck with those guys, they pull all the strings, they have all the contacts if you know what I mean.'

'Let's go,' I said and this time we turned and walked back towards the pub. He shouted after us.

'Hey, I hear you boys are flavour of the month again; if you ever need an engineer for your next album, remember, DON'T call me … haha!'

'Twat,' mumbled Geordie under his breath.

We got back to the pub where our vigilant sentinel, Robbo, was busily reading a discarded newspaper.

'Some fucking lookout you are!' I scolded. He stopped reading and looked up.

'How'd you go?'

'Yeah, okay. We've got it, or at least something that looks like it. We need to get hold of a reel-to-reel to check it out.'

'Bit fucking late now, don't you think?' said Robbo.

'Yes, your right. It's either the tape or it isn't. We've either been ripped off or we haven't.'

'Nah, that's the tape alright Billy Boy. He'd nay have the balls to sell us a lemon. Right, I'll tell you what, I'm going to get the first shout,' he said rubbing his giant mitts together. 'Pints all round?' Robbo and I nodded as Geordie made good haste through the doors of the pub. I stared up at the sign high up on the pub wall "The Oddfellows Public House".

'Now that's irony,' I muttered to no-one in particular. Robbo had re-accustomed himself with his newspaper and I breathed a sigh of relief. I was about to sit down when I sensed rapid movement towards me in my peripheral vision. I turned instinctively to see Chas striding forwards.

371

'Ha! Ha! Boys, boys, well, well, well, fancy seeing you here, what a small world we live in!' he gesticulated with his hands as though he'd found some long lost sibling.

'You're our Tour Manager Chas, we're playing a gig here tonight, so it's hardly "Dr Livingstone I presume", is it?' responded Robbo pithily. Chas stopped a few inches away from me and stuck his hands into his tight jean pockets leaving his thumbs dangling over the edge, a habit that had annoyed the shit out of me ever since we first met him all those years ago. There were a few seconds of awkward silence.

'So where's Allan?'

'Getting the drinks.'

'Of course, of course, yes. And Flaky?'

'He's gone swimming.'

'Swimming, ah yes, wish I'd learnt to swim, but it's not natural is it, I mean we don't belong in the water do we.' I wasn't much in the mood for idle chitchat and let him know.

'Cut the crap Chas, what do you want?' I challenged.

'Well I won't beat around the bush, we all know each other too well for the old flannel, so I'll come straight out with it. Give me the tape.' I was momentarily stunned. How did he know we had the tape? He must have been spying on us.

'What tape?' I asked calmly.

'The tape in the bag,' he pointed to the carrier bag that I held loosely by the handles. I realised there was no point denying it; anyway, why should I.

'Yeah right. We've just paid thirty grand for this, do you think we're really going to hand it over to you?' He took a serious tone and stared up at the sky with closed eyes while he spoke, as though he were some Victorian headmaster giving a lecture to wayward schoolboys.

'You lied to me Will. I'm very disappointed in you; I thought we had a relationship; a successful partnership is built on trust, without trust what is there?' His words were preposterous but I think he actually believed what he was saying.

He continued his supercilious address. 'That tape is not your property Will. It belongs to GMC. You were under contract when you recorded it and any court in the land would back that up. Now I'll forgive the fact that you lied to me and I can guarantee that GMC will reimburse your outlay, and not only that, but I heard from Reed Lochlan this morning and he said GMC are already in serious negotiations with Heidelberg's people about the licensing rights.' I smiled at his bravado, it was quite impressive.

'Bit premature seeing as they don't have the tape eh? And as for lying, well, coming from Bobby Bullshit himself, it's a bit rich. Anyway, who gave GMC the right to negotiate on our behalf?' Chas laughed and slapped his thigh. It seemed there was a bad case of the hammy actors doing the rounds today.

'Will, you're still signed to them, they still have an option on you, don't you get it!' My heart sank, surely this couldn't be true, not after all this time.

'You get less time for murder! I don't believe you.'

'Sorry Will, but it's the truth. You're still under contract to GMC. So you see, even if you had ideas to sell that tape to another company you couldn't.' He must have noticed the expression on my face and softened his approach.

'Look, boys,' he raised one foot onto a bench and leant forward in a conciliatory gesture. 'I'll come clean with you, Heidelberg actually signed up for the deal two months ago, we've just got to cross the "T's" and dot the "I's". One of his stipulations, no not stipulations, let's say requests, was that we raise the profile of the Tsars back into the public consciousness once more. Hence the tour,' then he added with a flourish, as though we should have been pleased, 'he's even funded half the project.' I was completely flabbergasted.

'You mean to say, that even with a six-and-a half foot Scottish psychopath, with an astonishing propensity for violence, aggression and stupidity, holding a gun to your head in a game of Russian Roulette, you still lied?'

'I don't like the word "lie" Will. It's an ugly word. Anyway, all that blubbering and crying and pissing my pants, it was all an act. You didn't really think I'd fall for the old gun trick did you? The gun may have appeared authentic but there were never any bullets in that barrel.' He seemed pleased with himself.

'I'm afraid, Chas, that you are wrong. There was a bullet in there. I accidentally discharged that gun and it left a hole in the plasterboard the size of a watermelon.' For a few seconds he appeared extremely concerned. It didn't last.

'Ah well, looks like I dodged a bullet—if you'll pardon the pun,' he smiled happily. 'So, just be a good boy and hand me the tape.' Okay, fuck him, now it was my turn to ham it up. I chuckled to myself and nodded my head up and down and then tightened my lips. I could see it unnerved Chas slightly and he pushed his glasses back up the bridge of his nose as he was apt to do when a little tense. I waggled the plastic bag in front of him.

'Come and get it,' I taunted.

'I will take it off you Will, I promise, by force if necessary.' Robbo stood up and suddenly got tough, which was not a good look.

'Yeah, you and who's fucking army?' he threatened. The thought of Chas and Robbo getting into fisticuffs almost made me laugh. Neither could knock the skin off the top of a cold rice pudding. Chas suddenly puffed his chest out and got all stern. The whole thing was farcical and I had a sudden vision of a school playground. Chas folded his arms and stood back.

'Gavin!' he yelled.

'Who the fuck's Gavin?' asked Robbo turning to me. I shrugged my shoulders. There was a teeth grating squeaking sound as a bench was pushed across concrete. I turned to see the man I had noticed earlier. The guy with the short cropped blonde hair and wide shoulders wrapped in a leather bomber jacket. He slowly rose to his feet to confront us. He walked forward until he was no more than a few inches away. I tightened my grip on the handle of the plastic bag. This was getting ugly. I assessed the threat. He was as tall as Geordie if not taller and twice as wide. He had cold piercing blue eyes and a crescent shaped scar running from below his left eye to the edge of his cheek. Arthur's words came floating back into my mind like leaves on a breeze, "big lad, short hair, great big scar under his eye." His body rippled with hard, over-developed, taut muscle—he was fit and mean. Blue denim jeans bulged at the seams as his thighs tried to burst through. A pair of well polished and menacing Doc Martens enveloped his leviathan sized feet. His arms hung limply at his sides yet his fists were clenched into two huge anvils. Ex-services, no doubt about it. I felt Robbo shuffle slightly to his left so he was now directly behind me, his sudden bravado of a few seconds ago deserting him as quickly as an alcoholic at a free wine tasting night once the drinks dried up. I felt my heart pound against my chest.

'For fuck's sake, it's bloody packed in there,' Geordie reappeared from the pub carrying three pints clenched between his large paws like thimbles, 'doesn't anyone fucking work these days or what? No wonder the countries gone to the dogs.' He was concentrating intently on not spilling a single drop of the precious ale and placed the drinks down tenderly on the bench with all the love and care of a mother with her newborn. He was side on and oblivious to the unfolding scene. He lifted a pint to his lips and began to pour the liquid down his throat. At first his eyes were intent on the bottom of the glass but as the amber fluid slowly disappeared, his eyes began a slow orbit to his left. They rested on me momentarily, then Chas and then Gavin. He stopped drinking with only a quarter pint left and replaced his glass watchfully onto the table. He wiped the suds from his top lip onto the back of his coat sleeve and stared at Chas.

'What a very unpleasant surprise,' he said with a smile on his face. He waggled his thumb in the direction of Gavin whilst still eyeballing Chas.

'Who's the girlfriend?'

'That's Gavin. They've come for the tape,' I informed Geordie.

'Is that so,' he responded slowly and calmly.

'That's right Allan,' echoed Chas confidently.

'Pigs fucking arse!' snarled Geordie. Chas winced and took a tentative step back.

'Allan let me introduce you to Gavin,' Chas held his arm out in a theatrical way and Geordie's attention now focused on the Goliath in front of him. 'Gavin has seen active service in the Falklands and the first Iraq war, ex SAS,' he spat out the words SAS with over exaggerated significance.

'I don't give a fuck if he's ex BBC. You ain't getting that tape,' replied Geordie calmly, now in a stare-a-thon with Gavin.

'Allan, Allan, Allan,' chuckled Chas, 'I know you're a hard man, a street fighter, a big Scottish brawler, but Gavin is a trained killer, he's a professional. You're out of your depth. Now we can either make this easy or we can make it hard.' He turned to me, 'Will, hand over the tape like a good boy, save your friend from a hiding.' He was right, despite Geordie's prowess at violence this was different. This wasn't some drunken prop forward or loud mouthed local hero this was Union Jack Jackson and Tommy Gun Tompkins all rolled into one. I made a move forward to hand the tape to Chas. Geordie's large arm thumped into my chest.

'Don't even think it Billy boy,' he ordered in a hushed tone. I noticed that some of the other patrons outside the pub had sensed the conflict and were now steadily melting away to the outer fringes.

'Geordie mate, it's not worth it, let me give him the tape, we can fight them in court if we want.' They were worthless words but they were all I could find. My heart was racing and my mouth had gone dry. Chas took another step back and removed his glasses and began to clean them, a sure sign of an escalation in his nervousness.

'Okay Gavin. Do what you have to do, but try not to damage his fingers, he's got to play a gig tonight.' Gavin twitched and then in a blink of an eye he dropped into a karate stance, palms facing inward, fingers pointing towards his target. Geordie didn't move an inch.

'Fuck me, it's the Karate Kid,' he commented in a sardonic manner. It happened fast. Gavin spun around with all the grace and balance of a ballet dancer and unleashed his left leg towards the right side of Geordie's head. The oversized boot honed in on Geordie's cheek and jaw. I braced myself for the sickening sound of splintering bone. Something darted out, quicker than a flash of light. It was Geordie's arm. He reached up and grabbed the express travelling limb at the ankle bringing the movement to a jarring halt. Geordie smiled, Gavin looked worried and could see what was about to befall him. He was left defenceless as all his weight was on his back foot, which was busily trying to keep him upright. In one swift and forceful movement Geordie yanked the captured leg down and behind him, Gavin was unbalanced and was propelled up and forward towards Geordie, who at the same time extended his left arm powerfully forward. The sledgehammer on the end of it smashed into Gavin's nose. Now, the sickening sound of breaking bones. Geordie let go of Gavin's leg and the hapless ex-SAS trained killer pirouetted backwards and landed comatose on the table he'd been sat at a few minutes earlier. There were a few "ooh's" and "ah's" from the onlooking crowd of people. Chas and I edged slowly forwards towards Gavin. His nose had taken a definite detour to the left and a thin stream of blood began to flow freely from both nostrils.

'I th ... th ... think you ... you've kill ... killed him,' stammered Chas. I had to agree, there were no signs of life from the hired heavy.

'Fucking hell Geordie, you've done it this time,' I whispered slowly. Robbo edged between Chas and me to gawp.

'Shit! What a mess,' he conceded. Geordie turned around, grabbed a pint, strode over to Gavin and threw the beer in his face. There was a sudden groan and moan as Gavin came round and slumped into the bench seat, pulling a tissue from his pocket to try and stop the crimson flow.

'I bet that wasn't your own pint you used was it?' challenged Robbo.

'Don't talk daft, it was yours,' Geordie replied.

'Fucking typical!'

Chas made a sudden charge and caught me off guard and before I knew it he'd yanked the plastic bag from my grasp leaving me with nothing but a pair of plastic handles. He was off and running hard towards the bridge. I immediately gave chase and heard the clonk of Geordie's cowboy boots behind me as he also set out after the quarry. Chas was quick, unbelievably quick. His skinny little legs in tight blue jeans were going at ten to the dozen and he soon put a good twenty metres between us. Geordie couldn't even keep up with my mediocre pace. We were in danger of being outrun by a badly dressed, bullshitting southerner. I began to feel a stitch and slowed down even further. Chas was now at the halfway mark of the bridge and extending his distance. *How come he's so fast—the little git!* I remembered our telephone conversation in Whitstone and how he said he'd been off the smokes for three years. That was it. Undone by the cigarettes. Damn those tobacco giants. I slowed to a fast walk, hoping the hand of fate may trip Chas up or that he'd suffer a heart attack or something worse. I stopped and caught my breath. I then heard the sound of an "Ooh, ah, ooh, hiss". I lifted my head to see a grinning Robbo, spliff in mouth, riding along at a cracking pace on a purloined bicycle, he waved as he went past and began singing,

'Riding along on a push bike honey, when I noticed you.' I began to run again and threw a glance behind to see Geordie also trotting along on the opposite side of the bridge. Robbo yelled out,

'I'll cut him off at the pass!' Robbo soon overtook a surprised Chas. He got a good ten metres in front of him and swung the bike across the path and dismounted. Chas halted and turned to run back the way he had come but I was now closing in on him fast. He stalled and then took off diagonally to try and get around me but stopped once again when he saw Geordie heading his way. He was trapped in the classic three pronged pincer movement. We all closed in for the kill. He hopped onto the low wall of the bridge and balanced precariously as his head twitched between looking at his pursuers and the murky water below.

'The games over Chas, give me the tape, there's a good boy.'

'D ... d ... don't come any c ... c ... closer Will or I'll j ... j ... jump!' he yelled back.

'Chas my old friend,' I continued in the clichéd acting style that seemed to be the order of the day, 'remember, you can't swim, you don't belong in water.' Chas suddenly realised it was over, there was no escape.

'B ... b ... boys, let's t ... talk.'

'You hand the tape back to me and we'll talk.' He was holding the dishevelled and rapidly disintegrating plastic bag at arm's length out of our reach and over the water.

'You promise?' he pleaded.

'Yes of course, nothing wrong with talking.'

'You mean it? If I don't get some resolution here I'm as good as dead, GMC will be after my sorry arse.' He appeared genuinely terrified and despite his underhand, nasty tricks I still felt a tinge of sympathy for him, it was hard not to like the guy.

'Okay, it's a deal, we'll talk, you have my word on that. Now give me the tape.' Chas smiled sheepishly,

'You're a good boy Will, always have been.' He slowly retracted his arm and swung it towards me. I reached out. I could see what was coming but was powerless to stop it. The reel-to-reel swayed in the bag and a little arc of the cylinder popped through the seam at the bottom. There was a barely audible splitting sound as the seam widened and the

379

canister grew bigger as it eased smoothly through the bottom of the bag. I lunged for it but to no avail. We all watched in dumbstruck awe as the tape, our multi-millions and possibly Chas's life rushed towards the water. A gust of wind whistled under the arch of the bridge and managed to dislodge the lid off the canister. The tape began a mad dash for freedom and in a seemingly never ending stream of ticker tape it spun free and wild and into the air, dispersing in a hundred different directions until it freed itself from its reel. It floated gently and majestically down to the water below and lay on top like some exhausted Prima Donna on the set of Swan Lake. The sound of a twin stroke engine grew louder. A small speedboat appeared from under the bridge and ploughed straight through the fragile and delicate serpent that lay sleeping atop its watery bed. It quickly disappeared from view as it was sucked unceremoniously beneath the river. Chas jumped down off the wall and dusted himself down. He cleaned his glasses as we all stared at him.

'Well I guess that's that,' he said quite matter-of-factly. 'Right then, I'll be off.' He stuck his hands in his pockets, thumbs on the outside, and strode confidently away. I even thought I heard him break out into a whistle. When he was a good ten yards away he turned around and yelled back,

'Don't forget, sound-check at five, don't be late.' He turned and wandered off as happy as you like. No one said a word. We just stared open mouthed, as he got smaller and smaller until he disappeared out of sight.

32: INSTANT KARMA

London – Wembley Arena

We played our final gig to another sellout crowd and retreated to the backstage party that was already in full swing. Champagne, boutique beers, scotch, vodka, speed, cocaine, blow; backslapping, bonhomie, congratulations, hugs and kisses; friends, friends of friends, family, loved ones, rock stars, pop stars, shining stars, fading stars, egos, associates, fans, groupies, sycophants, press, TV personalities, football, rugby, cricket players, hangers on, dealers, complete unknowns, losers, dropouts, deadbeats, Chas and Uncle Tom Cobley and all in a swirling, clattering, clamorous fandango of euphoria. I was on a high, higher than I could ever remember and I bathed in the warm radiation of adulation. I had all but forgotten that radiation could give you cancer. I was in such a state of agitated excitement, natural and chemical induced, that I forgot to phone the people close to me—Mother and Fiona. I also had five missed calls from John Peterson but still could not find the time nor courtesy to return his calls. As the party entered into a new day Chas gathered us together in a small ante-room away from the hullabaloo and madness. Things had been frosty between us and Chas ever since he let our precious "Bloom" tape fall into the drink, but that was all water under the bridge now, quite literally. Even the bellicose Geordie seemed placated by Chas's effusive platitudes. As we all sat down Chas walked around with a bottle of fine malt in one hand and an arm full of glasses in the other.

'Boys, boys, boy, you were magnificent, the greatest rock 'n' roll band in the world! Now listen boys, this may be the end of the tour but it is the beginning of something huge, I mean fucking massive!' Chas poured generous amounts of the whisky into each glass and handed them out in turn. Even the normally sober Flaky accepted the offering.

'Here's to the Shooting Tsars!' Chas proclaimed lifting his glass in the air. We all followed his lead and lifted our glasses.

'To the Shooting Tsars!' we all yelled in unison. The clink of glasses and congratulations and handshakes went on for a few seconds between us all before we relaxed back into our seats and each took a large gulp of the liquor, except Flaky who genteelly sipped his as he pulled a pained expression.

'Of course Reed would have dearly loved to have been here but he had prior obligations—but he sends his best wishes.' Chas was referring to Reed Lochlan, head of GMC. I cannot say that this statement soured the cream, for it did not. But if our mood was a brand new, shiny Ferrari, then it had definitely chipped a small piece of paint off the passenger door.

'Why would Reed have dearly loved to have been here?' I asked. Chas cradled his glass in a contemplative way and leaned forward to converse with us all.

'Because he likes you, he likes you a lot. In fact he likes you so much that he's got an offer for you that you'll find very hard to refuse.'

'Oh no, not the fucking horse's head in the bed is it?' remarked Robbo sardonically. Chas smiled with his mouth but his eyes were like an eagle's that was overdue lunch.

'No, no horse's heads. But he has bestowed upon me to be the bringer of good news. Here's the deal.' He suddenly got all businesslike and matter-of-fact. Robbo lit a spliff, I lit a cigarette and Geordie drained his glass, which Chas charitably refilled. 'We have managed to procure a copy of Bloom ...' he paused for effect. Geordie, Robbo and I exchanged glances; Flaky had a bemused look on his face like he hadn't the foggiest what Chas was talking about, which in truth, he hadn't. When no comment was forthcoming Chas continued. 'Yes, it appears your little sound engineer friend had been double dipping. The day after you handed over thirty grand for the so-called "master tape" he contacted GMC and was offering to sell us a copy for one hundred big ones.' I blew smoke from my mouth in one long slow breath. Still no-one commented. 'Needless to say, we, I mean GMC, weren't about to be blackmailed over something that is legally ours, I mean theirs, anyway.' He stopped and chortled to himself, staring cockily into his glass. 'Let's just say that Gavin paid him a little visit and made him see the error of his ways.'

'Which hospital is he in?' sneered Geordie.

'Haha! Not sure. But put it this way, he won't be twiddling knobs in a mixing booth for at least six months.' I suppose I should have felt some sympathy for the pocked marked extortionist but the thought of being duped by him pushed that particular emotion out of the back door. I flicked a glance at Flaky whose look of bemusement had now turned into one of complete muddlement.

'Who's Reed Lochlan? And who the hell are Gavin and Deano? And when you talk about the Bloom tape are you talking about our Bloom tape from all those years ago?' Chas seemed a little surprised.

'Oh sorry, is Flaky still out of the picture, I didn't realise,' said Chas apologetically.

'What picture?' asked Flaky evidently annoyed.

'Don't worry Flaky, I'll fill you in later, okay?' I stated with authority.

'Fine, very well, as long as you do. I'm a part of this band as well you know,' I nodded in acceptance. The chipped paint on the passenger door had now turned into a rear end shunt. Chas sensed the change of atmosphere and quickly moved on.

'Now, the deal with Heidelberg is about to go through. We just need to iron a few things out. The film is due to be released in eight months time. If it is a box office smash like his other films, then you boys are going to be catapulted into mega-stardom, especially in the States, which I don't have to remind you, we never did manage to fully crack last time. The soundtrack will be our springboard. Eight months gives us time to record a new album and get a nationwide US tour set up. And this won't be small venues, it will be big stadiums. So, having said that, Reed is ready to offer you, wait for this, he is ready to offer you, that is the Shooting Tsars, four million pounds and a two album deal. This is not an advance that will be recouped, it is a sign on fee if you like, a sweetener. If and when you sign tomorrow the money will be immediately deposited into your respective bank accounts. You'll all be a million pounds richer by Monday morning, plus the new two album deal will have a vastly superior royalty rate compared to your previous deal. Not sure on the exact figure, but twenty two percent was mentioned, and also, I'm not finished yet, all costs, I mean *all* costs, expenses, recording, promotion, everything, will be fully funded by GMC. No catches, no hidden clauses, no clawbacks, no fine print, just a bloody great deal.' He slapped his knees in unison and leant back in his chair with arms outstretched. 'Now what about that for the deal of a lifetime.' I was speechless. It was too good to be true.

'Four million pounds?' I repeated in a sceptical voice. 'Four million pounds!'

'Oh and lastly,' continued Chas, 'you have complete artistic control, complete artistic control. A deal like this is unheard of, in fact I think it's the first ever, not even U2 would get terms and conditions like this.' I stared at my comrades who all gawped back in astonishment. Suddenly the Ferrari had been traded in for a fleet of customised Lear jets.

'You said two albums, what about Bloom?' I inquired.

'Well, Bloom will be released under the previous deal. As I've pointed out to you before, it is GMC's property, and whether you take up this new offer or not, Bloom will still be released and licensed to Heidelberg for his new movie. What I would say to you is this; forget about "Bloom" that's history as far as you're concerned, even though you're still going to make a mint out of it. Concentrate on the future, leave the past behind.' He stood up and handed the bottle of whisky to me.

'I'll leave you boys to think about it. The only stipulation is that the deal must be signed tomorrow otherwise it's off the table— Heidelberg is already getting impatient. If you want to go ahead, then meet me at GMC headquarters tomorrow at 11:30am. Don't be late; Reed hates tardiness. Right, I'm off to mingle, chow.' With that he disappeared out of the door. Every ounce of my logic and reason should have made me scream NO! Every fibre of my being should have been twitching with suspicion and mistrust. But, instead, I was smiling inside and as I turned to the others, they were smiling on the outside.

'Okay Will, please explain,' demanded Flaky.

'Okay Flaky; well, it all started when ...'

#

My pursuers are a long way behind. I have a good start on them but I know I have to keep running until I find a safe haven. I try to increase the pace but instead of my legs moving faster they actually begin to slow down. The ground becomes soft and slushy, my shoes find no purchase and I begin to slip and slide. With super human effort I force my legs to move but they are leaden and sluggish. I look behind. I cannot yet see my tormentors but I sense their impending presence. I begin to panic. Why won't my legs move, I'm fit and healthy; I had been a fast runner at school; school? What was I talking about, that was twenty five years ago, why would I think that any physical attributes I possessed as a child would still be intact a quarter of a century later. I can see the old stone houses in the distance, if I can just reach them the narrow streets and alleyways will be my saviour. I know every nook and cranny, every laneway and hidden ginnel; I will melt into the surroundings like a chameleon and my trackers will never find me. If only my legs would move! I stop trying and take a breather. I'm panting hard and I'm thirsty, so thirsty. I peer nervously over my shoulder again. Still no visible sign although I catch the faint echo of a gruff voice followed by a shrill reply carried on the blustery wind. I stare again at the safety of the houses in the distance. The cold black stone offers a benevolent smile but its roots are deep in the earth encased in concrete, unable to assist me in my plight. The park is too wide and vast to cross. When I'd set off it appeared as a short distance; I'd traversed this park a thousand times as a kid; I ran with the wind, I flew, I glided, I hopped and skipped and my eager legs would gobble up the distance like a hungry dog wolfing a raw steak. But not now. The sound comes again, closer. Thirsty, I'm so thirsty, I need a drink of pure, icy cold water. The houses are straight ahead but too far to reach. To my left is the steep slope that heads down to the school; to my right is the uphill incline to the high stone walls of the reservoir. I turn right and urge my legs on. They ache and feel numb, they're incapable of receiving instructions. I curse them. Slowly, inch by inch I make painful progress up the grassy slab of earth. The voices are clearer now. No point looking behind anymore, I know what I would see. It's all over, I'm finished. It wasn't meant to end like this! I wistfully remember my sunny childhood when I would start at the top of the park and run with all my heart, downwards towards the school, arms outstretched; I was faster than a gazelle, I could almost fly, I would reach the school before I had even set off, I was Superman! I need a drink. Gruff, dark voices are nearly upon me, it's definitely over. I turn to face my attackers for the last time; they race up the hill after me but despite their fervour, even they find the precipitous nature of the terrain to be difficult going. Well, if I was going to go, there's one last thing I want to do, one last taste of my golden childhood. I set off downhill, steadily at first, but gravity was pulling me and for the first time I have the wind behind my back. My legs begin to slowly regain their suppleness. Messages from my brain begin to crackle through to my limbs. I'm racing now! I've taken my pursuers by surprise and have already doubled my distance between them and myself. By the time they turn to follow me I'm accelerating with such force that I take my own breath away. I open my mouth wide and gulp in the air, it isn't water but it's the next best thing. I spread my arms out like the wings of an albatross and zigzag down the grassy slope. I flap my arms, I feel a butterfly born in my stomach and with an overwhelming sense of freedom and happiness my feet lift off the ground. Only a few inches at first but then higher and higher and higher. I'm flying, really flying! The ground swiftly disappears under me; soon I'm higher than the trees, I get a sharp but short lived feeling of vertigo. I turn and catch the thermals. I swoop down towards earth. Twenty feet above the park I pass over the heads of my aggrieved predators. They stand, mute in the ground shaking their puny fists at me, their words nothing but silent confetti. I soar high and gaze down at the tiny little school below, the row of houses that stand there like a line of blackened teeth and finally I soar over the reservoir, a small splash of blue besieged by green. Then I'm gone; into the clouds—lost to all but myself.

#

11 am and we are all ensconced in the back of a black cab. Everyone has severe hangovers, everyone that is bar Flaky and hopefully the miserable looking taxi driver. I have been up less than an hour and even after copious amounts of water, three cups of coffee, a bacon and egg sandwich and a good line of speed, I still feel like shit on a stick. The mood is sombre and heavy. No-one wants to speak, no-one does speak. I'm dying to say how I feel but I can't. I won't be the doomsayer, the grim reaper on the wedding day, the scabby dog that pisses on summer's sweet strawberries. So, instead, I hold my peace, stomach like a knot of

lead, head hot and fuzzy and heart hiding and skulking like a scolded cat. I replayed the previous night's film in my head and as more fragments crept back into my consciousness, my mood became ever blacker. I remember ordering champagne after Chas had made the offer. I remembered the beautiful women that seemed to be everywhere I looked, and Robbo cutting up cocaine on the table. I recalled the showbiz personalities and other rock and pop icons coming up to shake my hand and tell me how much I had inspired them to form their first band. I remember feeling like a big shit in a big town, and thinking how much I deserved all of this. As each splinter came back to me I squirmed just a little more. Is this what I had become? A caricature of the archetypical rock star—a drug snorting, lecherous, puffed up, pompous, self-absorbed, pretentious tosser whose only purpose in life was to ensure the drugs never ran out, to impose myself on girls half my age and to massage my own ego in the company of fawning sycophants. At the moment the answer seemed to be "yes". A short burst of electronic beeps broke my trance.

'Who's that?' barked Geordie, 'Who's fucking beeping?' Flaky, Robbo and I all pulled out our mobiles. Flaky shook his head,

'Not me.'

'Nah, me neither. Must be you Will,' stated Robbo. I checked my screen and sure enough there was a message "Battery Low". Before I got chance to turn the thing off a final offensive beep sounded and the phone temporarily ceased to be.

'Shit, the batteries gone.' I moaned to no-one in particular.

'I don't know how you put up with those things. They're like a monkey on your back. I mean how come the human race survived hundreds of thousands of years without mobile phones and now it's a pre-requisite for existence,' whinged Geordie. No one had the stomach today to confront the Luddite. I prayed for the journey to continue indefinitely which was quite ironic as I'd spent the last few months praying for the journey to end. As each minute departed I farewelled it like a lover to the grave. *What is wrong with me? Why can't I be normal? Why can't I relax and enjoy these precious moments?* We were on our way to put our paltry, measly signatures on a piece of paper and in return see our bank accounts immediately swell by a million pounds each; and that was just the start. By the end of the two albums we would probably have quadrupled that amount.

Our hearse finally pulled up outside the gleaming glass edifice that represented the headquarters of GMC Europe. It stood tall and arrogant, sneering down on the rest of the world, omnipotent and omnipresent. I thought of Inglegor Pike and how it too was all knowing, all seeing. But its aura was in a natural earthy way, a vibration through time, a link between the past and present and forever the future. GMC's Reichstag was cold and soulless, a grinding mechanical money machine whose only master was the market. The streets were quiet, well why wouldn't they be, after all it was 11:20 am on a Sunday morning. Even this financial citadel slowed a little on the Sabbath. I paid the driver and turned to follow the others who were already entering a large revolving glass door. They had the demeanour of men sentenced to death, and yet why did they hold their tongues? As we entered the large reception area we were greeted by a chubby and dour looking guard who seemed to be about as happy as we were to be there.

'Morning, we're here to see Reed Lochlan and Chas Dupont,' I mumbled to the guard.

'You lot the "Shooting Cars" then?'

'Shooting Tsars, that's right,' I replied courteously.

'Yeah, whatever. They're expecting you. Take the lift to the tenth floor.'

'Not room 101 I hope', I laughed nervously and Geordie for the first time that day, let a smirk briefly pass his lips. The guard seemed irritated by my comment as though I was trying to take the piss out of him.

'Nah mate, it's room 111.' We turned and walked across the opulent reception area towards the lift passing a row of gold discs and portraits on the wall; Pink Floyd, Van Morrison, Pet Shop Boys, U2.

'Oh no, please don't tell me they're signed to GMC?' exclaimed Geordie. I didn't have to ask who he was referring to. Flaky spotted the numerous "No Smoking" symbols on the walls and smugly pointed them out to us as we waited for the lift to arrive.

'So Flaky, have you consulted the astrological charts today?' asked Robbo with the merest hint of sarcasm.

'Of course. I did a chart for all of us.'

'And?'

'Bit odd really. We all basically got the same reading,' Flaky explained with a furrowed brow.

'Is that unusual?' Continued Robbo

'Highly unusual.'

'Come on then, spill the beans?' badgered Robbo who now seemed genuinely interested.

'Well it said that today our destiny lay in our own hands and success awaits us if we choose wisely. '

'Is that it? Bit fucking vague isn't it?'

'It's an art, not a science Robbo. It gives advice on what is the best course of action. Oh yes, there was one more thing, it said "beware the tiger" ... or was it lion?'

'We're not planning a trip to the Zoo are we,' sniffed Geordie.

'I'm just relating what the oracle said, interpret it as you will.'

'Fucking quackery,' I murmured—I wasn't in the mood for Flaky's astrological bullshit and tried to block out the petty bickering that erupted. The lift arrived and we entered. The doors shut and the lift slipped effortlessly heavenward. I peered at our reflections in the floor to ceiling mirror that lined the lift. Old, haggard, weary and fucked stared back at me. *What am I doing here?* I began to hyperventilate and broke out in a cold sweat. I don't remember leaving the lift and only vaguely remember shaking hands with Chas, Reed Lochlan and a GMC lawyer called Mitchell. *Why does every fucker have a last name as a first name these days!*

Reed Lochlan sat behind a lavish, half moon desk that was made of some extremely expensive timber … probably old English Oak or Cedar. It would have been fifteen feet long if it was an inch. His smug, self-satisfied arse was ensconced in a leather chair that would be better described as a throne. Chas stood to his right and Mitchell to his left. The rest of us sat opposite Reed in chairs that were purposely lower, so we had no option but to gaze up at Mr Reed Lochlan.

I asked for a glass of water, which Chas promptly provided. I had a sip and then stared down at the carpet. It was lush, a deep luxurious brown with a gold monogram running through the pile at an acute angle, spelling out the initials "GMC"—definitely bespoke. Mitchell, the lawyer, began his waffle.

'… and hereby … there within … all contractual … shall be deemed … reasonable expectations … notwithstanding … blah … blah … blah, bullshit, gobbledegook … ten day cooling off period … and the aforementioned said signatories …' I glanced at a large ticking clock on the wall; 12:05, 12:15, 12:20. My head began to spin. I felt the cold clammy sensation of sweat trickling down my spine. I could feel all eyes burning into me, but whenever I dared to raise my head it seemed everyone was oblivious to my existence. 12:30, an hour had passed in the space of minutes.

'Okay, thanks Mitchell, if you have any questions please feel free to fire away,' Reed addressed us all.

'Yeah, I have a few,' piped up Geordie.

'Yeah me too man,' Robbo agreed. I said nothing. I couldn't say anything. I was physically incapable of speaking. It was enough just to keep my shallow breathing going. I didn't hear the questions and I didn't hear the answers. Just jumbled meaningless words that aggravated my senses. 12:40, 12:45, not that I was clock watching. I felt I was having some sort of attack. It could have been my heart or maybe a stroke or

391

asthma or an overdose, or liver failure or the onset of kidney disease. It could have been any or all of these things but it wasn't. I realised it was a simple, commonplace anxiety attack. Just fixating the problem made me feel a whole lot better. The voices droned on. 12:46, 12:55, and then they all abruptly stopped.

'Okay gentlemen, well I hope that explains things more fully. Thank you, Mitchell.' It was Reed Lochlan, again directing proceedings. 'Well, I guess it's—time—to—sign.' Reed laughed when there was nothing really to laugh at. Chas, sycophantically followed suit and let out a pathetic guffaw.

'Will? Will? Will?' I looked up to face Flaky. 'Will, have you any questions before we sign?' My mouth was dry. I swallowed the last dregs of tepid water from the glass and placed it with trembling fingers onto the large polished desk that encircled Reed. I studied him intently for the first time. Mid to late forties. Clean shaven with a slight pinkish hue around the gills. Jet black hair, well groomed. Dark piercing eyes, heavy lids. Stocky and well honed, must work-out. Expensive suit, probably Saville Row, light pink shirt with silver cuff-links. A pungent, cloying aftershave. Two ostentatious gold rings on his left hand. A heavy looking gold fountain pen in his right hand. A slight air of impatience, a thin wisp of arrogance.

'Will, do you have any further questions?' Reed asked, like a Judge to the accused, before sentencing. My fog cleared momentarily and I took the chance.

'Do you like us?' I whispered, barely audible.

'Pardon?' He appeared confused.

'Do you like us?' I repeated. He laughed, Chas laughed, Mitchell laughed.

'Like you? Well of course I like you. You all seem like terribly decent chaps. Why wouldn't I like you?' His thin veil of a smile could not hide his disgust.

'No, I don't mean us personally. I mean the music, our music.' The veil fell. He cleared his throat.

'Well, it's neither here nor there whether I like your music or not. What I see is a quality product with a clearly identifiable demographic. I neither like, nor dislike, shares and bonds, but when the price is right I will buy and sell.'

'But do you like us?' I asked again. I could feel the eyes of my fellow band members staring at me. If Chas's eyes spoke, they said one thing and one thing only, "don't you fucking blow this thing Will, I'm warning you!" Reed was now clearly agitated and threw an impatient stare at Chas as though this was all his doing.

'Will, Chas has lauded your attributes for quite some time and I have a great deal of respect for his judgement. If he says you've got that magic x-factor then I believe him.'

'But do you like us?' I stared unblinking into his eyes. He was now uncomfortable and let out a deep sigh.

'Really, Will, I don't think I can make it any clearer.'

'Do you like us?' I repeated.

'Look, to be brutally honest, I haven't really heard anything you've done, but like I said, that's beside the point. I don't know how they mine gold, I don't know how they extract oil from the ground and turn it into petroleum, but that doesn't stop me investing huge amounts of money into it. It's commerce Will, it's the free market, it's demographics, it's industry, it's buying and selling. We are buying you for X amount and we will sell it to our defined market for X amount plus thirty percent. You're better off, we're better off and the fools who buy it think they're better off. It's a win, win, win situation. It's sensible economics. There's a slight element of risk as with all trading, but as to the question as to whether I like you or not, well it really doesn't enter into the equation.' A thin bead of sweat appeared at the top of Reed's furrowed brow. 'Does that answer your question?' he banged his gold pen on the desk authoritatively.

'Yes, perfectly thanks,' I replied graciously.

'Good! Now here are the two contracts. The first one is for the Bloom licensing deal and the other one is for the new, two album deal.' He pushed a quire of papers neatly across the table. 'Will, you're closest, so you may as well go first.' I stared down at the contracts. They both had "Sign Here" stickers embedded at the appropriate spots within. Mitchell sidled up behind me and turned the leaves to the signatory pages.

'Right, yes, here we are. If you'd like to put your signature here Will, and then we'll pass it down the line.' Mitchell's aftershave was almost as overpowering as Reed's. I looked around for a pen and just as Mitchell retrieved one from his breast pocket Reed intervened.

'Here, use mine,' Reed offered as he leant across the table and handed me his pen. I rolled the pen around in my fingers and stared at it for a few seconds before placing it millimetres above the heavily starched paper. I could hear the second hand of the clock, tick. I stared at Reed— Reed the businessman. I eased the pen down until it barely touched the white sheet. A small round blob of black ink bled from the nib, leaving a tiny indelible stain behind. I glanced at Chas. A new bead of sweat had emerged on his brow like a mushroom from the earth. It hung in the one spot momentarily, expanding with age, before gravity implored it to make a mad rush down the bridge of his nose. He nudged his glasses up without once removing his eyes from the pen and paper in front of me ... hmm. I rolled the pen around in my fingers, again and again. Something ... what was it ... a roughness. I pulled the pen away from the paper, staring at the black blob on the whiteness. My gaze shifted to the pen. I lifted it to my eye line and studied it carefully. The roughness I had felt was an engraving—"To My Tiger, All My Love". Reed broke the silence.

'Present ... from my wife,' he offered quietly, almost embarrassed. The clock ticked and I shot it a glance. 12:59—for the first time I noticed a calendar and the date: **Sunday 21st August 2005.**

Sunday, Sunday? I thought of the Mamas and the Papas. Sunday? Now why would anyone, especially someone in the music business, organise a meeting to sign a contract on a Sunday, less than twelve hours after the offer was first made?

'Erm, can you excuse us for a moment, I'd just like to discuss something with the guys.' I put the pen down. Reed was clearly losing patience. Despite this, he played the gracious host.

'Why of course. Please feel free to step next door,' he opened his palm, indicating towards a glass fronted adjoining room. 'You can use my secretary's office. Take all the time you need. Maybe we are rushing it all a little. How about I order some refreshments?'

'Yes thanks, that would be good.' We trooped disconsolately into the adjoining room and closed the door quietly behind us.

#

'What's the go Billy Boy? Cold feet?' inquired Geordie calmly.

'It's not right, it just doesn't add up. Here we are on a Sunday morning signing a four million pound deal with no representation; a deal that was first discussed late last night. And another thing, why the two contracts?' I paced the room as I talked. Geordie and Robbo, by their demeanour, were open to debate. Flaky, on the other hand, leant against a filing cabinet with arms folded and defended the machine.

'Reed explained all that. One contract is for the new two album deal and the other contract is for the licensing of Bloom. For a million pounds each, I don't see a problem, I really don't.'

'Well that's just it; how often has Chas told us that "Bloom" is GMC's property, they own it under the old contract. They're our publishers as well as our record company.'

'Your point being?' said Robbo as he began rolling a spliff.

'So, why would we need to sign a licensing deal? GMC can license it to whoever they damn well want—they own it! They don't need our permission. Publishing companies licence music all the time—to films, adverts, TV programmes. They don't need the artist's permission—unless there's a specific clause in the contract. My point is, if the old contract was still valid, they would have licensed Bloom to Heidelberg already. Which raises the question, why do they want us to sign a licensing deal? The whole thing stinks.'

'He's got a point,' said Geordie, taking a deep breath, 'and as for that Reed, well, I don't like the cut of his jib, and we all know the track record of Chas and for that matter GMC. No, I'm with you Billy Boy, it smells worse than a knackers gash.' I was thankful for Geordie's allegiance if not his terminology.

'Did you notice Chas began to sweat just as I was about to sign?' I added as extra ammunition to my cause.

'You can't turn down a deal like this just because someone begins to sweat. I mean you were a complete shambles in there, does that mean you're up to no good?' countered Flaky.

'That was a panic attack. I can stand in front of 80'000 people and sing my heart out; cameras, TV, I don't give a shit once I'm in the moment; but sat in an office with corporate vampires calendaring my future, well, then something kicks in. Call it ESP, sixth sense, call it intuition—whatever—it's not right.' Robbo finished rolling his spliff and deposited it in his mouth but did not light it.

'Okay, well what are we to do?' asked Robbo. Flaky put forward a suggestion.

'How about we ask to take the contracts away and we get that John Peterson chap of yours to look them over?' I was still chewing over the events that had just occurred and wasn't really listening to Flaky.

'What? John Peterson ... of course! John Peterson!' I exclaimed. I remembered his missed calls to my mobile. I had to call him. I pulled out my phone and my heart immediately sank. The dead battery; I had his number in my contacts but without that, I was lost.

'Shit!'

'What is it Will?' asked Flaky

'I can't remember his number and my mobiles dead.'

'Give it a go. You can sometimes get a few seconds before it closes down again. Just go straight to your contacts and shout out the number and I'll write it down,' explained Robbo helpfully.

'Good idea Robbo! Ready?' I switched on the phone and it blinked into life. It immediately let out a warning beep - "Battery Low". I navigated to my contacts and located Peterson, John.

'Okay Robbo, get this.' I read out the number as Robbo jotted it down. The phone let out another warning beep and instantly closed itself down. 'Did you get it?'

'Yeah, no probs.'

'Lend me your phone Robbo.' He handed it over and I began to punch in John Peterson's number while having a sideways glance through the glass window at our supposedly magnanimous benefactors. I heard a ringtone and prayed that John had his phone switched on. As I waited, I now gazed out through the window to the metropolis below. It was a bright summer's day and the sky was an aqua blue without a trace of cloud. At the end of the street lay a park that was busy with young families. Kids raced up and down slides as parents sat on benches, chatting or reading newspapers. It appeared inviting and civilised and seemed to put things in perspective.

'C'mon c'mon, bloody answer,' I pleaded aloud.

'Hello, John Peterson speaking.'

'Hello John, it's Will, listen can you talk?'

'Will thank God you've called! I've been trying to get hold of you for days. I've left several messages with your Tour Manager for you to get in touch ...'

'You mean Chas?'

'Yes, that's right, Chas. Where are you now?'

'We're all in the MD's office at GMC?'

'Oh Jesus Christ! Please tell me you haven't signed anything?'

'No, not yet, we were just about to ...'

'Thank God for that! Listen, do not sign a thing and listen very carefully to what I'm about to say ...'

#

Ten minutes later we walked back into Reed's office, confident and jovial. An invisible weight had been lifted from our shoulders and our normal inane, argumentative, mindless, schoolboy banter had returned—for better or for worse.

'It's not an ATM machine, it's just an ATM. ATM already has machine in its name you dickweed,' explained Geordie to Robbo.

'You're playing with syntax you highland ignoramus. Everyone says "I'm just going to the ATM machine to get some cash out". No one says I'm going to the "AT machine" now do they?' argued Robbo as he lit his spliff, much to the look of annoyance on Reed's face.

'Aha! But normal people—and I exclude you in that sentence—would say, "I'm away to the ATM to get some cash out". So stick that in your pipe and smoke it! And I think I've just won the argument.'

'Listen fart-breath, you couldn't win a wanking contest in a room full of one armed wankers!' Chas thankfully interrupted the playground bravado.

'Boys, boys; we're not here to argue the virtues of the ATM machine or masturbation competitions. Mr Lochlan is a very busy man and we have some very important business to put to bed—so if you please ...' Chas indicated for us all to take our seats. Reed's demeanour was growing more impatient by the second.

'Yes, if we could hurry things along. I'm already late for my child's hockey match,' Reed said staring impatiently at the clock on the wall.

'Oh, I'm sure your daughter will understand that Daddy's a very busy man,' said Geordie helpfully. Reed stared coldly at Geordie.

'It's my son, actually, that plays hockey,' Reed replied brusquely. Geordie seemed confused.

'Oh sorry. I thought that hockey was a girl's ga ...' Chas cut him off.

'Okay, enough is enough. Let's get these contracts signed and then we can all move on with our day. I'm sure we all have better things to do than be stuck in this office.' It was time to make my move.

'Well that's just the thing you see, Chas, Reed, we're not signing today. We've decided that we'd like to take a copy of the contracts away with us and get them looked over by our own lawyer.' Chas froze. For once he was lost for words. Reed stared at me with barely concealed contempt.

'I've really wasted enough time on this project already. Now listen up and read my lips,' he addressed us impatiently. 'This offer is on the table right here, right now. You either sign today, otherwise the deal is off—for good!' he slammed his palm onto the desk to emphasise his intent—intimidation had never worked with me.

'Thought you might say that. Okay, it's off,' I smiled benevolently.

'Would you really turn down a million pounds each and one of the best record contracts that's ever been offered?' Reed shouted at us, incredulously. Chas was red in the face and the sweat, again, began to seep through his oily skin.

'Will, b ... b ... boys, what are you saying, I thought we had it all sorted. You can't do this to me ... I mean us, you, all of u ... us.'

'Sorry Chas. I know you're going to miss out on your twenty percent but we've decided that life is too short to get hooked by the same shysters twice. We won't be signing now or in the future.' Reed began to laugh.

'Big, big mistake boys. Anyway, it's your call. You've just saved GMC four million and I'm glad you did. I really don't like your type, your attitude, your manners, your dress sense; in fact, everything about you makes my skin crawl; I really don't enjoy doing business with people of your ilk at all. Of course, we do have the Bloom tape and it will be released, and it will be the soundtrack to Heidelberg's epic. The only thing that irks me slightly, is that you lot will profit from it.' He laughed a big hammy laugh and turned to smile at Mitchell who stood mute in the corner. 'Of course, after all the claw-backs, production costs, editing costs, manufacturing, publicity etcetera, etcetera, etcetera, there won't be an awful lot left coming your way. And sometimes those damn royalty cheques can take years to come through.' Mitchell sniggered understanding Reed's inferences, as we all did. Chas sat down and stared in to some private hell. Reed's spiel was predictable and I was more than ready.

'Well, I'm not so sure about that. You see I've just spoken with our lawyer. He's been searching the internet for the last couple of days trying to find a report on the court case, remember—the court case you won? The Judge sided in your favour. He said that we had to deliver one more album to GMC or, and I quote "The members of the Shooting Tsars have a choice to make; fulfil their contract with GMC by providing them with one more album or they will be prohibited from releasing any new material into the public domain for a period of no greater than ten years". Bit harsh, don't you think?'

'Very harsh,' echoed Geordie and Robbo in unison.

'Your point being?' asked Reed suspiciously, his smarmy grin long since gone. I sensed he knew what was coming, after all, he was smart, he'd reached the top.

'… prohibited from releasing any new material into the public domain for a period of no greater than ten years—from the date of the verdict.' I was drawing it out as long as I could as I wanted to watch Reed squirm, but he did not oblige. 'Now what was the date of that verdict? Ah yes, I remember, 18th of August 1995, a Friday if I remember correctly. Which happens to be exactly ten years and two days ago. Funny about that, isn't it?' Reed glared at me maliciously. 'We are no longer signed to you. And tomorrow morning, landing on your desk will be an envelope by registered mail. In the envelope will be a writ challenging you, GMC, on the rightful ownership of the Bloom tape. Now I'm no lawyer, but, something about "adverse possession". As the Bloom tape will be the main evidence in any upcoming court case it would be foolhardy to license it out to a third party such as, erm, David Heidelberg, when the rightful ownership is still in question; you could be opening yourselves up to a massive lawsuit.' Reed shot a quick glance at Mitchell, who nodded slowly in agreement. 'And as for the million pounds each, well, I wasn't paying much attention as Mitchell went through the contract, sorry Mitchell, but I do remember him saying that there was a ten day cooling off period. I assume this would be applicable to both parties. I'm not a betting man, but I would wager my life that within ten days GMC would have pulled out of the two album deal. So all up, we, that is, "the Shooting Tsars" as of two days ago are free agents and you'd be courting disaster to try and licence Bloom to Heidelberg and I guess we'll see you in court—again—you may or may not win.' A sneer spread across Reed's face and he began to clap slowly.

'Chas, it seems like you underestimated your protégés,' Reed acknowledged with a hint of respect. Chas sat motionless and did not respond. Reed put down his gold pen and leaned across the table and stared at me intently for a few seconds.

'What I don't understand, is that you could have still made millions from the Heidelberg film. Why would you throw that away?'

'Whatever we would have made, then you, GMC, would have made ten times as much. And I would gladly sacrifice every penny due to me to ensure that you make nothing off our backs ever again.' Reed leant back into his throne and shook his head with a quizzical smile.

'You'd cut off your nose to spite your face? It's just business Will, just business and you're no businessman,' he replied, almost regretfully.

'You're right, I'm not a businessman and to be brutally honest, I don't much care for their *ilk*. The day I become a businessman is the day I walk through the gates of hell.' Reed picked up his phone and hit a button,

'Ah, yes, security, Reed Lochlan here, could you send a crew up to escort the Shooting Tsars from the building, yes, straight away please.' He hung up.

'No need to get shitty,' accused Robbo.

'Oh, I'm not getting shitty, but my time is very valuable and I've wasted enough of it on you.' He turned to Chas as we all began to shuffle towards the door.

'Chas, I want you in my office 8 am tomorrow morning—understood?' Chas nodded silently, his gaze still transfixed on some unseen object. Reed now addressed us as we made our way out—some fuckers always have to have the last word.

'Oh, and by the way, two things: one—I always win and people would do well to remember that and two,' he glared at Robbo, 'put that noxious weed out before you get into the lift. I don't want that foul smell permeating the whole building.' Robbo retrieved the spliff from his mouth and gazed at it in all innocence, as though some evil imp had magically implanted it between his lips. He took one last gargantuan heave and then dropped it onto the lush bespoke carpet and twisted it into the pile with the heel of his shoe.

'Oops, sorry. Bad habits are hard to break, don't you think?'

\#

We were stood on the pavement outside GMC headquarters. I stared up at the monstrosity of a building and began to laugh hysterically. My band-mates all patted me on the back.

'Bloody hell Billy Boy, it was worth a million quid just to hear your little speech in there. Did you see the look on Chas's face—I will remember that for the rest of my days!'

'So what now?' Asked Flaky. I regained my senses and smiled at them all.

'What now, I'll tell you what now. It's time for the new Punk!' I stuck my arm out straight in front of me, with hand flat and palm facing downwards. 'All for one and one for all!' The other three all placed their hands on top of mine and yelled in harmony,

'All for one and one for all!'

'Hey, I know of a great little boozer just down the road, sells real ale and does great grub ... who's up for a pint or three?' teased Robbo.

'That's the most sensible thing you've said all day Robbo,' replied Geordie, 'your shout ... right?'

'It's always my shout, you great big lumbering Scottish git. How about Flaky's shout for a change. I don't think I've ever seen him buy a round.'

'Yeah, good point, your shout then Flaky,' ordered Geordie.

'Now hang on a damn minute, I only have a soft drink, that's way cheaper than buying pints of beer.'

'Oh shut your great cakehole and get your wallet out you big wet tart.' I watched them as they ambled down the road, bickering and bitching with each other. All three, in their different ways, were a regal pain in the arse—but they were my pain in the arse. It had been a long, long time, since I'd felt this happy.

--

CLAIM YOUR FREE SHORT STORY

BELOW

--

403

FREE SHORT STORY

Thank you for reading and I hope you enjoyed Arc Of A Shooting Star. I would love you to sign up to my sporadic and spam free newsletter so I can let you know of any new releases or special offers or discounts that are happening with my other books.

If you would like to find out more about Will, Geordie, Robbo and Flaky before they became The Shooting Tsars, then you can download, for free, **The School Report: Before We Were Tsars** once you've subscribed to my newsletter. This is a short book looking at the School Reports of our heroes when they were still teenagers in high school. Yes, I'd like to sign up to your newsletter and claim my free copy of The School Report.

THE SHOOTING STAR SERIES

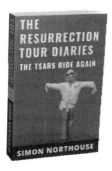  

Arc Of A Shooting Star – Book 1
Fall Of A Shooting Star – Book 2 (due out Nov 2018)
The School Report: Before We Were Tsars (Short Story)
The Resurrection Tour Diaries: The Tsars Ride Again (Novelette)

ALL REVIEWS ARE APPRECIATED!

Reviews are very important to authors as they add a little bit of social validation for other potential readers. And, it's also great for me to see what you—the reader—think about my work. So if you could please find the time to leave a fair and honest review I would be very grateful. It doesn't have to be long, a quick sentence or even a couple of words will do – thank you!

Yes I would like to leave a fair and honest review for Arc Of A Shooting Star

DON'T GO JUST YET! Below is an excerpt from book 2 in the series to give you a little taster of what's in store.

It was a warm night and the gymnasium roof was open to let in fresh air. The Rocky music was playing on constant repeat in the background. Heidelberg had walked in, to great fanfare, dressed in a red silk boxing robe and wearing a black head guard. The fight was nearly called off earlier, due to the fact that we couldn't locate a head guard that would fit Geordie's enormous melon. Eventually, one was found and the fight was most definitely on again. I have to admit that Heidelberg did look like a boxer, apart from the extra pounds that he carried. Whereas Geordie—well what could one say? He wore a blue head guard and sported a pair of Ranger's Football Club shorts that were excessively small. His groin protector protruded rudely out against the thin material looking more like a codpiece than protective gear.

I was determined to keep a close eye on proceedings, so I had nominated myself as Geordie's trainer and cornerman. As I stood on the canvas ring I tried to get Geordie's attention as he shadow boxed at the corner post whilst skipping from foot to foot letting out snorts through his nostrils as he did so.

'Geordie, are you listening?' I repeated for the umpteenth time.

'Yeah, yeah, I'm all ears,' he replied, bristling with nervous energy.

'Okay, good. Now let's go through it one more time. Three rounds of three minutes each,' I directed.

'Yep. Three rounds—three minutes each,' he echoed.

'First round, you come out and skip around the ring. Keep out of his way, okay? Maybe throw a few little jabs and dabs, nothing to the body or head, just glancing blows to the arms or shoulder—yeah?'

'Yep. Got you. Glancing blows to arms and shoulders.'

'The first round you let him win on points—get it?'

'Yep, got it, first round he wins—points.'

'Good. Second round, same again, dance around the ring, bit of shadow boxing, a few little jabs. Again, nothing to the head or body, just the arms and shoulders. Make sure you're out of his reach. He's a big hefty bloke, but I think you can outdo him on speed and agility. Now, towards the end of round two just throw a few gentle jabs at his helmet, nothing too aggressive—understand? You win the second round on points—got it?'

'Yeah, yeah. Towards the end of round two, a few gentle taps to the helmet. Yep, got that Billy Boy.'

'Round three, same again …'

'Yep, same again…' he repeated as he continued his shadow boxing and snorting.

'Half-way through round three, get in a bit closer, throw a few punches that miss and then, at some point he's going to let one go. Now watch out for it, because it may come fast. Let it connect with some point of your head guard and then fall to the deck. Make it look realistic but not over-dramatic—otherwise he may smell a rat. Have you got that?'

'Yep. All over it. Third round, half-way through, let him connect and then take a dive, no rats.'

'Good, good. Make sure you fall to the deck with arms spreadeagled and do not get up again until after the count of ten.'

'Sure, sure. Arms spreadeagled, count of ten.'

'And Geordie, this is the most important part—that guy has got an ego bigger than the San Francisco Bridge—do not, I repeat—do not for one second let him think that you are going easy on him. Do I make myself clear?'

'Yeah, got it. Don't let him think that I am going easy on him.'

'If he thinks for one moment that you have let him win, then that will be a massive hit to his ego and either he'll cancel the deal altogether or he'll massively screw us down in negotiations. Do I make myself clear?'

'Yep. Ego, deal, screwed. Got it.'

'Okay, good. Feeling nervous?'

'About the deal? Yeah, a little bit.'

'I meant about the boxing!'

'The boxing! Give me a break. He's a fat fucker!'

'Geordie, he's a big bloke, a powerful bloke—don't underestimate him.' I rubbed him down with a towel as Jackie, who had elected herself as Master Of Ceremonies, climbed through the ropes into the ring, lifting her skirt up as she did and accidentally flashing a black G-string.

'Look at the woman,' said Geordie, 'she has no shame.' Fiona and Julie were sat on a bench perpendicular to the ring, behind them were Rory the chauffer, the cook and the cleaner. Heidelberg's personal trainer and physio were in his corner, opposite. There was a convivial atmosphere of good-natured excitement that permeated the night. I turned and looked at Robbo, who was my "cutman"—well, sometimes you've got to take what's available. He was holding a bucket that contained a drizzle of water and a sponge.

'This may turn out alright, don't you think?' I suggested optimistically. Robbo stared back at me as though I was a complete dick. I nodded towards the bucket and sponge. 'Do you even know what that's for?' I asked.

'Yeah,' he replied. 'It's for mopping up blood.'

Jackie began the announcements.

'Tonight, we have the heavyweight fight of allllll time! Forget the rumble in the jungle, discard the thriller in Manila—tonight we bring you the "Massacre from Lassiter", whoop, whoop, whoop!' The tiny crowd erupted into a chorus of whoops and cheers—apart from

Robbo and Geordie who looked on impassively. Jackie continued.

'Tonight, in the blue corner, we have the contender—the no-go-from Glasgow, the kilt from the silt, the Spartan in the tartan—the one and only—Gorgeous Geordie!' There were more eruptions from the corralled spectators as Geordie complained bitterly.

'Gorgeous Geordie! She makes me sound like some twat from a cross-dressing boy band.'

'And in the red corner, we have the undisputed heavy-heavyweight champion of the world—the bull from the Bronx, the Manhood from Hollywood—the Reducer Producer—the one and only H-Bomb Heidelberg!'

The crowd exploded once again as Jackie slipped back through the ropes and took up her seat with the other girls.

'Okay, Geordie my son, remember the plan. Stick to the plan and everything will turn out sweeter than a nun's fart.'

'Got you Billy Boy, the plan, nun's fart,' he replied positively, but there was a look in his eye, which made me feel just a tad uneasy.

DING! DING! DING!

The bell reverberated across the room. Geordie skipped across the ring in two youthful bounds and unleashed a ferocious barrage of rapid-fire, bone crunching jabs into Heidelberg's midriff. By the look of astonishment on Heidelberg's face, I deduced that he wasn't expecting such a full-on, savage, frontal attack—especially so early on in proceedings, and, I could only assume that he didn't enjoy it one little bit. He let out an audible "humph" as he creased in the middle and his body contorted downwards.

Geordie now swung his left arm around his shoulder twice—much akin to a Pete Townsend windmill power chord move—and then unleashed a sledgehammer southpaw uppercut. It connected squarely with his opponent's chin.

I fully expected to see Heidelberg's head depart from his

body and fly out of the open roof and disappear into the night sky—but it didn't. It clung on to his neck with a stoic tenacity that I almost admired.

His heavy frame reeled back onto the ropes, which groaned and stretched as they absorbed the kinetic energy of his huge torso. Once again, Newton's third law of motion took almost immediate effect. The ropes propelled Heidelberg back into the ring at an undignified speed, and with a far greater velocity than the physical laws of science could have predicted.

I'm not sure if he was still compos-mentis at this point, but his bog-eyed and vacant expression led me to believe that maybe he wasn't. This could possibly explain why he didn't see, or anticipate, a perfectly timed, laser-guided Howitzer of a straight jab to the bridge of his nose.

Luckily, I was on the far side of the ring, so I wasn't splattered with the blood that erupted from Heidelberg's deconstructed conk. The same however, could not be said of Heidelberg, his cornermen or Geordie, who now all looked like they'd just participated in a free-form Jackson Pollock happening.

Ruddy, nebulous globs flew through the air and landed with a gloopy splat on the canvas. Heidelberg rocked gently back and forth on both feet, like a giant oak in a gentle breeze. For one horrifying moment, I saw Geordie winding up again, but thankfully, he showed unusual restraint. Heidelberg wobbled once more and then toppled and crashed to the canvas. A white towel was immediately thrown into the ring as his personal trainer and physio both rushed forth to render assistance.

There were more screams and whoops from the spouses as Geordie skipped back to his corner, still shadow boxing and snorting disconcertingly through both nostrils. I looked at the second hand on my watch—it had just ticked past twenty seconds since the bell first rang out.

'Whaddya reckon Bill? Do you think he noticed I was feigning?'

'Hmm … my gut instinct tells me "no", but one can never be certain.'

'I was in two minds whether to really let him have but I pulled out at the last second. Do you think he spotted that?' He asked with a worried frown.

'I think at that point, his brain, or what was left of it, was more preoccupied with shutting down non-essential organs than detecting if you deliberately withheld a punch.'

'So, you think I pulled it off?'

'Yeah Geordie—you did great! You may have diverged slightly from the plan and turned Heidelberg into a shuffling turnip, but overall, it went like clockwork. I couldn't have asked for more.' Robbo handed me the sponge.

FALL OF A SHOOTING STAR
IS DUE FOR RELEASE IN NOVEMBER 2018.

ABOUT THE AUTHOR

Simon Northouse has been many things: bricklayer, croupier, publisher, magazine editor, magazine writer, recording studio owner, sales rep, musician, rock star (not), delivery driver, draftsman, technical writer, window cleaner and now author.

He has spent the last decade working for a multinational company doing incredibly tedious things. However, he has won the company's
"Most Proactively Disenfranchised Employee of the Year" award for ten years on the trot, an achievement that he prides himself on, as the competition is damn stiff.

He began fiction writing a number of years ago and found he was rather good at it—although, that is open to debate.

He initially threw himself into writing literary classics, which was quite unusual, as he'd never thrown himself into anything before. However, he soon realised he was never going to be the next Harper Lee, or even Bruce Lee for that matter, so concentrated his efforts on producing mildly amusing commercial fiction.

He currently lives somewhere with someone and does some things he should not do and some things he should do—but not as often as he'd like.

Printed in Great Britain
by Amazon